Blossom by the Billabong

Blossom by the Billabong

Lucidus Smith

Other Titles by Lucidus Smith

The previous two books in the 'Blossom' Trilogy:

Oh for a Ha'porth of Tar

Blossom in Winter – Frost in Spring

Dedication

Will he bat or Will he bowl?
We'll have to wait and see.
Stu-pendous effort on the fourth,
A par five down in three.
Rob-ed in black shorts and matching shirt,
His whistle keeps the fun;
There's always hope for this sad world,
When there are men, like my three sons!

7th July 2011   LS

Table of Contents

Introduction

This book is the sequel to 'Blossom in Winter - Frost in Spring' and is the third book of the 'Blossom' trilogy.

It covers the period from August 1949 to March 1951 and once again follows the lives of Bertie Bannister and his family along with his young friend Arnold (Digger) Smith.

After Bertie and his new wife Victoria return to Upper Style from their trip abroad, they are re-united with Bertie's daughter Deborah, who proves to be as un-predictable and difficult to handle as ever.

Digger's fiancée Moira, is soon on her way to Scotland in readiness for her forthcoming marriage to Digger, who persuades his cousin Donny to be Best Man, which could prove to be a dangerous choice, in view of his past history for practical jokes.

After the wedding Digger and Moira emigrate to Australia, where a new job and a new way of life, offer better opportunities than the two believe are possible in Britain; but they are not prepared for the way things turn out there and a dull, safe job with another bank, soon has surprising ramifications!

Chapter 1
Digger's Cousin

Arnold old chap, I would be delighted to be Best Man at your wedding; I assume none of your other friends were prepared to travel that far north for the occasion."

"Donny I can assure you that you were always my first choice, I just did not want to bother you while you were still unwell," Arnold explained to his cousin.

"A likely story; but I have never been to Inverness before and will enjoy the trip, can you arrange accommodation for me, or do I have to try and find a hotel myself?"

"No, you can stay with me at a neighbour's house, a few doors down from where Moira's folks live, it's all been arranged."

"Talking of Moira, I insist on coming over and meeting this unfortunate young woman for myself, who knows there might still be time to save her!"

"Donny, if you say anything that embarrasses me with Moira, I will cancel your invitation and pay someone off the street to be Best Man in your place," Arnold said, knowing from past experience, that his older cousin was quite adept at dropping him in it.

"I called round to see Vi and Mick the other week," Donny continued, "and your sister tells me that this Moira is a real good looker and young Brian was really taken with her and even showed her his 'Fag Card' collection; high praise indeed."

"That's right and since neither Vi nor Moira have a sister, they are both looking forward to getting to know each other."

"A quick look at my appointment book Arnold, tells me that I am completely free this coming weekend, why don't I come over and visit you, assuming that you are both going to be around, that is?"

"Let me check my diary, Saturday the sixth and Sunday the seventh of August, sounds good to me and we will both be here for the whole weekend, but I will just clear it with Mrs. Black and warn Sissy that I have a guest staying with me in the cottage. I have got to dash Donny, the manger is giving me the evil eye again, ever since I handed in my notice at the bank, he has been particularly difficult."

"Sounds like my old C.O. Arnold, expect me over Saturday afternoon then, do you have a pub in that village of yours?"

"We certainly do and a very good one, I might say!"

"O.K. well book a table and I will treat you both to dinner. Bye for now," with which Arnold's cousin Donny ended the telephone call.

Just as Arnold, who usually went by the nickname of Digger, put the telephone receiver back on the stand, the bank manager walked over to his desk and said in a loud voice, so that everyone in the office could clearly hear what he was saying,

"I really should not be reminding you Smith that private telephone calls are not permitted during office hours. I know that you will be leaving us soon to travel to the Antipodes, but while you are here and the bank is continuing to pay your salary, you will continue to keep the rules or there will be serious consequences. Do I make myself clear?"

"Yes sir, you are perfectly clear," Digger replied, standing up and staring down at the shorter man.

"Good and make sure you have the figures I requested on my desk first thing tomorrow morning."

"But you said that you did not need them until Monday morning, I had planned to do them tomorrow, as I was finishing off the University documents today, for handing over to my replacement."

"Well you will have to work on them tonight then, won't you Smith?" With which the manager returned to his office and closed the door.

One of Digger's colleagues remained with him for a couple of hours that Wednesday evening, to help get the figures ready for the manager's inspection the next day and to show his appreciation, Digger took him out for a drink afterwards at a country pub and then drove him back to his home, in his 1936 Austin Seven AAL Tourer. It was a deep blue colour with black mudguards and a black hood and was Digger's pride and joy.

"I don't suppose you would consider selling the car to me, would you, when you sail for Australia?" his colleague enquired. "I have always liked the Austin Seven's."

"I don't see why not," Digger replied, "although I am loathe to part with her, my friend Bertie who was in Australia a short while ago, said that open tourers are not the most ideal car to have over there, what with the heat and insects, so I have been considering my options, whether to ship her over or sell her here, or even buy something more suitable and ship that over instead. I'll tell you what, make me an offer and I will let you know."

When Digger got home from work on the following Thursday, there was a note from the vicar telling him that Bell Ringing practice at St. Luke's church, had been cancelled that night, as Davy Jones the leader of the group, had gone down with some mystery illness and was not able to lead it that week.

Digger's home was in fact, an old cottage that was attached to a large stone house called Millstone House, that lay a short distance down a narrow lane which ran down the side of St. Luke's Church in Upper Style, Buckinghamshire, England .

The house was owned by two ladies, Mrs. Amanda Black, who was the widow of a wartime army chum of Digger's and her widowed sister, Mrs. Penny Duffy-Smythe who was an author of children's books.

He had only been indoors a short while when he heard Mrs. Black calling to him.

"Arnold are you decent, can I come in?"

"You're quite safe Mrs. Black, I am just making a cup of tea, what can I do for you?"

Mrs. Black came in and sat down on a kitchen chair, "My sister's Morris Eight is misfiring; I don't suppose you would have time to check it over for me this evening would you, as we have to drive into Aylesbury to do some shopping tomorrow. Oh, and Moira rang to say that since the Bell Ringing practice had been cancelled, she was going to wash her hair tonight, so she will meet you in the Stag tomorrow at seven thirty, as per usual."

"Right thanks, I did buy some new points and plugs last week for your car, when I got some for mine, so I will swap them over once I have changed out of my suit and had something to eat, I don't suppose Sissy left me anything did she?"

"We are about to eat ourselves, so come and join us, there is plenty of food to go round and Sissy has put some scraps in the bowl for the dog. I should mention that we are running low on wood again, if you could see to that over the weekend please Arnold."

"Most certainly I will, it is already on my 'to do' list. While I think of it, I have invited my cousin down for the weekend, he has agreed to be my Best Man at the wedding, would you mind if I borrow the 'chair bed' from the laundry for him, so he has somewhere to sleep?"

"Help yourself, but it is not very comfortable, as I am sure you will remember. I will get Sissy to look out some spare bedclothes for him tomorrow. I am really sorry that neither of us will be able to make your wedding, but Penny is halfway through a new book, with a deadline to meet and if she stops writing, it can sometimes take her months before she gets going again."

"That's O.K. I understand, you have both been so good to me since I arrived here last year, that it would have been nice to have you there, but not to worry, it's a very long way to go, as all my friends keep telling me."

After dinner Digger changed into his working clothes and got his tools out of the garage and changed the plugs and points in the Morris Eight and then took it for a short run to Lower Style and back, to make sure it was running smoothly, before putting it into the garage, next to his own car. He then took his dog Mac for a walk in the nearby wood and picked up a few stout branches from a pile he had collected previously and deposited them in the far corner of the garden, which lay to the rear of the main house; for sawing up into logs on the following Saturday. He gave Mac a bowl of water and made a hot drink for himself and then settled down for a quiet evening with the 'steam radio' and the newspaper.

Friday night at the Stag pub had become a bit of a ritual over the last few months, with Digger and Moira challenging anyone present, to a game of darts, with the losers buying the next round of drinks. By the time they had won their third game of darts, it was almost half past eight and they were ready for a bit of supper, which Sheila, the publicans wife was happy to provide. They were just about to start on the Fresh Bread, Cheddar Cheese and Pickles when their good friends,

Bertie Bannister and his wife Victoria came into the pub and sat down beside them.

Bertie was a retired sea captain and he and Victoria had only met the previous year, and in a whirlwind romance married each other shortly afterwards. They were both in their sixties and it was Bertie's second marriage and Victoria' third and whilst Victoria did not have any children, Bertie had a grown-up daughter named Deborah who lived in London.

Victoria had come into some money the previous year, but was told that she had to go to Australia to claim it and as a result she and Bertie had spent most of the past year sailing to Australia and back. It was, in fact, through them, that Digger had gone for the interview with the Perth Mining & Commerce Bank Ltd of Australia and had been offered a position, which he had accepted, at their regional office in Perth, Western Australia. He and Moira had already booked their passage to sail to Australia shortly after their wedding which was to be held in Inverness, Moira's home town, on Saturday the 27th August 1949.

"Don't tell me you two have been winning again," said Bertie, "when was the last time you had to buy a drink for yourselves on a Friday night?"

"Just beginners luck," Moira answered, "do you fancy a game after we have finished eating?"

"No thank you dear," said Victoria, "you are far too good for us, but we thought we would find you here, so we just popped in to see if you would like to come to dinner tomorrow night. We are celebrating the third anniversary of Bertie buying the cottage here in Upper Style."

"We would love to," said Moira, "what time shall we come?"

"Six thirty to eat at seven," Victoria replied.

"Err, hold on," said Digger, "slight problem. I have invited my cousin Donny to come over for the weekend."

"You never told me you had invited him over this weekend," said Moira, a little indignantly.

"I'm sorry, I didn't realise I had to clear it with you first!" Digger snapped back.

"Not a problem, bring him too," Bertie interjected, " assuming Donny is a man, that is, mind you, you can still bring her if he isn't!" he said chuckling to himself.

"I think I know what you mean Bertie, but he is a man alright! He is just six years older than me and there is never a dull moment when my cousin Donny is around. I hate to think what stories he is going to tell in his Best Man's speech at the wedding; I could try and vet them, but that would probably make him even worse! He was a bit of a big brother to me, when I was small, which was great at school in the playground, but not so good in family circles, if you know what I mean."

Digger walked Moira home from the pub and went in for a coffee and a cuddle and yet another discussion about all things 'wedding'.

On Saturday morning Digger and Mac fetched some more large branches from the woods and then set about sawing them up into logs and then chopping up some of them for kindling. He filled the large log box for the two sisters and then his own supply of slightly smaller logs that he used to burn on the range in his kitchen.

It was only the sight of the bedding that Sissy, the maid at Millstone, had left on his kitchen table, that reminded him of Donny's impending visit and the need to carry the heavy old 'bed chair' from the laundry room, where it normally resided, into his parlour.

"Donny is going to love this!" he said to himself.

Sissy had a real soft spot for Digger, so she also left him some cold pork pies and salad for his lunch, along with the bedding for his guest and after washing his hands in the sink, he sat down outside the cottage with Mac and ate his lunch and consumed a large mug of tea, while enjoying the summer sunshine and the gentle breeze. After lunch he started to read a book that someone at the office had lent him and managed a dozen or so pages, before he dozed off in the chair and he and Mac were happily snoring away when Mrs. Duffy Smythe walked down the garden path towards him, accompanied by a man wearing a flying jacket and helmet.

"Arnold, you have a visitor. Arnold, your visitor has arrived," she called out, disturbing his dream of blue skies and gold coloured kangaroos.

Mac was awake first and stood up and wagged his tail and walked over to where Mrs. Duffy Smythe was standing.

"Good boy, but don't jump up, this is a clean dress," she said, patting his head and stroking his back.

Arnold stretched and stood up, "I must have dozed off for a second, good to see you Donny, thanks Mrs. Duffy-Smythe, I assume my cousin has introduced himself?"

"He certainly has and told us all sorts of interesting tales about you Arnold."

"Donny, what have you been saying, I am regretting asking you to my wedding already."

"Well I am just delighted to have found two such attractive and intelligent ladies that refuse to call you by that ridiculous nickname of Digger. You are not Australian and you don't dig, I just don't understand why you do it."

"I don't know how you can stand there and tell such bare-faced lies Donny Smith. The reason I asked people to call me Digger, Mrs. Duffy-Smythe, is that my dear cousin here, won a competition, which allowed him to name one of the baboons in London Zoo. So he named it after me. You may have seen the type of baboon in question, it has a brightly coloured bottom and gets up to all sorts of antics, which meant that he could tell people that he saw Arnold doing this or that revolting thing and everyone assumed it was me."

"Very ingenious Mr. Smith, I must use that in my next story. Anyway gentlemen, I must go now and thank you for filling the log box this morning, but to be honest, I am now not sure whether I should continue to call you Arnold or start calling you Digger. How bizarre!"

With which she laughed to herself and went back down the path and into the house, where she related the 'baboon' story to her sister.

"Where did you leave your motorbike?" asked Digger.

"Outside the front of the house. Is it alright if I wheel it round and put it under cover?" Donny enquired.

"I have cleared a space for you in the garage and the forecast is rain tonight, so it would be a good idea to go and get it."

The two men and the dog went out of the large back gates, down the track that went behind Digger's cottage and round to the front of the house. As the path was rutted and muddy, Donny decided to push the bike rather than risk riding it and getting the working parts covered in mud.

The two men chatted and went for a walk in the wood with the dog and were having a drink in the parlour when Moira called in at the cottage a few minutes after six. She heard them chatting and called out,

"It's only me Digger, I'll just make myself a drink and come through."

As she walked into the parlour, the two men were sitting on the couch facing the fireplace and stopped talking and stood up as she entered. Digger kissed his fiancée on the lips and then introduced her to Donny.

"Moira, this is my cousin Donny,"

Donny walked over and held her hands and smiled at her as he said, "It's a real pleasure to meet you Moira, you have chosen one of the nicest, most decent men I have ever known and if half of what he has told me about you is true, you are a most wonderful lady yourself and I hope you both will be truly happy together."

Fortunately Digger had warned Moira about the scarring down the side of Donny's face and neck, a memento of the war, so she had the self control not to gasp or flinch, but to return the smile and say,

"Well thank you kind sir and if half of what Digger has told me about you is true, I am amazed he has asked you to be his Best Man," which caused both men to laugh heartily out loud.

Digger and Moira sat down together on the couch and Donny attempted to make himself comfortable on the old 'bed chair'.

"Have you told Donny about the change of plans tonight?" she asked.

"On no, I forgot. Why don't you fill him in, while I have a quick wash and change," Digger suggested.

"So what has changed?" asked Donny. "Are we not going to the pub for a meal?"

"No, we have been invited to have dinner with some good friends of ours, Bertie and Victoria Bannister. They are celebrating the third anniversary of Bertie buying his cottage and moving to the village."

"I see, did Victoria not move here at the same time as him then?" Donny queried.

"Err no, they were both widowed. Victoria was actually cook here at Millstone, when Digger first arrived and it was really through Digger and a nasty accident that happened to Bertie, that brought him and Victoria together last year. They have only been married for about a year."

"So where did this Bertie move from then?" Donny asked.

"I am not sure, to be honest. He was a merchant navy captain and has travelled the world and I know he met up with some friends in Gibraltar on their cruise out to Australia, but you will be able to ask him yourself when you see him."

"So are we the only ones invited, or will there be sons and daughters there as well?"

"As far as I know it will just be us, but they are aware that you are coming, there is no problem there. Ah, just one thing, Bertie has a daughter and she and Digger do not get on and I mean, they really do not get on."

"Perhaps she has not been invited, does she come here often to visit her father?"

"She came a lot to start with, but since she and Digger fell out, her trips have been a lot less frequent and she only came down twice to check the cottage, the whole time they were away in Australia. Anyway, we will soon know if she is visiting her father, as her motorbike will be parked outside the house."

"A motorbike, strange transport for a young woman," Donny commented.

"A big red one, an Indian, so I am told. She learnt to ride it in the war, Bertie told us once and I think he said that they were abroad somewhere at the time."

"She is not really that young then!" Donny said thoughtfully.

"I would say she was nearer your age than mine," Moira replied.

Digger came into the room, clutching a bottle of wine he had bought from the pub the previous night.

"Don't tell me you have taken up drinking again Arnold?" Donny said.

"No, but being the unselfish chap that I am, I got this for 'them's that do', time to get going."

They walked down the path by the house and then along the track until they came to the path which led to Bertie's cottage.

"Oh, Oh, tyre marks," shouted Digger, "looks like 'you know who' will be at the dinner tonight; did you warn Donny about her."

"Don't panic, he has been warned, which is probably why he is wearing his flying helmet, in case any projectiles should come his way," Moira suggested.

They were walking carefully down the path when Mac suddenly came bounding up behind them and almost knocked Donny over.

"Hello boy, have you come to join us for dinner as well?" Donny said, giving Mac a pat.

"Oh Digger, you forgot to leave Mac in the house, that will really wind Deborah up," said Moira, "do you think you should take him back home?"

"I certainly do not! Look Moira, it's Bertie and Victoria's house we are going to, not Deborah's and Mac can do no wrong as far as they are concerned, so don't worry about it."

They went through the gate and down the path and saw Deborah's motorbike sitting by the front wall, underneath the parlour window.

"Wow what a beauty," said Donny, "you two go in, I want to take a closer look at it."

"It's a bit bigger than yours Donny, but don't touch it or she will kill you," Digger warned his cousin.

Moira knocked on the door which was opened by Bertie who greeted his guests and ushered them into the parlour.

"I thought your cousin was coming with you tonight," said Bertie.

"He is mate," said Digger, "he is outside looking at Deborah's motorbike."

"Well he had better not touch it if he knows what's good for him," Deborah exclaimed, getting up from the couch and walking across to the window that the bike was parked under.

"Deborah, where are your manners, say hello to our guests," Bertie instructed his daughter.

"Hello guests." Deborah said. "Of all the cheek dad, he is now sitting on my Indian, if you please."

"I will go and give Victoria a hand in the kitchen," said Moira, sensing a major incident was about to happen.

At that moment the big 1200 cc engine of the Indian Chief roared into life and Donny turned the throttle and released the clutch and slowly drove the bike forward, so that it was right next to the front door, where he continued to rev the engine.

Deborah had never been more incensed about anything in her whole life and she did no more than turn round and walk to the fireplace and lifted the large heavy poker out of the rack.

"No one touches my bike, especially one of your moronic relatives," she snarled at Digger as she walked towards the door, "I'll give him something to remember me by!"

Everyone was too stunned to move as Deborah flung open the front door, lifted the heavy poker with two hands above her head and stood their glaring at the man in the flying jacket and helmet, sitting on her prized motorbike.

Donny cut the engine and looked up at her and said quietly, "I wouldn't do that Debs, if I were you."

That one short sentence changed Deborah's life forever.

She dropped the poker, which fell onto the front light and mudguard, scratching and denting as it went. She was unable to speak and just stood there transfixed, as Donny got off the bike and walked to where she was standing and held her in his arms and kissed her.

Victoria, Moira and Digger, stood behind Bertie in the doorway of the house, totally transfixed by what was happening in front of them. When Bertie had got over the shock and found his voice again, he walked up to his daughter and said, "Deborah, what exactly is going on here. Who is this man?"

"It's Mac dad, Digger's cousin is my Mac!"

Chapter 2
The Bravest of Men

Donny and Deborah stood on that front doorstep for more than fifteen minutes while they hugged and kissed and cried together. Victoria, Digger and Moira stood watching for a while, but then went indoors, completely bewildered by the scene being enacted before them.

Bertie broke the pair up for a minute to hug Mac and to shake his hand. He tried to speak, but words failed him, so he smiled and followed the others into the house leaving Deborah and Donny to hold each other close, once more. He sat down and dried his eyes, as he too had been completely overcome by the occasion and Victoria was the first to speak.

"Bertie are you all right dear?" she asked.

"Whew, I think so Victoria, that was just amazing!"

"How do Deborah and Arnold's cousin know each other," Victoria asked him, "and why did Arnold call him Donny and Deborah call him Mac? I thought she was talking about the dog at first."

"I can explain the name confusion," said Digger, "his real name is MacDonald Livingstone Forbes Smith, but everyone in the family calls him Donny, but when he joined the R.A.F. there was already a 'larger than life' Donny on the base, so he got everyone to call him Mac, which is probably how he introduced himself to you Bertie."

"That's right Digger, we knew him as Mac and of course now I have seen the two of you together, I can see the family likeness, which I guess, is why you gave Deborah such a problem. Plus calling your dog Mac, I assume now after your cousin, only made matters worse."

Digger went on to relate the 'baboon' story and how he said he would always get his own back some day on his cousin, hence calling his dog Mac.

"But how did you and Deborah get acquainted with Mac, Bertie?" Moira asked.

"It was June 1940 and Deborah and I were living in Roses in Spain. It is a small town on the Mediterranean, close to the French border. I was a skipper with a Spanish Steam Ship company, mostly carrying passengers and cargo around the Mediterranean Sea and down the West coast of Africa. We had to call in at Lisbon in Portugal to drop off some passengers and pick up some cargo when I got chatting to a man in a bar; or rather he got chatting to me."

"So was this man Arnold's cousin then?" Victoria asked.

"Yes he was, but he had a very real problem, apart from speaking awful Spanish, that is. He was working as an undercover agent for the British and was supposed to be going to southern France to liaise with the Resistance there, but there had been a security leak and he could not travel on the original planned route. He had been told to contact me and to find an alternative way into France; so he asked me if I could take him to Roses and then help him to get across the Spanish/French border, as Spain was of course neutral in the last war."

"But why was he told to speak to you and how did he know that you would be willing to help him?" asked Victoria.

"That's another story Victoria and as I have told you before, there are certain aspects of my work during the War, that I am not free to discuss with you or anyone else for that matter," Bertie replied.

"What on earth am I supposed to conclude from that?" Victoria responded, in an offended manner.

"You are to conclude that he is bound by the Official Secrets Act Victoria, just like Donny is and thousands of other men and women who worked behind enemy lines," Digger replied. "So what happened next Bertie?"

"I agreed to help him, but I had to go back to the ship for fresh clothes and papers for him and while I was absent he got set upon by two German agents who robbed him and left him badly wounded."

"I guess that explains the knife scars on his arm and chest then," commented Digger.

"Yes, he had lost a lot of blood and somehow I managed to get him to the ship where the Mate and a New Zealand friend of mine, who goes by the name of Brock, carried him to my cabin where we stitched him up. When we docked at Barcelona, two of my Spanish friends, Paco and Luca were there to meet us and between us we managed to smuggle him off the ship and into my car and Brock and I drove him to the house at Roses."

"You never mentioned before that you actually had your own car Bertie," said Victoria.

"Not had, but have, Victoria. It is a Renault Juvaquatre and is currently being used by John and Annette in Spain. I have not actually sold it to them yet. But let me continue please, or we will never get to the end of this story."

"I am sorry dear, so much new information," she replied.

"Deborah nursed him through June and July and the two of them became close friends and fell in love. He was with us and was there to comfort Deborah, when my mother died at my house in Benicarlo, which is also in Spain on the Mediterranean Sea. We buried her in the same cemetery where my first wife Deborah and our stillborn son are buried. Please, not now Victoria, I will talk to you later about all this."

Moira went and fetched a glass of water from the kitchen and gave it to Bertie, who then continued with the story.

"On Monday the 22nd July 1940, Mac had recovered from his wounds and was fit and well and was ordered to travel into Southern France. We drove up to Rialp in the Pyrenees, where my friend Luca had a house and waited to be contacted. My contact was a Frenchman named David, the same David we met in Gibraltar, Victoria and he had with him an injured British airman named John. We picked up John from where David had left him and took him back to Rialp, where our friend Annette, who was Luca's niece joined us on the Tuesday and she took over the care of John and they also fell in love and eventually got married in England in April 1944 and now live in that same house at Roses."

Bertie had another drink of the water and then continued,

"Anyway, on the evening of Wednesday the 24th July 1940 Deborah and I bid farewell to Mac and he and David crossed the Pyrenees to join the Resistance movement in southern France. The next time we heard about Mac was June 1941 when David informed us that Mac had been captured by the Germans and had been killed, along with his interrogators, in an Allied bombing raid. All that was left of him were burnt remains and the back of the watch which Deborah had given him as a farewell present. As you can imagine we were both devastated and Deborah has not been the same since. As to how he is alive and well today, we will have to ask him that question."

At which point, Victoria jumped up and flew into the kitchen, closely followed by Moira.

"It's O.K." Moira announced, "but we really should sit down and eat the food now."

Digger went to the door and opened it, to find Deborah and Mac still locked in each other's arms, as if they were afraid to let go, in case one of them disappeared again.

"Grubs up Donny," was all he could think of saying.

The table was re-arranged so that Deborah and Mac could sit together and Victoria served the roast lamb and fresh vegetables she had spent the afternoon preparing. While they were eating, Mac picked up the story from where Bertie had left off.

"I had been in the cellars of that awful building for several weeks and seen my friends in the Resistance broken by torture and starvation. We were all regularly beaten and abused, but it was not until one of the others told them that I was a British agent, that I was chosen for their special attention. They tell you at training school, that everyone breaks under torture in the end, but they encourage you to hang out for as long as possible, so that what you finally tell them will no longer be relevant."

"Oh Mac, I have had nightmares ever since over what they might have done to you, before you died in that dreadful place," Deborah confessed to him.

"Well I lasted just under a week and then told them everything I knew, I just could not take any more and wanted to die. The chief interrogator had given the instruction to take me outside and shoot me when he noticed the watch I was wearing, Deborah's gift to me and removed it from my wrist and put it on his own, giving his watch to one of the guards."

"So that's why the watch was found on the corpse inside the building," said Bertie.

"That's right; but because I was in such a terrible state, it took two of them to carry me outside and two more to act as guards. There was a post in the grounds at the rear, that they tied prisoners to who were being shot and I was being carried there, when an Allied plane flew over and dropped a stick of bombs on the place. The house took a direct hit and one of the outhouses must have contained ammunition as it blew up at the same time, sending a deadly shower of metal and a wall of fire across the compound. The four guards were caught by the blast and three of them were killed outright and the fourth was badly injured, but because I was being carried by them, I was almost completely protected, except for the burns I suffered to my back, neck and face."

"But if you were so badly injured already, how could you possibly get up and walk away from all that?" asked Deborah.

"Well that is the most amazing part of the story Deborah, let me explain," said Mac, "it appears that a team of three British soldiers, comprising a junior officer, a sergeant and a corporal, had been sent to guide the plane to the correct target, with the orders to withdraw immediately the bombs had been dropped. They knew that there were thousands of German soldiers in the vicinity and they did not want the three men to be discovered by them. The officer in charge of the team along with his sergeant followed orders precisely and left the second the first bomb was released. The corporal had tried to persuade them to stay and look for anything in the building that might be useful, but the others had refused. He had been nearest of the three to the compound and had seen me through his binoculars, being carried out of the building by the guards, just as the bombs fell and he could not bring himself to leave there, without checking to see who I was, not expecting any of us to be alive."

"Don't let your food get cold Mac," said Victoria, "but do tell us what happened next."

"I was lying there and managed to roll onto my good side and saw this British soldier approaching and then realised that the fourth guard had also seen him coming and was maneuvering his machine gun into a firing position. Without thinking I shouted out a warning and at the same time kicked back into the man's chest, which spoilt his aim. The British soldier fired one shot which hit the guard in the chest and killed him outright. He then bent down and said to me, 'Well I guess you saved my life Froggy, so I had better save yours now,' with which he picked me up in a fireman's lift and carried me out of the compound."

"So he thought you were a member of the French Resistance then?" said Digger.

"Yes, they had not been told of the possibility of a British agent being in the building, so he had quite a surprise after he had banged my head against a tree for the third time when I said to him, 'You bang my head against a tree again, you ignorant Tommy basket case and I'll bite your ear off.'"

"So what did he say to that?" asked Moira.

"He was so surprised that he tripped over a tree stump and we both fell to the ground. Which was actually most fortunate, as a German patrol was just passing within a few feet of where we would have been if we had not tripped over."

"Surely they heard you fall though," said Deborah.

"A couple of them were arguing about something and did not notice us; it was just our lucky day. We realised that we were surrounded by German soldiers, so when we spotted an old woodsman's hut, we just took the chance to rest up and he bandaged my wounds as best he could and strapped up my broken wrist and we ate the rations he still had with him. In the end we stayed there for a couple of nights and each night he would go off foraging and bring back supplies along with a couple of German guns and some ammunition and some fresh clothes for me."

"And no-one discovered your hiding place?" asked Bertie.

"A French peasant came past with his dog the first day and saw me, but said nothing and the next day he came past again and brought us a bottle of wine and some bread and cheese. He told us that he had lost his son in the Resistance and was glad to help and told us which way we should go to avoid the

Germans and more importantly, he told us where a British Field Hospital was located.

My 'Good Samaritan' carried me for another two days through hostile countryside, along the edge of a minefield and across a river before we finally made contact with a British patrol. They took me to their Field Hospital and he went back to his unit."

"So what was his name, this 'Good Samaritan of yours," asked Moira.

"I don't know Moira, he called me 'Flyboy' and I called him 'Tommy', sounds silly now, but that's just the way things were then."

"How long were you in the hospital for?" asked Deborah.

"I was there just a few days when the decision was made to bring me back to England for treatment and de-briefing. I was transferred to various 'Burns' hospitals and was constantly being questioned about what I had seen and done, but because of the 'top secret' nature of my mission, I was not allowed to make any contact with my family, but they were told that I was still alive and somewhere in Europe; so I was grateful for that."

"So were they able to treat all of your wounds?" asked Moira.

"No, the burns were not responding to treatment, so in the end I was taken to the Queen Victoria Hospital in East Grinstead, where they had established a specialist burns unit, which finally sorted me out and got me back on the road to recovery. By now we are into December 1941 and of course on the 7th December that year, the Japanese attacked Pearl Harbour and on the very next day the U.S.A. entered the Second World War."

"I knew a nurse who went to a hospital in East Grinstead," said Moira, "how long were you there for?"

"I was there for New Year and then I was shipped to the States to be part of a liaison team between the British and American forces fighting in Europe, before finally being sent to Germany at the end of the war to participate in the final surrender and all that followed on from that."

"So when were you finally demobbed?" asked Bertie.

"The end of January 1947," said Mac.

"Why didn't you come and find me?" said Deborah.

"Who say's I didn't?" said Mac. "You had moved from Roses Deborah and had not left a forwarding address."

"Annette had my address, you could have asked her."

"I went across to Spain in the summer of 47 on my motorbike and went to Roses, but the place was locked up. I tried several of your old neighbours and even spoke to the chap who bought your horse, but they all said the same thing, 'she has gone back to England with her father and has sold her house to a Spanish lady, who is away on holiday at the moment and we don't know when she is coming back'. I never dreamed that the Spanish lady was Annette, how was I to know?"

They finished the meal and were still talking late into the night when Moira decided it was time for her to go. Deborah flatly refused to let go of Mac, so he spent the night on the Bannister's sofa and Digger walked Moira back to her house.

"Did you have any idea of all that your cousin had been up to during the war?" Moira enquired as they walked along.

"Well I knew he had joined the R.A.F. and had been shot down and had then been sent back to France and of course I knew about the burns and the various hospitals, but all the rest was a revelation to me. Some men are never the same again after such experiences and others like Donny, seem to revert to what they were before it all happened. Pretty amazing bloke really, my cousin."

"He certainly is and the change in Deborah was unbelievable, she was a different person, almost likeable, she must really have loved him. Talking of unbelievable, what was all that about Bertie and Spain and a son and a car and a house, what a dark horse he has turned out to be."

Digger kissed her goodnight on the doorstep and walked back to the cottage, where he found Mac sitting quietly outside the door.

"Hello boy, I forgot all about you, let's get you a drink of water and some biscuits, what a night we have had."

Digger was woken around seven the next morning by his cousin, who after a terrible night's sleep on the sofa, had slipped away from Deborah to return to the cottage for his things.

"Arnold are you awake? Arnold it's me, I have just come for my things."

"Well I wasn't awake," said Digger, as he came slowly down the stairs, "I thought you were staying with Bertie, don't tell me the girlfriend's father has rumbled you already, shee, that's quick even for you."

"Very funny, pretty amazing last night wasn't it?"

"You can say that again," said Digger, "so what happens now?"

"I don't suppose you would care to turn your wedding into a double wedding would you, as I actually proposed to Deborah after you two left last night?"

"Never on your life and congratulations," Digger replied, "but I will be your Best Man if you want me to and if I am still in England, that is."

"Only joking about the double wedding. There is a slight complication though, whilst Deborah accepted my proposal, she said she wants to get married at Benicarlo in Spain, so that is going to take some organizing. Getting the aged parents to travel to the R.A.F. base at Lincoln from Bedford was bad enough, but the thought of getting them to cross the English Channel and go to distant Spain is a task of mammoth proportions."

"I don't agree, I think they will be so relieved to see the back of you, that they would travel to the Moon and back if necessary. Your mum only asked me the last time I spoke to her, if I knew any nice girls that would suit you. Funny enough I thought of suggesting Deborah, but that seemed too cruel, even for you."

"Watch it cousin, you are talking about the woman I love, mind you, my first encounter with her was a bit interesting!"

Digger put some wood on the stove and boiled the kettle and made a cup of tea to go with the bread and marmalade he had laid out on the table.

"So seriously Donny, what happens next?"

"I am going to follow Deborah back to London this afternoon, to find out where her flat is. We both have to work this week, but she will come out to Bedford next weekend and meet the folks."

"I would love to be there to see how she gets on with your mum, that will be a most interesting encounter."

"Come over if you want, they are dying to meet Moira and are bitterly disappointed not to be going to Inverness for your wedding."

"Thanks mate, but no. When Moira told you that Deborah and I did not get on, she failed to mention that she and Deborah do not see 'eye to eye' either. So it's best if we leave you two lovebirds alone for a while."

"Bertie's wife Victoria was saying something about them going back to Australia, has that anything to do with you and Moira?"

"Indirectly yes, it does. They met a banker over there who told them he was coming to England to recruit for the bank and they told me about it. I went for the interview and was offered a job, which is where we are going after the wedding, to Perth in Western Australia. Come to think of it, Bertie and Victoria were planning to go back there later in the year, as Victoria has inherited a farm or something like that and I know Deborah did say that she wanted to go with them; almost put us off going."

"New horizons, sounds good to me, I wonder if there is any work for a civil engineer in Western Australia?"

After breakfast the two men took the dog for a walk in the woods and collected some more timber for the fire and while Digger got ready for church, his cousin got his motorbike out of the garage and headed back to Bertie's cottage.

"There you are Mac," said Deborah, who was standing by the gate, waiting apprehensively for his return. "So what has Digger been saying about me then?"

Mac said nothing, but after putting his bike on the stand, he walked up to Deborah and started feeling with both hands in her hair.

"Well he was wrong there," he said.

"Wrong about what? What has he been saying?"

"He said quite clearly that you have three horns, but I could definitely only find two."

"Perhaps you should check again, I enjoyed that," she replied laughing.

Bertie and Victoria were watching their antics from the window, "I couldn't believe the change in Deborah last night

Bertie," Victoria said, "she is a completely different person to the woman I thought I knew."

"That Mac certainly has a way with her," Bertie said in reply, "it's so good to hear her laugh and to see her smile again. Any thoughts about lunch today Victoria, as Deborah said that she wants to head back early to London as Mac is going to follow her?"

"It might be just as easy to go the pub and have something to eat there and then they can go off straight away afterwards," Victoria suggested.

"Good idea, we are too late for church now, so I think a glass of something in the garden is called for."

Digger met Moira in church, but as she sang in the choir, he sat in the usual pew that he, Bertie and Victoria normally sat in, on his own; until Sissy joined him, that is.

"Hello Arnold, mind if I join you today?" she asked.

"Of course not Sissy, bags of room. Your mother not with you today?"

"No. She and dad had the most awful row and he just stormed out of the house, in a terrible mood he was. Mum was too upset to come with me, crying and everything. 'My mother warned me that the Small family were a violent lot, but I knew best' she said. Poor mum she is such a gentle woman and dad gets so angry these days."

The service finished at a quarter past twelve and Digger walked Moira back to her home and as they passed the Green they spotted two motorbikes outside the Stag Inn.

"Looks like the Bannisters' and Donny are having lunch at the pub today Digger, did you want to join them? I do have some salad prepared for us at the house, if you don't," she said.

"No, Donny and I said our goodbyes this morning; anyway, if Sissy's dad is in there it might not be a very pleasant lunch time for anyone today. He is in another of his foul moods again."

They walked back to the house Moira rented from the local Brickworks and enjoyed their salad and listened to the radio and did some more planning for their forthcoming wedding.

Meanwhile in the Stag, things were starting to get interesting. While Tom Small, Sissy's dad, was relieving himself in the 'Gents' an old antagonist from the Brickworks had come into the pub and had sat down on his stool.

Del, the pub landlord was in the process of asking the man to sit on another stool, when Mr. Small returned to the bar.

"Mr. Case, you know perfectly well that Mr. Small sits on that stool when he is in here and that is his half finished pint of bitter to prove it."

"Can't see no sign to that effect, this stool don't have no-one's name on it, that I can see, Del me old mate." Mr. Case replied, "so get me a pint and lets be having no more of this nonsense."

"Casey, I warned you before," roared Mr. Small, "get off before I throw you off."

The sudden outburst interrupted the quiet, but animated conversation that was going on at the other end of the bar, between Bertie, Victoria, Deborah and Mac.

They looked up to see this big angry man, standing with his fists clenched, by the side of the man who was occupying his favourite stool.

"Mr. Small, we don't want any trouble, Mr. Case was just about to go, it was just a simple mistake."

"The only simple mistake in here, is this bag of wind on my stool," replied Mr. Small.

Everyone in the bar sat there quietly waiting for the volcano to erupt, when Mac turned to Bertie and said rather loudly in his very best R.A.F. voice, "I say Bertie old chap, who is that great oaf over there, with that ridiculous tattoo on the back of his neck?" implying Tom Small.

Bertie gulped, knowing that even his friendship with Tom Small would not prevent his young friend from receiving a most vicious bashing.

Tom slowly turned round and glared down the bar at his new antagonist. A 'flyboy' complete with flying jacket and still wearing his flying helmet.

"What have we here, an all 'mouth and trousers flyboy' I might have guessed," Tom snarled.

His son, Young Tom, tried to grab his father's arm, but was pushed aside.

"I suppose you know all about 'flyboys' do you Tommy?" Mac replied.

Tom Small took a couple of paces down the room towards Mac and stopped but said nothing.

"What does that Tattoo say Tommy? Go on tell everyone what it says."

Tom Small took another pace forward.

"No don't bother Tommy, I know what it says, it says 'TOM3Engineer' with your service number underneath it, doesn't it?"

Tom Small nodded, the room was hushed, everyone waited for the action.

"Do you all want to know how I know what it says?" Mac asked no-one in particular.

"Go on then, tell us how you know," one of the customers eventually called out.

"I know because I had to stare at that damned tattoo for the best part of three days while this man carried me on his back in 1941 through the forests and countryside of enemy occupied France. He carried me safely through the enemy lines and round a minefield and even across a river, before he deposited my shattered body at a British field hospital."

"I never even knew your name, so I couldn't ask about you," said Tom, as he stepped up to Mac, "I didn't know if you would survive those terrible injuries you had suffered, but I would recognise that voice of yours anywhere! For three whole days you never stopped talking, you drove me half mad with your jokes and comments, but you did have me fooled to start with just now, Flyboy."

"My name Tommy, is MacDonald Livingstone Forbes Smith, but all my friends simply call me Mac. I stand before you all today, thanks entirely to the courage, strength and integrity of this man. Tommy, I owe you my life, you are one of the bravest men I have ever met, you are without doubt a hero."

He got no further as he was engulfed in a bear hug that would have squeezed the life out of him, if he hadn't said quietly in his ear,

"If you don't let me go now, I will bite your ear off."

No sooner had Tom and Mac parted than Deborah stepped up and hugged Tom and thanked him for saving her man and even Mr. Case was caught up in the occasion and bought his old adversary a pint and vacated the stool.

After finishing their meal and saying goodbye to her dad and Victoria, Deborah drove her Indian motorbike back to Fulham with Mac following and they both parked their bikes in the back garden and were both very late for work the next day.

Tom Small was a hero and everyone in the village soon came to hear about it. People that had considered themselves 'above' the Small family, were suddenly inviting Mrs. Small round for afternoon tea and their sons and daughters were allowed to date Sissy and her brother Young Tom.

The management of the Brickworks came to hear about it too and soon Tom was promoted to 'Charge Hand' and within a couple of years, he was 'Works Manager', a position he held until the day he retired. He still enjoyed his pint at the local, but the aggressive behaviour was gone and people regularly pointed him out as being the hero of the village.

Chapter 3
'Ow-zat'

It was just around mid-day on Monday the eighth of August 1949 when Mac arrived at the Council Offices where he worked; he parked his bike round the back of the building, next to the Royal Enfield combination and covered it with the tarpaulin that he had left by the wall. He then went in through the back door and past Helen the receptionist who called out after him,

"Your boss has been out looking for you twice already this morning Mac, be warned he is not in a good mood."

"Thanks Helen, speak to you later," he called back, as he raced up the two flights of stairs, two at a time.

As he entered the Planning Office, which occupied most of the first floor of the building, he greeted the secretary as he hung his coat on the hat-stand by the door.

"Morning Mrs. T. how are you today?"

"Good afternoon Mr. Smith and where have you been so late in the day?" she enquired knowingly, "Mr. Rose was expecting you in at 9:00am to go over the plans for the new library with him, you had better go straight in to his office, but I should warn you that he is not in a good mood!"

Mac walked over to his manager's office in the corner of the room and knocked twice on the solid oak door.

"Enter," his boss called out imperiously.

Mac opened the door a little and looked in, "You wanted to see me Mr. Rose?"

"I wanted to see you at nine o'clock this morning Smith, what time do you call this?" he shouted out so loudly that the whole office stopped work and looked towards the corner of the room where Mac was hovering by the door.

Mac stood in the doorway looking at his boss, who had now got up from his seat and was walking round his desk towards him.

"I am really sorry sir, but I was delayed and could not get to a telephone to let you know that I was going to be late in," he tried to explain.

"Delayed, man, delayed! Delayed is ten to twenty minutes not three and a half hours, I needed you here for nine o'clock to assist me with these plans. I am tired of your lame-duck excuses Smith come in and sit down, this will have to go on your record this time," he stormed.

Mac turned round to the rest of the office and pulled that, 'I have cooked my goose this time' sort of face and then went in and sat down, while his boss slowly walked across to his secretary and said very calmly to her, "Mrs. T. would you mind making me a cup of strong coffee please, my throat is quite hoarse after all that shouting and you had better get Smith one as well, he is going to need it."

"Yes of course Mr. Rose, I will do it right now and bring them into you."

Mr. Rose went back to his office and slammed the door and Mrs. T. went to the kitchenette and made them a drink.

"Well, tell me, how did it go?" Mr. Rose enquired in a most congenial tone of voice.

"Like a dream Henry, whatever your brother did, he fixed the problem completely. She never cut out on me once and I was cruising along without a care in the world, easily the best she has ever gone."

"And the new tyre and inner tube he got for you?"

"Perfect, as good as he promised, wherever your brother gets them from, I think they are the genuine article, which reminds me, would you mind giving him the fiver I owe him, when you see him next?"

Mac was reaching into his jacket pocket to get his wallet, when Henry got up from the desk and walked towards the door.

"Hold on Mac, coffees are coming."

Henry opened the door for his secretary and she came in and put them down on the desk and noticed that Mac was wearing his very best 'sheepish' look.

"Thank you Mrs. T. please see that we are not disturbed for at least an hour, while I decide whether the council should continue to employ this so called engineer or not."

"Certainly Mr. Rose, leave it to me," she replied.

Mrs. T. left the room and gave the thumbs down to those that were watching her and shook her head in that, 'you would not want to be in there' manner, that senior secretaries can do so well.

Henry closed the door firmly and put up the 'Do not Disturb' sign on his window and sat down opposite Mac. He took the five pound note that Mac gave him and put it in his wallet.

"So I assume you lost the match yesterday," Mac said after sipping his coffee.

"We were all out for fifty three and you really will have to take your old man to the optician's and buy him some new spectacles."

"Why, what did he do this time?"

"He gave me out L.B.W. on a ball that bounced so far outside the leg stump that he should have called a wide."

"How many runs did you make?"

"Two. My lowest score of the season. But our wicket keeper was the main problem again. He dropped a vital catch and missed an easy stumping by at least two feet and was out for a duck himself. I am sure you could do a lot better than him, why not come along to practice on Wednesday and give it a go."

"Henry, I haven't played since before I got this," Mac replied, pointing to his face, "but I am free on Wednesday evening, as it happens, I guess I could come along for a practice, it would certainly please mum and dad to know I was playing again."

"Great, we can go straight from work and get a bite to eat at the pub by the green."

"Ah, hold on a minute Henry, next Sunday could be a bit tricky as I have invited a guest for the weekend."

"That's O.K. bring him along as well, he can keep score or something. I assume you are talking about your cousin, whom you went to visit this weekend."

"Arnold, no it's not him. It's a lady friend in fact, who is coming for the weekend. To tell you the truth Henry, I got engaged this weekend, she is my fiancée!"

Henry had just taken a mouthful of coffee when Mac made this announcement and he almost chocked as he tried very hard not to spray it all round his office.

"My giddy aunt Mac, did I just hear you right? Your fiancée!"

"That's right, quite amazing really. I went out to dinner with Arnold and Moira, his fiancée, to a friend of theirs in the village and who should I meet there, but a young woman and her father, that I got to know in the war, while I was overseas," Mac said.

"Not that little 'Popsy' in Spain that you are always going on about, surely? I thought she had completely disappeared from the scene," Henry replied.

"The very same. Turns out that her father Bertie, who was the sea captain who rescued me, moved to the village that

Arnold lives in, a couple of years before him and she was down for the weekend visiting her dad."

"Well I'm blowed!" said Henry.

"You and me both, old chap," said Mac. "I haven't told the Mater yet that we have a visitor this weekend, that should be interesting!"

"Too true and I assume this lady is the reason you were late in today?"

"Afraid so, sorry about that Henry, she lives in London and the traffic getting out of town was awful this morning."

"I'll believe you, thousands wouldn't! While I think about it, just sign the plans, there and there and initial the one change I have made," Henry said, passing the plans to Mac, who duly signed where intimated.

"If it's not too delicate a question, how did she respond to the injuries and the escape story?" Henry asked, after sipping his coffee.

"She was so blown away by seeing me alive and kicking, that I don't think she hardly noticed my face and to make the weekend even more incredible; I met the man in their local who actually rescued me form the compound and carried me to safety."

"Small world," said Henry.

"It sure is." said Mac.

"So about the cricket match on Sunday," Henry said, getting the conversation back to the really important matter of the week, "don't you think it would be an ideal opportunity for everyone to meet her and for her to work with your mother and Deidre preparing the afternoon teas?"

"I really cannot see Deborah with a pinafore on serving teas to sweaty cricketers, but you are right, it would be a great opportunity for them to get to know each other and saves me having to think up something to do to entertain her."

"Great, I will warn Deidre that she could be in for an interesting afternoon. So where does this Deborah live, if she is not living with her father?"

"Well her father has married again since I knew him and Debs told me that she much prefers the town to the country, so she has a very nice flat above a shop in Fulham, which is very convenient for her job in the centre of London, where she works for an insurance company, before you ask."

"It is a long way to travel to Bedford each day from Fulham, as you found out this morning, or maybe you can persuade her to live out this way, once you are wedded and settled," Henry suggested.

"I am not so sure Henry, that I will be staying with the council, once we are married."

"Go on then, what are you hiding? I can see you have something up your sleeve. Don't tell me you would be prepared to move to rural Buckinghamshire or Oxfordshire to work and live near your cousin and her father?"

"Good grief no, try a bit further afield. Perhaps it would help if I told you we plan to get married in Spain."

"Spain, that's a long way to go, I am not sure the wife would risk a journey of that distance in the sidecar with the nippers; assuming we will get an invite to the wedding, that is!"

"Of course you are invited, I was hoping you would be my Best Man."

"Did your cousin turn you down then?"

"No, he will already be in Australia by then," Mac replied.

"So by saying 'he will already be there by then', implies that you could be there, shortly afterwards. Am I right?"

"Spot on Henry. Her step mother Victoria, has recently purchased a part share in a fruit farm and she and her father are going back to help run it, or something like that and

Deborah had already decided that she wanted to go over there as well and do something different with her life. It appears she went to New Zealand when she was a lot younger and just loved it there."

"I thought you said that she preferred town to country, so why would she want to settle on a fruit farm, in the great 'outback' of Australia or New Zealand?"

"She lived in Auckland, during her time in New Zealand and it appears this farm is only about sixty miles from Perth which Victoria really loved and has been telling her all about it, so Debs wants to go there and live."

"I see, so where does that leave you?"

"I said that I was willing to go with her and give Perth a try; lots of British people are emigrating to Western Australia at the moment and Bertie says there are great opportunities for everyone; so my friend, what do we know about civil engineering projects in Western Australia?"

"Not a lot at the moment, but I will make some enquiries; hey, this could be our opportunity to start the partnership we have always dreamed about."

"My thoughts precisely Henry. Bertie was telling me about two British builders he met over there who are doing really well and Arnold was told the same thing at his interview with the bank, that there are opportunities right now, for bright young men and women, with imagination and a will to work."

"Now you have gone and spoilt it. I thought you could just walk down the main street of the mining towns and find nuggets of gold at the side of the road," Henry joked.

"That reminds me," said Mac, "didn't you start off your engineering career in mining, up north somewhere."

"That's right, I did five years at the Seaham Harbour coal mine in County Durham before coming down here to work. You know, we really should start making enquiries about emigrating to Australia while we are both still positive about it. I will discuss it with Deidre tonight and see what she thinks, I am sure a friend of hers emigrated last year, but I am not sure where she went to. Anyway, we both have things to do and I have a Lord Mayor to placate, so I will see you later and good luck with your mother tonight and don't forget the spectacles for your dad."

Mac worked through till six thirty p.m. that evening, to show willing and then went home to inform his parents about the events of the weekend.

"Of course I am pleased dear," his mother said, "why wouldn't any mother be pleased to hear that her son, who ostensibly went away for the weekend to discuss being Best Man at his cousin's wedding, has returned home, practically married to some mysterious woman he met in Spain during the War and which no-one else has ever met!"

"Well you will get the chance to meet her this weekend, I have invited her over here," Mac replied, "she will arrive on her big red Indian motorbike, around lunch-time on Saturday."

"Well, a motorcycle indeed, whatever next?" said his mother, who sniffed twice, 'sniff - sniff', always a bad sign, "I suppose I had better get the spare room aired, if we have a guest."

Mac looked at his dad, who pulled that glum sort of smile and then said, "Did Henry mention the match to you son?"

"Don't change the subject Angus," his wife said, cutting off any 'cricketing' deviation in the bud.

"Sorry dear, I thought you had finished, please continue," Angus replied.

"So you did actually propose to this woman then and I presume, she accepted, which I conclude, is the reason you did not return home last night. Is that correct?"

"I proposed, she accepted and we are going into Bedford on Saturday afternoon to buy her a ring, mother," Mac replied.

"So if her father lives in Buckinghamshire and she lives in London, where do you propose to get married, or perhaps you would like to get married here and I could possibly be persuaded to help with the arrangements."

"That's very kind of you mother, but she actually wants to get married in Spain," he replied, but actually mumbled the 'Spain' bit.

"I'm sorry dear, I didn't quite catch that, but I thought you said Spain. My ears must have deceived me."

"I did say Spain mother. She wants to get married in the town where she was born in Spain and where her mother, her granny and her baby brother are buried. It is the one place that she thinks of as home and it holds good memories for her."

"I see," said his mother, "well you will never get your father to Spain Donny, it was bad enough getting him up to Lincoln to see you at the Air Base and your aunt Violet has never been further east than Clacton, remember the holiday we all had there, so I am sure it will be impossible to talk her into crossing the English Channel; besides which, I don't have a hat suitable for Spain! No, we will have to discuss this whole matter with your Deborah at the weekend, my word we will!"

"No Hazel we will not," said Angus, in a surprising show of family headship.

"I beg your pardon Angus," said Hazel, "what did you just say to me?"

"You heard Hazel, I said we will not be discussing this matter with Donny's fiancée this weekend, or any other weekend, for that matter. Tradition states that the Bride chooses where she wants to get married, not the Groom's mother, and kindly do not use me as your excuse for not going to our son's wedding. I will most certainly be there and I expect you to be at my side and if your sister Violet chooses not to come, that is her decision, but I should say, it will the first time in all the years that I have known her, that she has turned down the opportunity for free food and drink! Is that clear Hazel?"

Hazel did not reply but went upstairs to check on the supply of sheets and blankets for the spare bed; the next day she went to visit her elder sister who lived a few streets away and to give her the good news about Donny.

"How exciting Hazel, I always said that your Donny was a dark horse," Violet exclaimed, "I have always wanted to go to Spain and we can have a nice long holiday while we are all there. Did he say when he thought the wedding would take place?"

"No he didn't Violet, I don't think he knows himself yet. It turns out that it was her father who rescued him from Lisbon and stitched up his wounds after he had been stabbed by the Germans and she nursed him until he got better, at the house she used to own at this other Spanish town near to France. But she doesn't own it any more, or something like that. It's all very confused, but he is so in love with her, I was so thrilled when he told us about her."

"I wonder what they wear in Spain at weddings," Violet asked aloud.

"No idea, but I told Angus that I have absolutely nothing suitable and will need a complete new outfit."

"Good for you Hazel, we can both go up to London and visit all the big shops, it will serve the old skinflint right, he never spends any money on you."

"That's a bit harsh Violet and he speaks so highly of you," Hazel replied.

"Pull the other one dear, it's got bells on it," Violet responded, "I have no illusions of what your husband says about me behind my back; he is blunt enough to my face!"

The cricket practice on Wednesday went well for Mac and as they were a man short for the game on Sunday, he agreed to 'keep wicket' but only on the understanding that he would be the last man into bat.

He and Henry had spent a lot of time discussing the 'Australian option' and had written off for details of emigrating to Western Australia. They both decided not to discuss the matter with anyone else, until they had a better idea of what was involved.

By the time that Saturday arrived Hazel had almost convinced herself that a Spanish wedding was a great idea and was looking forward to meeting this woman who had stolen her son's heart.

Deborah turned up at the house just after one thirty and after a very quick introduction to his parents and the handing over of the requisite bunch of flowers to Hazel, Mac jumped onto the pillion seat and they both went into Bedford to look at rings, returning home about four p.m.

"Oh what a beautiful ring my dear," Hazel said to Deborah, as she stood in the living room next to Mac, with her left arm partially extended and her hand at a slight angle, to display the sign of their betrothal on her finger.

After Hazel had relinquished the hand, Angus came over and had a quick look, then said, "That's nice Deborah," and went off into the kitchen to put the kettle on.

"Why don't you and I go through to the sitting room Deborah and start to get acquainted, while the men get the tea sorted. It will probably take the two of them at least ten minutes to accomplish such a tricky task," she said smiling and intimating the minimum amount of time she expected to be alone with her future daughter-in-law.

"That ring must have cost you a packet, Donny," his father exclaimed, once the ladies had left the room.

"Almost a month's wages dad, but I would have spent more if I had it, what did you think of her?"

"Not your usual lady-friend this time Donny, this one appears to have a personality and not just a pretty face and a nice figure, not that I am saying she was not pretty, just appears to have a bit more depth to her."

"Yes, I suppose she does, what with her mother running off back to Chile where she was born and having to be rescued by her father and then all the things they got up to in Spain during the war, she has had a hard time one way and another and is a pretty unique lady, that's for sure."

"Has your mother had her ten minutes yet, we don't want to leave Deborah un-supported for too long son?"

"Don't you worry about Debs, she is more than capable of looking after herself."

"Well Deborah, why don't we sit on the settee and leave the armchairs for the men," Hazel suggested.

"I am afraid my trousers are a bit muddy Mrs. Smith, do you mind if I go and change first," Deborah replied.

"Of course dear, Angus put your bag in the guest room, which is at the top of the stairs and the bathroom is the next door along."

Deborah went upstairs and changed into a skirt and blouse and freshened up in the bathroom and brushed her hair before returning to the sitting room, just as Mac and his dad brought the tea and cake in and put the tray on the coffee table.

"Sorry Debs," said Mac, "never thought that you might want to change your clothes."

"Not to worry Mac," said Deborah, "shall I pour the tea since I am the one standing up?"

"Thank you dear," said Hazel, "that would be most kind, but can we just clear up what name you like to be called, as Donny said that you hate having your lovely name shortened, but he just called you Debs, so which do you prefer, Deborah or Debs?"

"I would like you to call me Deborah please, Mac is the only one who is allowed to call me Debs. Do you take milk and sugar Mr. Smith?"

"A little milk and one spoon of sugar please Deborah and Hazel is the same."

The teacups were handed over and the plates and cake circulated and Deborah sat down on the settee next to Hazel.

"What beautiful pictures," said Deborah, admiring the two landscapes that hung in the alcoves either side of the fireplace.

"They are aren't they," said Angus, "been in my family for yonks. They are by a Scottish artist named B. Ward and we presume they are of the highlands. Probably quite close to where Arnold is getting married in a couple of weeks time, up near Inverness."

"Will you be going to the wedding Deborah?" asked Hazel.

"No, I don't really know Digger and Moira that well, but my dad and Victoria are going up there and of course Mac is Best Man."

"Victoria is your father's second wife I presume," said Hazel.

"That's right, my mother died in January thirty five and dad re-married last year, she is really good for him and they get on so well together."

"Donny told us that you were a year younger than him, but did not say when your birthday was," Hazel continued, mentally ticking off the questions on her list.

"It's in a couple of weeks on the thirtieth of August and I will be thirty four."

"Will you be back by then Donny, or still in Scotland?" asked his dad.

"Good question, the wedding is on the twenty seventh and I am travelling up with Arnold in his car, if it gets that far, but I haven't actually booked a ticket for the return journey yet, so I guess I could be back for the thirtieth, I will go to the station on Monday and see what I can organise."

Deborah beamed at him across the room, "It would be wonderful if you could be here, dad and I normally book some tickets for the theatre with a meal beforehand, but of course he and Victoria will still be in Scotland, so I had nothing planned as yet. Perhaps your parents might like to come with us as well," Deborah suggested.

"That would be lovely," said Angus, "we have not seen a show in the West End since before the War, it's high time we started to enjoy ourselves again Hazel."

"Tell us about this town in Spain, where you want to get married," Hazel asked, "we are all so excited at travelling to Europe for your wedding. Does your father still have property there?"

"I don't think so. He was asked to sell it a while ago to the couple who were renting it from him, but I am not sure what happened. He sold his first house in Benicarlo in order to finance the rescue mission when my mother was in prison in Santiago, in Chile, so he had the second house built in nineteen thirty three, which is where my mother spent her last two years before she died of T.B."

"I am so sorry my dear," said Hazel, putting her hand on Deborah's, "my mother died of T.B. also, in this very house; sometimes at night when I can't get to sleep, I am certain that I can still hear her coughing."

So an unlikely bond was formed between Deborah and Hazel, much to the surprise and pleasure of father and son. The two women seemed to genuinely enjoy each other's company and when Mac announced that he was playing cricket on the Sunday and that his father was an umpire and his mother was in charge of catering, Deborah immediately offered to go along and help her with the teas.

Mr. and Mrs. Smith discreetly went upstairs to bed around ten thirty, leaving their son and his fiancée in the sitting room with the wireless. They held each other tight and kissed and chatted quietly and talked over the events of the day.

"Your parents are really nice Mac," said Deborah, "and they seem to like me too."

"I can honestly say that you are the first girl that I have brought into this house that my mother has approved of," Mac replied.

"So how many other girls were there before me, lover boy," she asked, leaning over and nibbling his ear.

"Too many to count; hey that hurt you hooligan. They were all before the War, before I met you, there have been none since then, honest."

"Well that's all right then," she replied, releasing his ear lobe from her teeth. "So what time does everyone get up here, on a Sunday."

"Dad normally gets up about seven thirty and brings mum up a cup of tea about eight. She then brings me one up at eight thirty and we have breakfast together around ten past nine. We all then get changed and head off for church about ten thirty.

It's about a fifteen minute walk, so we have time to greet our friends before the service starts at eleven."

"You never used to go to church, I remember you telling me that you didn't believe in all that anymore," Deborah commented.

"What do you think kept me going in that dreadful Gestapo prison. I prayed for hours each day and not only found strength and courage but found my faith again. I asked God to save me and he did. If I had cracked a few hours earlier, I would have been executed before the bombs struck the building and if I had lasted a few hours longer, I would have been killed by the bombs. Apart from that, along comes Corporal Small, in truth a man prepared to disobey orders to check out who I was, who had the brute strength and tenacity to carry me for three days and deposit my battered body in a Field Hospital," Mac replied, with a slight tremour in his voice.

"I understand Mac, don't go getting emotional on me again or I will start crying again just like I did on Sunday night and I don't want to embarrass myself in front of your parents. Can I come to church with you tomorrow morning?"

"Of course you can and it will give you a chance to meet Henry and his family before the match in the afternoon. His wife Deidre is a real scream, she helps mum with the teas. She is younger than Henry and pulls his leg mercilessly, you will love her."

Hazel took Deborah up a cup of tea about eight thirty five Sunday morning, just after she had given one to her son.

"Good morning Deborah," she said, "I trust you slept well last night?"

"Thank you I had a really good night's sleep and thanks for the tea, I am not used to tea in bed. Mac said it would be alright for me to come to church with you today."

"Of course it is, but I would advise you to get into the bathroom early as he seems to spend forever in there on a Sunday morning."

Deborah took the advice and finished her tea and visited the bathroom and was fully dressed and ready for breakfast at nine o'clock. They ate in the living room around the large family table and breakfast consisted of toast and marmalade, tomatoes, bacon and sausage, with a fried egg and brown sauce for those who wanted it, all washed down with copious amounts of tea.

After breakfast, Mac and Deborah walked to the corner shop and bought a Sunday paper and a packet of Polo's and slowly walked back home. By the time they had arrived there, the washing up was done and put away and after everyone had paid a visit to the bathroom, they all set off for church.

It was a large Baptist Church on the corner of the street and they were greeted at the door by one of the deacons who was introduced to Deborah and who shook everyone's hand and warmly welcomed them to the church. Once inside, they made their way to their usual pew and found Henry and Deidre already sitting in the pew in front, with their little boy in the process of being told off, for pulling his little sister's hair.

"So this is Gloria," said Henry, shaking Deborah's hand, "Mac has told me all about you and I simply adore opera, just like you."

Deborah stared at him and her jaw dropped, when Deidre pushed him out of the way and held both her hands and said to her, "Take no notice Deborah, these two continually compete with each other, for winding each other up. He knows precisely who you are, don't you Henry?"

"Sorry Deborah," said Henry, "but you should have seen your face. Morning Mrs. S. and Angus, how are the eyes today?"

"No better for seeing you Henry," Angus replied, squeezing the outstretched hand.

They settled down for the service which lasted just over eighty minutes and they were back home by a quarter to one having a light lunch of salad and cold meat, before heading off for the cricket match.

Hazel piled all the food into the back of their Austin Seven and she and Angus got into the front seat and drove off, leaving Deborah and Mac to follow behind on the Indian, as Deborah had said that she wanted to leave straight after the match, as there was something she needed to prepare for work the next day.

The afternoon was dry and the sun decided to put in an appearance for an hour or so and the visiting team batted first and managed to score seventy four runs in the allotted overs. Mac did quite well behind the wicket and managed to catch one and stump one, so he was pleased with his performance.

Deborah had managed to watch some of the game, whilst helping Deidre and Hazel get the tea ready, but did not really understand what was going on. The players were all ravenous and Deborah had not seen so much food disappear so quickly in all her life and there was almost a fight over the last plate of homemade cakes.

"I am sure that half of our team only play so that they can have the free food," Deidre commented, as she struggled with a giant teapot to replenish the empty cups.

The home team batted after tea and since Mac was batting last, he was able to sit with Deborah and explain what was happening on the field of play. They were doing quite well to start with and had knocked fifty runs off the first twelve overs for only two wickets and were feeling mildly confident, when things started to go wrong. The next six wickets fell for just twenty two runs and much to everyone's surprise Mac was told to 'pad up' and be ready to play.

"I didn't practice batting on Wednesday, just wicket keeping," he complained to his mother, "not sure I am up to this."

"Nonsense, you will go out there and score the winning run, or I will want to know the reason why!" she replied, as she found a pair of gloves in the bag, that did not have too many holes in them.

A cheer went up from the spectators, "They just scored a two Mac," Deborah informed him, "your friend Henry did it, looks like you won't be needed after all."

"Ow-zat!!" Came the shout from the field.

Angus, who was the umpire at the bowlers end, looked down the pitch towards Henry and held up his finger, indicating that for the second week in a row, he had been bowled out L.B.W.

Henry stood there in disbelief and stared at Angus down the wicket, but was too good a sportsman to say anything, so he turned and walked towards the pavilion; as he met Mac coming towards him, he passed him his bat and wished him well.

"Stand near the Off stump Mac, it will throw him off a bit," he suggested.

Mac walked to the crease, casually looked around him, to give the impression that he knew what he was doing and stood near to the Off stump as Henry had advised. He saw his father signal 'play' and watched the bowler running up to the crease. In all honesty, he never saw the ball coming and only felt the slightest of jars, as he took a half pace forward and connected with the ball, which hit his front pad and whistled off behind the wicket.

"Run Mac, run," shouted the batsman at the other end, which he did with great gusto and the team scored a 'leg bye' which won them the game.

Deborah played her part and gave him a hero's welcome, his mother said, "See Donny, I told you that you could do it," and Henry complained that if Angus had not wrongly given him out again, he would have scored the winning run and been the hero instead of his friend.

The engaged couple hugged and kissed after the match and everyone waved as Deborah rode off into the sunset on her majestic stead, she having agreed to meet up with Mac again the following weekend, at her place.

Chapter 4
A Scottish Wedding

Both Digger and Moira finished work on Friday the 19th August 1949 which was also the day that Moira's tenancy ended on the house she had been renting from the local brickworks. She and Digger had moved all of her things to his cottage during the week, as Mrs. Black had told them that they were both welcome to stay there until their voyage out to Australia on the fourteenth of September.

When Digger got home from the bank at six forty p.m., Moira had already changed out of her District Nurse's uniform and had the kettle boiling on the hob and had prepared a salad ready for their tea and had fed the dog.

"Goodness me, Moira," said Digger, "if I had known this was all part of the deal, I would have got married long before now."

"Would you indeed?" she queried. "Since I have only known you for a year or so, tell me who you would have 'got married to' Mr. Smith?"

"Good point! Remind me, what time does your train leave from Euston tonight?" he asked, changing the subject.

"Ten past ten, the same as last time you asked," she replied. "Do you still intend to go round to see your sister after you have dropped me off at the station?"

"Yes, Mick rang me at work today to confirm it. Patty wants to show me her bridesmaid's dress that Vi has made her. It appears your other bridesmaid Joyce, has been really helpful to Vi, who is not the world's greatest seamstress."

"Oh good, I have arranged to see her on Sunday after church, so I am sure she will tell me all about it and show me her dress as well. I hope you have not been peeking at mine, while it has been hanging in your wardrobe!"

"Boys Brigade honour. I said I wouldn't and I haven't; I assume it is now safely packed in that large suitcase which I fell over when I came in just now," Digger replied.

"Do you want to eat now or are you changing first, before we leave for the station?"

"Give me five minutes to change and then we can eat and as long as we are away by just after eight, we will have plenty of time to get to Euston and park before the train departs and yes, the car is running well at the moment, thank you."

Digger washed and changed out of his business suit and was back downstairs in his sports jacket and slacks by seven fifteen. They had a hot drink and ate the salad and Digger washed the dishes while Moira said her goodbyes to Mrs. Black and her sister, who presented her with a wedding present, carefully wrapped in some silvery paper.

"Can I open it now?" she asked.

"I don't see why not, I am sure Arnold won't mind," replied Mrs. Duffy-Smythe.

She carefully unwrapped the parcel and found a beautiful cut glass fruit bowl, with a card inside, from the two sisters.

"Oh, it's truly beautiful, thank you both so much," she said, "and not too big to take to Australia with us, as well."

"We know you have always admired our fruit bowl, so it is as near the pattern as we could get to it and as you said, we wanted to get you something that you would be able to take with you and not have to wait months for it to arrive," explained Mrs. Black.

Moira returned to the cottage to find Digger sitting by the front door with his coat and hat on. She passed him the bowl and said, "Isn't it beautiful Digger, it's the very finest cut glass."

"It's a fruit bowl! Vi got four fruit bowls for wedding presents, so one down and three to go. Are you ready to leave now?"

Moira did not know what to say, so decided to say nothing, as fruit bowls are a favourite presents in Scotland, the home of the finest 'cut glass'.

They left Millstone House at five past eight, with two large suitcases for Moira and an overnight bag for Digger. The car behaved itself all the way into London and they had managed to park at Euston Station without any problems and were walking down the platform, with the luggage by a quarter to ten.

Digger accompanied her into the sleeping compartment and stowed the larger of the two cases away for her, when the young woman who was sharing the compartment with her, who was about the same age as Moira, arrived with her young man. They all chatted for a while and then both couples said their fond farewells and the two men descended onto the platform and after a few minutes more, they all waved frantically to each other as the train steamed out of the station on its way to Glasgow.

Digger managed to get lost somewhere around Kingsway and the Aldwych, so instead of going over Waterloo Bridge he ended up going over Blackfriars Bridge and down past the Borough and Kennington and was beginning to get a bit worried as to where he would end up, when he spotted the Oval Cricket Ground and realised exactly where he was. He drove down alongside Clapham Common and arrived at the house where his sister and her family lived, just after ten past eleven.

Vi had been looking out for him since ten thirty, despite Mick telling her that he could not possibly be with them until about eleven o'clock. She was down the stairs and outside in the street before he had even managed to get his bag out of the boot and gave him a 'big sisterly' hug, before reprimanding him for not having brought Moira over to see them, before she left for Inverness.

"Give the man breathing space Vi, he has only just arrived," said Mick, as he joined the pair on the pavement. "I told her earlier that you would not be arriving until about now Digger, but would she listen?" He then pointed at the boot of the car and said, "Have you got a dent in your boot? Looks fresh!"

"Blast, you are right," said Digger, "must have happened while I was parked at Euston, it was fine when we left home tonight. I'll check it out tomorrow, make sure nothing is damaged."

"I thought you might be hungry, so I saved you some steak and kidney pie," said Vi, as they were walking up the stairs, "and Mick has bought a bottle of Tizer from the off-licence for you."

"Funny you should ask, but I am starving. Moira got us some salad for tea and I had a liquid 'farewell' lunch today, with the boys at work, so I could eat a horse."

His niece and nephew were awake early the next day and were in the lounge where Digger was sleeping on a camp-bed, at about three seconds after eight, having been threatened with all sorts of dire consequences, should they waken him before eight o'clock.

"My dress is pale blue with short sleeves and is tied at the back with a big bow," Patty informed him, as he was trying to come to and remember where he was.

"I scored a great goal at football on Thursday and had a fight with my best friend Freddy and you have got a dent in the back of your car," Brian stated with confidence.

"Come on kids, give your uncle time to come to, he is here for the whole weekend," said their mother, as she set a mug of tea down beside his bed, "and don't kick the tea over, do you hear me?"

"Yes mum, we hear you!" they replied in concert.

"So are you both looking forward to the wedding and in travelling up to Inverness by train on Wednesday?" Digger asked, as he carefully sipped the tea.

"Oh yes," said Brian, "dad has booked a sleeping compartment for the trip up but said he couldn't afford one for the trip back."

"Are you travelling by train uncle, or going by car?" asked Patty.

"Your cousin Donny and I are driving up on Tuesday and Wednesday Patty."

"Dad said that Donny was going to be your Best Man, but if he is the Best Man, why is auntie Moira marrying you and not him?" Brian asked.

"Don't even attempt to answer that one Digger," Vi interrupted from the kitchen next door, "I heard Mick putting him up to it last night, when he was tucking him in."

"Ah mum, you spoil everything," Brian retorted quietly.

"I heard that too," she said.

After breakfast Patty was allowed to show off her bridesmaid's dress, which Digger duly praised and thanked his sister for all her trouble and then informed them that he could divulge no information about the bridal gown, as Moira had refused to let him see it. She had been making the dress herself, over the last few months, with the assistance of her Great aunt Mary who lived in Buckingham and had travelled to Inverness two weeks earlier, to be there to assist Moira and her mother with all the wedding arrangements and to make any final alterations to the dress.

Vi then put on her new dress to show her brother and lastly Brian paraded up and down in his new black shoes, which creaked as he walked in them.

"That just leaves you Mick," Digger said with a smile, "new suit, or blazer perhaps?"

"I got a new tie for a present last Christmas which I have been saving for the occasion and a new pair of braces that Vi got for me, mustn't forget them!" he joked back.

"I assume you have treated yourself to a new suit Digger," Vi asked.

"What with us travelling to Australia so soon afterwards, it would have been a waste of money, so Moira's dad has arranged for me to hire a wedding suit up there. Saves it getting creased in the back of the car, when I drive up with Donny."

"What's this I hear about Donny and that Devilish Debbie you are always going on about?" Vi enquired.

"Don't call her that in front of Donny, please, but talk about a co-incidence," Digger replied, "that she, my worst night-mare should turn out to be Donny's long lost love, whom he met during his time in Spain."

"I never knew Donny went to Spain," said Vi, "Hazel always said he was in France or Germany when I asked her."

"She didn't have a clue where he was, most of the time, it just saved any awkward questions I expect," Digger told her and then proceeded to tell them the whole story of Donny and Deborah meeting up again at Bertie's cottage.

"So does that mean she is travelling up to Scotland with you for the wedding then?" asked Mick.

"Thankfully no. She was never invited to the wedding and Donny never asked and Moira would never have agreed to it, if he had!"

"How far is it from Bedford to Inverness?" asked Brian, "and will your old banger make it O.K?"

"You cheeky little blighter," Digger replied, grabbing his nephew and wrestling him to the floor. "It's about five hundred and fifty miles and my 'old banger' as you dared to call it, will get there with no problem at all."

"What time does Donny finish work then on Tuesday," asked Vi.

"He said that he would finish at mid-day and I could pick him up around two and I reckon it shouldn't be more that a six hour drive to Kendal from Bedford where we are spending the night."

"Stopping somewhere nice?" asked Vi.

"We are as it happens, we are stopping at The Highgate Hotel in Kendal. Our good friends Bertie and Victoria from the village are travelling up by bus this weekend and stopping there for a few nights before they catch the train to Scotland, so we are meeting up with them."

"Isn't that the same Bertie who is Deborah's father and could end up as Donny's father-in-law," enquired Mick.

"Yes, fascinating isn't it. Donny is quite different around Bertie, I have been contemplating all the things I can say about him, to get my own back for all the rotten tricks he has pulled on me over the years," said Digger.

"Just remember he is going to give a Best Man's speech at your wedding, I wouldn't wind him up too much if I were you brother," said Vi, warningly.

They all had a drink and then Digger put together a kite he had bought the children in Oxford the previous week and then they went onto Clapham Common to fly it. There wasn't a lot of wind around but eventually a gust took hold of it and lifted it high up into the air. Brian was just getting the hang of it when Patty decided it was her turn and demanded he hand the kite over to her.

"Come on Brian, your uncle bought the kite for both of you, so give your sister a turn," said his father.

"Here take it," he said, thrusting the chord at her.

Patty was in the middle of giving her sweetest smile of triumph to her brother, when another gust of wind caught the kite and wrenched the string from her grasp.

"I knew that would happen dad," said Brian, "girls!"

"He did it deliberately dad, he never gave me the string properly."

"Did so," Brian replied.

"Enough you two," said their mother, "what on earth must your uncle be thinking?"

Digger laughed and was about to speak, when Vi cut him off.

"That was not a question but a statement Digger, thank you."

"It's caught in that tree dad," said Brian, "give me a bunk up uncle and I will climb up and get it."

"You most certainly will not, it's far too dangerous," said his mother.

"You heard your mother son, why don't we all walk over to the bandstand and see if there is anything on today," Mick suggested.

"You go," said Vi, "I have some things to do at home. Do you want to come with me or stay with the boys, Patty?"

"I'll come with you, mum, before I get blamed for anything else I didn't do," Patty replied, staring at her brother and poking her tongue out, when she was sure no-one else was watching.

The men and Brian strolled over to the bandstand but there was nothing going on, so they watched the model boats being sailed on the boating lake and then started a slow walk back home.

"The kite is still there dad, come on, let me go up and get it. I can easily climb that tree once I am up to that branch there," he said, pointing to a branch that was about five feet off the ground.

"Are you sure about this son," his father asked.

"Me and Freddy often come up here with his elder brother and go tree climbing, believe me dad, I can do it."

"Well all right, but be careful," with which he lifted Brian up to the branch and stood there watching as he climbed up and rescued the kite and then dropped it to the ground, close to where the two men were standing."

"Don't jump from there Brian, the ground is uneven and you might twist your ankle," Digger called out to him, "just lower your tummy onto the branch and we will lift you off," which is exactly what happened.

"Well done son, you are a good climber, but don't say anything to your mother, I will tell her later, understood?"

Digger and Mick checked the car over in the afternoon and decided there was no serious damage to it, just a dent and the loss of a bit of paint. Once the children had gone to bed, after countless games of Ludo and Snakes and Ladders, Mick got out the papers he had received from Australia House and laid them out on the table.

"You two are really taking this emigration idea seriously then," Digger said, as he started to read his way through the paperwork.

"The more we talked about it, the more interested we got, especially knowing that you and Moira would already be there in Western Australia, since we knew we would have some sort of base to start from and not have to go into one of those camps that they talk about," Vi explained.

"On my wages, we are always going to be struggling here," said Mick, "and the bloke I spoke to at Australia House said they were crying out for plumbers in every state in Australia and that we would easily be able to buy our own place in a year or two, something we could never hope to do over here."

"The fares will cost us ten pounds each for Mick and me and the children go free. We have to stay for two years, after that we can come home if we don't like it. Honestly Digger, what do we have to lose? We can stop with you can't we?"

"Of course you can, but you need to give us at least six months to get a place of our own and to get ourselves established. When I told Moira that you were thinking about emigrating, she was really pleased about it and it actually made her a lot more comfortable about going there. What about your folks Mick, have you told them yet?"

"Goodness no, you know what my mother is like. We will wait till we have got everything booked and then I will tell them, but not a word until then. We have been thinking about May next year, as a departure date. It will give us time to save a bit more cash and give you time to find out about the cost of housing, schools, job opportunities and the like. It would also be useful if you could let us know which of our furniture and things are worth shipping over and which we can buy just as cheaply over there."

"It's asking an awful lot of you Digger, are sure you don't mind?" said Vi.

"After all you two have done for me over the years Vi, I will be only too pleased to help and so will Moira. Goodness if Donny and Deborah decide to come as well, we will have half the family over there with us."

The next day being Sunday they had a bit of a lie-in and then went to the Methodist church which was just down the road, where the children were members of the Cubs and Brownies and it was the monthly church parade.

They both looked very smart in their uniforms and waved to Digger as they filed into church.

Digger left for home, straight after lunch, leaving Mick to explain to Vi, how the kite had mysteriously appeared in the boot of Digger's car, when he opened it to put his bag in.

He spent Monday doing a whole load of odd jobs for the two sisters, who assured him that they would look after his dog while he was away.

"Will you take him to Australia with you Arnold," asked Mrs. Duffy-Smythe, "or find a good home for him here?"

"To be honest, I haven't thought about it, what with the wedding and everything, poor old Mac, how could I forget you, eh boy?"

Mac wagged his tail and went over for a pat, before sitting down again by the chair of Mrs. Black.

"To be honest with you Arnold, we have been thinking about it and would be most happy to look after Mac permanently for you, or at least until you are settled in Australia and can send for him," Mrs. Black informed him.

"That is very kind of you, can I think it over and let you know when I get back from Scotland?"

On Tuesday he packed his bags and left for Bedford around ten o'clock and had a pleasant drive across to Donny's home. He parked outside the house, closed the gate behind him and then rang the bell which was located at the side of the front door. As no-one had answered the door after a couple of minutes, he rang again and was on the verge of ringing a third time when the door was opened by a breathless Angus.

"Hello Arnold, good to see you, come in. Sorry for the delay, but I was in the shed and Hazel has popped out to the shops."

"I wasn't expecting to see you here Angus, are you on your holidays or the late shift?"

"I am on 'lates' this week Arnold, which was one of the reasons that we couldn't come to the wedding, that and Hazel's phobia of steam engines."

"You could have gone by bus, like Deborah's parents of course!"

"I know son, I feel rotten about it, but that would have needed another week's holiday and I didn't have that many days left, I'm afraid."

"That's all right Angus, I understand, but if she wouldn't travel to Scotland, how on earth are you going to get her to Spain for Donny's wedding."

"She and that sister of her's, have it all worked out; but tell me what you know of this Deborah and her family, she and Hazel got on like a 'house on fire', quite amazing really."

"What's amazing Angus?" said Hazel, as she appeared in the doorway of the dining room, carrying two large carrier bags of shopping."

"I wished you wouldn't do that Hazel, creep up on me like that, you'll give me a heart attack one of these days."

"Guilty conscience my lad. Hello Arnold, how is everything, you have a dent in your boot, did you know?"

"Hello Hazel, it was amazing that Donny and Deborah met up again the other weekend; everything is wonderful, yes I have a dent and yes I know about it and how are you?"

"Was that a little bit of sarcasm creeping in there, that I detected Arnold?" she asked, as she pecked him on the cheek and put the shopping away in the larder.

"So what did you make of Deborah when you met her the other week?" Digger asked.

"Well she is certainly different to any of the other girls he has brought home before," Hazel replied, assuming that the question had been asked of her and not Angus.

"What is most important of course, is that she is madly in love with him, as he is with her, so quite frankly if she had two heads and smoked a pipe, I would still like her, as she is going to be my daughter-in-law in the near future and hopefully the mother of my grandchildren, at some time after that."

"Well said old girl," said Angus, patting his wife on the back.

"Thank you Angus, but I am not a horse and I do not require a pat. Remind me Arnold, do you take sugar with your tea these days?"

Donny arrived home about one thirty and it took him five minutes to change, another five to grab a sandwich and they were on their way by a quarter to two and had travelled about two miles on their journey, when Donny remembered he had forgotten his Bartholomew's Road Atlas, so they had to return home to get it and were finally on their way again around two o'clock.

"Do you want to stick with the A6 all the way and go over the hills, or would you prefer the flatter route Arnold and go round via Stoke on Trent and Wigan?"

"I am not sure what the weather will be doing over the hills and the roof leaks a bit in heavy rain, so let's play safe and go via Stoke, it will be a good place to fill up with petrol as well, before we have to go round Manchester."

The miles seemed to flash past and Donny was engrossed in his war time story about Deborah and Bertie when Digger realised that they were still on the A6 and had not turned onto the A52, so he had do a three point turn and retrace his steps, to pick up the correct road again. They stopped for petrol in Stoke and again in Preston and arrived at the hotel in Kendal at a little after eight o'clock. When they signed in at Reception they were told that Mr. and Mrs. Bannister had gone through to the dining room already and that they could leave their bags at Reception if they wanted to and pick them up again after they had eaten. Bertie spotted them as they walked through the door and stood up and beckoned them over.

"Hello Digger, Mac, good to see you both, sorry but we were famished so we started without you, come and join us."

"Good evening Mrs. Bannister, nice to see you again," said Mac.

"Please Mac, call me Victoria, after all, I even allow your cousin Arnold to call me by my first name nowadays!"

They sat down and ordered a main course and another bottle of wine and chatted and ate until well after ten.

"I gather from Arnold that you used to live in this area and still have family here, Victoria."

"That's right Mac, my first husband was a gamekeeper on one of the large estates and my second husband owned a grocers shop in Penrith and my brother Eddy lives in a small village not far from here, with his wife Dolly."

"Is he the chap you were telling me about that used to play football in his youth?" asked Digger.

"He certainly is," said Bertie, "the last time we called on them we caught them by surprise, but this time he was ready for us and I think he must have showed us every medal and mention in the press that he ever received. Nice chap though, never a dull moment when Eddy is around."

"His wife Dolly had us in stitches though," said Victoria, "it appears that Eddy often cannot sleep and has to get up in the night to make himself a drink, but Dolly regularly reorganizes her kitchen shelves, so he often ends up with salt instead of sugar and gravy instead of tea!"

"When are you travelling up to Inverness?" asked Mac.

"We are catching a train on Thursday and Moira's mother has very kindly booked us into a hotel quite near the station and has invited us round to their house on Friday, isn't that nice of her?" said Victoria.

"Her mum and dad are fine," said Digger, "just count your fingers after shaking hands with her granny though, there are no flies on that one!"

After a good night's sleep and a full English breakfast, they said goodbye to Bertie and Victoria and were on their way just after nine. They took the A6 to Carlisle and then the A74 over the hills to Glasgow and then across to Stirling and up to Perth where the A9 took them all the way to Inverness.

The scenery up the A9 was breathtaking and they kept having to stop so that Donny could take some photographs with the new camera he had bought himself. They arrived at Moira's parents house just after seven and after Moira had greeted Digger and introduced Donny to her parents and her Granny, she took the two men down the road to their neighbour, Mrs. McKay, who ran a Bed and Breakfast and was putting them up for a few nights. Mrs. McKay was not just a neighbour and good friend of the family, but in her younger days she used to be Moira's dancing teacher. Having deposited their bags, they returned to the Leith's house, where they were soon all sitting down together for their evening meal.

Once the meal was over, Donny escorted Granny home and then went back to Mrs. McKay's house to get acquainted with her, while Digger and Moira went for a walk along by the river.

"You must be exhausted after that long drive," Moira said, "how were Bertie and Victoria when you saw them and how did Donny behave himself with them?"

"They were fine, having a great holiday and said they would see you on Friday. Donny is really anxious to impress them, no fooling around, no practical jokes, this engagement lark seems to have taken all the fun out of life for him."

"And has this 'engagement lark' taken all the fun out of life for you too?" she asked sheepishly.

"I will let you know after the honeymoon," Digger replied and then quickly walked ahead of her.

"Joyce is coming round tomorrow morning and then we are going off to the church about eleven for a practice with the minister; Oh, and what was Patty's dress like?" Moira enquired, once she had caught up with him and grabbed hold of his arm.

"Blue with a bow, I think," he said and then pulled the sort of face that men pull, when they know that the answer they have given, was not quite what had been expected, but did not want any follow up questions to be asked.

"Donny and I will call round about ten and we can meet Joyce and then all walk to the church together."

The practice went well at the church and Joyce and Donny seemed to enjoy each other's company and all the guests from the south arrived safely on time at the station and were met by Digger or Donny, who escorted them to their different lodgings.

Saturday the twenty seventh of August was dry but overcast and Digger and Donny arrived at the church in good time, just after one fifteen. They parked the car down the side of the church and went inside to meet the minister, who was waiting for them in his vestry.

"Welcome gentlemen and may I say how resplendent you both look in Highland Dress, you were both made for the kilt."

"Thank you," said Digger, "it takes a bit of getting used to, but I knew it would make Moira's day and it has gone down well with the rest of her family too."

They chatted for a bit longer and then went over the order of service and walked through into the church at around twenty to two. Brian's eyes almost popped out of his head when he saw his uncle dressed in a skirt, but as he saw other men come into the church who were also dressed in kilts, he realised that it was perfectly all right.

Moira's mother arrived with her sister and family around ten to two and by now the church had pretty much filled up with, family, friends, workmates and neighbours of the Leith's.

When Bertie and Victoria arrived, they made a point of coming up to speak with Digger and Donny and to wish them well.

At exactly one minute past two, the church organ started to play 'Here comes the bride' and everyone stood and turned to watch Moira, escorted by her father and followed by her two bridesmaids, slowly make their way down the centre aisle of the church.

Digger could not take his eyes off her and just could not believe how beautiful and graceful and totally fantastic she looked.

"Moira, you look fabulous," he whispered, as she stood next to him at the front of the church.

The whole service passed seamlessly and they both spoke their words loud and clear when they made their vows to each other, so that even people at the back of the church, could hear every word they said.

The Minister finally said those wonderful words that every couple longs to hear,

"I now pronounce you husband and wife. What God has joined together, let no man separate. You may now kiss the bride."

Which he did with great gusto.

The registers were signed, the photographs taken and by four o'clock, they were sitting down in the church hall for the wedding meal, which was served by some of the ladies from the church. The Minister said grace and the meal was consumed along with copious amounts of squash and lemonade.

As was the custom, the Minister acted as Master of Ceremonies and called on the bride's father, Mr. Leith to make the first speech. He was both lucid and witty and extolled the virtues of his daughter and welcomed Digger into the family and made particular mention of Digger's sister and her family along with Mr. and Mrs. Bannister who had made the long journey to Scotland for the occasion. He then asked everyone to be upstanding and proposed the toast to the Bride and Groom.

Donny was next to speak and true to form, he did his very best to embarrass Digger with tales of their youth and especially of trips they had made to the London Zoo; but he did end up by telling them all, what a great chap Digger was and how he had helped him personally, through a most difficult period of his life.

He then thanked Joyce and Patty, the two bridesmaids, for the excellent job they had done in assisting the bride on this very special day and he proposed the toast to the Bridesmaids.

Last of all, Digger was invited to say a few words. He had deposited the notes for his speech in his sporran, which took him several minutes to open and caused some mirth among the assembled guests.

"Ladies and Gentleman," he started, "on behalf of my wife and myself, I want to say thank you to everyone who has contributed in any way, to making this such a wonderful day for the two of us. In particular I want to thank Mr. and Mrs. Leith for having such a beautiful daughter and for all their hard work over many months in preparing for today. Thank you for welcoming me into your family and for allowing my cousin and myself to wear your family tartan today.

I am, of course, disappointed that my own parents and some of my army buddies are not here to share in today's celebrations, but I am so pleased that my big sister Vi and her husband Mick along with Brian and Patty were able to be here and share this day with us.

Thank you also to my good friends Bertie and Victoria Bannister, who not only made the long trip from Oxford to Inverness, but actually cut their holiday short in Australia, to be here with us today."

There was a short pause while Moira's family clapped at this point, much to the embarrassment of Bertie and Victoria.

"Lastly I want to thank my cousin Donny, for being my Best Man and for all his help and support and in particular, for not telling any of the stories that he had threatened to tell. As I said earlier, there are many old army friends, family and neighbours who were not able to be with us today, so could I ask you to stand for one final toast - To absent Friends."

"To absent Friends," echoed round the hall, which was followed shortly after by the Minister who wound up the proceedings and offered a final blessing on the happy couple and their future.

While the meal was being cleared away and the tables arranged around the outside of the hall, the Bride and Groom circulated among their guests, opened cards, read telegrams and posed for a few more photographs.

Several of the guests were musicians and while all this was going on, the platform at the end of the hall was cleared, so that the two violinists, the accordionist and the pianist could set up their instruments ready for the Ceilidh, which started around six thirty. One of Mr. Leith's Boys Brigade officers acted as 'caller' for the dances and before long everyone was on the floor, giving it a go, with Moira and Digger and Donny with Joyce, leading from the front.

They started with The Gay Gordon's and then Strip the Willow and the Dashing White Sergeant, but when it came to The Eightsome Reel, all the folks from south of the border, decided to sit down and watch the experts dance.

An Intermission was held around eight o'clock which gave Moira and Digger a chance to change into their 'Going away' outfits. Before the music started up again half an hour later, they had said their goodbyes to everyone amid a shower of confetti, hugs and kisses and had left for their honeymoon in Digger's car, which had coloured ribbons tied to the handles and tin cans attached to a string which was tied to the rear bumper.

As soon as they were out of sight of the church, Digger pulled over to the side of the road and got out of the car. He took his penknife out of his pocket and cut the string with the tin cans and put them into a dustbin, that was conveniently close by. He untied the ribbons and gave them to Moira, he then took a large screwdriver out of the boot and removed all of the hub caps, which Donny had kindly filled with small stones.

He was about to get back into the car, when Moira called out to him,

"I am sure there is a funny smell coming into the car Digger, almost fishy, I think."

"I bet I know what that is," he replied, opening the bonnet and removing a kipper, which some kind soul had left there and put it into the dustbin on top of the tin cans.

"Unless Donny has learnt some new tricks, that should be it," Digger said as he climbed back into the car and started the engine.

"Why didn't you hide the car so that they couldn't do all this to it?" she asked naively.

"You must be joking Moira," he replied. "One of my friends in the army did that, big mistake."

"Why, what happened to him and his poor wife?" she asked.

"They got into the case and tied knots in all of his shirts and pyjamas, as well as adding two or three bricks, to make it heavier and then they found out which hotel they were going to for their honeymoon and rang up and cancelled the booking. No, it's much safer to let them have a bit of fun with the car, much safer."

"That's awful, who would do such a terrible thing as that?" Moira commented.

Digger did not answer that particular question, he just stared hard at the road ahead, looking for the sign to Beauly.

"How far did your dad say it was to Beauly," he asked.

"About thirteen miles and the hotel is on the main road, you can't miss it," she replied, "every time we went there when I was young, I would ask if we could stop at the hotel for a night, but mum always said that it was too expensive."

They chatted about this and that and how the day had gone and before they knew it, they were pulling up outside the hotel, ready to spend their first night together. Digger got their cases from the boot, locked the car and walked into the hotel lobby and went up to the Reception desk.

"You sign us in Digger, I need to go to the cloakroom," said Moira.

He stood there for a minute, but no-one came, so he rang the bell 'Ding-ding'. No-one appeared, so he rang the bell again, 'Ding-ding, ding-ding'.

"There is no need to be impatient young man, I was just coming," said a middle-aged lady in a tweed suit, who emerged from the back office. Digger smiled.

"Name please," she said, once she had opened the Register.

"Smith," said Digger, "Mr. and Mrs. Smith."

She lowered her head slightly and peered at him over the rim of her spectacles,

"Smith you say, Mr. and Mrs."

"That's right, Mr. and Mrs. Smith, we are booked in for one night," said Digger, in a slightly exasperated tone.

"Well Mr. err Smith, I do not have a booking for you, so you and your lady friend will have to find somewhere else to spend the night, I'm afraid."

Digger stared in disbelief and wondered if indeed, someone had telephoned and cancelled their booking.

"No-one has telephoned you and cancelled the booking, by any chance have they?" he enquired.

She made a big play of opening the Register once again and running down the list of names with her finger, before replying to his question.

"As I said before Mr. err Smith, there is not a current booking, there is not a cancelled booking and this hotel is full tonight, so you and the lady will have to leave. Good-night!"

"What do you mean 'Good-night'? My wife's father made this reservation for us weeks ago," he shouted at her, "and I don't like the tone of your voice or the implication of your sarcasm, my good woman, so I suggest you go and fetch the manager."

Digger had just finished this tirade, when Moira came running from the cloakroom and the duty manager emerged from the back office.

"Digger, what's all the shouting about," she asked, at the same time as the duty manager said,

"Is there some sort of problem here Miss McTavish?"

Before Digger or Miss McTavish could answer, Moira and the duty manager recognised each other.

"Moira," he said.

"Dougal," she replied.

Miss McTavish suddenly became a tad uncomfortable and softened her tone as she explained the dilemma to the manager that was confronting them all.

"Did your father telephone and make the booking Moira?" he asked.

"Yes Dougal, probably a couple of months ago, so the booking may of course be under the name of Leith, rather than Smith."

"I have it here, of course today was your wedding day, many congratulations to you both. I am sorry I was not able to attend myself, but I am sure my mother and father enjoyed themselves."

"Thank you Dougal, they were certainly up dancing together before we left and we had a lovely day, until now that is," she added, scowling at the crest fallen Miss McTavish.

"Quite, quite," he said diplomatically, "let me escort you to your room Moira, I think the Bridal Suite tonight for our guests, don't you Miss McTavish?"

Chapter 5
Vive la Difference

Dougal and Moira chatted as they walked up the two flights of stairs and then she followed him down the long corridor to the Bridal Suite that was located at the far end of the building. Dougal carried the case that Moira had indicated was hers, leaving her to carry her coat and handbag. They chatted about old friends, life 'down south' and working in a hotel, until he opened the large door and led her into the suite. It was a spacious room, with a high ceiling and a very grand 'half tester' bed, which was undoubtedly the centerpiece. The remainder of the furniture consisted of two Victorian mahogany wardrobes and a chest of drawers, with matching bedside tables and a dressing table with a large mirror, that was situated between the two windows, which stretched almost from the floor to the ceiling.

A chaise longue and an old fashioned high backed arm chair were in a corner of the room, along with a small table which had some out of date magazines on it.

"Would you like me to have tea or coffee sent up this evening Moira and would you like to have breakfast in your room tomorrow morning or will you be coming downstairs for breakfast?" he asked in a pleasant, friendly sort of way.

As he was just finishing the sentence, Digger arrived in the room, having carried the heavy case and the overnight bag, along with his coat, hat and umbrella.

"There you are Digger," said Moira, "Dougal was just asking if we wanted a hot drink this evening and whether we would like breakfast in our room tomorrow, wasn't that nice of him?"

"No. Yes. Goodnight," said Digger, dumping the case down in the middle of the floor with a loud thump.

"Well, I will be going then," said Dougal, "if there is anything that you want Moira, just let me know. I will have your breakfast brought up at eight thirty. Goodnight."

Dougal left the room and Moira turned on Digger.

"That was very rude Digger, to speak to Dougal like that, it was not his fault that the Receptionist was unpleasant."

"If there's anything else you want Moira," Digger mimicked, "did he have a crush on you when you were at school together or something?"

"Don't be silly, we were just good friends. You're jealous Arnold Smith! We have only been married a few hours and you are acting the 'jealous husband' already."

"It's your own fault for being so beautiful, now come and give me a big kiss," he said, putting his arm around her waist and pulling her to him.

"Down boy," she said, when she stopped kissing him to get her breath, after a couple of minutes of his embrace, "it is almost ten thirty, perhaps it's time we went to bed."

In thinking about it later, she did not ever recall seeing him move quite so quickly before. He lifted her case and put it on top of the large blanket chest, which had a padded top on it, to take the luggage of patrons and put his own case on top of the chest of drawers. He opened his case, took out his pyjamas, toothbrush and toothpaste and disappeared into the bathroom which was part of the bridal suite.

He could not have been more than three minutes in the bathroom, but when he emerged, she was sitting on the foot of the bed in her brand new Marks and Spencer's nightdress and holding her hairbrush in one hand and her toilet bag in the other. He noticed that there was no sign of the clothes she had been wearing and assumed she had hung them in the wardrobe and decided that he should do the same to save his new trousers from getting creased.

He went over and closed the window, which was wide open and went and lay down on the right hand side of the bed, which was next to the door. Like most men, he had thought about his wedding night on more than one occasion in the past and lay there going over in his mind the various scenarios he had considered.

He slowly became aware that something was digging into his back and heard Moira saying, "Digger, are you asleep? Digger, wake up, you are on my side of the bed."

He slowly rolled over onto his back and saw Moira standing at the side of the bed, holding her hairbrush by the brush end and digging the handle into his back.

"I must have dozed off," he said, by way of explanation, "you were a long time in the bathroom Moira, what did you just say to me?"

She had a sort of cross, perplexed look as she answered this question,

"I said, you are on my side of the bed. And did you close the window that I opened?"

"Window! It was blowing a gale, of course I closed it. What do you mean by your side of the bed? This is the first time we have been in a bed together, so how can it be your side? Anyway, I was here first, so I get to choose."

"You most certainly were not here first, as you so nicely put it! I turned the corner of the sheet down and this is my book on the bedside table, if you care to look. Now move over please," she said firmly, giving him a bit of a push.

"You brought a book to read on your honeymoon?" he said incredulously.

"I normally read at least two or three chapters every night in bed, before I turn the light off. It helps me get to sleep."

Various answers to this statement went through Digger's mind, but he decided against them all and went on to explain, why he thought he should sleep on the right side of the bed and not her.

"Look Moira," he said, sitting up, "I could tell you that I wanted to be by the door side of the bed, in case we had intruders and I could jump out and protect you, but I am afraid the real reason is not quite as romantic as that, but it is still 'gallant' in its own sweet way."

"Go on Mr. Gallant, I am listening," she said in a threatening sort of way.

"While I was in the army in France, we all slept in tents, six or eight of us together and all the other blokes used to insist that I slept by the door, because they said that I used to get really bad wind, while I was asleep. They made a really big thing about it, the way that blokes do, but it happened so often, that I sort of suspected that there was some truth in the matter and since I sleep on my left side, it means if I should get wind in the night, that if I am laying on the right side of the bed, then it won't affect you. Is all that clear?"

"Oh that is charming! The vicar never mentioned that in his pre-marriage chats. What happens if you happen to roll onto your other side, what do I do then, get a gas mask out? And you want to sleep with the window closed!"

"I think this could be the very first compromise of our marriage," Digger suggested, "you can have the window open and I will sleep on the right side of the bed, agreed?"

"Agreed," she replied and picked up her book and walked round to the other side of the bed and climbed in."

"I thought you wanted the window open," he said.

"I do, but I am sure that a jealous and protective husband such as yourself, would not want his young and beautiful wife to stand at the window in her nightdress, would he?"

"Oh, of course not," with which he climbed out of bed and opened the window about half an inch. Moira coughed twice, so he opened it another half an inch, before climbing back into bed.

"What about the light Digger?" she asked.

"I thought you said that you wanted to read first," he answered.

"No Digger, I said that I normally read first. This is the first night of our honeymoon and I thought you might object if I 'read first' tonight."

Digger jumped out of bed and switched the light off and then tripped over his bag which he had left in the middle of the room and stubbed his bare toe on the foot of the bed. "Ahhh!"

"Are you all right, what was that noise?"

"It was me stubbing my toe on the bed. I think I have busted my big toe."

"It is probably just bruised, go and put it under the tap."

Digger hobbled over and put the light back on and went into the bathroom. Moira sat up and watched him through the open door as he attempted to put his big toe under the cold tap in the sink.

"May I suggest you use the cold tap in the bath Digger, before you injure yourself anymore," she called out.

"Good idea," he called back, removing his foot from the sink and hobbling over to the bath, "shee, its freezing. My whole foot has gone numb."

"Are you always such a baby when you hurt yourself?" she asked. "My Great aunt Mary says that if men had to have the babies, then the human race would have died out a long time ago."

"Such pearls of wisdom coming from someone who has been a spinster all her life," he retorted, turning off the tap and drying his foot.

"Talking about having babies," he said, as he hobbled back into the room, moved his bag to the side of the wardrobe, turned the light out and climbed back into bed.

"I would love to have babies of my own, one day Digger, but not till we are over there and settled in Australia, I don't want them just yet, thank you. I assume you have brought some 'thingies' with you?" she tentatively enquired.

"Some 'thingies' with me," he replied, "not quite sure what you are alluding to there, do you mean something like bed-socks or a pair of braces."

"You know exactly what I mean," she answered, a little embarrassed.

"Yes, I have some thingies," he said, "but I can't help thinking that the risk of you falling pregnant on our honeymoon is pretty low."

"Well you would be very wrong then," she replied indignantly. "I deliver no end of babies to women who said they had only taken a chance, once or twice and managed to get themselves pregnant."

Digger attempted to remove the thingy from its packet, but found it quite difficult.

"Have you ever done this before?" she whispered to him, as she rolled onto her side facing him.

Now this particular question had been debated by Digger and his mates over a drink on several occasions and the advice of the married men in the group, was quite unanimous, you must always answer 'No'.

"No, never," he replied, "have you?"

"What did you say?" she said horrified. "What sort of a girl do you think you have married?"

"What. What's the matter? What did I say?" he asked in bewilderment.

By now she had turned onto her other side and was facing away from him.

"You know very well what you said, how could you!"

"How could I what? You asked me if I had ever done it before and I just asked you the same question. How come it's all right for you to ask me but not all right for me to ask you?"

"Don't touch me; it's different for a man and anyway, we all know what soldiers are like." Now as she said the last sentence, she realised she had probably gone too far and bit her lip and waited for the riposte that she knew would be coming her way.

"Moira, we both know that is unkind and I am sure you did not really mean it, just as I did not mean to offend you. Please turn round and talk to me."

"Sorry Digger, of course I did not mean it, I love you so much and you really are my knight in shining armour," with which they embraced and consummated their marriage.

It was a little after eight thirty when the maid knocked on the door and getting no reply, let herself in and wheeled the trolley over to the table and pulled open the curtains a little way. Moira came too and sat up in bed and thanked the maid.

"Is everything all right madam?" she enquired.

"Yes thank you, everything is just wonderful," she replied, looking down at her husband and then blushed.

The maid smiled and left the room and Moira got out of bed and went to the bathroom. By the time she had emerged, Digger had woken up and taken a jumper out of his bag and put it on over his pyjamas and was pouring the tea into the cups.

She sauntered over and put her arms round his neck and kissed him on the side of the cheek. He stopped what he was doing, stood up and embraced his wife.

"Looks like a full English breakfast to me, plus a couple of items I cannot identify," he informed her.

"Those are black puddings," she informed him, "I will eat yours if you don't want it," she offered.

"I will swap you my black puddings for your 'buttery'," he replied, "these are a bit different to the ones your mother has."

They ate their breakfast, made love again in the big bed, had a bath and were ready to leave the hotel by eleven. Neither Dougal nor Miss McTavish were on duty when they signed out and were delighted to discover that Mr. Leith had already paid in advance for the room. They loaded their cases into the car and Digger filled up with petrol before heading off for Bonar Bridge, where they were to spend the next four nights.

"Do we know how far it is to this place?" asked Digger.

"Dad said it was about forty miles; so we head off first of all for Dingwell and then we take the road alongside the Cromarty Firth for a few miles. We then take the scenic hill road across to the Dornoch Firth and Bonar Bridge is just four miles or so from there."

"Sounds easy, we should be there in good time for lunch," he replied, as he stepped on the accelerator and headed off for Dingwell, where they stopped for a while as Moira decided she needed a few things from the Newsagent, which was still open.

While they were crossing the hills by Aultnamain Inn, they decided to stop and enjoy the view for a while and eat some of the biscuits that Moira had bought in Dingwell. Just as they were getting going again, a young lamb jumped into the road from no-where and instinctively Digger swerved to avoid it and grounded the exhaust pipe on a rock at the side of the road, almost breaking it in two. He climbed out of the car and looked underneath, before giving his prognosis.

"Rats, of all the luck," said Digger, "it's broken off about nine inches before the silencer, if it had been after it, we could have risked it."

"Can you fix it," Moira asked.

"Temporarily, do you think there will be a garage at Bonar, or will we need to go back to Dingwell?"

"I am sure it will have a garage, anyway, the local farmers will need to get their tractors serviced somewhere nearby."

"O.K. Help me unload the car, as I will need to jack it up, so that I can work underneath."

They unloaded the car and Digger took out an old shirt and working trousers he kept in the boot, along with a piece of tin and some large exhaust pipe clips.

"It's a good job we are married, standing there in your underwear, get a move on in case someone comes past," she said, as she folded his jacket and trousers and put them in the car and he changed into his old clothes.

"It certainly is my dear, that's for sure!" he said, in a sort of Machiavellian, West Country accent.

They jacked up the front nearside wheel and put a large rock underneath the tyre and then did the same with the rear nearside wheel. He then retrieved the piece of tin and proceeded to roll the tin into a tube and use it to join the two pieces of broken exhaust pipe together.

"Don't you want these then?" Moira asked, pointing to the two clips which should have gone onto the exhaust before he inserted the tin, "and wouldn't it be better to put the tin on the outside of the pipes, rather than the inside, otherwise it might just shake loose?".

Digger grunted, separated the exhaust pipe and tin tube, put the two clips onto either end of the broken exhaust and then wrapped the tin round the outside of the exhaust and put the two clips on over the tin, to hold everything in place.

He then jacked the car up again, removed the rocks and started the engine to see what it was like.

"What a din," said Moira, "are you sure it is safe to drive?"

"We will have to be careful, but yes, it is safe, that is why I always carry a piece of tin in the car. An old army habit."

"Well I have to say that I prefer that one, to a certain other habit you demonstrated during the night. I was very glad to discover that your nose was towards me and your tail was pointing the other way," she joked.

They drove very carefully over the hills and caused a bit of a stir as they drove through the normally quiet village of Ardgay and then over the bridge to Bonar Bridge.

"Which way do we go to the hotel?" Digger asked his navigator.

"Right. No hold on, yes , left, left," she replied.

"I will take that as a left, right?" he said, for which comment he received a punch in the arm.

They pulled up outside the Pilot Whale Hotel which overlooked the water and he carried the bags inside. This time Moira went up to the Reception desk and rang the bell once, ding. A short lady in her mid sixties came through from the back, smiled and said,

"You must be Mrs. and Mr. Smith, welcome and congratulations my dear," she said, giving Moira's hand a little squeeze. "Please sign the Register and I will give my husband a shout to help you with cases. Paddy," she called out.

"A Scotsman called Paddy," commented Digger out loud, "how unusual is that?"

"To be sure now," said Paddy, in a soft Irish lilt, as he stood in the doorway, "a fine Scottish lady with her English manservant, if my eyes don't deceive me."

"Ah, Irish then," said Digger without thinking.

"Mother, quick, put your coat on and get down to the bookmakers, there's a man here with real insight, who will make us a fortune."

Digger decided not to respond but to ask the obvious question instead.

When do we get to see the Pilot Whales then, at high tide I presume.

Paddy could not believe his luck that one person could be quite so naive.

"Tell me young man," he said, "if you went to a pub called the 'Pig and Fiddle' would you expect to see a pig playing a fiddle, or if it was called the Three Wise Men, would you expect to see their camels in the car park?"

Before he could reply Mrs. Kelly, Paddy's wife of over forty years, put her hands up to both men and said, "Enough boys, enough. We have been in this hotel for twenty years Mr. Smith and Paddy has had all that time to work out a clever answer to any question you might ask him, this is really not a fair contest. Paddy, show Mr. and Mrs. Smith to their room please. Now."

As Paddy and Digger dutifully obeyed and carried the bags up the stairs, Mrs. Kelly informed Moira that the hotel took its name from an incident in 1926, when a school of Pilot Whales ran aground in the bay between Bonar Bridge and Ardgay.

As the two men reached the top of the stairs and started to make their way down the landing, Paddy started speaking again;

"Do you want me to show you where the local garage is situated my friend," asked Paddy, "Oh and the bathroom is that door there, but there is no-one else booked in to the hotel at the moment, you have it to yourself."

"Yes please, we hit a rock coming over the hill and snapped the exhaust pipe, just before the silencer. I managed a temporary fix, but it needs a new pipe. My name is Digger by the way, is it all right to call you Paddy?"

"That's fine Digger. I thought you must have damaged your exhaust, I was looking out the front window when I heard you coming over the bridge, what a noise you made! Once you have cleaned up, I'll go with you to the garage, the owner is an old friend of mine and often works on a Sunday afternoon, I am sure I can persuade him to sort your car out for you."

Digger washed the dirt off his arms and face and left Moira to unpack while he and Paddy took the car along to the local garage. They pulled up and parked in the forecourt and then walked into the workshop together, where a head could just be seen in the inspection pit, underneath a Grey Fergie tractor.

The Pilot Whale Hotel   Artist - Peter Rugendyke

"Is that yourself down there in the pit Rory Wallace, hiding from your dear wife no doubt?" Paddy enquired.

"Oh awa ye go Paddy Kelly, bother some other poor soul for pity sake," Rory replied.

"Is that all the thanks a man gets around here, for bringing in a cash paying customer to you and an Englishman to boot and you know how gullible they are."

"Shall I just leave you two alone for an hour and come back when you have finished," Digger enquired.

"Nay need, Austin Seven with a broken exhaust pipe, just before the silencer," said Rory, "I don't have a replacement and it will take ten days to get one from Aberdeen, but I should be able to fix it for ten shillings and it will be ready on Tuesday afternoon."

"Many thanks," said Digger, "the keys are in the ignition, will they be safe or shall I put them in your office."

"This is nay London my friend, the keys will be safe," said Rory, "and for goodness sake, make sure ye tak that good for nothing Irishman with you."

"To be sure," said Paddy, "t'is the very last favour I do for you Rory Wallace, no more free drinks for you, at my hotel bar!"

Rory shouted something else back, but Digger's understanding of the local dialect was very poor, but he understood the gist of what was being said.

The two men walked back to the hotel and found the two ladies sitting in the lounge, enjoying a natter over afternoon tea.

"You can't come in here in those dirty clothes, go and change first Digger," Moira instructed him.

He duly changed into the casual clothes he was wearing before the accident and went down and joined the ladies.

"Since we did not have any lunch, Mrs. Kelly has suggested that we eat at five thirty today, isn't that nice of her, Digger?"

By now, Digger had come to realise that any sentence ending with the phrase ' isn't that nice of her, Digger', is not actually a question which requires an answer, but is a statement which expects the response 'Yes dear', so he said,

"Yes dear," and proceeded to chomp his way through a large slice of fruit cake.

It was the first time that Digger had eaten venison and although he found it a little dry to his taste, he thoroughly enjoyed the steak, along with all the trimmings which accompanied it. With Sticky Toffee Pudding and custard to follow, all accompanied by a large glass of Irn-bru, he needed at least half an hour to recover before they went for a walk along the water's edge.

Monday was wet, so since they were without transport, they mostly stayed indoors and chatted to Mr. and Mrs. Kelly and Moira was able to catch up on her reading, while Digger read the newspaper and listened to the wireless.

Around lunchtime on Tuesday, Rory Wallace drove up in Digger's car, to announce that the exhaust had been fixed and that the car was ready for use; so Digger handed over a ten shilling note, which Rory took into the Hotel and sat down at the bar accompanied by Paddy. He and Moira went for a short drive in the afternoon up to Lairg and back and managed to avoid loose sheep and large rocks and when they returned, they found the two men, still seated at the bar, a little the worse for wear, but still able to exchange banter.

On Wednesday they went for a longer drive to Dornoch and after having a bite to eat in town, they drove down to the beach and walked along the sand barefoot and paddled their feet in the sea. It was a bright sunny day when they left

Dornoch and foolishly they decided to leave the hood down for the return trip. It started to rain around Spinningdale and it got heavier and heavier and by the time they arrived at the Hotel, they were soaked through, which for some unknown reason, seemed to give some sort of zest to their lovemaking, once they were back in their room and out of their wet clothes.

They said goodbye to the Kelly's on Thursday and after paying their bill and swapping jibes with Paddy, they packed the car and headed back to Inverness, arriving at Moira's parents house around two o'clock.

"I meant to ask, what are the sleeping arrangements for the next two days," asked Digger.

"Mummy thought it best if you were to sleep in the shed, to save daddy getting upset. ...Oh, you should see your face," she said laughing, "we are stopping with Mrs. McKay for the two nights."

"I never know when you are being serious and when you are teasing me," he said, "it's not fair, because you always seem to know when I am teasing you."

"Ah, didums, not fair is it! Why don't you take our things into Mrs. McKay's and I will let mum know we are back and then we can go to the shops."

Digger drove along the road to where they were staying and knocked on the door, which was opened by Mrs. McKay.

"Hello Digger, do come in, your usual room, upstairs. Can't stop to chat right now, I'm baking; must dash."

Digger carried the cases up the stairs, put them on the bed and opened them, before walking back down the stairs to chat with his hostess.

"Smells good," said Digger, "that's the problem with coming up here, you can't help putting on weight."

Meanwhile down the road, the conversation was not going quite so cordially.

"What do you mean, you have arranged to stay with Mrs. McKay? You never told me, I have got your room ready for you, what will people think?" her mother said.

"I simply told Mrs. McKay that Granny would probably be stopping with you, for the two days we are in Inverness and quite honestly mum, I don't really care what people think any more, I am a married woman and I will do as I please. Besides which, dad can be really funny when Digger is with me and I don't want any more scenes and don't look like that, you know exactly what I am referring to."

"That was ages ago and he was just being loving and protective, that's all."

"And now I have a husband who loves me and wants to protect me, just as dad does for you."

"Very well Moira, I assume you and your husband will be joining us for dinner tonight."

"Of course we will, but we need to do some shopping right now, so we will come round at six, see you later."

Moira went back to get Digger and then they both walked into town and bought a few things from the shops and got a bunch of flowers for Moira's mother.

Their time in Inverness passed without incident and a lot of the conversation naturally centered on Australia and the trip they were about to undertake and what they expected to be doing, once they were out there.

They set off for home on Saturday, straight after breakfast and spent the night in a Bed and Breakfast at Luss, on the shores of Loch Lomond, but it rained for their whole visit, so they were happy to move on the next day.

On Sunday they drove down to the Lake District and from Penrith they took the road which ran alongside Ullswater and then over the hills and down into Ambleside. They stopped for a while by Lake Windermere, before taking the road into

Kendal, where they spent the night in the Highgate Hotel, where Digger and Donny had stayed on the way up.

On Monday they drove almost two hundred miles down to Worcester and found a Bed and Breakfast just on the outskirts of town. Digger had written several times to the parents of an army buddy who was killed in the War and who also happened to be the husband of Mrs. Black, who was one of the sisters who owned Millstone House in Upper Style, where he lived.

"So let me get this straight Digger," said Moira, "Ronnie Black's parents don't actually know we are coming to see them."

"I told them we were getting married and that I had accepted a job in Australia and that we would be leaving Britain in September and they wrote to say that if there was any way I could pop in before I left England and tell them something about Ronnie's army days, then they would be most grateful."

"Well in that case, I think that you should go round and see them right now, to make sure they will be in tomorrow, they would be devastated to find out later that they had missed you, just because they had gone shopping," she suggested. "Do you know where they live?"

"Yes, Mrs. Black wrote down directions for me, I left them in Donny's Road Atlas. You won't mind if I leave you here on your own then?"

"I have managed on my own for the best part of twenty seven years, another hour or so, will not be too much of a hardship. Off you go and remember that the landlady has kindly offered to cook us a meal tonight, so be back by seven at the latest."

If truth be known, Digger was a little apprehensive at meeting his dead friend's parents on his own. But he parked outside the house and knocked on the door, which was answered by a middle aged man in a battered suit, the trousers of which, were held in at the ankles by a pair of bicycle clips.

"Yes, can I help you?" he asked warily, eyeing up the man on the step, who was smartly dressed, if perhaps a bit casual, for an Insurance Agent, which is what Mr. Black thought this stranger might be; as he himself was an agent for the Liverpool Victoria Insurance Company and had only recently signed up some new clients, who had previously been with a competitor.

"Are you Mr. Percy Black?" Digger asked deliberately, looking at the man behind the door, who was still wearing his trilby hat and bicycle clips.

The man on the step's tone and question, now definitely had Percy Black worried and fearing some sort of retribution from the other aggrieved Agent, was about to inform the newcomer that he had been trained in un-armed combat, without mentioning, of course, that it had been during the First World War; when his good lady wife pushed past him and took over the conversation.

"That'll do Percy. I am Mrs. Black and who might you be?"

"I am Digger, Ronnie's friend from the army. We have written to each other several times Mrs. Black."

"Digger of course, do come in," she replied, "how nice to see you, on your way home from your wedding in Inverness I expect. Percy, do get out of the way and let Digger in and kindly remove your hat and those ridiculous bicycle clips."

He went in and had the requisite cup of tea and a digestive biscuit and told them that he and Moira could come round on the Tuesday and chat with them, if they would like them to.

"My name is Myrtle by the way and unfortunately I have a Women's' Institute meeting in the morning which I cannot avoid, but I should be back by twelve thirty, why don't you both come round for lunch. Percy, you will have to finish early tomorrow, you won't want to miss what Digger has to tell us about our son."

"Of course dear, but I will not be able to get back before one fifteen, could we delay lunch until then?"

"One fifteen, Percy, no one eats lunch at one fifteen," Myrtle replied.

"Well actually that would suit us a bit better, as Moira has a few things she needs to do in the morning," said Digger, coming to the rescue of the hapless Percy, "and if you will both excuse me right now, I do need to get back for our evening meal."

With which he stood up and headed for the door.

"Don't just sit there Percy, show our guest out," Myrtle instructed him.

The next day Digger and Moira arrived at the Black's house at one twenty, just in case Percy had been delayed. They had a light lunch and Digger gave them an overview of what he and Ronnie and his other two friends, who were all army drivers, were doing in France, around the time of Ronnie's death in March 1944.

"So he simply drove over a land-mine in his lorry, you say Digger."

"That's right Percy, it was a risk we all faced every day on those roads in France."

"He would have died straight away then," said Myrtle.

"Oh yes, instantaneously," Digger replied.

"Did anyone else die in the incident, or just our Ron?" asked his dad.

"His co-driver, a young Irish guy got killed and most of the soldiers in the back were badly injured, it was a most tragic incident," Digger answered.

"Thank you so much for coming to see us Digger, we really appreciate the trouble you have gone to and on your honeymoon as well," said Myrtle, wiping her eyes with a handkerchief.

"You are very welcome Myrtle, Ronnie was one of the best friends I have ever had and this was the least I could do for him."

"And thank you also, for whatever you said to Amanda, Ron's wife, she came to see us, as you know, so it's good that we will be having some contact with her again," said Percy, "it was just awful when she refused to speak to us and she wouldn't tell us why."

Moira and Digger stayed all afternoon but left around five on the pretext of going back for dinner, but to be honest, the afternoon had been so emotionally charged for Digger, talking about his dead friend, that Moira could see that he was completely drained and that she needed to get him home.

The landlady cooked them some fish and chips and was her usual jovial self, which was just what the pair needed that Tuesday evening.

On Wednesday they drove back to Upper Style arriving at the cottage in the late afternoon, to be welcomed by Mac and Sissy and the two sisters who wanted to hear all the news about the wedding; well not Mac that is, he just wanted to be petted.

Chapter 6
Charing Cross

"What time did you say you arranged to meet Deborah here?" Hazel asked Donny for the umpteenth time.

"For goodness sake Hazel, the boy's told you at least ten times already, six o'clock underneath the clock at Charing Cross," Angus replied on his son's behalf.

"Don't you get shirty with me Angus, it's not me who is ten minutes late," Hazel snapped back, "I am telling you that Deborah is not the sort of person to be late, something must have happened or we are waiting at the wrong place!"

"Believe me mum, there is only one Charing Cross and this is it. The Wyndhams Theatre is just a short walk from here, in Charing Cross Road and the restaurant that Debs has used before is just round the corner from it, in Cecil Street."

"Hold on son, I hate to admit it, but your mother does have a point. Deborah lives and works in London and has done for years, but she uses buses, taxis and the Underground, she never uses the Railway, does she."

"No, so what difference does that make?" Donny enquired.

"Well I would guess it makes all the difference in the world," Hazel exclaimed. "I would also guess that she is patiently waiting under the clock at Charing Cross Underground Station, wondering what has happened to us. You just run down and have a look for her Donny and your father and I will wait here," suggested Hazel, in a particularly smug tone of voice.

It took Donny just a few minutes to run down the road to the Underground Station where he found a very worried fiancée pacing up and down outside the station entrance.

"Mac over here," she called out as she saw him running towards her, "where have you all been, I have been waiting for almost half an hour and have been getting some very strange looks from people."

"Sorry Debs, big misunderstanding, we have been waiting in front of the Railway Station Clock, never mind, it's great to see you and 'Happy Birthday'," with which he gave her a big hug and a kiss.

As they walked up the road, they spotted Hazel and Angus chatting to a policeman and could see that Mac's parents were having a very animated conversation with the officer, so they approached carefully and quietly,

"I am truly sorry madam, sir," the constable was saying, "but I noticed you standing here at least ten minutes ago and you were looking very furtive as you and this gentleman chatted with the other gentleman, who suddenly ran off down the road as I approached."

"What do you mean exactly by furtive? Angus, what is he implying, get his number, I have never been so insulted!"

"Calm down Hazel, he was just doing his job. Here are Donny and Deborah now, so we can go and have something to eat. Thank you officer, no damage done. Goodnight."

"Goodnight sir, enjoy the show," the officer replied, as he continued on his beat.

"Hello Mr. and Mrs. Smith, sorry for the mix-up, the restaurant is not too far," Deborah interjected as they crossed the road and headed for Cecil Street.

As Donny had paid for the theatre tickets, Angus insisted on paying for the meal at the small Italian restaurant round the corner from the theatre. They had finished their meal and were in their seats, in good time for the show called 'Daphne Laureola', which starred Edith Evans.

A good time was had by all and after the show, Angus and Hazel took a taxi to St. Pancras Railway Station, where they caught the train back to Bedford and Donny and Deborah had a couple of drinks in a pub, before they got a taxi back to Deborah's flat in Fulham.

"I remembered to get a bottle of beer for you Mac, it's on the marble slab in the pantry, help yourself," she called out from the bathroom, "I'll have a small glass of sherry please, you'll find it in the dresser cupboard."

Mac located the beer and found an opener in the drawer with the cutlery and even managed to locate a large glass to pour it into, by the time Deborah appeared in the kitchen.

"What on earth have you been doing Mac, you are still pouring your beer, for goodness sake. Where is my sherry?" Deborah asked him.

"All in good time Debs, pouring beer is an art, you can't rush it. You just sit down on the settee and I will bring your sherry over."

He opened every cupboard in the dresser twice and still could not find the sherry.

"I thought you said you had a bottle of sherry in here somewhere, blowed if I can see it."

She got up from the settee, walked to the dresser, opened the bottom cupboard, moved a glass biscuit barrel two inches to the right and retrieved the bottle of sherry, which she handed to him, without saying a word and sat down again on the settee.

He took the cork out of the bottle of sherry and then proceeded to look for a suitable glass.

"Top cupboard, middle shelf, three inches back," she called out, giggling.

He opened the cupboard, took a glass, poured the sherry and presented it to Deborah.

"Happy thirty fourth birthday," he said, and they both took a sip of their drinks after which he sat down next to her, having taken the precaution of putting his glass onto the side table first.

"That was a lovely evening Mac, even though it did get off to a shaky start and you must find out what that policeman said to your mother, she was really livid about it."

"They certainly appreciated your inviting them to join your celebrations this evening; I expect it will be a talking point for weeks to come."

"Talking about celebrations, how did the wedding go last weekend and is it true you and Digger wore kilts? I wasn't sure if dad was pulling my leg or not when he telephoned."

"It was a really good time and everything went off very well. Moira looked wonderful of course and even made her own dress, but if I am honest, Digger and I probably stole the show, in our highland outfits. Moira's dad had hired kilts in the family's tartan, with jackets and sporrans and everything to match and we really did look good. Victoria took lots of photographs, so you will be able to see for yourself."

"Where did they go for their honeymoon?"

"Not sure. Arnold was very cagey about the details, somewhere north of Inverness I believe. If he ever made it, that is."

"What on earth do you mean, what did you do, you beast?"

Mac explained about 'doing up the car' but said that the kipper in the engine was not his idea.

"That's awful, I hope no-one does it to us, at our wedding."

"Well Arnold won't be there as he will be in Australia, but Henry has said he will be my Best Man, so I hate to think what he might be planning, after what I did to him."

"I will talk to Deidre about that, no one is messing with my motor bike!" she said in a most resolute tone of voice.

Mac was up early the next day and got the underground to St. Pancras and then the train out to Bedford and was only twenty minutes late for work.

They did not meet up the following weekend as Deborah had an R.S.P.C.A. conference to attend on the Saturday and Mac had a cricket match on the Sunday.

On Friday the ninth of September, Mac took the train into London and went to the cinema with Deborah in the evening and they both drove out on the Indian to Upper Style on the Saturday morning, to help Digger and Moira with a final clean and tidy up of the cottage.

"Well I am sorry mate, but I had no idea that you were interested in the car," Digger explained, "the chap at work made me a fair offer, which I have accepted and he is coming to collect it on Monday. You should have said earlier."

"I just assumed you would be taking it with you, never crossed my mind that you would leave 'Matilda' behind in England. She will be devastated, poor thing," Mac replied.

"So who is this Matilda, you will be leaving behind?" asked Deborah as she came in from the garden with Moira and the dog.

"It's his car," said Moira, "he calls it Matilda!"

"I see, how quaint! Never mind the car, what are you doing with the dog," asked Deborah.

"The two sisters have offered to keep him here for us, until we are settled and know what we are doing. Digger wants to have him sent out, but I am not so sure, we will just have to wait and see," Moira replied.

"Good solution," said Deborah, "the dog is going to miss you and needs to be with someone he knows and will properly care for him. A lot of animals don't handle the long sea voyage very well, so it may be kinder to leave him here."

"So how are you getting to Southampton then," Mac asked.

"Mrs. Black has offered to take us down on Tuesday and when we were talking to Bertie and Victoria about our plans, he recommended the Star Hotel on High Street, which he had stayed in before, during the war, so we have booked a room there for the night. We have already had three large trunks containing most of our possessions, taken down by lorry to Southampton, last week, so it will just be the two of us and a couple of cases, this time."

"Did dad mention to you that he has a car in Australia Moira?"

"Not exactly, Deborah. Victoria told me that they bought one last year while they were out there, but she never said what they did with it when they left to come home. I assumed that they sold it."

"No, I am sure they didn't. I think they left it with the local Undertaker, or something like that. He uses it when he needs it and keeps it in good order for them, in return."

"Sounds like a good arrangement, but why did you ask?"

"Well, when dad was in New Zealand before the war, he used to have a Ute, it stands for a Utility Vehicle, the Americans call them a 'pickup' truck and he has decided to buy another one for use on Victoria's farm, when they return to Western Australia. So he may well be prepared to sell you his car, which I think is a Morris Eight, just like the one that the ladies have here."

"Digger, did you hear what Deborah just said about Bertie and Victoria having a car in Australia and that they might be interested in selling it?"

"I did indeed, very interesting, perhaps you could mention it to your dad when you see him next. If he is not interested in selling it, maybe he might be interested in letting me use it, until he comes back out again and I would pay him for the privilege."

"But to change the subject, have you set a date for your wedding yet and where exactly in Spain will it take place?" asked Digger.

"Not exactly set in concrete yet," said Deborah, "but it is looking like March next year, as dad and Victoria want to return to Australia in April/May time and Mac's parents like the idea of a March wedding as well. It will be in the town of Benicarlo, where dad used to have a lovely seaside house and where I spent a lot of my childhood."

"So will you be coming out to Australia with them, when they come?" asked Moira. "Digger's sister Vi and her family are planning on coming out to join us next year some time, so we could have a little community of Brits out there at this rate."

"That's a good question Moira," said Mac, "and at the moment, we just don't know. Deborah has a hanking for going back to Auckland in New Zealand and I fancy Sydney in Australia, so we will have to wait and see. Who knows, maybe we will decide to stay in Spain or even settle down in England somewhere."

Monday was spent saying their 'goodbyes' to all their friends in the village and in parting with Matilda, to Digger's workmate. They ate with the two sisters on Monday evening and on Tuesday, after saying goodbye to the dog, they all piled into the Morris Eight and Digger drove them down to the hotel in Southampton. After a quick lunch in the restaurant, Mrs. Black said her tearful goodbye to the couple and drove the Morris back home to Upper Style on her own.

They had a quiet meal in their room that evening and got a taxi next morning to the pier where the ship was moored. The steward escorted them to their first class cabin, where their trunks were already waiting for them. The ship sailed out of Southampton just after mid-day and slowly steamed past the Isle of Wight on its way to the Mediterranean and its first port of call, Gibraltar.

They arrived in Gibraltar on Saturday morning and Digger managed to obtain a map from the Purser's Office.

"It seems an awful cheek Digger, to knock on the door of someone we don't know and just say 'Hi, we are friends of Bertie Bannister', it looks like we are on the scrounge or something."

"Not at all Moira. Bertie has given me a letter of introduction and he said his friends will be delighted to see us and that we should buy some jewellery from them, as it will be a better investment than taking cash into Australia."

"Look, there is the shop, 'Joseph's Jewellery and Antiques', it looks closed Digger, we are too late."

Digger walked up to the shop and tried the handle, but it was locked, so he peered through the glass door, "I can see someone in the back," he said and knocked loudly on the door. No-one came, so he knocked again. A lady came to the door and mouthed, "We are closed," at him.

He held up the letter and mouthed, "I have something for you, please open the door."

The lady walked away and returned with a man, who opened the door slightly and said, "I am the proprietor, we are closed. What is it that you have for me?"

"We are friends of Bertie Bannister and he has asked us to deliver this letter to you," said Digger.

The man took the letter, closed the door, read the letter and opened the door wide and welcomed them into his shop.

"Come in, come in, Digger and Moira. I am David and this is my wife Esther. You are most welcome. Come through to our flat, we have just finished for the day and are having afternoon tea, as you English call it."

They climbed the stairs to the flat above the shop and sat down at a small table where Esther served tea and cakes.

"Bertie says in the letter that I am to ask you about Mac," said David.

"Mac, my dog, why should he think you would be interested in him," queried Digger.

"Perhaps Bertie is referring to your cousin Digger, remember they all call him Mac and not Donny," suggested Moira.

"Why would a man in Gibraltar, be interested in my cousin Donny, unless you happened to have met him in the war, that is."

"I met a man we knew as Mac, in the war, when I was with the French Resistance. But he was sadly killed in a bombing raid in 1941," said David.

"No he wasn't killed," said Digger, "he is my cousin and he is very much alive and in fact was best Man at my wedding a few weeks ago."

Digger then explained what had happened to Mac and how he had been saved from the bomb and then rescued by a British soldier and eventually taken back to England. He went on to describe the reunion between Mac and Deborah in Bertie's cottage and of their intention to get married early next year in Benicarlo.

"I cannot tell you how much this news means to me," said David, "Mac was a good man and did outstanding work for the Resistance, but when he was captured by the Germans, it was my decision to call in the air strike to destroy the Gestapo headquarters and him along with it. I have had to live with that awful decision, every day since then. I am just overjoyed to hear that Mac is alive and well, thank you both so much, for coming to see us and for bringing this wonderful news."

"Thank you David," said Digger, "and whilst Mac has not mentioned the name of anyone in particular that he worked with in France, he has often spoken of the courage and sacrifice of the people he worked with and I know for a fact that he does not hold any hard feelings over the bombing incident."

They all chatted for a bit longer but then Moira looked at her watch and announced it was time for them to return to the ship.

"Just one thing before you leave," said David, "Bertie says in his letter that they will be travelling to Australia again next year, but may well go via the Panama Canal next time and therefore will not be able to visit us in Gibraltar, although, of course, we will hopefully be able to catch up with them at the wedding."

"Oh right," said Digger, "I didn't know that."

"I was wondering, therefore, since I am holding several items for Bertie, if you would mind taking one of them with you, just in case we are not able to see them."

"Of course," said Moira, "we would be pleased to help."

David disappeared down to the shop and returned a few minutes later with a jewellery box, which he opened and put on the table. It held the most beautiful, gold and diamond bracelet.

"Ah, that is beautiful David, are you sure you are prepared to trust two complete strangers with such a valuable piece of jewellery?"

"It isn't that valuable Moira, as we have had to replace some of the diamonds with imitations, but it is a piece we have been holding for Bertie since the end of the war and it is time it went back to its rightful owner."

"Talking of jewellery, I don't suppose you would have a nice necklace to sell me as a gift for my new wife, would you?" asked Digger, "let's say for about twenty five pounds."

"Of course we do, come downstairs with me Moira and you can choose one that you like," said Esther, "and Digger can give David the money."

While David wrapped the bracelet and took Digger's twenty five pounds, Esther showed Moira some necklaces and in the end she chose a single strand of pearls, which Esther fastened round her neck.

"What do you think of these love?" she asked Digger excitedly, after she had rejoined the men upstairs.

"Wow, they look great, are you sure they are within my budget?"

"Esther said they were a little bit over, but since it is a wedding present and we brought them such good news about Mac, she would let you have them for the twenty five pounds; isn't that kind of her?"

The ship left Gibraltar on the Sunday and they had a leisurely cruise through the Mediterranean and then passed through the Suez Canal and the Red Sea at the end of the week, calling briefly at Aden on Sunday the 25th September 1949.

Bertie and Victoria had told them about their taxi ride when they were in Aden, so along with another young couple they had become friendly with, they hired a taxi for a day and set off to see the sights of Aden together.

"Tell him to go the Bazaar first Digger, Victoria showed me the silver filigree necklace she bought there and I would like something similar and she said that on no account should we pay more than two pounds for it."

The driver dropped them at the edge of the Bazaar and told them which shop to go to for the necklace and said he would return in a couple of hours. After twenty minutes of bargaining, they ended up paying three pounds for the necklace, but did get a pair of filigree cuff links for Digger, thrown in as well.

The taxi got them back to Steamer Point in time to catch the last boat back to the ship, which set sail for Colombo later that evening, arriving at that port on the thirtieth of September.

"It seems a terrible cheek Digger, imposing on complete strangers like this," said Moira over breakfast the next day.

"Not really love, we are picking up this Pariah Dog for Victoria, I just hope all the paperwork is in place and remember that the dog is not for us, but someone else."

"If it is as adorable as she said, then it might well be for us!" replied his wife. "What time should we expect the car?"

"According to Bertie's telegram, it should be here at ten thirty and we are to look out for a Riley Kestrel. It's the only one on the island, so it should not be too hard to spot."

They finished breakfast and packed an overnight bag and wandered down onto the quay about ten fifteen.

"There it is over there," said Digger, "just stopping by that bullock cart, come on, let's go and introduce ourselves."

They wandered over to the car, just as a lady was getting out from the back seat;

"Mrs. Van Royt I presume," said Digger, holding out his hand, "we are Moira and Digger Smith, friends of Bertie and Victoria, nice to meet you."

"Moira, Digger, lovely to meet you," she replied, shaking their hands, "we don't get many visitors these days, so this is a super surprise, do get in, we can chat while we are driving home."

The drive to the villa took just over an hour and the house was situated just a couple of miles outside of Negombo on the edge of the lagoon. High walls surrounded the villa and after they had driven through the heavy iron gates, the chauffeur got out and closed and locked the gates, behind them. As they got out of the car five or six dogs came running up barking wildly at them, but when Caroline spoke to them, they quietened down and allowed the strangers to stroke them.

"Which one is Victoria's?" asked Moira.

"Duke, come here boy," said Caroline and a young dog came running up to her and sat down in front of her. "Say hello Duke," she said to him.

He held up his paw for Moira to shake, which she did and then made a big fuss of him.

"Isn't he adorable Digger, I am not at all sure that we will be able to part with him, when the time comes."

They spent two nights with the Van Royt's and saw a large part of the island and had a boat ride on the lagoon. During their short stay with them, they became firm friends and were even planning on a get together in Australia, later in the year, around Christmas time; over dinner on their last night.

"The bank has promised to find us accommodation as part of the deal for the job, so you will certainly be most welcome to come and stop with us, when you come over to Perth, we just can't be sure where that will be exactly, at this stage of the game," Digger explained.

"Oh that will be lovely," said Caroline, "once we have set up an import company for the glassware, we hope to be frequent visitors to Perth and who knows, we may even emigrate ourselves, one of these days."

"What, leave this paradise location!" said Moira.

"Unfortunately, paradise has started to change since Independence last year," said Samuel, "we have to be practical and look at our options, staying here may not be in our best interests in the long term and Australia is a land of opportunity, which of course is why you, yourselves, are making the change."

Caroline got up from the table and left the room, returning a few minutes later with a box, which she gave to Moira.

"It's just a small memento of your visit my dear, it was made in our factory, I hope you like it."

Moira opened the box to find a glass vase with coloured birds on it, "Oh thank you Caroline, it's beautiful, how kind you have been to us, I really look forward to entertaining you in our home in Perth when you come over."

They said their goodbyes the next morning and the chauffeur drove them back to the ship, along with Duke who travelled with them. All the paperwork for the dog was checked and he was taken on board and put into a waiting kennel, that had been reserved for him.

They set sail for Fremantle on the fourth of October and arrived in that port on the tenth. True to his word, Mr. Johnston from the bank, was there on the dock to meet them and was able to give the Purser's office an address to send the bulk of their belongings to, the next day. Someone from the quarantine kennel arrived for Duke and Digger signed the papers for the dog, saying that he would be along to collect him in about three months time, once they were settled in their own house.

"I thought it would be easier if you came and stopped with my wife and myself for a few days, while you get acclimatized," said Mr. Johnston as they drove off in his car. "My secretary has spoken with a letting agent, who will call round tomorrow and take you both to see a selection of apartments and houses that are within the bank's budget. I suggest you come into work with me on Friday, Digger, so that you know where the building is and more importantly, where your office will be."

"Thank you sir," said Digger, "that is most kind of you and your wife to go to all this trouble on our behalf."

"Please Digger and you too Moira, things are very informal in Australia, everyone calls me Nugget and my wife is called Junie and just to warn you Moira, Junie is a sister at the Royal Perth Hospital and when I mentioned that you were a nurse, her eyes just lit up, as I know they are looking for staff there at the moment."

"This is just too wonderful," said Moira, "do you think your wife would be willing to come house hunting with me, if Digger is tied up at work and she is off duty, of course?"

"Just you try and stop her, anyone would think that it was her who was looking for somewhere to live, the amount of information she has prepared for you, but for the moment, just relax and enjoy the ride and I will point out the Fremantle and Perth landmarks to you."

Chapter 7
Ruth Street

Nugget and his wife Junie had a large house in the Highgate area of Perth, which they shared with Junie's elderly mother, who was known to everyone as Dora. She was a third generation Australian and had known very hard times for most of her life, living on a Station in the outback, running sheep and cattle.

Junie and Nugget had met at a Young Farmers weekend, which he had attended with a friend from the bank and after a swift romance had married and settled in Perth; moving to their current home when her father died and her mother decided it was time to sell the farm and enjoy the fruits of her labours. They had one son, who also worked for the bank, but who was now based in Melbourne.

The guest room was very large with ample space for a table and two chairs along with a large bed, a wardrobe and several chests of drawers. They got to know Nugget, Junie and Dora very well during the three weeks they stopped with them and were able to enjoy at first hand the famed Aussie hospitality.

As Nugget had hinted, Junie was very keen to find a job for Moira in the Royal Perth Hospital and she duly started there in the Medical Ward on Monday the 24th October, a week after Digger started at the Bank.

Finding a home of their own was not quite so easy as finding a job, especially one that was in easy travelling distance of the Perth Mining & Commerce Bank Ltd, which was situated at the far westerly end of Hay Street and the Hospital which was situated at the far easterly end of

Wellington Street; the two streets running parallel to each other and only about three hundred yards apart.

"Surely Digger you can ask Nugget if we are allowed to add to the Housing Allowance, so we can get a home that suits us and not the bank!" said Moira, after yet another unsuccessful 'viewing'.

"Mr. Davis is not my greatest fan at the moment Moira and to go over his head and speak to Nugget directly, would not be a good move."

"I see," she said and let the matter drop.

The next day, however, she was chatting to Junie at work, who asked how the house hunting was going and the whole story came out as to how the allowance, was not sufficient to get the sort of house they wanted in a suitable area.

"Well couldn't you just add a bit extra yourselves?" asked Junie, "after all, the allowance is only for the first three months, so you will be paying all the rent yourselves after that period anyway."

"Funny, but I asked Digger the same question last night," answered Moira, "but he seemed unwilling to raise it with Mr. Davis, his boss."

"Don Davis is his boss, you say. Hmm. I know that he has a reputation for being a bit awkward, I'll have a word with Nugget, I'm sure it will be alright," replied Junie.

The next day, Nugget called Digger into his office and explained, that whilst Don Davis was indeed his line manager at the moment, his whole welfare and job package was still Nugget's responsibility, so if he did have any issues with 'the package', then he should talk with him directly and not Mr. Davis.

Needless to say that when Digger went home that night and shared the good news with Moira, she already had the details of a house which was situated on Ruth Street, which lay just over a mile north of the hospital and about two miles to the east of the bank. The agent had agreed to meet them there the next day at seven a.m., so that they could inspect the property before they went to work.

"Good morning Mrs. Smith, it was me who spoke with you yesterday," the agent said, as he walked up to Moira who was standing by the front gate, "my name is Denis, was your husband not able to come then?"

"Oh, he is here all right. I am afraid he was a bit impatient Denis and has already gone down the side of the house to take a look at the back. Hope you don't mind?"

"Not in the least. As I explained on the telephone, the house is owned by an old lady, who has gone to live with her sister in Albany. She would prefer to rent the house furnished, at least for the first three months, just in case she and her sister do not get on and she has to come back to Perth. That means the house is just as she left it; so I am afraid it is a bit untidy and some of the rooms could do with being decorated."

"That suits us fine, here is my husband now. Digger this is Denis; shall we go in then?"

It was a good sized plot measuring one hundred and forty feet long by forty five feet wide and the house, which was single storey, was set back about fifteen feet from the pavement.

It had three bedrooms, a lounge, kitchen, bathroom and toilet with a large dining area at the back of the house, overlooking the garden, which was laid to lawn with flower borders down each side. The garden had access onto Edith Street at the rear of the property and Digger was told that the old lady would not object to him putting in a gate, if he wished to park a car in the rear garden, on the hard-standing next to the shed.

"No pressure folks, but I do have two other couples booked to see it later today, so to be sure that you are the ones to get it, I need to know right now, I'm afraid," Denis informed them.

"Digger, it's ideal, I just love it, please say we can have it," said Moira.

"You heard the lady Dennis, we will take it; when can we move in please?"

"You can move in tomorrow if you like, but there are a few jobs that must be done first and I have arranged for them to be seen to this week, so realistically, how does next Monday sound?"

"Sounds perfect," said Moira, "our first home of our own Digger, isn't it exciting?"

"Mum, mum, it's a letter from Australia," shouted Brian, as he raced upstairs from the front door, with the precious letter in his hand.

"Can I have the stamp for my collection, please mum?" said Patty.

"That's not fair mum," exclaimed Brian, "I wanted the stamp for my collection and I brought the letter up."

"Quiet the two of you, give me the letter and neither of you can have the stamp for arguing over it."

"See what you've done now," said Patty.

"You only said you wanted it because you knew I did, you don't even collect stamps!" exclaimed Brian.

"Enough, go to your room and tidy your things up; I am getting tired of you two always arguing!"

She sat down at the kitchen table and taking a spoon out of the cutlery drawer, used the handle to open the letter, being careful not to damage the stamp, as she did. She poured herself a cup of tea and started to read Digger's letter.

1st November 1949

Dear Vi, Mick and the two Sprogs,

We arrived safely in Perth after a great trip out on the ship and were met by Nugget, who was the head of the Interview Team in London. We stayed with him and his wife Junie and her mother Dora for the first three weeks, which was a great way to find out about Perth and the way things are done here.

It's a beautiful City with lots of parks and open spaces and Moira and I just love it here. You will be interested to know that my various work colleagues with children all seem pleased with the local schools and the education their children are getting. The temperature has been around eighty degrees most days and we have already been to the beach at least half a dozen times and just love swimming in the warm waters of the Indian Ocean.

Yesterday we moved into our own rented house, which we have leased for an initial three month period. It belongs to an old lady who has moved south to be with her family, so we are hoping to be able to extend the lease and possibly purchase some of the furniture, once she is certain of her own plans.

The house has a good sized garden, plenty of room for the kids to play in and it has three bedrooms, so lots of room for you all to come and stay with us. Have you made your final arrangements yet? Nothing to stop you now, is there?

Moira has already got a job at the local hospital and loves it and a colleague of mine at the bank, has a brother who is a builder and would be delighted to give Mick a job working for him, the moment you all land here. He also asked Vi, if you were used to handling the accounts for Mick's business; so maybe a little job for you too, if you were interested.

We have had permission to put a telephone into the house, so will ring you with the number, once it is installed.

Bye for now, write soon,

Love Digger and Moira

X X X X

When Mick got home from work that evening, he saw the letter from Digger, sitting behind the clock on the mantelpiece and immediately took it down and read it.

"Well Vi, this is it, decision day. Are we going or are we staying?"

"It sounds so wonderful Mick, but everything inside me is warning that it is 'too good to be true'. I want to say 'Yes lets go' but I am frightened of making a big mistake."

"OK," he replied, " we will do this scientifically," with which he took a penny out of his pocket, tossed it into the air and catching it with his right hand, placed it on the back of his left hand.

"Heads we go, tails we stay," he said to Vi.

"Are you mad Mick, we can't decide something this important on the flip of a coin!" she said to him.

Ignoring her comment, he said again, "Heads we go, tails we stay. What do you want it to be Vi? Deep down, what is your heart saying to you. Heads or tails?"

"I want it to be heads, but I'm frightened to look, in case it is tails."

"We don't need to look at the coin," he said, putting it back in his pocket, without looking at it. "You wanted it to be heads and so did I and we know the kids do too. We have made our decision and tonight after tea we will fill out the papers and you can post them tomorrow."

Vi walked over and gave her husband a big hug and a big kiss, just as Brian walked into the room.

"Oops sorry. Did you see the letter from uncle Digger dad?"

"I certainly did son, what do you say if we try and join him for the end of March next year?"

"Really dad, really! Next year with uncle Digger in Australia, fantastic!"

The next few weeks passed quickly for Digger and Moira and they were delighted to get an Air-Mail letter from Vi and family at the end of November, saying that they had sent the paperwork off to Australia House and would be joining them somewhere around the end of March 1950.

It was also around the same time that they received a letter from Bertie and Victoria which informed them, that Deborah had mentioned that Digger would be interested in using their car, with the intention of buying it from them, when they next went out to Australia. Bertie gave them the details of the Undertaker in Pinjarra who had custody of the car and that he had written to him on the subject and that he would now be expecting a telephone call from Digger to arrange a convenient time to pick the car up.

Bertie also said that they would be obliged to Digger and Moira if they could call on Ray and Jenny Thomas and introduce themselves to them and take some photographs of the new Fruit Farm, that Victoria was a part owner of.

Digger telephoned the Undertaker and arranged to meet him at the Pinjarra Railway Station at eleven twenty five the following Saturday. Moira had decided to pack an overnight bag, just in case the car was not ready for them, but also because she was feeling that it was about time she saw somewhere in Western Australia, other than Perth, the hospital and the shops.

There were a few other passengers who got off the train with them at Pinjarra, but these soon disappeared from view, leaving them standing on their own, on the deserted platform.

"Are you sure he understood it was this Saturday that we were coming?" Moira asked, "after all, it was only Thursday that you telephoned him Digger."

"He said that he had a small funeral for later this afternoon, but this morning would suit him fine. We'll give him another ten minutes and then walk into town. It looks like there might be a hotel over there," he said pointing to a large building down the road from the station.

They waited the afore-mentioned ten minutes and then a few minutes more and had just started to walk across the dusty station forecourt, when a beat-up old pick-up truck came roaring down the road and stopped in front of them. A huge man got out and walked towards them:

"G'day mate," he said to Digger, "would I be right in thinking that you two are Victoria's Pomey friends?"

"We certainly are," Digger replied, offering his hand to the big man, with some trepidation, if the truth be known, "I'm Digger and this is my wife Moira."

"Good to meet you both, I'm Ray, I expect that Skipper mentioned me to you. My wife Jenny and I, own a farm with Victoria."

"Of course Ray, good to meet you, has the Undertaker been delayed or something?" Digger enquired.

"It appears that the funeral for Mrs. Spade had to be brought forward and that there were a lot more mourners than was at first expected, so he is in fact in need of the Skipper's car, so asked me to come and meet you."

"That's very nice of you Ray," said Moira, "we were hoping to come and visit you and your wife while we were here."

"I know," said Ray, "we got a letter this week as well and when Jenny told Vicky that you were coming, she said that you could stop with her for the night, as our place is a bit cramped."

"I am sorry Ray, but we don't know who Vicky is," said Moira.

"Right then," said Ray, "I will try and explain, but get into the truck and we can go to the hotel, where the wake is being held. Jenny and Vicky went to the funeral, but I had some work to do."

They all climbed in, with Moira wedged in the middle, as the passenger door was a bit suspect and drove down the road to the hotel, while Ray tried to explain who Vicky was.

"Did you know that Victoria had been married before and had a step-son, who died while she was out here last time?" Ray asked tentatively.

"Yep, we knew that," confirmed Digger.

"Ah, well then, Vicky is the step-son's daughter. Not sure what relation that makes them, but they became very close, during the short time they were together."

"Right, thank you Ray. Are you sure it will be alright for us to 'gatecrash' a wake?" asked Moira, "won't the relatives of this Mrs. Spade object."

"No relatives left to object, luv, in fact no-one ever knew what her real name was, we just all called her Mrs. Spade, I don't even know why. But you stay by me, I'll see you right, 'No worries'."

Ray pulled up outside the hotel and they all got out and Moira started to carry the overnight bag into the hotel with her.

"You won't need that in there Moira and it will be a lot safer in my truck, as everyone knows this is mine and no-one will mess with it, I promise!" Taking the bag from her, he threw it through the window onto the seat and they all walked into the bar, where the wake was being held.

There was a loud hub-bub in progress, so Ray did no more than shout out, "Quiet please, I said quiet please and that includes you Johnny Buckler," the room quietened and everyone turned towards Ray, "these two folks are Digger and Moira and are friends of mine, so I expect you all to be friendly and make them welcome and I don't want to hear any Pomey jokes either."

"Would you two like a drink," he asked.

"That would be great Ray, but nothing alcoholic please," Digger replied.

Ray nodded and then pushed his way to the bar and got a beer for himself and two bottles of ginger beer for his guests.

"I don't know if you drink ginger beer Moira, but it's all they have at the moment, with which he twisted the top off and gave a bottle to her and the other to Digger.

"Thanks Ray, good health mate," said Digger and then turned round to Moira and tapped her bottle with his and watched her enjoy the ice cold drink.

"Where is your wife Ray?" asked Moira.

"Probably helping out with the food in the kitchen, come on, I'll introduce you."

They followed Ray into the kitchen where several ladies were working feverishly preparing food for the folks in the bar.

"Jenny, Vicky, come and say hello to our Pomey visitors," he called out across the kitchen.

Two ladies put down what they were doing and walked over to Ray; one was a few years younger than Ray, in her late thirties and the other was just a young woman in her early twenties.

"You must be Moira, good to meet you, I'm his better half; Jenny."

"It's very nice to meet you too Jenny," said Moira, "this is my husband Digger and I assume this young lady is Vicky, nice to meet you."

They all shook hands and Jenny and Vicky used the opportunity to escape the kitchen and handed out some plates with food on and they all made their way to a quieter corner of the hotel, where they started to eat and get acquainted.

"Mr. Smith," said a man in black, who had come rushing into the room, Digger nodded and smiled. "So sorry to have changed our arrangement like that, hope it was not too inconvenient for you both, the car is parked under the trees and here are the keys. It has half a tank of petrol, which will get you back to Perth with some to spare. Must rush, things to do. Oh, the engine seems to be misfiring occasionally," with which the undertaker, rushed back the way he had come.

"I don't think he was too pleased to get Bertie's note saying that you were coming for the car," said Jenny, "he was only supposed to use it occasionally, but I often saw him and his wife driving round in it when I came into town."

"I'll give him misfiring occasionally," said Ray, "he hasn't had it serviced the whole time he has had the car."

"Not to worry, but it is a good job I brought my tools with me then," said Digger, "I can give it a check over when we get it back to Perth."

"I thought you worked with Nugget in the bank," said Vicky, "I didn't know you were a mechanic as well. You sound like a useful friend to have in these parts of the country."

"I wouldn't call myself a mechanic Vicky, but I was a driver in the army during the War and we had to be able to look after our own vehicles, so I know enough to get by," Digger replied modestly.

"Well mate," said Ray, "I for one would be most grateful if you would bring your tools next time you come here and give my old Ute a once over for me, you heard how rough it is running. If you don't mind, that is."

"Of course not Ray, I would be delighted to," Digger replied.

"Are your two farms far from town?" asked Moira.

"Not far, about five miles or a fifteen minute drive to mine and just a bit further to Jenny and Ray's," replied Vicky. "Why don't we finish our drinks and head off, I have prepared the spare room for you both, so I do hope you are able to stay the night with me, it's not often we get visitors."

Vicky led the way in her big fawn Chrysler and Digger and Moira followed in the Morris Eight with Ray and Jenny bringing up the rear in the old Ute.

"What lovely people Digger, I am so glad we brought our things with us and can stop the night here. It would be so good to get to know people and make friends away from work."

"I agree Moira, I really liked the people we met in the Hotel in Pinjarra, reminded me of some of the Aussie blokes I met in the War."

They waved goodbye to Ray and Jenny and followed Vicky into the old farmhouse. She led the way to the guest bedroom pointing out where the bathroom was to her guests.

"I am afraid that the toilet is outside Moira, you just go through that outside door over there and you will see a small shed at the edge of the veranda, that's what we call the 'dunny' or the toilet to you. I don't have an electric light in there, so you will need to use a torch or a paraffin lamp. We always have one on the table by the door at night and don't worry about the frogs, they are quite harmless."

"No worries mate," said Moira laughing, "I have become used to the frogs at our own home in Perth, but we do have an inside toilet, I am pleased to say."

After un-packing their bag and freshening up in the bathroom, they wandered through the house and found Vicky on the verandah with a pot of tea and some cakes.

"I thought you two would enjoy this tea as it is some that Bertie and Victoria picked up in Ceylon, when they were coming over here," said Vicky, " normally I eat a bit later than this, around seven thirty, will that be OK with you?"

"That's fine," said Moira, "we are just so grateful that you have gone to all this trouble on our behalf."

"No trouble at all, but a real pleasure to have some company, now tell me all the news about Victoria and Bertie and about this Spanish wedding that is coming up soon."

Chapter 8
The Northam Matter

Digger and Moira had a good night's sleep but breakfasted on their own as Vicky had left a note saying she was going for a ride on her horse, Midnight. They had just finished eating when she arrived in the kitchen, breathless, having run from the stables.

Moira stood up and greeted Vicky and said, "Why don't you sit down and I will make you a cup of tea. You look like you have been rushing."

"Oh I have Moira, its ages since I rode Midnight and it is the one thing I really miss while I am at college, so I simply lost track of the time while I was out riding. I normally go to church on a Sunday, hope you don't mind, but I need to have a quick wash and be on my way, it starts at eleven. Did either of you want to come with me?"

"Yes we would love to," said Moira, "wouldn't we, Digger?"

"Err, yes, but I guess we will need to change, can't go like this in shorts, can we?"

"That's good," said Vicky, "see you in ten minutes, do you mind driving Digger?" with which she left the room, not waiting for an answer.

The church was situated in the town, just over the bridge and they made it, with at least two minutes to spare. It was a short service and they were home, changed and enjoying a cold drink by twelve thirty.

"What about the photographs Bertie asked you to take Digger, did you mention that to Ray?" said Moira.

"Not a problem," said Vicky, "I saw Jenny this morning and we are all invited to their place for lunch, so you can take some snaps while we help to get things ready."

They finished their drinks and then drove up to Ray and Jenny's farm and while Vicky helped Jenny with the meal, Ray took Digger and Moira on a tour of the fruit farm. Ray explained what they had done since Victoria and Bertie had been there and Digger took a whole reel of photos, saving just a couple which he used up over dinner.

"What are you doing for Christmas?" Jenny asked Moira at the end of the meal.

"We had thought that some friends we met in Ceylon might be coming out here to spend Christmas with us," Moira replied," but we recently heard that they have changed their minds, so we have accepted an invitation from Nugget and Junie to spend it with them,"

"That's a shame, you would have been most welcome to come here," said Jenny.

"What about New Year," interrupted Ray, "come and spend New Year with us. Welcoming in the New Year under the stars, with all of our friends, will really be something to write home about. Vicky will put you up, won't you?"

"I would love to," Vicky replied, "but look, I am coming into Perth on Monday the twelfth, to see Nugget, why don't I call past your place and we can sort out the details."

"Why don't you come and spend the night and give us the opportunity to extend our hospitality to you," replied Moira.

"That would be lovely, thank you; do you know what shift you will be on at the hospital yet?"

"I think so, but if you give us a call on the Sunday evening, I can confirm what time I will be home, but Digger is normally in by six, aren't you love?"

Digger nodded and was about to say something when Ray interrupted him, "Hey we always visit our accountant in Perth on the third Friday of each month; I don't suppose you could put us up too, could you?"

"Ray! You've got a cheek," said Jenny.

"We would be pleased to mate," said Digger, "if you stop for both the Thursday and Friday night, perhaps we could go out together, see a show or something."

"That sounds 'bonzer' mate. We normally see our accountant first thing Friday morning and could get to you for six on the Thursday, if that suits," Ray replied.

They left Pinjarra at four p.m. and arrived home just before six, by which time, the car was sounding like it badly needed that service.

The following week was busy for both of them and with Moira having to work the night shift at the hospital, they did not see a lot of each other, which gave Digger plenty of time to service the car and to replace the points and plugs and purchase a couple of new tyres. He also managed to buy some chicken wire, to cover over some of the gaps in the hedge, ready for when Victoria's dog Duke, would be living with them.

Vicky rang Digger at work on the Friday to say that she had a nine thirty meeting with Nugget on the Monday, so would it be OK if she arrived on Sunday afternoon, rather than Monday afternoon.

He had only just put the phone down on Vicky, when Nugget's secretary rang to say that he wished to speak with him right away. When he arrived in Nugget's office, he found that his manager, Mr. Davis was already there and was obviously in the middle of a heated conversation with Nugget.

"I'm sorry to interrupt, but your secretary said you wanted to see me right away Mr. Johnston," Digger said.

"Get out Smith," shouted Mr. Davis, "didn't they teach you any manners at your fancy London bank?"

Digger stood there, glowering at the man, waiting for Nugget to confirm or deny the instruction to leave.

"Would you give us a moment please Digger," said Nugget quietly.

Digger nodded and closed the door and went over to chat with the secretary.

"Excuse me Mrs. Redcar, but when you rang just now I was under the impression that Mr. Johnston wanted to see me right away, but he seems to be discussing something important with Mr. Davis at the moment. Should I come back later?"

"No, please wait," she answered, "I am so sorry for the confusion Mr. Smith, but he had invited Mr. Davis to his office, as well as yourself, to discuss the Northam matter, with you both, but Mr. Davis appears to be very agitated about something."

"What 'Northam matter' might that be?" replied Digger.

"The camp that has been set up for the immigrants to Western Australia, didn't Mr. Davis talk to you about it?"

Digger was about to reply, when a red faced Don Davis came out of the office and pushed past Digger as he was standing by the secretary's desk.

"You had better go in now Mr. Smith," said Mrs. Redcar, "and I will bring you both in a cup of tea in five minutes time."

"Sit down and I will ask Mrs. Redcar to get us a drink."

"No need sir, she said that she would bring us some tea, in about five minutes time," Digger replied.

"I asked you to come and see me Digger, as I needed your answer about the 'Northam matter'. But Mr. Davis has just informed me, that contrary to my clear instructions to him, he has not yet discussed the matter with you."

"We have both been busy with the Foreign Currency Review this week, so I guess it must have slipped his mind," Digger replied skeptically.

"Very generous of you, my boy, but it means you have not had time to discuss it with Moira and I require an answer today!"

"What exactly is the 'Northam matter', something to do with a camp of some sort, I believe!"

"Northam is a small town about sixty miles north east of Perth. During the Second World War, it was the location of a large military camp but has now been chosen as a reception camp for new immigrants from Europe. It is well situated close to the two main routes heading North and East and to the railway. It is also near to the Kalgoorlie pipeline, which means it has a reliable supply of good drinking water. It is assumed that over the next ten to fifteen years, the camp will be home to thousands of new immigrants to Australia."

"And all new prospective bank customers, I presume," added Digger.

"Exactly, you have it in one. The Board has decided to open a branch in the camp, probably only two days a week, to start with and we need someone to run the operation for us and I asked Mr. Davis to see if you would be interested in the position."

"Well thank you for thinking of me, would I continue to report to Mr. Davis, or would I have a new manager and would it mean moving to Northam or could I just drive down and stay overnight?"

"Can you imagine what Junie would say if I took her newly recruited nurse away from her? No, since you now have the use of a motorcar and the Board members have decided to open for just two days a week to start with, probably Thursday and Friday, you could drive down after work on Wednesday and come back Friday evening. As regards your manager, Mr. Davis is about to become the new manager of the branch at Kalgoorlie, starting next week, which is why he was in such a bad mood."

"I thought he wanted to take over a large branch somewhere; he has been talking about it for weeks."

"Oh he has," said Nugget, "but Sydney, Melbourne and Adelaide have all refused to have him; in the end it was Kalgoorlie or Broome, so he chose Kalgoorlie, only to discover that Mrs. Davis would have preferred to go to Broome!"

"So is it a promotion Digger, or just something else to test you out on?" asked Moira, after he had recounted the events of the day to her, over dinner that night.

"Neither really, I don't think anyone has gone into those sorts of discussions yet. It appears the matter was first discussed by the Board a couple of weeks ago and Mr. Davis should have told me about it on Monday."

"So why didn't he tell you? He hasn't liked you right from the start, has he?"

"Look Moira, he is a difficult man to work with, everybody says that, not just me, so I don't think it is personal; but us spending the first three weeks of our time here with Nugget and Junie, was probably not the cleverest of things to do, with hindsight. It has caused some friction at work and not just with Mr. Davis."

"I know what you mean," she replied, "some of the other nurses can be quite catty towards me, when it suits them."

"Still, on the bright side, they were terrific hosts and we have found some good friends for life, so the positives far outweigh the negatives, don't they?" Digger asserted.

"Of course they do, but you haven't managed to tell me what decision you gave him yet. I assume you said yes!"

"I would have preferred to discuss it with you first, but he needed a decision right then, as he was seeing Mr. Newgate, the Director who is overseeing Northam, straight after seeing me and I couldn't leave without giving him a decision, not after all he has done for us."

"Of course you couldn't, but what was your decision for goodness sake!"

"I said yes," he replied, giving her that 'what else would I have said' look. "They wanted me to be away from home for two nights of the week Wednesday and Thursday, but I said no to that. It is only sixty miles, so I can drive up Thursday morning and come home Friday evening, which is what I have suggested. I didn't want to leave you on your own any more than for one night."

"Well that's very nice and protective of you love, but I was on my own for all the years before I met you, so I am sure I will be able to manage for the short time you are away and anyway, we are due to pick Duke up from the Quarantine Kennels in mid-January, so I will have him for company, won't I?"

"That's true and we should go and see him again soon, perhaps after work, one day next week. Anyway, Nugget suggested that we take a drive up there this weekend to see the town and he also said that we can charge the whole trip to the bank. He said that there was a nice hotel in town, so it would give me a chance to check everything out."

"I do need to give the house a good clean and make up the spare bed with Vicky coming on Monday," said Moira.

"Sunday, she is coming on Sunday afternoon," said Digger, "she rang me first thing at work today."

"Oh, well thank you very much Mr. Smith and when were you going to tell me about this change to our schedule? Sunday afternoon I suppose!"

"Don't go all huffy on me Moira; after all, I have had rather a lot to think about since her phone call."

"Huffy, huffy, I'll show you huffy," she said and immediately attacked him with the feather duster she had been using earlier on the ornaments on the dresser.

Moira was up early on Saturday and gave the house a thorough clean and put clean sheets and pillowcases on the bed in the guest room. She then woke up Digger and they had breakfast together, before going to the shops to stock up for the weekend. They returned home and had a sandwich before putting their weekend bag in the back of the car and heading off for Northam.

"Did Nugget suggest somewhere to stay," she asked, as they left the outskirts of Perth and drove through the area called High Wycombe.

"He did say that there was a hotel in town called the Shamrock, built in the eighteen sixties and that it offered good accommodation with reasonable food and that the rooms at the rear overlooked the Avon River."

"Did he say where it was in town?"

"On the main street I presume, Fitz something or other."

"So is that where you intend staying when you are there?"

"Probably not, it appears the bank is a bit mean with expenses, so I will be expected to find a B & B, but that is not today's problem, so let's enjoy the trip."

It took almost two hours to get to Northam and locate the Shamrock and to negotiate for a room 'with a view'. They strolled through Bernard Park and walked up and down the river and went back to their room with a couple of ginger beers they had bought from the hotel bar.

"What time did the manager say that they serve dinner here?" Digger asked, as he kicked off his shoes and stretched out on the bed.

"Six thirty," Moira replied.

"That's an hour and a half to kill before we eat and I forgot to bring a book," said Digger, sipping his drink and looking perplexed.

Moira kicked off her shoes and sat next to him on the bed and sipped her drink, before saying, "Oh, I'm sure you will think of something to do Digger!"

And he did!

"Did you enjoy the meal mate?" asked the waiter as he cleared the plates away.

"I most certainly did and what were the vegetables that were with the potatoes?"

"They were 'Sweet potatoes', have you not had them before?"

"I don't think so, but I certainly will again."

"Would you like some apple pie and custard for pudding?"

"Yes please," said Digger.

"Not for me," said Moira, "I am full."

"We do have some fresh peaches in the kitchen, if you would like one, they are delicious," the waiter replied, as he walked away.

"Where do you put it all Digger? That steak was huge and how you can eat a sweet as well is completely beyond me," Moira exclaimed.

"It must be a combination of practice, dedication and the heat, I would say. Why don't you take the peach the waiter offered you and then we can always eat it later, in the room, if we want to."

The waiter returned with a large bowl of apple pie and custard and a large juicy peach with a sharp knife and an extra serviette for Moira.

"I would suggest you tuck the serviette down the front of your dress, that peach is really juicy," he warned.

Moira took the advice and enjoyed the best tasting peach she had ever eaten.

"Didn't Ray and Jenny have some newly planted peach trees on their farm?" she asked Digger, who was now struggling with the last of the pie and custard.

"I think so," he replied, "peaches, nectarines, plums and something else; that one was good I presume."

"I have never eaten anything like it. I am going to keep the stone and see if they will let me plant it in a spare corner of the farm somewhere. Do you fancy going for a nice long walk down by the river, to work off all that food you have consumed."

"Not a good idea," said a customer on the table behind them. "I don't mean to be rude, but I couldn't help overhearing your last comment. My wife and I went for a walk down by the river, after our meal last night and we both got at least a dozen mozzie bites each, for our effort."

"Well thank you for the warning," said Moira, "so what does one do here, instead then?"

"We were going through to the bar for a drink, why don't you come and join us," said the man's wife.

And that is exactly what they did; before retiring for the night at around ten forty.

The birds woke them early on Sunday, so they went for a walk before breakfast, after which they paid their bill and left for home, arriving back at Ruth Street around noon.

Moira cooked a roast dinner for Vicky, who arrived there in the late afternoon and they spent the evening, eating and drinking and chatting, as if they had been friends for years rather than just a few days.

On Monday morning Digger and Vicky walked to the bank together and Digger left her in the capable hands of Nugget's secretary and he went off for his first meeting with Mr. Newgate, his new boss.

"Well Mr. Smith, what did you and your wife think of Northam?" asked Mr. Newgate.

"To be honest, I am not sure what I was expecting, sir, as apart from Perth and Pinjarra, we have not actually seen a lot of Western Australia as yet. The journey only took a couple of hours and the town seemed to be full of life, but the camp was off limits, so we only saw it from the outside."

"While I think of it, if you get an Expenses form from the Stationery Cupboard and complete it and hand it to my secretary, I will sign it and pass it to the Cashiers Department for you."

"Thank you sir," Digger replied.

"Is your wife happy about this new assignment and comfortable with the extra risks you will be taking?"

"Yes she is, but what extra risks are these that you are talking about?"

"The currency transfers of course. You will be taking Australian pounds with you to Northam and bringing the different foreign currencies back. Surely Mr. Davis explained all this to you; after all, he was the one who first set up the system that we operated in Melbourne before the War."

"I was not aware of these particular risks; Mr. Davis has not been very forthcoming about such matters. I had assumed that the new office would have its own safe and that the currency movements would be carried out via an armoured bank vehicle of some sort."

"Goodness me; whatever gave you that idea? We would be running the operation at a loss if we had to do that. No, the sums involved are not sufficient to warrant such an expense. We expect you to take a thousand pounds a week, at most, and bring the equivalent amount of foreign currency back with you. There will be a small safe installed in the office, but it will not be anything more than a strong box, cemented into the wall."

"Oh, I see," said Digger dubiously, "and has there been any history of robberies of bank employees in the past, when doing such journeys?"

"Not since Ned Kelly was around, you will be quite safe and we are happy to provide you with a firearm, if it makes you feel more comfortable. Just let my secretary know what you would like and she will make the necessary arrangements."

"Do we know where these immigrants will be coming from and what languages they will be speaking? I picked up a little French and German and a bit of Italian during the war, but not enough to handle complex financial negotiations."

"The camp will recruit its own translators, mainly from among the immigrants, who will be there to assist you with the various languages. In addition to this, we have the basic Account Forms in a number of languages already printed, but if Don Davis's experience still holds good, three quarters of the people will just want to exchange their own money for pounds, without opening an account."

"Three quarters, that high a number, you surprise me," Digger replied, "so when do you want me to start Mr. Newgate?"

"Why, this week of course! Time is money, my boy and we don't want any other bank to get there before us, do we? I suggest you book into the hotel you used over the weekend, for at least three nights this week and go back to Northam tomorrow and visit the camp and set up the office. I have arranged for a builder to meet you there on Thursday morning and install the safe for us. If that is agreeable, I will get my secretary to make all the necessary arrangements with the camp."

"So you are off to Northam tomorrow then! That was quick! When will you be home again?" Moira enquired.

"Well for this week, I will stay at Northam all week and get the office sorted out and introduce myself to all the appropriate people at the camp and in the town. As soon as I have arranged for a telephone, I will call you with the number, but I will not be home before Friday night at the earliest."

"But what about Duke at the kennels, you said we could go and see him this week and they might even have let us bring him home with us Digger, so I would have had some company while you were away!"

"I am really sorry Moira, I thought you said you would be all right while I was away this week. Why not ring the kennels tomorrow and see if they will allow you to go up there after work to visit Duke. You can get a taxi to take you there and if they will allow Duke to leave the kennels, you can bring him back home with you, after all we do have everything he will need here and you can always call in at the butchers for some meat scraps for him."

Which is exactly what she did the next day, so Duke came home to Ruth Street and kept Moira company while Digger was away at Northam.

Chapter 9
Christmas Revelations

"So how did the weekend go with Ray and Jenny," Junie asked Moira as they had a cup of tea together at the hospital, on the following Monday morning.

"They were fantastic company, we didn't stop laughing the whole weekend and I am sure that Ray must know every pub and restaurant in Perth. We had so much fun with them both, but I really had to put my foot down when it came to the dog. They both fell in love with Duke and tried to persuade us that he would be better off with them at the farm, but he was such good company for me, while Digger was away at Northam last week, that I just said no, my need is greater than theirs."

"Good for you Moira and what with all the snakes and other dangers at the farm, you do not want to be the one to tell Victoria that her dog got bitten by a Tiger snake and is no more. Are you going to bring him with you on Christmas Day?"

"I would love to, if you are sure you don't mind, but I was a bit worried if Dora would be able to cope with him?"

"No worries there, it was my mother who told me to mention it to you. Living on a farm all her life, she really misses the animals now, especially the dogs; do you allow him inside the house at Ruth Street?"

"To be honest, it never crossed our minds not to allow him into the house, Digger's dog in England just went wherever he wanted to. It was only when the rental agent called round on Friday for the first inspection, that I discovered we should have asked for the owner's permission, before we let him inside. Anyway, he met Duke when he called and spoke to the owner when he got back to his office and told her that I would be on my own for two or three nights a week while Digger was at Northam, so she said it was O.K. for him to come in the house."

"That was good of her," said Junie.

"While we are on the subject of Christmas, I have made a traditional Scottish 'penny pudding' which I was going to bring round, if you don't mind that is."

"Sounds intriguing and I assume traditional for you, of course you can bring it round, just don't expect to take any of it home with you again!"

"Have you heard when your son will be arriving from Melbourne yet?" Moira enquired.

"Assuming nothing urgent crops up at work today, he is hoping to leave Melbourne tomorrow, so he should be here Thursday afternoon if he comes by train and a bit earlier if he decides to fly. You never quite know with Rusty, what he will do, until he has done it!"

"Digger and I want to go to the morning service at church and then come along to your house afterwards, if that will suit, say about half past twelve."

"That will be fine Moira; we normally sit down for Christmas dinner about two o'clock and then go for a swim in the sea about five, when it has cooled down a bit, so don't forget your bathers."

"You know, this is the one thing I have been looking forward to most, being able to walk on the warm sand and going for a swim in the sea, on Christmas Day, I can't wait."

Meanwhile, at the bank, Digger is in the middle of a meeting with Mr. Newgate and reporting on the first week's activities at Northam.

"The people at the camp were very helpful and have allocated three rooms for my use. There is a large room, which has been furnished as a waiting room, a smaller room, which I can use as my office and a separate room where I meet the clients and transact the business. The builder you organized came on Thursday and has installed the overnight safe in my office. As luck would have it, the room happened to have a suitable chimney breast in it, so the builder incorporated the safe into that.

I was not happy, however, with the strength of the doors and the quality of the locks on the windows and spoke with your secretary about it and she has organized for carpenters and locksmiths to visit the offices today and tomorrow, to change them all."

"Well done Smith, getting the basics right is so important and I gather that you have been able to recruit an interpreter already and that the pair of you were actually able to meet with your first customers and transact some business last Friday."

"That's right sir, I have arranged for the services of a young man called Pjetri Fulici. His mother was Albanian and his father Italian and he speaks five languages fluently and understands a few more. I have agreed to pay him fifteen shillings a day for the two days he works for us. I think he will prove to be a great asset."

"Seems generous to me, but it is your call Smith. Did you take the thousand pounds I suggested and have you arranged for a firearm yet?"

"I did indeed take the thousand pounds, even though I was not expecting to use even half of it, not just in a single day's trading. As regards the firearm, I have requested a Colt M1911, which is a single-action, semi-automatic pistol and happens to be the firearm I carried with me in the final stages of the War, so I know how to use it and look after it."

"Very good, so how much business did you do and how many new customers did you sign up?" asked Mr. Newgate.

"Eight hundred and forty three pounds, six shillings and ten pence worth of curreny trading, covering six different currencies and I was able to sign up seventeen new accounts, out of the twenty three people I saw."

"Goodness me you have done well and almost three quarters of them became bank customers, that is three times the rate we achieved in Melbourne, let us hope you can keep this up Smith."

"Did you remember to get the Johnston's a Christmas present Moira?" Digger shouted from the bedroom, as he searched through his chest of drawers a second time, looking for his swimming trunks.

"Don't you ever listen to what I tell you Digger? I am giving them one of those spare 'cut glass' fruit bowls we got for a wedding present, that you dislike so much and what on earth are you looking for now, Duke and I have been waiting for ten minutes already?"

"My old red swimming trunks, you haven't seen them by any chance, have you, I was sure I left them in this top drawer?"

"You did, but I thought I told you that I had thrown them out, they were a disgrace, I bought you a new pair last week and they call them 'bathers' here, by the way, not trunks."

Digger was about to say something in response, but decided to let it go, so picking up the basket of goodies that Moira was taking with her, the three headed outside and got into the car and drove off.

"Did you turn the gas off under the stewpot Digger?" Moira asked, as they got to the end of Ruth Street. Showing even greater self control than earlier, he turned the car round and went back into the house and found the stewpot on the gas stove, with no gas alight under it.

He went outside, started the engine and turning to Moira said, "Mission completed, no harm done," and drove round to their friends' house.

No sooner were they in the house than Dora took charge of Duke and taking him out into their large garden, sat in her favourite chair and played ball with him until lunch was served.

While both wives had warned their respective husbands not to discuss banking matters over lunch, Junie had forgotten to warn her son to stay off the forbidden subject and all went according to plan until Moira served the 'penny pudding' with silver threepenny bits hidden in each portion.

"Hey, this is a great tradition you Scotts have, I bet the children love it," commented Rusty, "Oh, the pudding is delicious too, by the way, any chance of another piece?"

Moira cut him another slice and passed it across the table, as she said, "I'm glad you like it Rusty, but you only get the silver pennies on the first helping, do you still want it?" she teased.

"While you are there love," said Digger, "I could manage another slice too."

"Not for me Moira," said Nugget, in answer to her questioning look at him.

"Hey Digger, I expect you have taken a few odd silver coins at Northam, from the immigrants," Rusty commented.

"You bet I have," Digger replied, "silver, gold and copper coins, paper money, bank draughts, I have even been offered antique coins and jewellery, would you believe?"

"Have you indeed, so what did you say to them?" Nugget asked, ignoring his wife's angry stare.

"I told them I couldn't help them of course; I mentioned it to Mr. Newgate and he was going to find out what action the bank took in Melbourne, with regard to these sorts of queries."

"He doesn't need to speak to anyone in Melbourne, I can answer that question for you," said Rusty, "according to the rumour mill, Don Davis made a lot of personal profit from buying and selling those sorts of items."

"Rusty, you know better than to spread malicious rumours about a fellow employee, that sort of thing could ruin someone's career at the bank," snapped his father.

"Hold your horses' dad, my information came from an impeccable source who works in the branch I first started with in Melbourne. She believes Don Davis stole vast amounts of money from gullible, confused immigrants, over the whole time he was in charge and believes he should have been prosecuted for theft in Melbourne and not promoted and sent to Perth."

"What utter nonsense, I won't stand for such malicious speculation Rusty, who is this impeccable source who has poisoned your mind?"

"Only his wife, that's who! Good enough source for you dad?"

"Now I know you are talking rubbish, his wife is with him here in Perth, you couldn't possibly have met her in a branch in Melbourne."

"That woman is not his wife dad, she is his expensive mistress that he stole to support. He and his wife are separated, they are not even divorced, so that's the sort of honourable man that your Don Davis really is."

"O.K. boys, that is enough," said Junie firmly, "you can continue this conversation at the office next week, it is time for us to clear the table and then go for our swim. Mum said she was happy to stay here and look after Duke, so let's get cracking."

On Tuesday the 27th December 1949 at 11:00 a.m. precisely, in a little used conference room on the top floor of the bank, Nugget chaired a meeting to discuss the recent revelations concerning Don Davis. Present at the meeting were Nugget himself, Mr. Newgate, Digger, Rusty, Carl Kemp, the manger in charge of Internal Audit for W.A. and the manager in charge of Security.

Nugget opened the meeting and informed those present that this matter carried the highest level of confidentiality in the bank and was not to be discussed with anyone outside of the meeting.

"I spoke this morning on the telephone, with the Chairman about the information which has recently come to light, concerning Don Davis and he has asked me to head up this investigation, on his behalf. He has personally instructed my opposite number in Melbourne to liaise with me and informed him that he is to speak with Mrs. Davis, who I gather has been using her maiden name of Hunt, which is why the bank did not pick up that she was Don's wife.

He has asked us to compile a list of question for Mrs. Davis to answer, whilst making it quite clear, that she herself is completely above suspicion in this matter.

I gather that the Chairman has also spoken with yourself Mr. Newgate, so is there anything else you wish to add?"

"I have been asked to attend a weekly review meeting with yourselves and to make sure that you receive the fullest co-operation from everyone in the bank. So may I suggest that the first Review Meeting takes place at the same time next Tuesday the third of January and that you will notify me if anyone needs speaking to Nugget, or if there are any matters that need my urgent attention," with which he got up from his chair and left the meeting.

"Right Rusty, tell us all that you know about this sorry matter," instructed his father.

Rusty went over the information he had shared at the Christmas dinner table and then went on to explain how Mrs. Davis believed her husband had operated.

"She does not think he set out to steal from the immigrants, but told me that her husband had always liked to gamble on the horses and had managed to get himself indebted to a particularly tough bookmaker, at the same time as he started to run the New Immigrants Office. She told me that she believed he simply started looking for new ways to make a bit extra cash, to pay off his debts."

"Well that certainly fits, as he was always the one to run the Office Sweepstake each year," Nugget commented.

"Well, it appears that a few days after he opened the office for the immigrants," Rusty continued, "that he inadvertently used too low an exchange rate when changing some Italian Lira into pounds, leaving himself with several hundred Lira spare, when he came to balance the books at the end of the day. He thought he would get into all sorts of trouble if he admitted that he had made such a basic mistake, but luckily for him, the two people concerned did not wish to open a bank account, so he simply wrote out two fresh receipts for them, crossing the other ones through, to show a simple error had been made and corrected."

"Yes, something similar to that happened to me on my first day," confessed Digger. "I had been changing an amount of French Francs into pounds for a man and then he produced some Spanish Pesetas and I forgot to use a different exchange rate and only realized when I was counting out the pound notes, so I had to cross the receipt through and write out a new one; but I did ask the man to initial it as well. So what did Mr. Davis do with the spare Lira he had acquired?"

"His wife was not certain, but believed that he simply hid it somewhere in the office, while he considered his options over night," replied Rusty. "Anyway, the next day he had another man come in who had a whole range of different currencies and spent some time in the office. The man was going to open a bank account and had given Don Davis his address and some sort of proof of identity, but for some reason he left in a hurry, leaving his papers behind him on the table.

Don assumed that he would be back the next day for them and left them in the office. Mrs. Davis believes that the man never came back and Don realized that all he had to do was rent a room somewhere in town in the man's name and then open a bank account, having the relevant cheque book and papers sent to this bogus address."

"Let me guess what happened next," said Carl Kemp, "he used the Lira he had acquired to start with, to exchange for pounds and paid the proceeds into the bank account and from then on, he could cheat people at will and just pay his profits into the bogus bank account. Which probably also explains the low rate of take up for bank accounts, as he could only cheat the cash customers!"

"You have it in one Carl, but his wife does not know the name of the account he used, but believes that after a week or so he stopped renting the room and moved the address to a Post Office Box out of town somewhere," Rusty concluded.

"From what you have told me Rusty, the security of the Bank has not actually been breached and the bank has not suffered any pecuniary loss, as a result of Don Davis's actions," suggested the Security Manager.

"I guess that's true, but surely you are not suggesting we turn a blind eye to what he did!" Rusty queried.

"Of course not, I am merely suggesting that this is more of a matter for Carl's Internal Audit department than mine. What do you think Nugget?"

"I agree," Nugget replied, "besides, Internal Audit snooping around asking questions, will make far fewer waves internally than if Bank Security do it. We do not want Mr. Davis tipped off that we are investigating him.

Once we have all the facts, I am sure Security will issue some procedural changes, in order to make certain this unsavoury incident cannot be repeated. On balance, I agree that Carl's department should handle the day to day investigation and I have already spoken to their respective managers and have formal agreement that Rusty and Digger be seconded to the investigation as from now, as they are both already involved. Is that all right with you Carl?"

"Yes of course Nugget and perhaps we three can get together after this meeting, to decide exactly what each of us is to do in the next few days."

Rusty returned to Melbourne and Digger continued to run the office at Northam, keeping detailed records of each transaction and every unusual request/opportunity that came his way.

It took Rusty more than a week to track down the bogus Bank Account that Don Davis had used. It was in the name of Hans Schmidt and was originally set up for an address in Melbourne and then moved to a Post Office in Melton, which is a small town about twenty miles North West of Melbourne. It sat there for a few years and was then transferred to Fremantle about a month after Don Davis moved to the Perth office and had recently been transferred to Southern Cross, which lies on the Great Eastern Highway about one hundred and thirty five miles West of Kalgoorlie.

The account had accumulated several thousand pounds during the time that Don ran the Immigrants Office in Melbourne and had slowly been run down over the ensuing years, to where it currently held just a few hundred pounds.

"No wonder he was so annoyed that I had been asked to run the office at Northam and not him," Digger commented to Carl as they were discussing the latest information, "he obviously needs an influx of funds to support his lifestyle. But what do you make of this latest payment into the account of eight pounds fifteen shillings and ten pence?"

"Is there any additional information about it?" asked Carl.

"Well I'll be!" said a surprised Digger, "it was paid to him by his very own Kalgoorlie branch office"

"There have always been employees who fiddle their expenses and we even had a manager once, who employed and paid a bogus cashier, so who knows what he thinks he can get away with, now he is the branch manger," Carl replied.

"Has Rusty had any luck yet in tracking down the original Hans Schmidt?" Digger asked.

"He thinks so. He has been making discreet enquiries among the German community and discovered that a lot of people knew of Don Davis and his antics and many of them appear to have been cheated by him, so he thinks it is only a matter of time, before Herr Schmidt comes forward. In the meantime, before you travel to Northam on Thursday, leave a day earlier and drive out to Southern Cross and visit the Post office where his mail is being sent. Take this with you, it is a photograph taken of Don Davis last year at a managers' function, show it to the Post Office staff and see if any of them recognize him."

On Wednesday the eleventh of January 1950, Digger set out bright and early for Southern Cross. He called in at the Northam office first and deposited the week's money in the safe and then set off again, arriving at Southern Cross in the late afternoon. As he got out of the car at the Post Office, he noticed that one of his front tyres was looking a bit flat and found that a spike of some sort had got buried in the middle of the tread. He spotted a garage down the street and walked down to talk to one of the mechanics.

"First thing tomorrow mate is the best I can do," the mechanic informed him, "drive the car down and park it over there, by that pile of tyres and it will be safe for the night."

Digger walked back to the Post Office and went inside and made a phone call to Carl, telling him what had happened and saying that he would probably be late in getting to Northam on the Thursday and could Carl let Mr. Newgate know about the puncture. He then spoke to the manger of the Post Office and showed him the photograph and he instantly recognized Don Davis as being the new P.O. Box holder, Hans Schmidt.

"So is Hans a friend of yours then," the manager enquired.

"Err, yes, we used to work together, but then lost contact and a mutual friend told me that I might find him in Southern Cross."

"Oh he doesn't live here, he just passes through from time to time, in fact, I am expecting him to call in the next few days. He told me that he was a traveling salesman of some sort, machinery I think he said. Is that your car outside with the flat tyre, by any chance?"

"Yes I picked up a nail on my way here from Northam, the mechanic at the garage said that he would fix it for me tomorrow morning."

"My wife runs a Bed and Breakfast, if you need somewhere to stay tonight, Mr. err, what did you say your name was?"

"Smith, Digger Smith at your service. Thanks for the offer, but I am booked into the hotel, perhaps next time, if you have a card or something I can keep."

Digger left the Post Office, slowly drove the car to the garage and parked it by the pile of tyres, handing in the key at the office. He then took his overnight bag from the boot, walked to the hotel and booked in. His room was on the first floor overlooking the street, so he had a quick wash in the bathroom next door and stretched out on the bed to rest before dinner.

He woke with a start and looking at his watch realized that it was gone seven thirty, so he rushed down to reception only to be told that the restaurant had already closed and if he wanted something to eat, he should walk down the street to the little café on the other side of the road, opposite the garage.

He got there with ten minutes to spare and ordered a steak with potatoes and vegetables and a large mug of tea. He finished his meal and went outside to discover it was pitch black, with just the odd light here and there to light his path. As he was walking past the end of a narrow alley, he heard a woman groaning and calling out for help. He warily took a couple of steps into the alley and called out, "Is anyone there, show yourself."

"Over here," she replied, "I tripped on a log and have fallen and hurt my leg; I think it might be broken. The pain is terrible, help me please."

He walked over to where a woman was sprawled on the ground and as he bent down to look at her, he heard a footstep behind him and only caught the briefest glimpse of a man standing behind him, before he was hit on the head with a large lump of wood.

When he came to, he found himself on his side and tied up with rope. He realized that he was in the back of a car, which was traveling at speed over a rough dirt road. Not only were his hands and feet tied tightly, but he also had a sack over his head, so he could not see his watch and had no real sense of time or distance. As he lay there he was able to make out the conversation which was taking place in the front of the car.

"How much further is it Don, this road is giving me a headache?"

"Almost there Ursula, have you heard any noises from the back yet?"

"Nothing, you hit him so hard I thought you had killed him, come to think of it, why didn't you just kill him? It would have saved us a lot of trouble."

"Where would we have got rid of a body in town, don't be stupid, use your head for once. This way, if he is ever found, it will look like he went for a walk and simply got lost in the bush and fell down the pit. Whatever people may think, they won't be able to prove diddly squat! By the time anyone misses him tomorrow, we will be safely at home asleep in our bed, or already at work, giving us the perfect alibi."

After a few more minutes, the car came to a halt and Digger decided to pretend that he was still out cold. The boot was opened and Don Davis and his mistress peered in. Between them, they wrestled Digger out of the car and let him drop to the ground pulling the sack off his head as he fell. He let out a groan as he hit the ground and looking up saw the woman holding a torch in one hand and his gun in the other.

Don and Ursula stood there laughing at him and Don removed the ropes from his hands and feet, while Ursula kept the gun pointing at his chest.

"Well, well, our inquisitive friend is wide awake Ursula, not so cocky now are we Smith? In case you are thinking of trying something, Ursula is an excellent shot and certainly won't miss you at this range," with which he punched Digger hard in the face and kicked him several times in the stomach.

"You all thought you were so clever, you and Rusty and Carl, conducting your secret enquiry, tut, tut, tut, we didn't do our homework properly did we?"

"Just hit him again Don and get it over with, I'm getting cold out here, in the middle of nowhere."

"Patience Ursula, it will soon be over. In case you haven't worked it out yet, Ursula is German, as of course her uncle is, Hans Schmidt. Oh, I can see I have surprised you. Yes, that's right, he sent all the immigrants to me, for a percentage of course and Hans, being a jeweller by trade, told me what to offer for the gold and jewellery that came my way and then bought everything off me; wasn't that kind of him?"

Digger looked at him intently and then turned away and spat a mouthful of blood into the pit.

"I am sure you must have lots of questions about my work and how I knew you were here, but Ursula is getting cold and you wouldn't want that, would you? I have to tell you Smith, that I never really liked you and I don't believe that you ever liked me, so you will be pleased to know that this is the last time you will ever see me, in fact, it is the last time you will ever see anyone!"

"I'm cold and getting back in the car, for goodness sake get on with it Don," Ursula snapped, as she took her foot off Digger and turned towards the car.

Don raised the wooden stake to hit his unfortunate victim, for the second time that evening, but before he could strike the blow, Digger just rolled over the edge of the pit, not having Ursula's foot to keep him in place on the brink any more. Don rushed back to the car to fetch the torch and returned to the pit and shone it down the big black hole, but Digger had disappeared from view. As he listened, he could hear something splashing around in the water at the bottom of the shaft and then everything went quiet. Don got back in the car beside Ursula, started the engine and drove home to Kalgoorlie, for a good night's sleep.

Chapter 10
News from Spain

"Deborah, what time are you and Mac leaving for London?" Bertie called out to his daughter. "Deborah! I said what time-"

"I heard you dad, I heard you, please don't shout, my head is pounding," Deborah replied, as she slumped down into a kitchen chair.

"I warned you to lay off Del's homemade punch, two glasses of that stuff and Victoria is out for the count. Still it was a good New Year's Eve party and all the revellers enjoyed themselves at the Stag. I have to say that everyone I spoke to is a lot more confident about the Fifties than they were about the Forties, that's for sure."

"Here you are Deborah, a nice cup of sweet tea and a couple of headache tablets, it works every time for me," said Victoria, putting the teacup quietly down on the table next to her.

"Thanks Victoria. Mac said he would come by after breakfast and pick me up on the Indian and we would head back into town, but I am not sure I want to travel anywhere, feeling like this. Oh, did I mention there was some late mail arrived for you two yesterday, I put it in the glove box in the hallstand, on my way out to the pub."

Victoria walked out into the hall and opened the lid of the glove box and took out the mail and calling out to Bertie said, "You know that screwdriver with the ratchet, that you accused me of throwing away last week, well it is in the glove box and it wasn't me who put it there." Emphasizing her point, by closing the lid a little more firmly that she needed to.

"Thank you for that information Victoria, anything important or just late Christmas Cards?" Bertie said, when she returned to the room.

"Well there's one from Kendal, which probably means Eddy remembered he had not sent us a card when he got ours, an official looking letter for you from Spain and a small package from Australia, from Moira and Digger." She passed the Spanish letter to Bertie and then opened the card from Kendal.

"I was right, it's from Eddy and Dolly. Oh, he has twisted his ankle and damaged his elbow and has a black eye. She says that he was persuaded to act as linesman for an inter village game of football, slipped over in the mud, taking a middle aged lady with him. He damaged his ankle and elbow in the fall and she gave him a whack in the eye, with her umbrella for spoiling her new coat. For goodness sake Bertie, Eddy is almost seventy, will he never grow up? Men! You all right love, you look stunned, is it bad news from Spain?"

"Yes it is, the letter is from Paco's solicitor, to say that Paco died while out fishing three weeks ago. The solicitor says that there is a small bequest for me and that Paco has left his house to me as well, in view of the very low amount that I charged his niece for my old house the other year."

"Poor old Paco, he was always such fun and so full of life. What will you do dad? Will you go over there to see the solicitor?" asked Deborah.

"Yes, I guess I will have to. It sounds like he died from a fishing accident rather than health problems. Well, it is the way he would have wanted to go. Did I ever tell you Victoria that the house Paco was living in, was actually built by me, before I got married."

"No Bertie you didn't, but nothing surprises me any more where you are concerned; but how did a poorly paid seaman, afford a house in Spain?"

"I paid for it out of my ill gotten gains on the El Burro Volando. If I am being honest, I actually preferred it to the second house we built, it's in a great spot, just back from the beach, I am sure that you will love it."

Victoria smiled and nodded and continued to open the package from Moira.

"You seem engrossed with that package," he said, "what does it contain?"

"It's the photographs I asked Digger to take of the Fruit Farm in Pinjarra. It must have cost a fortune to send them to us. Still, he is getting the use of our car for free! Come and have a look Deborah, there is a picture here of my Step-son's daughter Vicky, as well as Digger and Moira, and Jenny and Ray, who own the farm with us."

"Moira is looking well and Ray is huge, but no sign of your dog, Victoria."

"No, that's right Deborah. Moira says in her letter that he is still in the kennels but they are hoping to pick him up quite soon. Sounds like a motorbike is drawing up outside, better go and get dressed Deborah. You don't want to let Mac see you looking like that, do you dear?"

Deborah went off to her room to get changed and Mac came striding into the room.

"Good morning everyone and how are we all today, on this bright, frosty New Year's Day. No Deborah yet?"

"Good morning and a Happy New Year to you Mac," said Victoria, "obviously no hangover for you then?"

"I stick to one drink, normally beer and know when to stop, that way I never have a problem. Is she fit to travel?"

"Putting my paternal hat on, I would say a definite no, perhaps this afternoon, probably tomorrow; but this is my Deborah we are talking about, so I am sure she will decide what to do, without seeking her old father's advice," commented Bertie.

"I have some photographs from Australia, Mac, which have just arrived from Moira and Digger, would you like to see them?"

By the time Mac had finished viewing the photographs and had drunk the requisite amount of tea and eaten at least three homemade mince pies, Deborah re-appeared, looking a lot more like her old self, than she had before. They kissed and wished each other a Happy New Year and then they all sat round the table to discuss the implications of the news from Spain about Paco.

"If we work backwards from our Wedding Day dad, the eighth of April, we only have fourteen weeks to go. I think that you really need to be in Benicarlo in the next week or ten days, to make sure the house is signed over to you and that the church, hotel and restaurant all know what they are doing. You told me it was all under control dad! Mac's family have already booked their tickets and arranged for time off work and if his mother asks me one more question about the ceremony and reception, I will scream."

"Calm down Deborah, I spoke with Paco at the beginning of December and he assured me that he had arranged everything for the wedding, just as you had requested. His death does not alter anything, but to put your mind at rest, I will book a passage for next week and go over and see the solicitor. I assume you would like to come with me Victoria?"

"I certainly would Bertie. I can't wait to see this new home of yours and paddle my feet in the Mediterranean Sea, who would ever have thought it?"

Bertie was able to book a passage for the two of them which left Southampton on Friday afternoon, the sixth of January and sailed overnight to Palma in Majorca, giving Bertie the opportunity to show Victoria some of his old haunts. They arrived in Barcelona on Sunday and spent the night in the same hotel where his first wife had announced that she was pregnant with Deborah, but he did not bother to mention that fact to Victoria.

He managed to hire a car on Monday morning and they drove down to Benicarlo in the afternoon and booked into a small hotel in town. They had a quiet meal in a local restaurant and a walk round town before going to bed.

They were up bright and early the next day and Victoria insisted on going to the florist to buy some flowers to put on the graves of Bertie's first wife Makaa, who died of TB in January 1935 and his stillborn son Roberto, who died in June 1919 and his mother who passed away in 1940. After visiting the cemetery they walked to the solicitor's office to sort out the legalities of Paco's Will.

"Well fortunately Senor Bannister, it was my father who arranged the original sale of land to you in nineteen hundred and four and the additional land you purchased for the extension in nineteen hundred and sixteen, so I am pleased to say that all the papers are in order and if you just sign here, here and here, I can get everything filed with the authorities and the house will legally be yours in about a month's time," the solicitor assured him.

"Would it be possible to visit the house today, so I can see what sort of state it is in and Victoria can decided what furniture we will need," Bertie said, after signing the various documents.

"But of course, the house is not occupied, you are welcome to stay there during your visit, just do not remove anything from the house that is on this list. In his Will, Paco left certain items of furniture to his family, but the remainder of the contents are to go to you, with the house and boat. This is a list of the items which are to go to the family, but anything that is still there when you legally own it, becomes yours."

"This is the first I have heard of a boat, what sort of boat is it Bertie," Victoria asked.

"When Deborah and I moved to Roses in 1939, I bought a thirty foot long fishing boat, with an inboard diesel engine in it, which we all used to go fishing in, from time to time. When I moved to England in 1946 I gave the boat to Paco to use in his fishing business, on the understanding that I would get it back if I ever returned to Spain."

"I see and does the boat have a name and can you take me out for a ride in it?" Victoria queried.

"Deborah named her Makaa, after her mother and assuming it is tied up at its old spot in the harbour, we can certainly go for a ride and see how she handles. I seem to recall that Paco told me that he had replaced the engine and made a few other modifications to it last year."

"Here are the keys to the house and boat Senor and of course your bank pass book, into which Paco paid the rent for your house that he received from his niece every month, until you sold it to her. The bank manager is a friend of mine and I did notify him of your visit, so he is expecting you to call in and see him some time. I hope you and your new wife will be very happy here and of course we look forward to seeing your daughter Deborah again, when she comes over for her wedding in a few months time. Everyone is talking about it."

As the bank was only fifty yards down the road from the solicitor's office, they went there next and spoke with the manager and drew out some of the money that Bertie had allowed to accumulate over the last four years. They had already checked the room reservations for the wedding guests at the hotel, so they walked down to the restaurant which was hosting the Reception, to find that once again, Paco had arranged everything down to the last detail, just as Deborah had requested. Having already spoken with the florist when they purchased the flowers for the graves, it meant that they simply needed to make a final visit to the church and the priest who was conducting the service, to confirm that everything was ready for the big day.

"Can we go and visit the house now Bertie, I am dying to see what it looks like," Victoria said, as they walked down the road away from the church.

"You see that cottage over there, with the big red bougainvillea growing on the fence, well that is it."

"Oh Bertie, it's just charming and to think you built it all those years ago and here we are in nineteen fifty and it is yours once again. You must be thrilled!"

"I guess I am," he confirmed, "I certainly never expected to get it back again, that's for sure."

As they walked into the garden, they saw that the front door was open and could hear voices from inside and obviously a lot of activity was going on.

"Hey, who is this in my new house," Bertie called out in his best Spanish as he stood in the hallway, "show yourselves at once, I am a law abiding citizen, what is the meaning of all this?"

A woman came from one room and a man came from another and almost crushed him between them in their eagerness to embrace him, Victoria just stood there, utterly amazed at what was happening in front of her.

"Enough, enough, cried Bertie, it is so good to see you both again. Let me introduce you to my wife; Victoria, these are my good friends and long suffering neighbours, Daria and Santo."

"Eet is good to meet you Victria, velcome Benicarlo," said Daria, who had been practicing her English all week.

"Hola. Tanto gusto! No hablo Espanol," Victoria proudly replied.

They all laughed and Santo produced a bottle of the local wine and some bread and cheese and they all sat out on the veranda chatting and exchanging news, with Bertie acting as interpreter.

Daria explained that she had managed to wash and iron the bed linen and give the house a quick clean and get rid of all the old fishing bits and pieces and other rubbish that Paco had accumulated during his time in the house. She then conducted Victoria on a tour of the house while the two men chatted and caught up with each other.

For Victoria, it was love at first sight with regard to the house and its location next to the beach. Whilst she liked the cottage in England, it was very much Bertie's home, but she felt that this was theirs and that she had free reign to change and alter it as she wished; which is exactly what she and Daria did over the next few days.

She kept the best of the two beds as a spare one and got rid of the other and then ordered a new one from a shop in town. She and Daria spent hours looking at curtains, bed covers etc. but the vast majority of the furniture and fittings received the Victoria seal of approval and were allowed to remain in the house, after they were thoroughly cleaned and polished.

Around lunch time on the Friday, the telephone rang and thinking it was the solicitor, Bertie picked it up and said "Hello."

"Dad, it's me," said the voice on the other end.

"Deborah, what a nice surprise. I assume you are ringing to see how everything has gone; well I am pleased to tell you that everything has been done that should have been done for your wedding and the whole town is looking forward to the occasion."

"That's really great to know dad, but it's not why I am ringing. We had a telephone call from Moira yesterday evening, with some really bad news. Digger went off on a business trip on Wednesday to a place called Southern Cross in Western Australia and has gone missing, just disappeared and no-one has any idea of where he has gone, or why he has gone off on his own."

"Poor Moira, she must be besides herself. Did he take the car or has he gone off on foot?"

"Well that's the strange thing. It appears he drove your car to the town but found it had a puncture, so put it in the garage overnight, to be repaired in the morning. He went out for a meal at a café down the road from the hotel, but never returned to the hotel. The manager's wife raised the alarm in the morning when he did not show for breakfast and she realized that his bed had not been slept in."

"Moira said that your friend big Ray was heading off to Southern Cross to help in the search for him and was taking one of his own dogs and wanted to take Duke along as well, to help find him. It appears his chances of survival are pretty poor if he is lost in the bush for more than a few days. Anyway, tell Victoria that I gave permission for Duke to go on her behalf, so I hope she does not mind, but how could I refuse?"

"You were quite right to give your permission Deborah, I am sure Victoria won't mind in the least, ring me again if you hear any more news. Victoria really loves it here in Benicarlo, so I think we will stay a few more weeks as it certainly beats the English winter. Bye for now."

"And what exactly won't I mind?" his wife asked skeptically.

"Digger has gone missing in the bush somewhere and they are mounting a search party and Ray wanted to take Duke with him, so Deborah gave permission on your behalf."

Ray left home at the crack of dawn on Friday the thirteenth of January, arriving at the hotel in Southern Cross at around four o'clock. As soon as he had booked in, he walked round to the police station, leaving the dogs in the back of the truck. As he entered the station he heard a discussion going on between a middle-aged man in a suit and the police sergeant, which was obviously about Digger."

"I am sorry Mr. Kemp, but there are hundreds of square miles of bush out there to search. We do not know where your colleague may have gone to, whether he is on foot, or got a lift from someone, or what. My officer and I have already checked the most likely places and I can organize a much wider search on Saturday, when I can mobilize some of the local farmers to help, but there is nothing more I can do in the meantime."

"By Saturday Sergeant, my colleague will probably be dead, if he is not dead already. The Bank is prepared to pay everyone who takes part in the search, make sure that fact is widely known please and as I said to you before, Mr. Smith was investigating a serious case of fraud within the bank and I think his disappearance might well be linked to that investigation."

"Excuse me," said Ray, "but are you Carl Kemp, Moira said you would be coming here today."

"I am and you must be Ray Thomas, good to meet you, let's go back to the hotel and I can bring you up to date on what I have found out so far. Which isn't very much, I am afraid."

They walked back to the hotel, got a drink and sat down in the lobby, where Carl told ray of Digger's movements on Wednesday night.

"So, do you have a photograph of this Don Davis with you?" Ray asked.

"I do and I spoke with the Post Office Manager, but he was very nervous and refused to talk to me, so I don't quite know what to make of that."

"Give me the photo and I will go and visit him while you get changed into your rough clothes. People often seem to be willing to talk to me when they won't talk to others, for some reason!"

Leaving Duke in the back of the truck, Ray and his own dog walked down to the Post Office. A lady was serving a customer and Ray waited quietly. When the customer had left he walked up to the counter and asked her where the manager was.

"I am not supposed to tell you," she said, "he doesn't want to speak to anyone, but," and pointed to the office in the corner.

Ray and dog burst into the office and found the manager with a glass in one hand and a cigarette in the other. Ray slammed the photograph on the desk and shouted at him,

"You tell me what you know about this man right now or you and I will take a walk into the bush where I have got six other dogs even hungrier than this one, who will enjoy the feed."

Blossom by the Billabong

"My goodness," said Carl, "you must have a very persuasive line of questioning Ray, to have got all that information from him."

Ray just nodded and smiled and patted the dog.

"So Don Davis and a woman, whom we can presume is his pretend wife, arrived just before closing time to draw out some money from the Hans Schmidt account and the Manager just mentioned that Digger had been there with a photograph, asking questions and looking for him," Carl summarized.

"That's right and your Mr. Davis had his car with him and could have taken Digger anywhere. But let's start at the café where he had his meal and see what they can tell us."

"Good idea, but perhaps I should handle the questioning this time," Carl replied, "and best leave the dogs in the truck, I think."

They walked down the road to the café and spoke with the waitress who was standing by the door.

"I have already told that policeman all this," the waitress said, "just get a copy of my statement from him, can't you see that I'm busy right now."

"Well I could, that's true," said Carl, "but then if your information leads to the apprehension of the perpetrators of this crime, you will not be eligible for the Bank's reward."

"Oh, no-one said the bank was offering a reward, why don't you two gentleman sit down and I will get us all a cup of tea."

They sat down and the waitress went over the events of Wednesday night.

"Your friend was our last customer, it must have been about five to eight when he arrived and he seemed such a nice man, that I still took his order and cooked the steak myself, since the cook had already left for the night."

165

"Did anyone else come in while he was eating or did he happen to mention that he was going for a walk after his meal," Carl asked.

"On the contrary, he told me that he was tired as he had been up very early and was going back to the hotel to sleep. No-one came in while he was eating, but I did see that posh woman walk past the window and stare in. She had a big hat on and pulled it down over her face, but I would recognize that coat of hers anywhere, it must have cost a small fortune."

"She has been in here before then?" Ray enquired.

"She and her man have been in several times, he is Australian but she is definitely foreign, although her English is very good."

"Would this be the man?" Carl asked, putting the photograph on the table.

"Yes, that's him, I seem to recall that he said he was a salesman of some sort."

"That's what the Post Office Manger said," Ray commented.

"Can you remember what our friend was wearing and what time he left," Carl enquired.

"A suit I think, but no tie or hat. He knew it was past closing time and hurried his meal for me and left about eight thirty. Since I had rushed him and did not offer him a sweet, I gave him a couple of Anzac biscuits to take with him and eat at the hotel. I warned him to be careful of his teeth, as he did not appear to know what they were."

"Did you happen to notice which way he went when he left here?" Carl asked.

"Yes I did, as I left shortly after him. As I was locking the front door I watched as he headed off towards the hotel, but I had to go back in for something and left again a few minutes later and went in the same direction as him, but there was no sign of him."

"There was no-one else about, no cars around, nothing unusual happened?" Ray asked.

"Nothing at all; well, apart from the car that almost knocked me down as I was crossing the road. It came out of that alley, just down the road, no lights on, throwing up the dirt, some people just don't care!"

"Did you happen to notice which way the car went?" asked Carl.

"I can't be sure, as I was a bit shaken, but I think it turned onto the main road heading for Merredin."

"Well thank you very much, you have been most helpful," said Carl.

"And the reward," said the waitress.

"You will most certainly be hearing from us if we catch these people," Carl confirmed as they left the café.

Ray went and got the dogs and then they proceeded to the alley that the mysterious car had come out of. They had only gone down the alley a few paces when Duke picked up something from the ground and started to eat it. Ray immediately grabbed the dog and made him give up what he was eating.

"Look at this Carl, an Anzac biscuit and there's another one which looks like someone has been nibbling."

Carl took a paper bag out of his pocket and put the nibbled biscuit into it.

"There are some stains on that stone which could be blood, I reckon Digger came down here for some reason and got clobbered in the dark and was then driven off in that car," said Ray.

"Can I stroke your dog mister?" asked a young lad who had come out of a house just down from where the two men were kneeling.

"Not today son, he is not in the best of tempers," said Ray, "stroke the other one, his name is Duke."

The boy bent over and petted Duke, who licked his hands and rolled over so he could stroke his tummy.

"What have I told you about stroking other people's dogs and speaking to strangers," said a very cross lady in a large apron who appeared at the door of the house the boy had come from.

"It's perfectly all right madam," said Carl formally, standing up and turning towards the lady. "Your boy did ask first and my colleague here, gave his permission, so the boy is quite safe. Let me introduce myself, I am Carl Kemp and I am a manager with the Perth Mining & Commerce Bank Ltd. I am here investigating the disappearance of a colleague Wednesday evening. I believe he may have been accosted in this street about eight thirty or thereabouts and was wondering if you happened to notice anything unusual that night?"

"We didn't see anything, sorry we can't help, Lennie, indoors now," she ordered.

"What about that car mum, remember? I told you there was a big black Riley parked outside and you said it probably belonged to her next door's, fancy man."

"I said no such thing Lennie, where he gets it from I just don't know Mr. Kemp. But he's right, there was a car parked just there and a man and a woman. It must have been parked there for well over an hour and then it got dark and we had supper and Lennie went to bed. That's all I know."

"I couldn't get to sleep mum, it was hot and my big toe was throbbing where I stubbed it on the doorframe and I heard them come back. He opened the boot and it looked like she was sitting on the running board and then I must have dozed off for a while. I woke up again a bit later because they were arguing and I then saw him slam the boot shut and then they drove off."

"Could you tell what they were arguing about son," Carl asked.

"Not really, she had a funny accent, but I heard her say Yellowdine and rocks and he said 'No, the pits are closer'. That's all I heard."

"You have been most helpful son and here is a sixpence to buy yourself some sweets tomorrow," said Carl.

The boy and his mother went indoors and Carl and Ray walked to the police station and informed the Sergeant what they had found out.

"Well, going on what you have told me, the closest disused pits on the Merredin side of town are out past the rubbish tip, on the Hyden road. I will get some ropes and lamps and a first aid kit and you two can follow me out there," the Sergeant suggested.

The Hyden Road was just a few hundred yards out of town and the disused pits were about three miles down the dirt road. The Sergeant and his officer pulled over to the side of the road and Carl and Ray pulled up behind them. Ray then sounded his horn three times, he then waited a few seconds and sounded three more times.

"Quiet everyone," he ordered.

He then repeated the sequence again, once more requesting silence as he watched the dogs for some reaction. Duke picked his ears up and started to bark and Ray let him off the lead.

"Follow that dog," he ordered, "he has heard something."

Duke had only run a few yards into the bush when they found him standing by the mouth of a disused mine shaft, barking loudly.

"Quiet boy," Ray said and then shouted down the shaft, "Digger, if you can hear me make a noise."

As they all strained their ears they could hear a distinct tapping, 'Tap, tap, tap' silence, 'tap, tap, tap.'

"Hold on sir," shouted the Sergeant, "I will be coming down with a rope, but first I will be lowering a torch, if you can grab hold of it that's good, but if you can't, just start tapping when it gets level with you."

They lowered the torch on a string, watching its decent, when suddenly a hand shot out from a dark corner of the shaft and grabbed the torch. They all shined their torches down the shaft and could see a man, half lying and half sitting on a ledge, which looked like it could collapse at any moment.

"That ledge won't take both your weight and his, Sergeant," the other policeman informed him, "we will have to lower a rope and some padding and just pull him up, whatever his injuries might be."

It took almost forty minutes and the combined strength of the four men to lower the rope and pull Digger to safety. The fall down the shaft had dislocated his right shoulder and badly twisted his left ankle and right knee, but he was still alive and able to tell his story.

They took him to the local hospital where his wounds were treated and he was given plenty of water to drink and some food to eat. Carl phoned the bank to give them the good news and Ray phoned Moira to tell her that Digger was safely tucked up in a hospital bed. The sergeant took his statement and immediately telephoned the police station at Kalgoorlie who sent officers round to Don Davis's house to arrest him and Ursula. Several of the officers carried firearms, as Digger had warned them that Ursula had taken his gun and apparently knew how to use it.

The house was surrounded and a senior officer with a loud hailer told them to come out with their hands in the air. After the second warning by the police, the front door opened and Mr. Davis came out of the house with his hands in the air as requested. Ursula was a few paces behind him, but her hands were at her side and in her right hand was Digger's pistol.

She called out "Auf Wiedersehen Don," raised the gun and shot him twice in the back and then put the muzzle to her own temple and pulled the trigger.

Don Davis died on his way to the hospital; it turning out to be a sad and unlucky Friday the Thirteenth, for two greedy, dishonest people.

"Deborah, hello Deborah; it's Moira from Australia. Hope I haven't disturbed you too early in the morning, but I am about to leave for the station to catch a train for Southern Cross."

"Moira, good to hear from you, what news is there of Digger?"

"Ray and Duke found him yesterday afternoon, alive, but in very poor shape. The man he was investigating tricked him to go down a dark alley and knocked him unconscious with a lump of wood. He and his lady friend then tied Digger up, bundled him into the boot of their car and drove him out of town to a disused mine and threw him down the open shaft."

"That's awful Moira, you must be devastated! What injuries does he have?"

"Mild concussion, a dislocated shoulder and possibly a broken ankle and a twisted knee and he is badly bruised from the beating and fall and he is dehydrated of course."

"Have they caught the couple who did this to him yet?"

"I gather so, but no-one will give me any details. I am just so relieved that he is still alive! Ray said his army training probably saved his life and please tell Victoria, that it was Duke who actually located his whereabouts down the pit."

"I will let everyone here know that he is safe and I will tell dad and Victoria in Spain. Do you want me to ask Mac to let his sister and family know?"

"Yes please Deborah. I overslept this morning and the taxi is waiting, so I have to rush, bye."

"Goodbye Moira and thanks for ringing."

When the train from Perth steamed into Southern Cross that evening, Ray was waiting on the platform with Duke. It was the dog who spotted Moira first and he went bounding down the platform and almost knocked her over in his excitement.

"Duke, come here," she said, "whose a clever dog eh?" and made a big fuss of him.

"Let me take the case for you Moira," said Ray as he greeted her with a big Aussie hug.

"Thanks Ray, have you seen him today?"

"About an hour ago, but he was in and out of consciousness, so I didn't stop long. Do you want to go the hotel first or straight to the hospital?"

"The hospital please and thank you so much for all you have done for us. Leaving the farm at short notice and coming out here with the dogs and being the one to find him and then help to lift him out alive; we will always be in your debt Ray."

"Nonsense Moira, that's what mates are for. Besides, it was a Pomey who saved my bacon many moons ago. Hold on tight and let's go and see that husband of yours."

Disused pit outside Southern Cross –
Photographer - Lucidus Smith

Chapter 11
Mad Sheep and Englishmen

"Mick, get the phone will you, I am in the middle of washing Patty's hair," Vi called out from the bathroom, to her husband who was in the middle of a very aggressive game of Snap, with Brian.

"Hello, Clapham South Underground Station, can I help you," he joked.

"Are you the Manager," the squeaky voice on the other end replied, "as my pet tortoise escaped from its basket today while I was traveling on your Underground train and it is somewhere on the line between Clapham South and Balham, I would like you to go down the tunnel and retrieve him for me please?"

"Ah no, actually I was joking madam, this is not really the Underground Station," said Mick a little flustered.

"Got you!" said Donny and laughed down the phone at Mick.

"Donny, is that you?" asked Mick.

"It sure is and I reckon that's six four to me at the moment. You must be losing your touch Mick."

The two men chatted for a while and discussed the football results for the previous weekend and then Mick said, "Hold on a second Donny, while I let Vi know you are on the phone, I am sure she will want to chat with you."

"No, don't do that just yet Mick, let me tell you why I am calling," with which he went on to explain all that had happened to Digger in Australia and the good news that he had been found alive and was now in hospital in Southern Cross and that Moira was traveling there by train and should have actually arrived by now and be there with him.

"Do we have a telephone number for the hospital Donny or the hotel where Moira is staying and is she on her own and if so, should someone fly over there to be with her? Once I tell Vi all of your news, she will not settle until she has personally spoken to Moira or Digger, you know what she is like as far as her brother is concerned."

"I know that Mick, but it is only three o'clock in the morning in Australia, so tell Vi that I will start making some phone calls this evening to try and find out the hospital's telephone number and I will then ring you again first thing tomorrow morning with the information. Moira told Deborah that it was her father's old friend Ray Thomas who found Digger with the help of Victoria's dog and that Ray is staying with Moira in Southern Cross for another day or so."

"I will explain all that to Vi right now, but she will want to speak with you herself, if I know my wife; I assume you are ringing me from home."

"Yes, as you can imagine, mum is being a bit hysterical about it all and has probably phoned a dozen people already, but I will keep her off the telephone for the next half hour if Vi wants to ring me."

Mick broke the news to Vi as gently as he could, but as soon as he had finished, she insisted on telephoning Donny and hearing it all over again from him. She then rang Deborah at her flat and got the same story for a third time.

"But why didn't Moira ring me, Deborah, after she had rung you on Thursday; for goodness sake, I am his sister," Vi exploded down the phone, " to wait for another two days before she lets me know and then I have to hear it from Donny rather than from her direct, it is just not good enough Deborah."

Deborah held her breath and counted silently to five and then replied, "It was gone eleven o'clock on Thursday evening when Moira called me and she must have been on the telephone for at least fifteen minutes and to say that she was 'beside herself with worry' is probably the understatement of the year. She hardly stopped crying the whole time she was speaking to me."

"That is understandable, but why did she ring you and not me Deborah?" Vi queried.

"She knew that dad and Victoria had gone to Spain, so she was asking me to give permission, on their behalf, for dad's dog Duke to go to Southern Cross with their friend Ray; who had the engine running in his truck outside the house, waiting to go. As soon as she put the phone down on me, she went outside to find the dog so that Ray could head off to Southern Cross in search of your brother; a journey of about three hundred miles which took him well over seven hours."

"I see," said Vi, "but surely,"

"Please let me finish what I have to say," said Deborah firmly, "after coming off the telephone to me and finding the dog to go with Ray, she then had to telephone the police station at Southern Cross with a detailed description of Digger and what he was wearing and then she had to telephone the man at the bank that Digger had been working with, as he was about to catch a train to Southern Cross to meet Ray when he arrived there. Finally Vi, may I tactfully point out to you, that Moira, like me, does not have any brothers or sisters and could not possibly understand the anguish she has inadvertently put you through."

"Oh I am sorry Deborah, but Digger is the only person I really care about apart from Mick and the children, I shouldn't have shouted at you like that, I am sorry."

"That's all right Vi, assuming Mac can find out the telephone number for the hospital or hotel, he will ring you first thing in the morning, so you can speak with Digger or

Moira yourself. When is your own trip planned to sail out to Australia, can't be too long now?"

"No it isn't, we leave on Monday the third of April and arrive in Fremantle a month later. We are so sorry we won't be able to attend your wedding in Spain, but we should be somewhere in the Mediterranean at that time and will be thinking of you and Donny and the children said they will wave to you from the ship."

The two ladies chatted for a bit longer and by the time Vi put the telephone back on the receiver she was in a much calmer mood and able to chat to Mick about what had been happening on the other side of the world.

"Please don't fuss Ray, I am a nurse, I am used to seeing sick and injured people in hospital," Moira informed him as they walked down the corridor towards the Men's ward.

They pushed through the swing doors and approached the desk of the Ward Sister, who looked up as they approached.

"Mr. Thomas have you forgotten what I said to you last time, do not bring your dirty boots into my clean ward, take them off and leave them outside the door, there is a mat there for the purpose."

"Sorry sister," said Ray sheepishly and went and did as he had been instructed.

"You must be Mrs. Smith, please sit down a minute will you."

Moira sat on the chair indicated and the two women weighed each other up.

"I am aware that you are a nurse Mrs. Smith and that you may well have your own ideas and opinions about your husband and his treatment, but this is my ward and you will remember that you are a guest here, just like any other visitor."

Moira smiled and nodded.

"Good, we understand each other then. In my opinion your husband is very lucky to have survived the terrible assault that he suffered, his natural strength, stamina, training and excellent physical health enabled him to live, when many men would have probably died in the same situation. Having said that, I do not expect to keep him here for more than two or three days and he should be fit enough to travel back home to Perth on Wednesday, by train that is, he won't be able to drive for a bit longer than that."

"Thank you Sister, may I see my husband now?"

"Of course, Mr. Thomas knows the way and judging by the state of his socks, they could probably get there on their own!"

When they got to Digger's bed the screens had been pulled round it and a nurse was changing the bandage on his head. Moira tapped the nurse on the shoulder and putting her finger on her lips, to indicate silence, offered to continue bandaging the patient, who was sitting up but had his eyes tightly shut.

The nurse handed the roll of fresh bandage to Moira and then stood back to watch Moira and to keep an eye out for the Sister. When she had finished she just stood there and held his arm gazing at him, with tears in her eyes.

"You know nurse," said Digger, "you must use the same perfume as my wife, you smell just like her," with which he opened his eyes and smiled at her, "hello Moira, I would know your touch anywhere," he said.

The nurse and Ray left them alone while they hugged and cried and comforted each other.

After ten minutes the nurse came back and removed the screens and Ray brought another chair and sat down next to the bed.

"The Sister said you can have another ten minutes Moira, but that's all" said Ray, "but she did say that you can come back in tomorrow morning at ten if you want to speak with the doctor."

"Did the Sergeant Major tell you how much longer I have to stay in hospital?" asked Digger.

"Did the who, tell me what?" asked Moira.

"The Sister, all the men in here call her the Sergeant Major," Digger explained.

"She said two or three days more and then you should be fit enough to travel by train to Perth on Wednesday. Do you think your work colleague Mr. Kemp, would be willing to drive the car back home for us?" asked Moira.

"I can answer that one," said Ray, "he is currently in Kalgoorlie helping the police tidy up the loose ends there and sorting out temporary cover at the bank until a new manger can be appointed. He plans to come back here on Tuesday or Wednesday and said he is quite happy to drive the car back to Ruth Street for you."

"Oh that's a relief," said Moira, "I was wondering how I was going to tell Bertie that his car was stranded at a small town, in the middle of no-where, a seven hour drive from Perth."

At which point the bell signaling the end of visiting hour was sounded and Ray took Moira back to the hotel. After registering at the front desk and arranging for some sandwiches and drinks to be sent up to their rooms, they both enjoyed the first decent nights sleep for several days. Moira was suddenly aware of a loud knocking on the door of her room and checking the alarm clock by her bed, found that it was eight a.m. precisely.

"Coming, coming, ouch – that hurt!" said Moira, as she practically fell out of bed knocking her elbow on the bedside table in her rush to answer the door.

"What's the matter? Is there some news from the hospital about my husband?" she asked, as she peered round the door at the desk clerk who was standing by himself in the hall.

"No Mrs. Smith and sorry to have woken you so abruptly, but I do have a gentleman on the telephone downstairs who is ringing from England and is after some news about your husband, who he says is his cousin. Does that sound about right to you?"

"It will be my husband's cousin Donny, I will be down in half a minute, just keep him talking please."

Moira did a lightening change out of her pyjamas into her day clothes and was down stairs in a minute to give Donny an update.

"Hold on Donny, I will ask the desk clerk," she said. "Excuse me, but do you have the telephone number of the hospital to hand, to save me going upstairs for it?"

The desk clerk wrote the number down for her and she read it out over the telephone and then said goodbye to Donny. By this time Ray had joined her in the lobby and the two of them went and had breakfast together, after which Moira and Ray went round to the truck where the two dogs were tied up in the back under an awning and after Moira had made a big fuss of Duke, they took the dogs for a walk around town.

"Are you sure you will be O.K. on your own here Moira?" he asked, "I can stay another day if you want me to."

"I will be fine Ray, but thanks for asking, you get off home, Jenny will be missing you; but you understand that looking after Duke is only a temporary arrangement, don't you" she said laughing. "Phone me tonight though, so I know that you got home safely and thanks once again for all you have done for us."

As Ray drove out of town in his truck, Moira walked to the hospital, arriving at the Men's Ward dead on ten o'clock to meet the doctor.

"As the Sister told you yesterday, your husband is lucky to be alive Mrs. Smith, but I am pleased to tell you that he has made a remarkable recovery from his injuries. All being well, we hope to release him into your charge on Tuesday afternoon, so that should allow you both to catch the train for Perth on Wednesday. How does that sound?"

"Sounds marvelous and thank you so much doctor for all the care you and the nursing staff have taken of my husband and if there is anything I can do to help you, during my short stay in town, please feel free to ask me," she said.

"Well actually there is Mrs. Smith. I understand that you were a District Nurse in England and have had some training as a midwife and now work at Royal Perth, is that correct?"

"Yes it is," she replied.

"Well our resident midwife is currently out on an emergency call at Bullfinch and I have a very pregnant lady who I think will start labour some time this morning, so if you don't mind helping out, I would be most grateful."

So that is how Moira spent her Sunday, when she was not in the Men's Ward talking with Digger. She delivered a very healthy baby boy in the afternoon and patched up several local children who had come off bikes, been bitten by animals and tripped over tree roots.

She was back at the hotel by five and was there to answer the telephone when Vi rang at five thirty.

Her Monday was spent in a similar way to Sunday, as was her Tuesday morning, but after Digger had eaten his lunch on

Tuesday he was discharged from the hospital into his wife's care and the doctor drove them back to the hotel in his car, as a sign of appreciation for all Moira's hard work at the hospital.

On Wednesday they caught the morning train for Perth and were delighted to find that Nugget and Junie were there to meet them at the station when they arrived. They drove them home to Ruth Street and helped them to settle back into the house, with the assistance of a large hamper of food, that Junie had prepared for them.

"Well Digger, this must have been one of the most difficult weeks of your life," said Nugget, as they sat around the table eating their meal.

"There were one or two weeks during the War which would have given it a good run, but yes, you are probably right Nugget."

"It has certainly been my worst week ever," said Moira and looking at Nugget, continued "and I hope your bank recognizes the danger they put him in. It could have cost him his life."

"Moira, that's enough, it's not Nugget's fault or anyone else's for that matter, we all underestimated what sort of a man Don Davis really was and what he was capable of. Mind you, it was that woman, Ursula, who was the one urging him to kill me, she would have just shot me, with my own gun, if Don hadn't stopped her. I am really sorry that he is dead though, he certainly didn't deserve that."

"Well just so you know Moira, the Board of directors did meet today and Digger's courage and injuries were discussed and Minuted. Furthermore, I have been instructed to tell you that no-one expects to see you at work until Monday the thirtieth of January and I have also been instructed to give you this, as a sign of the Board's appreciation of all you have both been through," with which Nugget handed Digger an envelope.

"Thank you Nugget and please thank the Board for their kind consideration," he said formally as he opened the envelope. "Wow, Moira, look at this, a cheque for two hundred and fifty pounds; that is most generous of the Board, thank you Nugget."

The following evening Carl Kemp arrived back in Perth in the Morris Eight and delivered it to Ruth Street.

"How is the invalid today," he asked Moira, as they walked down the garden path together, after parking the car round the back.

"He is improving every day thank you Carl, but come and join us for a drink and you can see for yourself."

"Carl, it's good to see you, how was Kalgoorlie?" Digger enquired, as he met the pair at the back door.

"Oh pretty hot and dusty, can I have a glass of water please, my throat is parched and do you mind if I telephone my wife to come and pick me up, she knew I was coming here first."

Moira got the water and Digger showed him to the telephone where he dialed home and arranged for his wife to come and collect him, they then all sat down on the patio and discussed the events of the past week.

"How much do I owe you for the tyre," Digger enquired.

"Nothing, in fact I replaced both front tyres for you, but the bank can pay for them, since they did not have to pay for my return journey to Perth, apart from the petrol that is."

"So who did you leave in charge of the Kalgoorlie branch office?" Digger asked.

"The assistant manager, for the present, but I have wanted to go back to branch banking for some time now myself and as my wife came from Kalgoorlie originally and would love to move back there, I am putting myself forward for the job."

"Good for you," said Digger, "and who will get your job?"

"I was going to recommend that you get it, if you are interested that is. There is no-one else in the Perth office at your level, with your width of experience when it comes to banking matters; what do you think?"

"Yes great, I would love to be the Internal Audit Manager; perhaps we could discuss it in more detail after I return to work."

"Sorry mate, but I am making my report to Mr. Newgate tomorrow morning, I really need to have your answer tonight."

"What would this job involve that is different from what he currently does Carl?" Moira asked.

"Most of the time you will be based in Perth but you will need to conduct regular reviews with the different branches in Western Australia and occasionally you may be seconded to another State to conduct an independent review there."

"Digger, you said all along that you wanted something different from your job here and this sounds like it would give it to you, I think you should go for it," she said, with a conviction she did not really feel.

"Well if you are happy Moira, then yes Carl, please put my name forward for the post and thank you!"

"Sounds like my wife has just pulled up outside, I would recognize that crashing of the gears anywhere. Why can't women learn to double de-clutch Digger, eh?"

"Can you ring me tomorrow and let me know how it goes please," Digger said to Carl, as he was climbing into the passenger seat and grimaced, as his wife attempted to find first gear and pull away from the kerb.

They sat down and started to discuss what this new job might bring in the way of changes to their lives and of course what it might mean in the way of increased remuneration, when the telephone rang and Moira jumped up to answer it.

"Oh hello Vicky, how nice of you to call; he is doing really well and should not need any more head dressings after tomorrow. Come to the farm for a few days, we would love to. No, I don't drive, but there is the train of course, we could come down tomorrow afternoon if that is convenient. I'll just ask him, hold on," with which she put the phone down on the table and walked into the lounge where Digger was reading a newspaper.

"Vicky has invited us to the farm for a few days, what do you think?"

Having overheard the previous conversation, albeit just his wife's side, he decided to go along with the offer, "Sounds good to me, I guess we could get the train down tomorrow afternoon, ask her if she can meet us at the station."

Moira returned to the telephone and chatted to Vicky for several minutes more and then gave Digger the good news that she would meet them at the station tomorrow afternoon and that they could stop with her, at the farm, for as long as they wanted to.

Carl rang them around eleven thirty on Friday morning, to say that he was the new Branch Manager at Kalgoorlie and that Digger would be appointed the new Internal Audit Manager when he returned to work.

The taxi arrived shortly after he came off the telephone to take them to the station and they caught the early afternoon train to Pinjarra, arriving there just before three, to find Vicky and Duke waiting for them at the station.

"Moira, Digger, over here she called out from the barrier, I am parked just to the right of that tree. I didn't want to risk bringing Duke onto the platform in case he knocked Digger over."

After embracing each other and stroking the dog, they all got into the car, with Duke on the front seat next to Vicky.

"Duke has been with me since Ray got back from Southern Cross. I could see he was getting attached to the dog and just thought it was a bad idea to leave him at their farm, hope you don't mind."

"Certainly not, in fact I am most grateful Vicky, he is our dog, I mean Victoria's dog, not Ray's," Moira replied.

That evening Ray and Jenny joined them for dinner at Vicky's farm and they all sat around until the early hours chatting about the recent events and what their future plans were.

"Well I will be going back to college in Sydney in the middle of February, so you two are welcome to come out and stay here any time you like," Vicky said.

"Oh thank you Vicky, that would be marvelous, I really like Pinjarra. I was telling Digger's sister about the town when she was on the phone the other day and she actually said that she and Mick would rather live in a country town than a big city, once they have got themselves settled here."

"You never told me that, I thought they would want to stop with us in Perth for at least a year," said Digger disappointedly.

"Two women in the same kitchen, for a year, rather you than me mate. We had Jenny's brother and his wife and baby stay with us for three months once, never again!" Ray said, raising his eyes to the ceiling.

"Don't forget the auction tomorrow Ray, the springs on our bed are completely gone and the advert in the paper listed the furniture to be sold, which included a nearly new double bed."

"I'm sorry Jenny but I have to be in Boddington tomorrow morning to help with clearing that timber. They are paying me for my time and I can have all the wood I can carry and you know how many of our fence posts need replacing, I couldn't turn the opportunity down."

"That's all right Jenny, I was going to the auction myself, just to be nosey, I can take you with me and if you do buy that bed, they normally give you at least a week to pick things up and take them back to your home; I know because I bought a saddle at an auction a couple of months back."

"What auction is this," asked Moira, "could we come with you? It must be years since I went to a roup."

"What on earth is a 'roup'?" asked Vicky.

"It's a Scottish term for an auction, normally at a farm," Moira explained.

"This isn't a farm sale Moira, it's the block and house and possessions of old Mrs. Spade, the woman whose wake you attended, when you first came out here. It appears she was better off than everyone thought and had actually made a Will, leaving everything to the Salvos, since they had looked after her for so many years."

"I assume the Salvos are another family in Pinjarra then?" asked Digger.

"No, the Salvation Army," said Ray, "you Pomes are an ignorant lot. They fed and clothed her and dried her out and fed her animals when she was not able to, so I guess it's only fair that they should get the proceeds from the auction."

"What animals did she have?" asked Moira.

"As far as I know, two sheep, a few chickens and two cats," said Ray, "which is why not many people will be bidding on that block of hers. Both the cats are feral and one of them is huge and must be descended from a mountain lion. It guards the front door of the house and hasn't let anyone inside since the old girl died."

"Can't they just shoot it," asked Digger.

"You would think so," said Ray, "but there was something in the Will saying whoever buys the block must look after the animals for as long as they live and if it is found that they have deliberately been killed before the auction, then the Salvos get nothing and no-one wants that to happen."

"Well are the sheep and chickens normal?" asked Moira.

"As far as I know the chickens are, but the sheep have a real attitude problem and have been known to head butt anything that invades their domain."

"So what sort of price do you think the house and block of land will go for Ray?" asked Digger.

"Hard to say. The house is just an old weatherboard house, so whoever buys it will probably have to knock it down and build a brick one in its place. The block is down the end of James Street, so it is a bit out of town if you are a townie and a bit near town if you want country and it only has about three quarters of an acre of land, so not enough to do anything with. Plus you have got to look after those animals of hers, I doubt if it will fetch much more than sixty pounds. The last block only fetched seventy and that was in a much better position."

"So what does your brother-in-law actually do for a living Moira?" Jenny asked, changing the subject.

"He's a plumber, runs his own business in South London Jenny."

"A plumber you say, fully qualified?" asked Ray.

"As far as I know," said Digger, "he served a full apprenticeship and has had more work since the War ended than he can handle."

"So why is he coming out here then?" asked Jenny.

"The usual reasons, a better life for him and his family, the chance to do well in a new country. He will never be able to earn sufficient to own his own home in London, but out here, anything is possible, it is up to the individual."

"Well that's certainly true and I am the proof of that," said Ray, "but you should persuade them to come here Digger if they want to live in the country, the town and district could do with another plumber, that's for sure."

When they finally went to bed, Moira could not sleep for thinking about the conversation over dinner, regarding the auction next day.

"How much did you get for your Austin Seven, Digger," she asked.

"Two hundred and fifty pounds, why?"

"And how much do you think Bertie will want for the Morris Eight?"

"Ray reckons he paid about three hundred for it. Why?"

"So if we take fifty pound from the two hundred and fifty that the bank gave us, to cover the extra cost of buying Bertie's car over what we got for yours, we will still have two hundred pounds left. Is that Right?"

"Yes. Moira, look, I am dead tired, is there some point to all this book keeping."

"I was just thinking about what Ray said, that the block and house would sell for under one hundred pounds and Vi and Mick want to live in the country. We could buy the house, do it up and let them live there until they can get their own place and it would mean we would have somewhere to come to at weekends once they had moved out, if we wanted."

"Ray implied the place was falling down and not fit for habitation, we would need to check it our first, before we went and bought somewhere that could be a millstone round our necks; wouldn't we?"

189

"True, but we could do that tomorrow before the auction if Vicky wouldn't mind. I wonder what furniture they are selling with it, maybe we could buy some of that as well, what do you think Digger? Digger, I said what do you think?"

"Zzzzzzzz," was the only reply she got.

"Good morning Moira, you're up bright and early."

"Morning Vicky, I wanted to catch you before you went riding. Do you know what time the auction starts today?"

"It's in the paper, the advertisements are normally around the middle, here, you look and I will make breakfast."

"I have found it, it's at eleven thirty, I was wondering what time you were going into town?"

"Jenny wanted to check the furniture over before the auction, so I said I would pick her up about ten, why did you want to come?"

"Yes please, I am trying to convince Digger to make a bid for the block of land and the house. I think it would be ideal for his sister and her family. He is afraid the place is uninhabitable, so we need to go down and check it over."

"You are not bothered by the stipulation in the Will about looking after the animals then."

"No, I spent a lot of my childhood holidays on the hill farms above Inverness, so I am used to sheep and cats and I am sure Duke will protect us anyway."

"I think that is a great idea for Digger's sister and her family. There is a good school in town and it's a great place for children to grow up and your brother-in-law would certainly have no shortage of work, I am sure of that."

Vicky went off riding and Moira enjoyed a leisurely breakfast and then made breakfast for Digger and took it in to him at around eight o'clock.

"Wake up sleepy-head," she said, as she shook his good arm and kissed him on the forehead.

"Oh, hello love, what time is it then?" he asked, rubbing his eyes.

"I have made you a lovely breakfast of fresh eggs that Jenny brought down and some bacon from the local butchers and there is some toast and marmalade. Do you want tea or coffee?"

"Tea please," he answered, as he struggled to sit up in the soft feather bed. She put the tray on his lap and left to get his tea, returning about five minutes later.

"What time is it love, as I can't reach my watch," he said, when she walked back into the room with his mug of tea.

"The eggs are lovely, certainly the best we have had since we arrived out here, don't you think?" she said.

"Moira they were great, what's going on, what time is it for the third time?"

"No need to shout! It's almost eight thirty and Vicky will be back soon and we are going into town with her in about an hour's time. Does that answer your question?"

"Is this all about that auction again? Why don't you just say that you don't want my sister and her family living with us and be honest about it! I hate all this underhand stuff."

"Vi was rude to Deborah and quite sharp with me on the phone when I spoke with her at Southern Cross. You would think I had stolen the Crown Jewels rather than just not told her immediately about you having gone missing."

"Oh I see. Yes she can be a bit protective I have to confess, but they were never going to stay for too long with us, just a couple of months or so; we don't have to push them out the minute they arrive Moira, she is my sister!"

"I know she is Digger and I am your wife and I really would like a country cottage in this area, that we could call our own. Your new job could take you anywhere and who knows in a year's time, we could be in Sydney or Melbourne or Brisbane or some place else, so to have a home of our own, that we could always come back to, would be just wonderful for me Digger."

"Fair enough love, we will go and check it out but we are not spending any more than one hundred pounds, as we might still need a deposit for a house in Perth, if the owner returns and we have to leave Ruth Street in the near future."

When they got to the block in James Street, there were already a few people there looking over the house and furniture and furtively discussing what they were prepared to bid on, at the auction.

Suddenly there was a loud scream from the side of the house and everyone went running outside to see what had happened.

"The big cat scratched me mummy," cried a little girl with blood oozing from deep lacerations on her arms and legs.

The girl's mother rushed over and picked her up and told her husband to start the truck as they were going to the hospital to attend to the little girl's wounds and to get a Tetanus jab.

"But what about the auction?" he said.

"I told you I didn't want to live here and if you had listened to me, this would never have happened. Start the car before I get cross," she shouted at him.

"The house appears to be in reasonably good condition Digger," said Moira after a careful scrutiny of the property. "The kitchen could do with being replaced but the wood burning stove seems to be in working order and all the windows are in place and the doors are not hanging off their hinges. Why is Jenny kicking all the posts and pushing that screwdriver in everywhere?"

"I asked her that and she said she was checking for white ants. Jenny, over here, tell us what you think of the place?"

"The house has a Jarrah frame and apart from a bit of white ant activity I noticed on the lean-to, the rest of the house seems to be good. I have to say that it is in much better condition than I was expecting and I am pretty certain that the block backs onto the Murray River, Digger, might be worth checking out, as I am not sure where the sheep are getting their water from, as the wind pump does not seem to be working at the moment."

"Good idea I will do just that," he said and went outside and started to walk down the block towards the trees at the bottom.

"Where are the bathroom and toilet located Vicky, I haven't seen them yet?" asked Moira.

"They are in that lean-to at the back that Jenny mentioned, but I expect they are pretty basic, but if your brother-in-law is a plumber, that is surely something he could easily sort out for you."

Moira nodded and stood there deep in thought.

"Well, have you decided if you are going to bid on it?" Vicky asked. "I think it is a good spot here and will make a great 'weekender' for you both and if Digger's sister and her family do decide to come here and use it for a few months while they get settled, it will be a real adventure and great experience for them all."

Just then the auctioneer arrived and everyone congregated in front of the house.

"Where has Digger got to?" asked Vicky, "it cannot take this long to walk a hundred yards and see if there is a river at the bottom of the block."

"Here he comes now, running towards us and something is chasing him, it's the two sheep, he is running from the sheep, goodness that was a big jump over the wire fence, good job he didn't fall with that damaged shoulder of his" said Moira.

Digger spotted the three waving at him and walked over to join them

"What on earth has happened to you, your trousers are soaked and you are covered in mud?" asked Jenny.

"Huh, huh, that big one crept up behind me, huh, huh, when I was standing on the river bank and butted me in the back and in I went. Luckily I caught hold of a branch with my good hand and managed to keep myself from falling over in the water. Huh, huh, I got out of the water and the smaller one came up all friendly like and nipped me on the leg, so I just ran for it and they chased me all the way to fence."

"We were watching you, that was some jump you did and with an injured leg and all. Does this mean that you don't want to make a bid then?" said Moira.

"On the contrary, if you think I am going to let a couple of sheep run me out of town, then you can think again, no I love this place, it has real character, let's join the auction."

A local builder opened the bidding with fifty pounds; a couple from Dwellingup bid fifty five and the builder re-bid sixty and the couple re-bid sixty five. The builder shook his head at this stage and Digger came in with a bid of seventy five pounds, which turned out to be the final bid and the block, house and animals on James Street became theirs.

The auctioneer asked if anyone was prepared to make a bid for the whole contents of the house and Jenny, who really only wanted the double bed offered five pounds. When someone else present offered seven pounds ten shillings, she shook her head and Moira then bid ten pounds, much to Digger's surprise, which was the final bid.

"It's all right Digger, I told Jenny that she could have the bed for four pounds if she didn't bid against me. Wasn't that clever of me?"

"It was certainly very clever, but I am not certain it was very legal my love. It is a good job I asked Nugget to pay that cheque into our account as the auctioneer's clerk is coming this way and will want his money."

"Are you paying for both the block and furniture Mr. Smith, or is your wife settling for the furniture separately."

"Assuming you will take a cheque, I will pay for both; to whom should I make it payable?"

The cheque was written out and a receipt issued and the clerk informed the new owners that the paperwork should be all through in about a month, but they could have a key today if they wanted it and start work on the property as soon as they wished.

"I don't envy you the task of looking after those animals though, that cat is positively evil and the sheep are not much better," the clerk informed them.

"Don't you worry about the cats," said Vicky, "Duke is a natural in getting rid of them. I had two or three on the farm that were a real nuisance and Duke had only been with me for a day and one of them was dead and the others had gone, just bring him down to the block next week a few times and I am sure he will see them off for you."

Sheep with attitude
Photographer - Lucidus Smith

Chapter 12
In-laws and Outlaws

"Let me take your coat for you Victoria," Hazel said, as she welcomed Bertie and Victoria into her home, which she and Angus had meticulously cleaned from top to bottom during the previous week.

"Angus, take Bertie's hat and coat, I am sure he is not in the least bit interested in your photographs of steam trains, thank you and tell Donny that our guests have arrived, he is doing something in the shed."

"Please do sit down, you must be tired after your long journey, what time did you leave Oxford today?"

"Thank you Hazel," said Victoria, "what a delightful room and may we say how very kind it is of you and Angus to invite us over for the weekend, to come and see you. Were you aware that we traveled up to London on Thursday and spent the last couple of days with Deborah, at her flat, as she was naturally eager to hear all of our news from Spain."

"No, Donny had not told me that, so do you expect her to be arriving here soon?" Hazel enquired.

"Well, she was going to the motorcycle shop first to get a new headlamp bulb as the previous one has blown, but once she gets into that shop and starts to talk with the staff and other customers, time just disappears for her, but she said she would be here by teatime, if that is of any help," said Bertie, smiling politely.

Just then, there was a knock at the door, 'Bom, bom , bom, **bom**.'

"That will be my sister, Violet, she always uses the same knock, excuse me a moment please," with which she got up and left the room to answer the frond door.

"Violet, how lovely to see you, our guests have just arrived, apart from Deborah that is, who is traveling here on her motorbike."

The two sisters entered the room, arm in arm and Hazel introduced her to Bertie and Victoria.

"It's nice to meet you Violet and I gather you are kindly giving us a bed for the night," said Victoria.

"Not me," said Violet, "it must be someone else," winking at Bertie.

"That husband of mine!" exclaimed Hazel, "Angus was supposed to arrange it with you Violet, Deborah is staying with us and Bertie and Victoria are to stay with you, just wait till I till I get hold of him," with which she went storming off to speak with Angus.

Violet smiled, "It's all right Victoria, everything is arranged, you are both staying the night with me and it is only a short walk from here, but I expect Angus will drive us round in the car anyway; he and I have a sort of constant battle of wits going on, but it's not really a fair contest," she said, as Hazel came back into the room with a red faced Angus.

"That was most unfair on our guests Vi," he said, "at least I just keep our battles between the two of us."

"So the whole of the W.I. waiting for almost an hour on a draughty station because you gave me the wrong train time Angus, is just keeping it between the two of us, is it?"

"You will have to just ignore these two I am afraid," said Hazel, "Violet is a widow, but her husband and Angus used to work together on the railways and they were always joking around, a bit like Donny and Arnold do and somehow Violet allowed herself to get sucked into their little game, but I refuse to be part of it. Would you like tea or coffee to drink? If you will excuse me, I will give Donny another shout."

"Let me help you," said Victoria, getting up and following Hazel through into the kitchen.

"Donny, there you are, what on earth have you been doing, you have been ensconced in that shed, hammering away for ages, wash your hands and say hello to our guests."

"Hello Victoria, good to see you, how was Spain? Sorry not to have been here to greet you, but I went over on the bike on an icy road the over day and bent the carrier, but it is fixed now and back in place. Pass the Vim please mum, I have got some oil on my hands."

"That stuff is for cleaning pots, not your hands, I hate to think of the damage you are doing. Your father is in the front room with Bertie, I think he is talking steam engines, so you had better go and rescue the poor man, we will be through shortly."

"Has Debs arrived yet?" he asked, as he dried his hands on the towel.

"Not yet, but she shouldn't be too long," Victoria answered.

"Donny, there are grease marks all over my clean towel, huh, boys and their toys! They just never seem to grow up, do they Victoria?"

Donny walked through to the front room to find Bertie and his dad discussing the merits of steam engines versus diesel engines, in boats and trains.

"Don't get up Bertie, good to see you," said Donny, shaking hands with his future father-in-law and kissing his auntie on the cheek. "Hello aunt Violet, have you warmed up yet from your long wait at the station?"

"That's enough cheek out of you, young man, your father has already paid for that little joke, haven't you brother-in-law, dear?"

As Hazel and Victoria came through with the tea tray, Deborah arrived on her motorcycle and after a brief greeting to everyone, she went upstairs to change and freshen up.

The wedding arrangements were discussed in detail and photographs of the church, restaurant and hotel were passed around for everyone to see. As they were all traveling to Spain together on the ship from Southampton, Bertie informed them that he had made a temporary booking for them all at a hotel in Southampton for the night of the 4th of April.

"Isn't that when young Vi and Mick are traveling to Australia?" asked Angus.

"No Angus, they leave on the third, but didn't you say that you were going down to wave them off Donny?"

"That's right mum, we can't let them depart on such an epic journey without someone to wave goodbye to them, can we."

"Well in that case, I will go down as well," said Deborah, "I have finally decided that I want to take the Indian with me to Spain, just in case we decide to stay there for a while and I rather fancy visiting all the old familiar places again, like Roses and Rialp and perhaps go across to France for a few days. What do you think Mac?"

"That's a great idea Debs, I had been wondering what to do for our honeymoon; Rialp would be marvelous, write to Annette and see if the old house is still in the family and if so, if they will let us use it for a few days; goodness that brings back memories."

"Talking of bringing back memories," said Angus, "Hazel and I would like to formally thank you Bertie for saving our son's life in Lisbon. Without your skill as a surgeon and Deborah's skill as a nurse, we have no doubt that our son would not be with us today, so from the bottom of our hearts, we thank you."

Bertie nodded and smiled, but was not expecting this speech and it caught him off guard, so fortunately Victoria came to the rescue.

"Talking of near dearth experiences, has anyone heard from Arnold and Moira lately," she asked.

"Yes, I spoke with him this week and he is feeling a lot better and is actually back at work and has been promoted to the position of Internal Audit Manager," said Donny.

"Goodness, in our company that job carries the poison chalice, as everyone dislikes the Internal Audit Department," said Deborah.

"Oh, and another thing, he told me that they went to an auction with a friend who wanted to buy a bed and ended up buying three quarters of an acre of land with a house on it, for seventy five pounds."

"Don't be silly Donny, you couldn't buy a house and land for that sort of money anywhere, even in the middle of Australia," said Hazel.

"Mum, that is what Arnold told me, it's located in that town where your fruit farm is Victoria, Pin something."

"Pinjarra!" said Bertie and Victoria together.

"That's the name, Pinjarra," Donny confirmed.

"It sounds like your friend Ray has been at work here again Bertie," said Victoria, "he won't be happy until we are all living in that town."

"Yes it does, doesn't it, so does this mean that they are tired of Perth already Mac?"

"Not from what he told me Bertie, he just said that they liked Pinjarra and that they would use it as a place to go at weekends. Oh and they bought some furniture to go with the house and a couple of old sheep, one of which butted Arnold into a river and the other bit him on the leg. He certainly has a taste for danger, does that cousin of mine."

The rest of the weekend passed pleasantly as the two sets of 'outlaws' got to know each other. Deborah went off home to her flat on Sunday, while Bertie and Victoria stayed on with Violet until the Monday, when they got an early train to London and then another train out to Aylesbury, where Mrs. Black picked them up in the car.

"So how did your mum and Victoria get on together Mac?" Henry asked, during their normal Monday afternoon 'Planning' meeting.

"Surprisingly good Henry and dad and Bertie hit it off really well, both having a love of engines, albeit for different transport systems."

"Did Bertie say if he had been able to book somewhere for my lot to stay in Benicarlo?"

"Yes, as I understand it, there is an old cottage next door to the one that he and Victoria now own, that used to belong to an old skipper friend and is where he first stayed when he was in Spain. It is now a holiday cottage and he has booked it for as long as you want, up to three weeks maximum that is. Now I will stay with you and Deidre before the wedding and then Debs and I are booked into a hotel for a couple of nights and then we will go off traveling on the bike somewhere."

"Sounds exciting, is that the same hotel that your parents are staying in?" Henry asked in a matter of fact tone of voice.

"No, it most certainly is not and just to make things very clear, you would be the absolute last person in the world, now that Arnold is safely out of the way, that I would give that information to," Mac replied.

"To change the subject then, where are you and Deborah at, on emigrating to the Antipodes?"

"Good question Henry. She is sort of going a bit broody on me, to be honest. She pointed out at the weekend, that she is thirty five this year and that her body clock is ticking away and if we wanted to have children, then we should be starting pretty soon after the wedding, like this year."

"Well she is quite right of course, so where does that leave our plans for an Engineering Partnership, preferably somewhere warm?"

"To be honest, I don't know. One minute she wants to go to Australia and the next minute she is talking about New Zealand, but that could just be all the current interest with the Empire Games being held in Auckland this year. Over the weekend she told me she wants to take the Indian to Spain with her, so we can go traveling in Europe after we are married."

"Tricky," said Henry thoughtfully, "it turns out that Deidre's friend who went to Melbourne the other year, was so homesick that she barely lasted ten months before she had to come home again, but hated the weather here so much, that she is now paying her own fare to go back out, but to New Zealand this time. Christchurch I think."

"Tricky indeed, my friend; we will just have to wait and see. Oh, oh, look busy the mayor is heading this way," Mac said, as he stood up and started to gesticulate and make comments about the plans they had cellotaped over the windows.

"It's very good of you to let me spend Valentine's Day with you both," said Vicky to Moira and Digger as they sat on the patio at Ruth Street, enjoying a meal and a glass of fruit juice together in the evening.

"We are delighted to have the opportunity to repay your hospitality towards us, while Digger was recovering from his injuries, the other week," Moira replied.

"What time is your flight tomorrow Vicky?" Digger asked.

"It's not until eleven twenty, but I have ordered a taxi for just after nine, to be on the safe side."

"Very wise, better to be twenty minutes early than twenty seconds late," said Moira.

"Do remember that you are welcome to stay at the farm while you are decorating your new house and I did check on the sheep before I came here today and they are both still there and seem to be surviving well, with the extra hay that Ray took down for them last week. Jenny plans to get the chickens next week some time and take them back to her place for you."

"That is good of you all, I assume the sheep are still drinking from the river, or has Ray managed to get someone to fix the wind pump yet?" Moira asked.

"He did it himself, Moira, something just came unhooked at the top and he climbed up and fixed it, but he did say that your rainwater tank needed replacing, so let him know Digger if you want him to get another one for you as they may have to order one in and you don't want to miss the Autumn rains, do you?"

"You are talking to the wrong person Vicky, Digger thinks water just comes from a tap, he has never had to operate a hand pump or get water from a well in his life, have you love?"

'If only you knew', he thought, but said nothing and just smiled and filled everyone's glass with some more juice.

Moira and Digger left for work at the usual time next day, bidding Vicky goodbye before they went. She in turn caught her taxi to the airport and flew off for another year at college in Sydney.

When Moira arrived at work she was met by the Sister, as soon as she arrived at the ward.

"You are to report immediately to the Matron, Nurse Smith,"

"Why, what has happened, what have I done wrong," Moira asked the stony faced Sister.

"Are you questioning my instructions?"

"No, of course not Sister, I am going there right now," Moira replied, as she headed off towards the Matron's office.

She knocked on the door and was told to come in and beckoned to a seat, which she sat upon for at least two minutes, while the Matron finished her telephone conversation.

"Sorry about that Nurse Smith, thank you for coming so promptly. How is your husband now, fully recovered I trust?"

"Yes thank you Matron, his shoulder and leg are healing nicely and the doctor says that he will be able to drive again very soon."

"I am sorry we were not able to pay your wages during the time you had off to be with him, I trust his company looked after him properly."

"I was not expecting the hospital to pay me, as I had only been here for a few weeks and the bank was most generous to us, thank you Matron."

"Good, good, quite right and I gather he has been promoted too, is that correct."

"Yes he has been promoted," Moira replied skeptically, guessing that Junie had been speaking with the Matron.

"Does that mean he will be posted to another town then?"

"On no, he will be based in Perth, but he may well have to travel to other towns from time to time, but I am not worried about that, as the dog keeps me company when he is away."

"The very same dog that found him down the mineshaft, I gather."

"Yes, Duke heard his tapping in answer to our friend sounding the horn."

"Well, I cannot tell you how delighted I am to hear that you will not be leaving us Nurse Smith. Everyone likes you and Sister cannot sing your praises loud enough and I even received a letter from the doctor at Southern Cross, to say how much he appreciated all that you did for them there."

"That is nice to hear Matron," Moira replied.

"You are obviously aware that the position of Staff Nurse has been vacant on the ward for several weeks now and I am delighted to tell you, Staff Nurse Smith, that we are appointing you to that position, as of the week commencing the twenty sixth of February."

"Why thank you Matron and may I say what a well run hospital this is and how happy I am working here."

"That is marvelous news Moira, congratulations," said Digger, as he hugged his wife on hearing about her promotion at the hospital.

"And when she told me that Sister had been singing my praises, I almost fell off my chair with surprise; she has hardly said a friendly word to me since I started on the ward."

"There's 'nowt so queer as folks' and that's for sure, when do you get your new uniforms?"

"I pick them up next week, and officially start my new duties on Sunday the 26th February, which is one of the drawbacks to the job, as I may well have to work more weekend and late shifts than I have so far."

"We will have to try and make sure that my trips away, coincide with your late shifts and I will build a kennel and run for Duke, so he can stay in the garden when we are both out of the house together."

"Did you remember to ring the Agent today, to find out about extending the lease?" Moira asked.

"I did and he has confirmed that it is ours for at least another six months and that the owner will probably be happy to extend it well into the future, as she has now settled in with her sister in Albany."

"That is great, I think we should go out and celebrate, how about that restaurant Ray and Jenny took us to, last time they were here?"

"Sounds good to me, I will get my wallet, while you powder your nose."

Moira started her job on the Sunday, which gave Digger just about enough time to construct the hutch and run for Duke, before he was off by train to Bunbury on Monday morning, to carry out his first Branch Audit. Whilst he found nothing untoward at the branch, he did consider some of the practices and procedures to be antiquated and a waste of time as well as having some concerns about the physical safety of the bank tellers.

His report was not well received, by the powers that be, one of whom asked Nugget if this young fellow from England was going to teach them all to 'suck eggs' in the near future.

Mr. Newgate, however, having gained considerable standing over the Don Davis exposure, quickly nipped these disparaging comments in the bud and supported Digger in his recommendations and personally chaired a committee to look into the whole matter of updating branch practices and procedures.

The Security Manager had the good sense to agree with Digger's security concerns and immediately made enquiries as to exactly what other banks were doing around the world, in the way of beefing up their branch security. As a result he had a very enjoyable four week trip to Paris, London and New York, speaking with his opposite number in a dozen different international banks and making contacts that would serve him well, for many years to come.

Digger saw the doctor on the seventh of March who pronounced him fit and well and he was back behind the wheel, driving again, the same day.

The following three weeks just flashed by and Digger only just remembered to ring Vi and family at home, at the end of March before their telephone was disconnected.

"Uncle Digger is that really you," said Brian, who had easily beaten his sister to the telephone.

"It certainly is Brian, are you all packed and ready to go."

"All the packing cases and big trunks were taken away yesterday, so we are having to manage with just a few things and mum has forbidden me from going on the Common, in case I injure myself again, like the last time we went away."

"Well it won't be long before you will all be sailing on the big ship and heading for Australia, how exciting is that?"

"Mum says you have bought an old house in the country and that maybe we can stay there some time and that you have some sheep, but no kangaroos; is that right?"

"Yes, pretty much so Brian. There are kangaroos in the area, which might well decide to come onto our land and eat the grass, but no-one owns them as such, they are free to wander wherever they want."

"So why don't you ever have any at your other house then?"

"Well Perth is a city with lots of traffic, I guess it wouldn't be safe to have Kangaroos hopping around everywhere, but I have seen some in the parks and on the golf courses, though. Is your mum there Brian?"

Digger and Vi chatted for a while and then Moira came on the phone and finally Mick went over all the details again with Digger of when they would arrive and where everyone would stay.

"Look mate relax, everything is fine. The house is not big, but it is big enough for all of us and I know at least three builders who will offer you a job the minute you arrive and if you decide to set up shop on your own, either in Perth or out in the country, then we will help you get established. This really is the land of opportunity, why already both Moira and I have been promoted, you can't ask for better than that, can you."

"Are you sure there is nothing else you want us to bring out for you, this is your last chance Digger."

"I think Moira has already given Vi a list of the underwear she wants from Marks and Spencer, but if you are going past a decent Men's clothes shop and could get me a couple of white Van Heusen shirts, collar size 16, I would be most grateful. They are like gold dust over here and just as expensive."

"Consider it done," said Mick, "nothing else then?"

"You don't happen to know which hotel Donny is using at Southampton do you, as I was going to ring him and wish him well for his wedding."

"It's funny you should ask, as he rung here the other day and said that I was not to give you that information, on pain of death."

"Really!" said Digger, "I wonder why he would say a thing like that."

"I can't imagine," said Mick, "but I can tell you that he is using the same hotel as us, as it was him who told us about it; anyway, Vi wants to say goodbye, so I will see you in a months time, cheerio mate."

He chatted a little longer with his sister and was about to end the conversation when he said to her, "You had better give me the name of the hotel you are stopping at, in Southampton Vi, just in case anything crops up and we need to contact you there."

"Good idea Digger, it is the Star Hotel on the High Street, I have the number here somewhere hold on a second."

She found the number and gave it to Digger who said goodbye and put the telephone down, smiling.

"Right Donny," he said out loud, "it's payback time," with which he telephoned the hotel and spoke with the duty manager there.

Vi, Mick and the children arrived in Southampton on the afternoon train and got a taxi to the hotel, they registered at Reception and went up to their rooms on the first floor.

"Do we know what rooms Donny and Debs are in?" asked Brian, as he burst through the connecting door between the two rooms.

"Now you just go back to your own room, close the door and knock twice and ask if it is convenient for you to come into our room," said his mother a little flustered.

"Sorry mum. Knock, knock can I come in?"

"You speak to him Mick before I get cross," Vi announced.

Mick got up from the bed, walked to the door, took his son firmly by the hand and walked him back into the adjoining room that he was sharing with his sister, closing the door behind them.

"I know you two are excited," he said, "but your mother and I are exhausted, with all the extra work we have been doing in the last few weeks and we have just about had enough of your bad manners. It is stopping right now, do you hear me?"

"Yes dad," they said in unison.

"As far as I know, Donny and Deborah, do you hear me Brian, Deborah not Debs, will be stopping in the rooms at the end of the corridor. But you are to leave them in peace, as they too have been very busy getting ready for the wedding."

"I still don't see why we couldn't have gone to Australia by way of Spain, my teacher said it was on the way and then I could have been a bridesmaid again," sulked Patty.

"Patty, we have already had this discussion, so cut it out and I don't want to hear another word out of you two before we go down to dinner. Is that clear?"

"Yes dad."

At a little after six, Vi and Mick collected the children and went downstairs for their evening meal. The waiter found them a table in a quiet corner by a window, so the children were able to look out onto the street while they waited for their food.

Shortly after they had been served their soup, a large red motorcycle drew up in the courtyard at the rear of the hotel and Mac and Deborah dismounted, untied their bags and went into the hotel.

"Names please," said the reception clerk.

"Miss Deborah Bannister and Mr. MacDonald Smith," Mac replied.

"Please sign here, madam, sir. Thank you."

"We have managed to carry out your instructions to the letter, sir; although getting the dozen red roses for the lady was difficult, but you did say money was no object? And we have reserved you a table, right next to the piano, as you did say that you are slightly deaf and just love piano music."

"Oh Mac, how romantic, that's just wonderful, thank you so much, but I didn't know you were slightly deaf and I thought you didn't like the piano, strange!" said a smiling Deborah, kissing Mac on the cheek.

"You know me Debs. Why don't you go up to your room, I just want a quick word with the clerk. Leave the bags, I will bring them up with me."

Deborah left the lobby and Mac turned to the clerk.

"To be honest with you, I have to tell you that it was not me you spoke to on the telephone. I did not order flowers for my fiancée, I most certainly do not want a table by the piano and I should imagine this whole thing has been instigated by my cousin, who is getting his own back for all the pranks I have played on him over the years. So what exactly were the other things he asked you to do for me?"

"It's strange you should say that, because I took the call and realized it was long distance, but you said, err he said, you had 'popped across the pond' on business, so I assumed you were somewhere on the continent, I am terribly sorry Mr. Smith, I was completely fooled. What do you want me to do about the flowers?"

"Leave the flowers and do not mention any of this to my fiancée, she and my cousin do not get on at the best of times and she will go ballistic if she finds out that he ordered the roses and not me. But what else did he ask you to do?"

"Nothing, apart from the bed, that is."

"What about the bed."

"You said you had hurt your back playing cricket and were sleeping on the floor these day, so you, err he, asked us to remove the bed."

"And did you?"

"No, it wasn't possible; we just moved it right against the wall and made up a bed on the floor for you. I will get a couple of the porters to go up with you and reposition it."

"That's good, thank you. What about the table by the piano, can you change that?"

"I am sorry, but the restaurant is full tonight Mr. Smith."

"I don't suppose Mr. and Mrs. Broomland are eating in the restaurant with their two children tonight are they?"

"I did notice a family go into the restaurant about twenty minutes ago, they are sitting on the far side by the window."

Mac walked over to the door and looked in and spotted Vi and family as they were just finishing their soup.

"Yes that's them over there. Could you put an extra two chairs at their table for us please?"

"Yes certainly sir and here are the porters now, they will take your bags up to your room and move the bed for you."

"Thanks for your help," said Mac.

"My pleasure sir," said the clerk, very relieved that everything had been sorted out, "that cousin of yours is a real bandit isn't he?"

"Considering what I did to him at his wedding, I have got off quite lightly; it is a good thing he is not coming to Spain though, just my Best Man to worry about now!"

Chapter 13
Getting to Know You

"Please hang on tight to him Mick, I don't want him falling overboard right at the start of the voyage," said a concerned Vi to her husband, as they steamed away from the pier at Southampton, on the start of their voyage to Australia.

"He's alright Vi, stop fussing, I'm holding his jacket anyway. There's Donny and Deborah over there kids, by that lorry, he's waving his white silk scarf. Wave goodbye to them."

They all waved frantically to Donny and Deborah until they were just a couple of dots in the distance and as the cold wind started to chill them through, they went back to their cabin and then toured the ship to find out where everything was located.

"So do you think that Donny and Deborah will eventually come to Australia as well?" Vi asked her husband as they sat in their cabin.

"Who knows?" Mick replied, "I can fully understand why Digger doesn't get on with her, I thought she was going to throw a fit when she found out that it was Digger who sent the flowers and ordered the table by the piano; I hope Donny fully understands what he has taken on, with that one!"

"That's as maybe, but on the other hand Mick, she is devoted to Donny, so maybe she will change or at least mellow a bit, but I doubt it somehow."

"Dad said that the shipping agent's office should be down this road here Mac," Deborah said, as they headed off to pay the extra fee for taking the Indian motorcycle to Spain with them, once they had finished waving their goodbyes.

"I see it, it's on the other side of the road, next to Woolworth's," he replied grumpily.

"What is up with you Mac? Are you still annoyed about the bike? I said I was sorry that I announced that I was taking it before I discussed it with you, didn't I? You seemed pleased about it at your parents, so what has changed?"

"I was being polite at my parents Debs. You also announced, if you remember, that we were going on a bike tour of Europe for our honeymoon, without discussing it with me and to cap it all, you positively humiliated me yesterday at dinner, when you berated Mick for giving Arnold the name of the hotel we were staying in."

"He deserved it. You told him to say nothing and he told Digger the hotel and gave him the telephone number, how irresponsible is that. You may think it hilarious to have stupid pranks played on us at our wedding, but I don't and when Deidre rang yesterday evening to ask for directions to the hotel, I made it very clear to her, that Henry had better not do anything stupid in Spain, if he knew what was good for him!"

"You did what?" he asked in amazement. "What did you say exactly, to my best friend's wife? Tell me?"

"You're shouting at me Mac, stop it," she said, "I just told you what I said to her."

"And what didn't you tell me, what else did you say to her, woman to woman?"

"Nothing; well apart from not wanting to be friends or business partners, with someone who spoilt my wedding."

"You said what to her? You stupid, selfish little fool Deborah. How dare you speak to my friends like that! Just because you don't have any friends of your own, doesn't give you the right to turn my friends against us. Do you hear me Deborah?"

"Mac, please don't speak to me like that," she said tearfully.

"See the agent on your own, I'm going back to the hotel," with which he turned round and went back the way he had come, leaving her standing outside the office, speechless and very upset.

She stood there for a moment and colleted her thoughts before going into the office and paying the fee for the bike to be transported to Spain. The agent's clerk, who was an elderly lady, stood there patiently while Deborah fiddled with her purse and the money. She could see that Deborah was chocking back her tears and said, "Are you all right dear, is something upsetting you?"

Deborah said nothing, but held her hand out for the receipt, so the lady asked again, "Are you sure you are all right dear?"

"What business is that of yours," she snapped back, glaring at the elderly woman, behind the desk, who stood there smiling at her.

"Oh dear," she said, "we are in a bad way. I was about to go over the road for my morning cup of tea, why don't you come and join me dear and tell me all about it."

To Deborah's surprise, she heard herself saying, "I will, thank you, sorry for being rude to you."

The two went across the road to Joe Lyons and ordered a pot of tea for two and some biscuits and sat down in the corner and started to chat. It was the first time that Deborah had confided in another woman, since her father's friend Rosie, had returned to New Zealand in 1940 and just about everything came out that had happened to her since.

"Goodness me Deborah, you have had more than your fair share of ups and downs, haven't you?" she said, when Deborah finally came to halt.

"I guess I have, but the last ten years have not been easy for anyone have they?"

"Well that is certainly true dear. My poor husband was vicar at the local church and managed to come through the war completely unscathed, but got run down by a bus a few months after it finished and was killed outright."

"Oh, Mrs. Thompson that is awful, I am so sorry, you must have been devastated," Deborah replied, with real conviction.

"Thank you dear, I was, but life goes on. Now about this young man of yours, does he really love you?"

"Well I think so."

"Not good enough my dear. You are about to make a contract between this man and yourself, in front of your friends and family and before God, that is going to commit you to a relationship, 'until death' parts you. My dear late husband loved me through and through and I never doubted his love or questioned it and I loved him back in the same way. That way, when trials and tribulations came our way, our love for each other and our love for our Lord Jesus, enabled us to overcome all those problems and to stay true to each other and the vows we had made."

Deborah listened in silence, thinking about what was being said to her.

"Let me ask you another question, do you truly and completely love him?"

"Yes, of course I do, I loved him right from the start, I have never loved anyone else."

"So for the whole time you two were apart, did you or he have another boyfriend or girlfriend."

"No, certainly not."

"Is he an honourable man, do you think he will always be there for you, to care for you and support you? Will he put you before all others and himself?"

"Yes to all those questions. He is honourable and trustworthy and kind, he will be there for me, he will always support me and put me first, why are you asking me all these questions?"

"I asked you if he really loved you and you answered, 'I think so'. In answering my questions, you have told me that you don't just think so but that you really 'know so'. You have to understand Deborah that little girls, become big girls who become women. Little boys, become big boys and men are still just big boys at heart, but who have also become men. I have a brother who is older than me and still flies kites on the beach at weekends, just like we used to when we were children.

"Kite flying I can live with," said Deborah , "but it is these stupid jokes they play on each other that get me."

"The pranks and tomfoolery that men enjoy, leave most women cold, but it is part of who they are and you should not try and take that away from your Mac and his circle of friends, big mistake. Learn to accept it and live with it and believe me, it eventually reduces as they get older and you might even start to enjoy some of it yourself one day."

"Thank you Mrs. Thompson, I really appreciate your taking the time to speak with me like this, a complete stranger. So what do you think I should do now?"

"You first need to telephone his Best Man's wife and apologize to her before she leaves home. You then need to tell Mac that you are sorry for upsetting him and for not appreciating how important his friends and their pranks are to him and lastly you need to explain that you have been making decisions on your own, for a long time now and that you will try very hard to speak with him first in the future."

"And that will make everything alright again?" Deborah asked.

"Men like to have closure on unpleasant incidents with the one they love. In my opinion, if you apologize and he loves you, that will be an end to the matter, you wait and see."

When Deborah returned to the hotel she telephoned Deidre and apologized for what she had said the previous day. She made no excuses, but did tell Deidre how much she actually enjoyed their friendship and hoped she would not hold her outburst against her.

Deidre told her that the whole matter was forgotten already and laughed when she heard that Digger had tried to get Mac's bed removed from the room. She also confided that whilst she had not minded the confetti in the cases and the sewn up pyjamas, the visit by the police to the hotel, in the early hours of their wedding night, after a tip off about a bank robber, was just a bit too much, although Henry had thought it hilarious.

She then went up to Mac's room, knocked on the door and went in. She blurted out her apology, said she had rung Deidre and apologized and told Mac how much she loved him and was sorry for hurting him in that way.

"Thank you Deborah for ringing Deidre and for apologizing to her, that was good of you; please don't cry! I love you so much, I really hated myself for being so angry with you out in the street, but you just crossed that line and I unfortunately blew a fuse, so I am sorry too.

I know you don't enjoy these boyish pranks that we play on each other, but for Digger to have wheedled the name of the hotel and telephone number out of Vi and then to have made a long distance call and set everything up, was really very impressive and showed me how much he cares about me and was thinking of me, despite all that he has got on his plate at the moment. Do you understand?"

"I think so, but Deidre said that someone called the police and said that a bank robber was stopping in their hotel room, surely that was going too far and please tell me that it wasn't you Mac!"

The following day Hazel, Angus and Violet arrived first at the hotel, having caught the early train from Bedford to London and then the train down to Southampton. In the end, no more of Donny's friends or relatives had been able to afford to make the journey to Spain, so they had all got together one night after work the previous week, to give him a good send off.

Bertie and Victoria arrived by coach an hour later and Deidre, Henry and the children arrived later still, having had to contend with a puncture in the sidecar wheel, shortly after they had left Bedford.

Deborah had managed to book three tables quite near each other in the restaurant, so it was a very raucous and enjoyable meal they had together that evening.

Deborah did make a point of talking with Deidre during the evening, who assured her that the whole matter had been completely forgotten, but Deborah was never quite certain!

They all caught the boat for Spain the following morning and arrived in Valencia on Friday afternoon. Bertie organized for a couple of taxis to take them to Benicarlo, while Deborah and Mac waited for the Indian to be unloaded and then followed them all there a little later.

Bertie and Victoria went to their own house and showed Henry and family to the old cottage they had rented for them, next to theirs. Angus and Hazel unpacked their things in their room and then walked down to the beach to share a light snack with Deidre and Henry. Violet decided she was too tired to do anything and stayed in her room and slept for the afternoon.

"So Henry, what have you got planned for my son tomorrow," asked Angus innocently.

"Oh, you know Angus, the usual, assuming he is going off somewhere by taxi that is. Not too sure that Deborah would appreciate anything untoward, happening to her precious motorbike."

"Good point Henry, not sure that young lady appreciates the English sense of humour, having spent so much of her life abroad. Still, it was most amusing what young Arnold got up to back at the hotel, good for him."

"Quite so Angus, jolly good show; for him to arrange all that from Australia was outstanding; more wine Hazel?"

"Why thank you Henry, but Angus has had quite sufficient, haven't you dear. He is wearing his 'Cheshire Cat Grin', which is always a sign that he has had enough."

The rest of the day passed most pleasantly and when Hazel returned to the hotel, she discovered that Violet had struck up a friendship with an ex-pat from Denmark, who spoke excellent English and whose company, she was obviously enjoying.

The Wedding was well attended by all their friends from the village as well as John and Annette, who had traveled from Roses and David and Esther Josephs, who had traveled from Gibraltar; all of whom were staying in the same hotel as Angus and Hazel.

The priest repeated the key words in English and Spanish and kept the service quite short and a photographer had been employed to take some photographs after the ceremony at the church and again at the reception in the local restaurant.

Angus assisted Henry in tying some tin cans onto the rear bumper of the taxi and Hazel managed to pour a carton of confetti into one of their cases, as Deidre and Henry seemed unwilling to participate in that particular prank.

The happy couple left the reception just after nine and were driven to the hotel in Valencia, that they had managed to book the day before and where they had left the Indian for safe keeping.

They had intended in just spending a couple of nights in Valencia before moving on, but enjoyed the hotel and each others charms so much, that they stopped a full week.

"Are you absolutely certain you want to do this Deborah?" Mac asked on the Sunday morning, as they were packing the Indian to return to Benicarlo.

"Yes Mac, I am certain. Dad told me that he and Victoria were going to go back to Roses with John and Annette and that they were then going to bring his Renault Juvaquatre back to Benicarlo. He said that we could use the car, if we wanted to go to Rialp on our honeymoon, which means that Deidre and Henry could use the Indian to explore Spain for a few days, on their own, if they want to."

"Well it is very kind of your father to lend us the car and John and Annette for that matter and I am sure that Henry will be delighted with the opportunity, he has always admired your bike."

"To be honest with you, dad was furious that after having had the use of the car for free, for all this time, that John still asked for a little longer to find the cash to purchase it; besides, I am sure that he and Victoria will be spending a lot more time in Spain in the future and the car will come in very handy for them."

They returned to Benicarlo that morning and joined everyone as they were having lunch outside of Bertie and Victoria's house.

"Well thank you for your kind offer Deborah," said Henry, "but who is going to look after the children?"

"We will," said Hazel, "Angus is in his element building sand castles and messing about on the beach."

"And we will too," said Bertie, "I have already promised the children a ride in my boat, so you two go off and enjoy yourselves, the children will be fine with all of us here."

"I have always wanted to go to Madrid," said Deidre, "if we leave now Henry, we could be there and back by Wednesday, in time to catch our boat back home on Thursday. What do you think?"

"Great idea old girl; lets do it."

Deborah accompanied Henry for a short ride on the Indian, to make sure he knew how to handle all of its features and an hour later, he and Deidre were off on their 'second' honeymoon, to Madrid and after getting some clean clothes from his case and money from his dad, Mac and Deborah set off in the Renault for a week up in the mountains at Rialp.

On Thursday Angus, Hazel, Violet and her ex-pat friend caught one taxi to Valencia and Henry Deidre and the children caught another taxi and they all boarded the ship for England, apart from Violet's new Danish friend that is, who traveled to visit her in Bedford a month later.

They arrived in Southampton on the Saturday and traveled back home to Bedford that afternoon and evening.

"Well Henry, have you decided what you are going to do yet? The safe job in England with Crawley New Town, or the risky partnership in Australia or New Zealand or somewhere else, with Mac?" Deidre enquired, as they sat at home drinking tea that evening.

"Good question. Mac is just a different person these days; he doesn't know himself whether he will stay in England or go to Spain or Australia or New Zealand or who knows where. I just don't feel I can rely on him anymore."

"Maybe it is just a phase and once he is back from the honeymoon, he will be his old self again."

"I don't think so Deidre and after the way that Deborah spoke to you; yes, yes, I know she apologized, but there will always be that worry, that something else will light her fuse. I don't think we can take that risk Deidre, we have to think of ourselves and the children and if I am being honest, that job with the Planning Consultants is just what I have dreamed of and who knows; maybe they will even offer me a partnership one day."

"I know Henry, I have thought about it a lot while we were away and have come to the same conclusion and Crawley sounds like a really nice place to live and it will not be that far from the seaside either; I think you should write and accept their offer, I really do."

When Mac and Deborah eventually arrived back at Benicarlo, they were able to say that they had not only visited Rialp but had also crossed the border and visited Toulouse and then taken the coast road back to Barcelona, where they had stayed the previous two nights.

"The car was misfiring, so we booked it into a Renault garage and had it serviced," Deborah informed her father, who had begun to get slightly worried about them.

"That's good, thank you, it saves me the trouble, I don't think it had been touched in all the years John had used it," Bertie replied. "So what do you two plan to do next?" he asked.

"We have a quandary Dad, we need some advice. I don't want to go and live in Bedford where Mac's job is and of course he doesn't have a place of his own there and I just couldn't live with his parents and he doesn't want to live and work in London."

"Does it really matter where you live?" asked Victoria, "the important thing is that you are together and are beginning to get to know each other. Having said that, you do both need to be comfortable with where you live and of course, where you are going to raise your children, assuming that is part of the plan."

"Yes, children most certainly are part of the plan," said Mac, "and whilst I can see that Western Australia is right for Arnold and Moira and Vi and Mick, it does not do anything for me and I am not really sure why that should be!"

"Each to his own," said Bertie, "I have been to South Africa and there is a lot going on there and of course there is America and Canada, New Zealand and South America but don't mention my name if you go to Chile."

"How would your parents react to you leaving the country and living somewhere abroad Mac?" Victoria asked.

"I don't suppose they would like it, but they certainly wouldn't try and stop me. Deborah was telling me that you spent a lot of time in New Zealand before the War Bertie, what was it like over there?"

Over the next couple of days Bertie related everything he could remember about all the towns and places he had visited in New Zealand, as well as the people and the way of life and some of the more notable experiences he had gone through whilst there.

They returned to England the last week of April and set up home in Deborah's flat in London, with the intention that Mac would travel to Bedford for work on his motorbike, staying over with his parents a couple of nights each week.

By the time he and Deborah returned to work on Monday the 1st May, they had made their minds up that they were going to emigrate to New Zealand, probably Auckland, if

Deborah could get a transfer there with her Insurance company.

When she arrived at work she had to attend a meeting with the Personnel Manager, to discuss her long absence.

"Yes, we did get your telegram from France Miss Bannister, or should I say Mrs. Smith, explaining why you would be late home from your honeymoon and quite frankly we considered your excuse to be very poor indeed. It is only because of your impeccable past record with us that you are not being dismissed and a note has been put on your file, to that effect."

"Thank you sir and what about my request for a transfer to the office in New Zealand?"

"I have looked into the matter for you and I can tell you that the company does have a large office in Auckland and a smaller office in Christchurch, and having telephoned both office managers, I am pleased to say that each of them would be delighted to employ someone with your considerable experience in the company. Do you have any preference as to which town you would like to go to?"

"I personally would prefer Auckland, as I spent some time there after leaving school and still have friends there, but it will depend on where my husband can find a job, would you mind if I come back to you with an answer, in a few days time?"

The next day during her lunch hour, Deborah went to New Zealand House in London and studied the newspaper advertisements for draughtsman jobs in North Island and soon realized that Auckland had twice as many as anywhere else. When she got home she discussed the matter with Mac that evening and was able to tell the Personnel Manager the next day, that she would like a transfer to the Auckland office, which was later confirmed.

They now knew that at least one of them had a job to go to, when they arrived in New Zealand and Mac started to write to potential employers himself, who had advertised for draughtsmen, with his particular type of experience.

And so it turned out that on the very day that Vi and Mick and Brian and Patty steamed into Fremantle and disembarked to a new life 'Down Under', Mac and Deborah embarked on the long process of emigrating to New Zealand.

Chapter 14
New Beginnings

It was a beautiful sunny day when Vi, Mick and the children arrived in Fremantle, after being a month at sea with hundreds of other new immigrants. The temperature was in the low twenties and the wind, which is called the Fremantle Doctor, was blowing gently. They all said goodbye to the new friends they had made aboard ship, promising to keep in touch, and headed off with great excitement, to their new lives in a new country.

Moira and Digger gave them a brief tour of Perth, driving through Melville and Applecross before crossing the Canning Bridge and then heading north to go through Como and Kensington, before going over the Causeway Bridge and then home to Ruth Street.

"So Brian, what do you think of it so far," Digger asked his nephew as they were all sitting round the patio table, enjoying a long cool drink.

"I like it uncle and Duke is terrific and it will be great to be able to play in the garden and not be moaned at, for once. There is one thing though, why do so many of the houses not have an upstairs? All the houses in our street in London had at least one upstairs and some of them had two, but nearly all the houses we drove past today, only had a downstairs."

"I suppose because there is so much more land in Australia, that people do not need to go upwards, to get more space, but can just go out sideways or backwards," Digger replied.

"What about you Patty, what are you looking forward to most in Australia?" Moira asked the little girl.

"That's easy auntie, the seaside. To be able to go to the beach whenever we want and to go swimming in any month of the year, because the water will always be warm and without worrying about those horrible stingy jellyfish that were at Clacton last time we were there and my teacher at my old school wants me to write and tell them all about it auntie."

"Well, we will have to take some photographs of you swimming in the sea, to send with your letter, won't we Patty."

"It was very good of you and Digger to have met us today at Fremantle Moira," Vi said, "seeing you both standing there on the wharf, waving at us, made us feel so welcome. And thank you for sharing your home with us; we really do appreciate all the help you have given us over the last few months and for putting yourselves out for us, like this."

"Hey Sis, after all you and Mick did for me, it is our pleasure, isn't it Moira?" Digger replied.

"Of course it is Vi; did Digger mention that I went in to see the headmistress of the local Primary School last week and have reserved two places for the children as from next Monday, but she did suggest that you take them along this week some time, to meet her and their teachers."

"Oh thank you, did you hear that children, wasn't that kind of auntie Moira?" Vi replied.

"She did say that several other children would be starting on Monday as well, who had just arrived from England, so maybe some of the children on your boat, will also be going to the same school."

Once the children had eaten their tea and played in the garden with Duke for a while, they went to bed to talk about all they had seen that day and eventually to go to sleep, leaving the adults to chat on their own.

"So how have you been since you were assaulted by that man and woman Digger? Any lasting injuries or effects?" Mick asked.

"Well I do get the odd bad headache from time to time, but no, nothing really to speak of; I guess I am very lucky."

"Luck does not come into it," said Moira, "you were hit twice by a big, vicious man, wielding a large piece of wood. You dropped ten feet down a mine shaft onto a narrow ledge, disturbing a wild cat that fell another twenty feet down the shaft and drowned in the water at the bottom of the shaft. Your injuries prevented you from climbing back up the shaft and if Duke and Ray had not found you, because the police had really given up on you, you would have starved to death down there. No Digger, someone was watching over you and keeping you alive, I have no doubt about that whatsoever!"

"But I assume that one bad experience has not put you off Australia though?" Mick asked.

"Absolutely not, we just love it here and now that you lot are out with us and we hear that Bertie and Victoria should be back out in another month or so, our happiness is complete. Isn't that right love?" he said, turning to Moira, who smiled back at him.

"So tell me about these three builders you know, who are lining up to give me a job," Mick said to Digger.

"Well I may have exaggerated there a bit Mick, but here, look in the newspaper, there are lots of adverts for tradesmen; I am sure you will find something there, no worries."

"Digger, how could you do this to us," said Vi, "Mick needs that job right away, we spent a lot more money on the voyage than we budgeted for and apart from our nest egg for a house, some day, we are broke. Mick needs to start work tomorrow so that we can pay our way."

"Calm down Vi, you are stopping with us, there is no panic here, Mick will get a job within a few days, trust me!" said Digger.

"Actually Mick, I did notice that there was a sign up for tradesmen at the hospital building site. They are in the middle of building a new wing at the Royal Perth and I am sure I saw plumbers on the list, but I was chatting to my friend Pat at the time, who is a student nurse, so I cannot be one hundred percent certain, but why not walk to work with me tomorrow and you can see for yourself."

Vi and the children stayed at home the next day and waited in until their large trunks and other luggage had arrived form the ship. Following the map that Moira had drawn, they then walked round to the school, arriving there just as the children were leaving and went inside to meet the headmistress and then the class teacher for each of them. They saw their classrooms and where they would be sitting and were made to feel very welcome.

They then went to the local shops, with a shopping list and some money that Moira had left out for them and walked back via Hyde Park, where the children stopped to play for a while.

In the meantime, Mick had walked to the hospital with Moira and introduced himself to the site manager of the hospital building site, who turned out to be a man who had emigrated from Yorkshire three years earlier. The two men hit it off straight away and after a quick demonstration of Mick's plumbing skills, was hired on the spot.

"I assume you have brought your own tools with you Mick?" the manager asked.

"I certainly have Mr. err, I didn't catch your name."

"Terry, call me Terry. The Australians tend to be a lot less formal than we Brits, I am pleased to say."

"I am hoping Terry, that they will arrive today, so I should be able to start tomorrow."

"No, no, my friend, you can start right now. Working for yourself all this time, I presume that you are used to sizing a job and listing everything you will need to complete it, am I right?"

"Well yes, but hasn't the architect done that already?" Mick replied.

"In general terms yes, but he is not the plumbing expert, you are; so what I suggest is that we walk round the first floor together and we can then discuss all the plumbing that is on the plans and you can go away and give me exact sizes and lengths of pipes, along with a complete list of all the materials and tools you will require to complete the job."

"Are you sure I won't be putting someone else's nose out of joint, if I take over the complete first floor of the building."

"Not at all. The existing plumber and his mate are already three weeks behind schedule on the work required for the ground floor, with a bit of luck, if you are as good as I think you are, you will help me to catch that time up and maybe get ahead for once. I will pay you the weekly rate we agreed, with a bonus for each week that you complete the work on time. How does that sound?"

"Sounds very fair Terry, thank you. What about a Plumber's Mate, I don't know anyone here yet, are any of those young lads you have working over there interested in learning the trade, do you think?"

"No idea, let's go and ask them," Terry replied, walking over to where five young lads were resting against a wall, having a cigarette.

"Oi, you lot, come over here," he bellowed.

They looked nervously at each other and then walked briskly over to the site manager, extinguishing their cigarettes as they went.

"This is Mick, he is a Master Plumber and he is prepared to offer one of you layabouts the chance to learn the trade, so put your hands up if you can read and write. Now put your hands up if you can read a drawing. Right the rest of you go back to work, you two stay here and talk with Mick."

"Hello lads, nice to meet you," said Mick, shaking their hands.

"I guess the obvious first question is do either of you want to become a plumber."

One lad said he wanted to learn to be a bricklayer and the other said he wanted to be a carpenter like his dad had been, but had never thought about plumbing and was willing to give it a go.

"Right, so thanks for your time and good luck with the bricklaying," Mick said to the first lad, "and welcome to plumbing and the mystery of the pipe," he said to the other lad.

"What is your name then," Mick asked.

"Before I tell you my name, I have one condition to make about working for you," the lad said, in a very serious tone of voice.

"Go on then," said Mick, "what is it?"

"No jokes about my name, or about books or authorship or anything like that. O.K.?"

"You are intriguing me, but if that is your one condition, then that is fine by me."

"My name is Walter Scott," the lad informed him.

Now Mick was in the very act of asking him if that meant he had to call him Sir, as in Sir Walter Scott, when he remembered the agreement he had just made and said in fact,

"Does that mean, you want me to call you Sscotttie, or Walter, or do you have a nickname?"

"My mates call me Billabong, or Bill for short," the lad replied.

"How on earth do you get Billabong from Walter Scott? I don't get it," replied Mick.

"A Billabong is a water hole. Walter, Billabong. Do you get it now?"

"I am with you now. Bill it is and we start work together tomorrow," so they shook hands on the arrangement, which turned out to be the start of them working together for the next twenty five or so years.

The children started school on the Monday to find that one of the boys Brian played with on the boat, Bobby by name, was in the same class as himself, but none of the girls Patty had become friends with on the boat, went to the same school, but she quickly became firm friends with a young lass from Edinburgh named Isabel, whose family had emigrated a year earlier.

Vi started off looking for a part-time job, but nothing was suitable which fitted in with the children's school times, so she ended up running the home at Ruth Street, while Moira carried on working at the hospital.

She was walking home from work one day, chatting to her friend Pat, who seemed agitated about something as they walked past the building site.

"Is something bothering you Pat?" Moira asked, "you seemed a bit flustered yesterday when we were walking home past here, has something upset you?"

"Didn't your brother-in-law tell you about it last night then?" Pat replied.

"Tell me about what?"

"I was working in the theatre yesterday afternoon and we were in the nurses room getting changed into our theatre robes, standing there chatting with next to nothing on, when suddenly one of the girls heard shouts and whistles outside and went over to the window to see what was happening and all the men from this building site, were standing there, having climbed up on the scaffolding, staring in and watching us."

"Oh, how awful for you all, so what did you do."

"We all sat down on the floor and called for Sister. She came in and saw what was happening and went and got the Staff Nurse to help her and between them held a blanket up to the window so we could finish getting changed."

"Did Sister make a complaint about the incident?"

"She went and saw Matron that afternoon and the window has been covered in whitewash now and we are having blinds fitted next week, but it was so embarrassing Moira."

"Have the men been made to apologize?"

"Sister wanted to have them brought over and made to apologize to us, but we all said that would be even worse, to have to face them in the flesh again, so to speak."

"I take your point and was my brother-in-law, one of the men?"

"Oh no, I don't think so, but I am sure he will know all about it, you ask him."

So she did and he did!

After a couple of weeks of living together in Ruth Street, Digger decided it was time to go to Pinjarra for the weekend and do some work on the house, having arranged with Ray to order and then to have installed, a new rainwater tank. The last time he spoke with Ray he was informed that it was in and working properly and that it had already collected a couple of feet of water.

"Can I come to Pinjarra as well uncle Digger and help you with the house," Brian asked, when Digger and Moira were discussing the trip.

"You won't all be able to fit in the car Brian, as I have to take some new stuff for the kitchen with us as well."

"Well I heard dad say he was working again on Saturday, so him and mum won't want to come and Patty is going round to play with that Isabel again, so it will just be me; please uncle Digger?"

"I am sure Vicky will not mind if we take Brian with us, he can sleep in that little room, next to the one we use and Ray and Jenny have been dying to meet them all. I will talk to Vi about it and see what she says," Moira suggested.

"Mum is on the patio with dad, auntie," Brian informed her.

"Are you sure you don't mind Moira, I thought the two of you would enjoy a weekend on your own for once and Brian can be such a pest some times," Vi replied, when told about Brian's request.

"He will be fine Vi and Digger enjoys having him around, but we do plan to leave after work on Friday and not return until Sunday evening, is that all right with you?"

"That will be fine, I will make certain he finishes any school work before he goes, which will give him an incentive to get it done, for once."

On Friday afternoon, Brian raced home from school, rushed through his homework and had his bag packed in no time at all. Moira and Digger loaded the car, put Duke in the back with Brian and set off for Pinjarra.

"I remembered to telephone Jenny today and let her know that we were coming for the weekend and that Brian was

236

coming with us," Digger announced, as they were driving down the Albany Highway on the outskirts of Perth.

"What sort of fruit trees do they have on their farm," Brian asked.

"Peaches, plums and nectarines mostly, but I think they have some apple and pear trees as well and Ray was talking about putting in some citrus trees, like grapefruit and lemons," Moira answered, "and yes Digger, I did remember to bring that peach stone I saved from the hotel in Northam, this time, so perhaps Brian can help me to plant it on our block, somewhere, if he wants to that is."

"Yes please and I think we should plant it by the front porch, so that when it becomes a tree, we will be able to stretch out and pick a peach without having to get up out of our chair," Brian replied thoughtfully.

They tried singing some songs as they were traveling, but Duke insisted on joining in, so that didn't work and after a few rounds of 'Eye Spy' they ran out of things to spy, so the last half hour or so, was traveled in relative silence.

"I thought we would go to James Street first and drop off the kitchen stuff, before going up to Vicky's," Digger announced, "but I need you to stay in the car and keep hold of Duke for me Brian, because if he gets out and goes down to the river, we will never get him back again tonight."

James Street House
Artist - Lynette Lilley

"Are there crocodiles in the river?" Brian asked, "my friend Bobby says that Australia has some of the biggest crocodiles in the world."

"That is true, but we do not have any down here, but there are plenty of snakes and mosquitoes and we don't know how those sheep will react to us in the dark, so to be on the safe side, you stay in the car tonight with Duke, do you understand?"

"Yes uncle."

They parked in front of the house and Digger left the engine running with the headlamps on, to give them some light and he and Moira unloaded all the boxes from the boot and the interior of the car and carried them into the house.

They then re-locked the door behind them and drove back through Pinjarra and out to Vicky's farm.

"Those cats have been in the house again Digger, I could smell them the moment I opened the front door, you will have to find out how they are getting in and board it up," Moira said, as they were driving along.

"I saw the sheep come round the side of the house as you were locking up," said Brian, "and Duke saw them as well and tried to get out, but I held on to him tightly."

"Well done Brian, I don't think he would attack them, as they seemed to just ignore each other last time, but he did fight with that big feral cat and got scratched on the back by it, so we will have to be careful tomorrow."

"Someone's in the house Digger, there are lights on, must be Ray and Jenny," Moira announced as they pulled up outside the farmhouse.

"Can I let Duke go now?" Brian asked.

"Yes, he will be fine now, he knows his way around the farm, but he will probably just go inside to say hello to our friends," Digger replied.

Brian opened the car door and Duke shot of like a bullet, first to a nearby tree and then into the farmhouse, almost knocking Moira off her feet as he brushed past her. He raced into the lounge and there was Ray standing in the middle of the floor, with his arms outstretched calling Duke's name. A smaller man would have been knocked off his feet, but Ray just caught him in the air and the two of them went slowly backwards together, onto the couch.

"Pleased to see me are you boy," Ray said to the dog, who responded by licking his face and hands.

"Are you teaching my dog bad habits Ray Thomas?" Moira asked, as she stood there at the door with Jenny who had joined her from the kitchen.

"Guilty," he managed to say, as he pushed Duke back onto the floor, whilst still playing with him and getting licked to death in the process.

"Come and see what I have in the kitchen for you Duke," Jenny called out and headed back in that direction, followed by the dog, who knew only too well what that call had come to mean. She gave him a big cow bone, which he proudly carried outside to the front porch, just as Digger and Brian were coming in with the cases.

"And this must be young Brian," Ray enthused, "the 'fag card King' of London, or so I hear."

"Well not the whole of London, just my old school in Clapham," Brian replied proudly, "why do you play as well then?"

Ray avoided answering the question directly but announced, "I have a cigarette card collection that will make your hair stand on end and your ears curl; cars, buses, trains, airplanes, you name it and I have probably got it."

"Wow, when I can I see them?" Brian asked, with his eyes almost popping out of his head,

"If your busy schedule permits, I thought I would show them to you tomorrow morning," Ray replied.

"Can I uncle, can I see them tomorrow morning, I haven't played fag cards with anyone for weeks and weeks."

"Well, we were hoping to make an early start tomorrow on the old house Brian, I won't really have time to take you up to Ray and Jenny's farm before we leave."

"Not a problem Digger, I will come down and collect him, just say the time."

"That's good of you Ray, say seven thirty," Digger replied, "you sure you don't mind."

"Mind, as soon as I told him you were bringing the boy with you, he has been like a kid himself, getting out his cigarette card collection and other stuff to interest Brian.," said Jenny, "Ray loves kids, you just leave Brian with him and they will both be in their element."

They ate the dinner which Jenny had prepared and after Brian had gone to bed and then got up for a glass of water and then gone back to bed again, they chatted for several hours before finally Ray and Jenny left for home and Digger and Moira went to bed themselves.

The alarm clock went off at six thirty and Digger turned it off and went back to sleep, only to be wakened ten minutes later by Brian knocking on their bedroom door.

"Who is it, what do you want?" Digger shouted.

"It's me uncle, Brian; the clock in the kitchen says it is almost seven and I am to be collected soon and I haven't had my breakfast yet."

"Go back to the kitchen Brian and give Duke some water please, I will be through in a minute," Digger replied.

"When you said seven thirty to Ray last night, I thought you were being optimistic," Moira informed him, "when was the last time you were up before eight on a Saturday?"

"I am often awake before eight on a Saturday Moira!"

"I didn't say awake, did I?" she said, poking him in the side as she jumped out of bed. "I will bring you a cup of tea and get Brian his breakfast, so you just lie there and rest, Oh Lord and Master."

"Off with you wench and see about your duties," he said softly as she was leaving the room.

"I heard that, just you wait," she said laughing.

She walked through to the kitchen and put the kettle on the stove and took some bacon and eggs out of the cool chest and opened a can of beans and put them on the stove to heat up.

"How many slices of bacon and how many eggs would you like Brian and would you like some toast?"

"Can I have two rashers please, but just one egg and some toast with the beans will be great, thank you. I gave Duke a drink of water and then let him go outside, as he wanted to lift his leg."

"Good boy, thank you, do you want a glass of milk or a cup of tea with your breakfast?"

"Milk please; do you want me to take uncle's tea through to him?"

"Thank you Brian, be careful not to spill it. Hold on while I open the door for you."

Brian took the tea through to the bedroom and was pleased to find Digger, sitting up in bed, looking out of the window.

"Your tea uncle," he said, putting it down on the bedside table, "can I ask you a question?"

"Of course Brian, what is it?"

"Your friends Ray and Jenny, what should I call them? Mr. and Mrs. Thomas sounds a bit unfriendly, if you know what I mean."

"I do; good point. What did you call your mum and dad's friends, back in London?"

"They didn't have many friends who we saw that often, but there was uncle Denis and auntie Yvonne who used to work with mum before she got married, they were just friends, I guess."

"There you have it, I am sure they will both be delighted to be called uncle Ray and auntie Jenny and if they are not, I am sure they will tell you; no worries mate!"

Brian polished off his breakfast and was just putting on his Wellington boots when Ray arrived.

"Hi Ray, do you want a cup of tea," Moira asked, as he walked into the kitchen, followed by Duke.

"No thanks Moira. I forgot to mention last night that I normally take Vicky's horse for a ride on a Saturday and hoped it would be all right for the boy to come with me as well."

"Oh great, can I auntie?" Brian interjected.

"That horse can be a bit difficult Ray, I am not sure it would be a good idea," Moira replied in a concerned tone of voice.

"Oh no, I agree, I have managed to borrow a little pony from the farm next door, it will be perfectly safe for him."

Brian rushed to the window and looked out at the horse and pony tied up under a tree. "Please auntie, please let me go," Brian begged.

"I need to ask Digger on this one," she said, and walked through to the bedroom, returning a couple of minutes later, with Digger in tow.

"Hi mate," said Digger, "Brian has not ridden before, have you?" he asked turning to his nephew, who shook his head.

"Well this little pony has been carrying children on her back for twenty years and never had a mishap, so she will be perfect for the boy," Ray replied.

"O.K. but listen to me Brian, no messing about, no misbehaving and you do whatever your uncle Ray tells you to; do you understand me."

"Digger, are you sure about this, what will Vi say?" Moira asked.

"I know exactly what Vi would say, but she is not here, so off you go and enjoy yourself Brian. Duke, you come here and sit; good boy"

Ray and Brian went outside and Ray went to the stable and found a suitable hat for Brian to wear and then gave him his first lesson in horse riding. When Ray was satisfied that he had understood the basics and was safe to be on a horse, the two set off out of the farm and down the road together, towards Ray's place.

As they drove down into Pinjarra, Moira took the opportunity to speak with Digger on one or two subjects that had been bothering her.

"You know Digger, this is the first time we have been alone together in almost three weeks."

"You said you didn't mind Brian coming, so don't blame me Moira."

"It isn't Brian or Patty, it's your sister Vi. She has just taken over my home. She interrupts every conversation you and I have together, she is now making all the decisions about what we will eat and when we will eat it, she has reorganised my kitchen at least twice and I am beginning to feel like a guest in my own house."

"Look, I know what she is like, but with you working different shifts and her being at home all the time, this was probably going to happen eventually, if we are honest with each other love."

"So you are saying that it is perfectly acceptable for your wife to feel like a stranger in her own home, is that right."

"Did the words acceptable and stranger, come from my lips? No, they didn't, so let's just try and discuss this rationally, shall we?"

They parked outside the hardware shop and went in and bought the items they had listed during the week, plus a few more they had thought of over night; which also gave Digger time to collect his thoughts and decide what next to say to Moira.

"I did chat to Mick the other night, after you and Vi had gone to bed, just to sound him out about living out here in Pinjarra, but he said that he is getting on so well with Terry at work, that they are thinking of putting a small team together and maybe getting involved in all that new house building out Melville way."

"That means we will have them with us forever then. Oh great! That is just what I needed."

"Moira, what is going on here? This isn't like you at all and it does not mean they will be with us forever; in fact it means the opposite. Mick was saying that Terry already lives in Melville and travels across to the hospital every day. It appears that he built his own house and another smaller one that he rents out, on a large block of land that he purchased when they first came out here."

"Oh, I see, so what is Mick hoping to do exactly and does Vi know about any of this, because she has not said anything to me about moving to Melville."

"Well it turns out that Vi was the one who fancied living in the country, not Mick, so he has said nothing to her so far, until he has sorted things out a bit more with Terry. He does know that the current tenants will leave at the end of June and they could move in at the beginning of July, so even if he continues working at the hospital, he and Terry could drive over together each day."

As she sat in the car, taking in this news, her whole demeanour changed and she smiled as she said, "Digger that's wonderful news, just another six weeks and we will be on our own again, but that sounds unkind and I don't mean to be and I have actually enjoyed having the children in the house with us, especially Patty, she is a real sweetie."

"I'm glad to hear it and I have enjoyed having Brian with us too, so having the children has been good."

"Having children in the house has been great and it may well be continuing into the future Digger."

"No love, I just told you that all being well, they will all be moved over to Melville by the beginning of July," he patiently explained again as they parked in front of the old house and let Duke out for a run.

"I heard that Digger, but it isn't what I meant," she said softly.

"Well what did you mean for goodness sake?"

"I am pregnant, we are going to have a baby Digger."

"What did you say? I thought you didn't want children for a couple of years, so how did that happen Moira?"

She looked at him unable to speak and tears started to roll down her cheeks.

"Hey, I didn't mean that the way it sounded Moira, come here and give me a hug. That's wonderful news, I just wasn't expecting it. When is the baby due?"

"The middle of January and are you really pleased, I didn't know how to tell you or what you would say."

"I am honestly delighted love, me a dad, fancy that!"

They worked steadily on the house all day, ripping out old shelves and cupboards, painting walls, repairing broken glass, nailing down loose floorboards and cleaning up after the cats. They managed to find enough wood to get the stove going and drawing some water from the rainwater tank, made themselves a cup of tea which they enjoyed on the front porch. They had not been sitting there for long, when Duke came up and sat beside them and a short while later, the smaller of the two feral cats came and lay down on the grass at the side of where they were sitting.

"Are you sure you haven't overdone it Moira, a woman in your condition needs to be careful."

"Digger, I have dealt with more pregnant ladies than you have had hot dinners, so stop fussing, I have not overdone it.

Look at those two, I can't believe that Duke has allowed that cat to come up to the house and sit so close to him."

"Well I did here that Pariah dogs were originally the feral dogs of India, so perhaps he recognizes a kindred spirit and they are both a similar golden brown colour."

"That's true and it's a she cat not a male cat, so perhaps he does not feel threatened," Moira suggested. "What has it just caught Digger, looks like a mouse to me."

"I think you are right, I hate to see one animal torment another like that, why doesn't it just kill it outright?"

Digger was contemplating the situation and wondering what to do, when suddenly, out of nowhere, the other big feral cat, pounced on the other one's back, took the mouse from it's claws and sat there eating it, in front of them.

They were all dumbstruck and even Duke looked on for a few seconds, before pouncing forward onto the big cat, who was still holding the other one in it's claws, so it could not defend itself from the dog. Duke bit deeply into the back of its neck, causing the big cat to meow loudly and release the other cat beneath it, as it franticly tried to attack Duke. The dog twisted his head back and forward quickly, as if dealing with a large rat and somehow managed to break the big cat's neck. Duke then walked a few yards away from the house and dropped the dead animal onto the grass.

To everyone's amazement, he then went over to the smaller cat and licked the wounds on its back until they had been cleaned and the two then went off together and lay down next to each other, at the side of the house.

"You know Moira, I think Duke may just have found his Duchess, what do you think?"

"It could well be, they certainly seem happy with each others company. I think I saw a spade in the shed Digger, we need to bury that animal, before it starts to attract any other unpleasant creatures," Moira stated.

The spade was found, a suitable site away from the house was located and a deep hole dug and the dead cat put in. Digger was in the process of filling the hole back in, when Moira remembered the peach stone, so she went and fetched it from the car and threw that into the hole with the cat.

"That dog never ceases to amaze me Moira, I really will hate parting with him when Bertie and Victoria arrive back here."

"I know, but he is their dog Digger and he loves being out here in the country, I am sure he prefers it to the town. Perhaps once the baby has arrived, we could get a puppy of our own, that way there shouldn't be any jealousy between the dog and the new baby."

"I said to Ray last night that something was different about you Moira," Jenny said, when Moira broke the news over dinner, about being pregnant.

"That's worth a drink in celebration; I will get the sherry, Ginger Beer for you and Brian, Digger?"

"Yes please mate. Will you be O.K. to drink sherry Moira?"

"Digger stop fussing. As I told you earlier, I have forgotten more about babies than you will ever know. One glass of sherry will be fine."

"So I will have my first proper cousin," said Brian, "that's great, I can teach him to climb trees and play fag cards and frighten the girls and ride a horse now, can't I uncle Ray?"

"Too true you can son, a real Roy Rogers you were today, you just need a big white hat and a six gun."

"I hate to interfere with this manly discussion," said Moira, "but the baby may turn out to be a little girl you know, there is no certainty that it will be a boy."

Brian just pulled a face in disgust and everyone laughed.

"Give him a few more years and I am sure his opinion of girls will mellow," said Jenny, looking at Moira enviously.

The news of Moira's pregnancy was well received by Vi and Mick who were thrilled at the thought of a new baby in the family, which is more than could be said about the other piece of news that Brian had been horse riding during his visit to Pinjarra.

It also gave Mick the perfect opportunity to talk about moving out of Ruth Street, to Terry's house in Melville, which would give Moira the extra space she would need for the new arrival, but leave Vi close enough to come across and be there to help her sister-in-law in the first few difficult weeks, following the birth.

In the end it was the beginning of August when Vi and family finally moved out of Ruth Street and went across town to the house in Melville, after Vi had insisted that it was re-decorated from top to bottom, as the previous tenants had left their mark on every room in the house.

The children settled into their new schools very quickly and made new friends and Vi found a little job, round the corner, serving in one of the local shops.

Mick continued working at the hospital for the remainder of the year and he and Terry formed their own building company in November and started work on one of the new areas in Melville, called Attadale, building new houses with a view over the Swan River.

Moira's family were delighted with the news and her mother would dearly have loved to have been with her daughter when she gave birth in the January, but it just was not going to be possible; but this did not stop her and Granny knitting baby clothes, from the moment they received Moira's letter.

Chapter 15
Hans Schmidt

On the sixth of August 1950 Vi, Mick and the children, along with all the boxes they had brought from England and the furniture and other things, they had acquired in Australia, said goodbye to Ruth Street and made the journey across town to the three bedroomed house, that sat next to Terry's in Melville.

"Vi, if you have forgotten anything, I am sure I can pass it to Mick at work and at worst, Digger and I will drive over at the weekend with it," Moira said, as her sister-in-law thought of yet another reason why she should come over to visit Moira later that week.

"Well we are only a few miles away, so if you feel you can't manage anything, promise you will let me know Moira and come over anyway for Sunday lunch, please say you will."

"That would be lovely Vi," Digger chimed in, "we will see you all on Sunday."

The Broomland's finally drove off just before eight o'clock in their old Ford car that Mick had purchased a few weeks earlier and Moira and Digger got themselves ready for work.

"Are you all right love, you look a bit flustered?" Digger enquired, as he was getting his briefcase from the bedroom.

"I just had a bad night's sleep," she said, "and your sister was beginning to get me down, I'll be fine, don't worry. Did I imagine it, or did you say last night, that you might have to go to Melbourne later this week?"

"Oh yes, Rusty called me Friday to say that they had finally located Hans Schmidt and asked me if I wanted to go over there to question him about what happened between him and Don Davis."

"And do you? Want to go over there, I mean?"

"Well yes, I would like to talk to him. I don't think we have enough evidence to accuse him of anything, but just to find out what actually happened and how they worked the scam together. I think it would be worth finding out and documenting, just so the bank can be certain it will never happen again."

"Could I come with you, to Melbourne, it would be nice to see what life is like in another state?"

"I don't see why not, if you think you could handle the train journey, but what about your job at the hospital, what are they going to say if you suddenly take a few days off?"

"To be honest Digger, I have tried to talk to you on several occasions in the last week about my job, but someone, who shall be nameless, always managed to butt in and get your attention."

"Well you have it now Moira, what do you want to say?"

"I am finding it all a bit much at work and would like to ask the Hospital to cut my hours down, or maybe just allow me to fill in when they are short staffed, or failing that, to stop completely. Since you got the new position and that large raise, we don't really need my salary to survive anymore, do we?"

"No we don't and I had assumed you were going to stop work anyway, when the baby came, so if you feel you want to stop earlier than that, then you do what you think best love."

"Thank you, I will speak to Sister about it today."

When Digger got home from work Monday evening, Moira was tucked up in bed and one of the nurses from the hospital was sitting beside her and the pair were happily chatting away when Digger walked into the room.

"Moira, what's up?" Digger asked, when he saw her lying there, looking extremely pale.

"It's nothing to worry about Digger, this is my friend Pat, she said she would sit with me until you came home."

"Hello Pat. What has happened? Are you and the baby all right?"

"We are both fine Digger. I just overdid it, lifting a patient and passed out in the ward, so the Sister sent me home."

"Do you want me to get Vi over?"

"No please, not that, anything but that," Moira replied laughing.

"Don't joke Moira, this is serious. I have been asked to fly to Melbourne tomorrow and I can't leave you here on your own like this, can I?"

"I can stay with Moira, if you like," Pat said, "if that helps at all."

"There you are Digger, problem solved. How long will you be away for?"

"The plan is that I fly over tomorrow, spend Wednesday and Thursday in Melbourne and fly home Friday. I know you wanted to come with me, but it is just not possible this time."

"I can understand that and it is fine; is that O.K. with you Pat?" Moira asked. Pat smiled and nodded so Moira continued, "if you run Pat home in the car, she can pick up enough clothes to last till the weekend and I am sure that with Pat to keep me company and Duke to keep us both safe, we will all be able to manage on our own somehow, for the few days you are away."

Digger was up early the next day and took a taxi to the airport where he boarded the Qantas Empire Airways, Lockheed Constellation for Melbourne.

Rusty was there to meet him at the airport at the other end and drove him back to the Melbourne Head Office, to go over everything he had found out about Hans Schmidt.

"I have checked with the local police and there has never been any complaint filed against Herr Schmidt. The German community know of him and his connection with Don Davis, but generally speaking, it is thought that he always gave a fair price for any articles of jewellery that he personally bought from them and no-one appears to be aware that he purchased anything that Don Davis bought directly from them; so we only have your conversation with Don, to support any allegations we might have wanted to bring against him."

"Well it doesn't sound likely that we are going to get very much out of this man, but if we make it clear to him that we are not intending to file any charges against him, then maybe he will be happy to talk with us; let's hope so, or this trip will have been a complete waste of time," Digger replied.

That evening, the two men went out for an enjoyable meal at a very good restaurant at the Bank's expense and afterwards Rusty deposited him at his hotel, where he was able to ring home and find out how Moira was doing.

"I am doing just fine, stop worrying about me, how was your flight?" she asked.

"It was very good, very smooth, the plane landed on time and Rusty was there to meet me; so you didn't faint at work again today?" he persisted.

"I didn't actually go to work today; Pat took one look at me this morning and told me to stay in bed and she reported me in sick, but I feel a lot better tonight and will probably go in to work tomorrow, I feel such a charlatan, to be off sick. What was Melbourne like?"

"I didn't see an awful lot of it, but what I did see was a lot busier than Perth, perhaps I will be able to bring you with me next time."

Rusty picked Digger up from the hotel the following morning and drove to the office where the pair started the interview with Herr Schmidt a little after ten o'clock.

"We are very grateful to you, for coming in to see us this morning, Herr Schmidt," Rusty started, "do we owe you anything for your expenses?"

"Thirty shillings will cover it young man," Hans replied.

Rusty popped out of the office for a couple of minutes and spoke with one of the clerks outside and then returned. A few minutes later, the clerk entered the office where the interview was being conducted, bringing with him an Expenses Form and the thirty shillings.

"Here is your money and would you please sign our receipt form sir," the young clerk asked.

The form was signed, the money handed over and the clerk left.

"As I explained in my letter, it has recently come to light that our former employee Mr. Don Davis, had been acting fraudulently towards the new immigrants he dealt with on the bank's behalf, when he exchanged their foreign currency for Australian pounds. As you already know Herr Schmidt, this has sadly led to the untimely deaths of Mr. Davis and of your own niece," Rusty stated.

Hans shook his head and bit his lip and then replied, "Very sad Mr. Johnston, she was a beautiful girl, but always so headstrong, such a waste of a life."

"Herr Schmidt," said Digger, "I am the man that Don and your niece kidnapped and may I say how sorry I am for your loss."

"Thank you young man and may I say, how sorry I am for what they did to you. Cheating a few people out of some of their money is one thing, but kidnap and attempted murder are something completely different, they must have been out of their minds!"

"One of the things that Mr. Davis said to me," Digger continued, "was that you not only sent some of the immigrants to him, but also purchased any jewellery from him, that they decided to sell to him; could you clarify that arrangement for us please."

"I am happy to, but it is only partially true. Until I met Don Davis, the immigrants of all nationalities were selling their foreign currency to anyone who would buy it, normally for less than half of what it was worth. Don was offering much better rates than that and I was personally satisfied with what he gave me in exchange for my money and simply told my friends about him and the word went round very quickly."

"I see, but how did the jewellery connection between the two of you start?" Rusty asked.

"Quite simple really, I sold him a ring for his wife. We got chatting and I mentioned that I was a jeweller and he said he had been looking for a ruby ring and I happened to have one on me, which I sold to him, for a fair price. He then said that several people had already asked him about selling jewellery and said that he would give them my name and address, which I was naturally very pleased about."

"So you didn't buy anything off Don then?" Digger asked.

"Very little to start with, but it got more as the weeks went on. I told him I was not happy about it, so he suggested that I sit in the waiting room and talk to the people waiting to see him and offer them my services. I thought about it for a while and in the end arranged for my niece Ursula, who I had been training in the business, to go along and act on my behalf."

"So that is how he got to know your niece," Rusty said.

"Exactly. When I realized that she was falling for his charms, I told her he was married and forbad her from going to his office any more, but she just laughed at me and told me she did not need me any more and that he was going to leave his wife to be with her."

"Which is what he did," said Rusty.

"Thank you Herr Schmidt for answering all of our questions so honestly," said Digger, "we really appreciate your assistance today, is there anything else you would like to say before you leave?"

"Simply that I have nothing to hide gentlemen, my conscience is clear, everything I did was fair and above board, but I cannot answer for anything my niece may have done without me. There is one thing however, that you may be able to clarify for me, about your Mr. Davis," the old man said.

"If we can, what is it you want to know," said Digger.

"The bank robbery at the branch in Sydney, where he worked before he came to Melbourne, did it really happen and was he the 'inside man' as he boasted to my niece, or was that just another one of his lies?"

The two men looked at each other in amazement and then Rusty replied, "Neither my colleague nor myself were working for the bank at that time, but I don't recall my father, who was working for the bank then, ever talking about a bank robbery in Sydney before the War and I am sure I would have remembered it, so I suspect it was just another of Don's lies. Anyway, thank you so much Herr Schmidt for coming in and speaking with us today and I will ask my secretary to order a taxi to take you home, goodbye."

That afternoon, Digger, Rusty, Rusty's boss and the Melbourne Security Manager, all met to discuss the information that Hans Schmidt had given them at the morning interview.

"I can confirm that the old man was correct when he told you that Don Davis worked in the Sydney City Branch of the Bank in January nineteen thirty eight when it was robbed of a shipment of gold coins and cash," the Security Manager stated.

"Was it ever suggested that the gang had an 'inside man', in the bank?" asked Digger.

"Officially no, but un-officially yes; at least one possibly two 'inside men'," Rusty's boss confirmed.

"How much did they get away with?" Rusty asked.

"If my memory serves me correctly, ten canvas security bags containing two thousand gold sovereigns in each and a further six thousand three hundred pounds in assorted notes."

"Was any of it ever recovered?" asked Rusty.

"According to the files, a couple of thousand pounds in notes, was recovered from some of the gang when they were arrested, but not a single sovereign was ever found," the Security Manager stated.

"Did this particular branch of the bank regularly take delivery of gold coins?" Digger enquired.

"Not according to the files," said the Security Manager, "it was a one off delivery, which is why it had to be an inside job, probably involving someone at the bank and possibly the security guards who delivered the coins. It also appears that Don Davis was interviewed by the police on several occasions, but since he had been knocked unconscious by one of the robbers, before they escaped with the gold coins, he was declared a hero by the Board and promoted to his next job, here in Melbourne, a few months later."

"Gentlemen, let us not rush into any idle speculation about Mr. Davis's role in this robbery," Rusty's boss declared.

"Where have we heard those sentiments before Digger?" Rusty whispered to him.

"Thank you Johnston that will do. I think the first thing we have to do, is to interview Don's wife Ivy, who I gather now works for the Bank. Firstly we need to find out if she can confirm the story about the ring he purchased from Herr Schmidt and secondly, whether she knew anything about his involvement in the bank robbery. You two do that tomorrow," he said to Digger and Rusty, "and we will all meet here again on Friday morning."

"Hello Rusty, this is an unexpected pleasure," Ivy Hunt said, when called into her manager's office, early the next day.

"Hello Ivy, nice to see you, how have you been?" said Rusty, rising from his chair and shaking hands with her.

"Not too bad considering all things, I assume this meeting is about the death of Don and his mistress, is it?"

"Yes it is Miss Hunt," said the manager, "these two gentlemen are from Head Office and would like to speak with you privately, which I have told them is most out of order and I will only leave you alone with them, if you feel completely comfortable about it."

"Thank you sir, that is very considerate of you, but I am sure I will be quite all right, I have known Rusty for some time now," she answered.

The manger got up and left and Digger was introduced, simply as a colleague of Rusty's and the two men went over the previous morning's discussion with Hans Schmidt.

"Well it is absolutely true, Don did buy me a ruby ring from a man he met while doing that job and I do still have it. It was probably the nicest thing he ever gave me and it was certainly the last thing he gave me, because it was shortly after he gave me the ring, that he met that Ursula woman and started to go out with her and ignored me."

"But what about the bank robbery in Sydney, did he ever talk to you about that?" asked Rusty.

"Not really, he certainly enjoyed being called a hero and all the prestige it brought him, Don was a very vain man. I do remember hearing him talking on the telephone late at night once and he was getting very agitated with whoever was on the other end and he finished up by saying, 'that huge ape should not have hit me so hard, he almost killed me'."

"That's interesting," said Digger, "you have no idea what the rest of the conversation was about?"

"Money that he owed to his bookmaker, I think. He was being pressured as usual and I think this person owed Don some money and wasn't going to pay up, or something like that."

"Are you are able to hazard a guess as to who this person might have been on the telephone?" asked Digger.

"I thought at one point it may have been his previous manager in Sydney, Mr. Offstrop, but he was getting so angry with him, that I decided it couldn't be, Don was always a bit scared of him when he worked for him, he was a peculiar man!"

"You were never tempted to ask him about the conversation?" said Rusty.

"Don had always had a violent streak, I learnt very early in our marriage not to get on his wrong side," she replied, rubbing her face subconsciously.

"Well thank you Ivy, you have been most helpful," said Rusty, "plenty of food for thought, eh Digger?"

"Are you by any chance the man that Don tried to kill?" Ivy asked.

"Yes I am," Digger replied, "but if it is any comfort to you, I really do not believe that Don wanted to kill me, the woman was urging him on the whole time."

"Makes no difference now, does it? But I am glad you are safe, I understand that you only recently got married and came out to Australia immediately afterwards, is that right?"

"It is and my wife is expecting our first child, so it has not been an easy year for her either."

"I didn't know Moira was expecting, you dark horse you, we should go out and celebrate tonight," Rusty suggested.

"Typical men! The woman does all the hard work and the men get to celebrate," Ivy joked. "I have just had a thought Rusty, Don had a whole file of newspaper clippings and other notes on the robbery, I was going to throw them all out in the near future, would either of you like them?"

"We certainly would," Rusty replied, "I don't suppose we could pop round to your house now could we and get them, I have my car outside?"

With the manager's approval, Ivy, Digger and Rusty went round to her house and they waited outside while she went in and got the box-file containing the clippings and notes.

"Here we are Rusty and good luck with them, frankly I am pleased to see the back of them, but I truly hope that Don was not involved in the robbery, it would be nice to have some good memories of him."

Early the next morning Rusty's boss, the Security Manager, Digger and Rusty met once again to discuss the robbery.

"I have spoken with the other Board Members Mr. Smith and they have instructed me to tell you, that as of this moment, you are appointed to head up a fresh enquiry into the 1938 robbery at our City Branch in Sydney. I am sorry Rusty, but I am also instructed to inform you that you are not permitted to take any further part in this investigation."

"But why sir, what have I done?" Rusty asked.

"You have done nothing young man, but your father was a manager with the bank at that time and whilst there is absolutely no suggestion that he had any involvement in this whole sorry affair, the Board have decided that Mr. Smith, who did not even work for the Bank or live in Australia when the robbery occurred, is the ideal person for the job."

Rusty had the good sense not to push the matter any further and the Security Manager then handed over the Bank's own files on the robbery to Digger, assuring him of any further support that he might require.

"I talked with Mr. Newgate yesterday," Rusty's boss informed him, "and he will make a separate secure office available for you as soon as you return to Perth, along with a document safe to keep all of these papers in. Is there anything that you would like to say to me Mr. Smith?"

"Thank you sir, for the opportunity to lead this investigation and for the Board's confidence in me. I will need to travel to Sydney at some stage to visit the branch and gather information and there may be a requirement to talk to people who no longer work for the bank. I suspect I will also need an assistant to help with the paperwork and since my wife is pregnant with our first child and has not been too well this week, I may need some time off in the ensuing weeks and months to be with her."

"We understand all that Mr. Smith and Mr. Newgate has been authorized to sign off your expenses. Please remember though, that this is not a police investigation but is primarily a Bank Internal Audit on our procedures, to make sure that this kind of event could not happen again. You can go where you want within Australia and speak to whomever you need to; no doors will be closed to you. Anyone you second to assist you from within the bank must have only recently come to work for us and should not be connected in any way, with anyone who worked for the bank in 1938. Is that all clear to you?"

"Yes sir," Digger replied.

"Would you two gentlemen mind leaving us now, as there are some personal matters I wish to speak with Mr. Smith about."

Rusty and the Security manager left the office and Rusty's boss turned to Digger and said, "I was not being quite honest with Rusty when I said that his father had no involvement in this affair. The Security manager had a quick read through the file yesterday and noticed that the original investigation had talked to Nugget about a parcel he had sent to the City Branch a few weeks before the robbery, but the supporting documentation and statements are missing from the file and we suspect that if Don Davis was involved, then he might have removed them. Now, whilst we have no reason to believe that there was anything suspicious about the parcel, I considered it prudent, to be on the safe side and leave Rusty out of the investigation."

"I have to tell you sir, that I view Nugget and his wife as friends of mine and I just cannot believe that he would ever do anything underhanded or dishonest, or that would not be in the bank's best interests," Digger replied, slightly shocked.

"I am very pleased to hear you say that, as I too have known him for many years and share your sentiments entirely, so please do not let what I have just said concern you. I should say Mr. Smith, that the Board has asked me to tell you that they are promoting you to the position of Senior Internal Audit Manager and are watching you most carefully to see how you handle this whole matter. The Bank needs fresh young minds and you have certainly impressed people during your short time with us."

"Thank you sir, that is most generous of the Board."

"Time is getting on and I know you have a plane to catch Mr. Smith, so I suggest you leave now and return to Perth and get yourself thoroughly grounded in all the details of the robbery. Here are my personal telephone numbers for work and for home, so feel free to ring me at any time, if you need my help or support."

It was gone seven when Digger finally got home and he found Moira and Pat sitting on the patio enjoying a cool drink and chatting together.

"Hello you two," he said, as he walked through to join them holding a ginger beer he had taken from the fridge.

"Digger, we waited dinner for you, how was the trip?" said Moira as she got up from her chair and kissed him, on her way to the kitchen.

"Great thanks, how have you been?"

"Much better, I went to work yesterday and today and managed just fine, but I have been told not to do any more lifting," Moira informed him.

"How has she really been Pat?" he asked.

"She has been well but very tired, I don't think she can carry on working for much longer, as we will start to get hotter days again soon and that hospital can get very warm and stuffy."

"Pat has to be somewhere tomorrow morning Digger, so would you mind taking her home after dinner please."

Digger talked about Melbourne and the restaurants he and Rusty went to but was evasive about the work he had done and Moira had the sense to realize he did not want to talk about it, so they talked about nothing important and then over coffee

Moira announced, "The agent came round this afternoon and said the landlord was happy to give us a full years lease, since we had been such good tenants. It appears she still writes to the lady, two doors down, who has been singing our praises, so that's one thing less to worry about. I said you would drop the papers round to his office tomorrow."

"Right-o, anything else come through the mail?"

"Yes, we had a letter from Donny yesterday, it's on the sideboard if you want to read it," she informed him.

Digger got up and fetched the letter and sat down and read it.

"I guess the troubles in Egypt prompted them to go to New Zealand via Panama rather than the Suez, but I don't suppose there is much in it, time wise. Did you know that they were traveling with Victoria and Bertie, Moira?"

"Yes, I told you, Vi got a letter from Hazel and she told her about their arrangements. Do you never listen to what I tell you?"

"Goodness, Moira, it's only next Wednesday that they arrive in Auckland and then Bertie and Victoria are going on to Sydney to spend a week there with Vicky, before they fly over to Perth arriving here on the second of September. Better put it in the diary so we can go and pick them up, in their car!"

Digger took Pat home and thanked her for staying with Moira and took the opportunity to say that he might have to go on one or two more trips in the next few weeks and would she be prepared to stay with Moira again.

"I would be delighted to Digger, we have really got to know each other this week and thoroughly enjoy each other's company," Pat informed him.

He drove himself home and found Moira had gone to bed as she was feeling tired, so he made them a hot drink and went to bed to join her and tell her what had been happening to him in Melbourne.

"You were a bit mysterious over dinner," she said, "what is this investigation all about, or can't you even tell me that."

"In short no, I can't I'm afraid. The Board have asked me to carry out a review of the Bank's procedures in light of some new evidence that has come to hand regarding a bank robbery which happened in January 1938."

"Goodness Digger, you sound like a lawyer. Let me guess, it has all to do with what happened to you at Southern Cross and that Don Davis."

"How did you work that out?" he asked in disbelief.

She rubbed her nose with her forefinger and said, "Let's call it women's intuition. I hope they gave you a raise to do this important investigation."

"Well they did actually, Miss smarty pants, I am now the Senior Internal Audit Manager. Impressed?"

"Ever so," she said, "you come here a moment please Mr. Smith."

Chapter 16
The City Branch

Digger spent the next week and a half, finishing off the Reports he needed to write on the Internal Audit work he had already completed and agreeing a list of modified procedures with the new man who was in charge of the Northam office. He then carried out a final Internal Audit on the branch in Collie and once more made recommendations to improve the security for the counter staff and then he spent a few days handing everything over to his assistant.

"Any idea how long this special project is going to take and whether there is any chance of this temporary appointment becoming permanent Digger?" the man asked, delighted to be appointed as the new temporary Internal Audit Manager for Perth.

"The project could take a few weeks or a few months, there is no way of telling where it will lead me and what I will discover about all that went on back then. To answer your other question, I think it will all depend on how the Board perceive the work I do and the results I achieve, but if I am being perfectly honest, I loved the pace of life and all the action in Melbourne, it was a lot more like London than Perth will ever be, so I doubt that I will be wanting my old job back, so I think you could well be here for the long term; but please keep that to yourself."

"Right you are and thanks. By the way, I was thinking about what you were saying yesterday, about needing an assistant to work with you on the project and I reckon that Roger Cousins in the Securities Department could be your man. He is in his early twenties, single and has only been with the bank for eighteen months and came out from England,

Manchester I think, about two and a half years ago. He seems a very decent chap and could well be worth talking to."

Digger followed up on the suggestion and as it turned out Roger was delighted to be asked to work with him, on the Special Sydney Project, as it had become known in the bank. His manager, however, was not willing to let him go for at least another two months, so it took a phone call from Mr. Newgate to the Securities Manager, to secure his immediate release.

On the seventeenth of August, Digger and Roger took up residence on the top floor of the bank, in a large office just down the corridor from Mr. Newgate's and with permission to use his secretary if required, to book appointments and make travel arrangements.

Digger explained in detail what the investigation was all about and asked Roger to sign a document saying that he would not communicate any of the findings at any point in time, to anyone outside the bank, a copy of which, Digger had already been asked to sign himself.

The first task was to analyze all the witness statements from the bank's own files, crosschecking, names, dates and timings with each other, looking for any anomalies that the original investigation may have missed. After a couple of days of independently doing this, they started to compare notes.

"Did you see that statement by a witness who was walking down the side street behind the bank, at the time of the robbery, that a car was parked outside the back entrance to the bank with its bonnet up?" asked Roger.

"Yes I did read that and of course, it later turned out to be the car that two of the robbers used to make their getaway in, with the sacks of gold coins," Digger replied.

"The police said that the driver claimed that the car had points problems and that the man, was out for a ride with his family when it happened to break down outside the bank and that he had just about got it going again, when the two men came out, held a gun to his wife's head and told him to drive off," said Roger.

"Most peculiar," said Digger, "surely no-one in his right mind takes his wife and kids on a bank robbery, if he is the getaway driver, for fear of them getting hurt; but when the police spoke to the children about it all, they were completely un-phased by what had happened and the wife never made a statement, apart from confirming what her husband told the police."

"How long do you estimate the whole robbery took, from start to finish?" Roger asked.

"Hard to say," Digger replied, "some of the bank employees said it took more than ten minutes, others less, about five or six minutes. As most of the robbers were already in the bank when the gold arrived, it did not take long for them to draw their guns and force the guards to carry the sacks through to the back office."

"No, hold on, I think I read somewhere, that there was a trolley already in the bank and that was used to transport the sacks through to the back office, so it may have just been one of the guards and one of the robbers who went through, we need to check that out, as it may be important."

"Good point, but anyway, all the security guards were brought to the front of the bank and made to lie on the floor, with all of the customers and just one robber stayed through in the back, where Don Davis had been working with one of the younger clerks. According to Don's statement, which we now know might not be correct, the robber forced him to open the back door, which allowed the big man to come in, who punched him in the face and knocked him out and whom the police presumed, had carried the gold out to the car."

"Surely that means that the car outside had to be the getaway car and whereas the police believed they were dealing with a highly professional team of bank robbers, they were in fact a bunch of amateurs, who got lucky," Roger suggested.

"Or un-lucky as it turned out," said Digger, "for we cannot forget the mysterious tip-off the police received, just about the time that the robbery started. It meant that they were on the scene pretty sharpish and were able to apprehend the driver of one of the other getaway cars which was parked in front of the bank, which they chased from the scene."

"What do you make of the manager's statement that he was in the basement, looking at some old ledgers, the whole time the robbery was in progress?" Roger asked.

"The police account states that they found him in the basement and the door had been locked from above, which of course Don Davis confirmed, saying that he had been ordered to lock it by the robber. What is worrying me about all this," said Digger thoughtfully, "is that I have not worked with any manager yet, who would risk getting his suit covered in dirt and cobwebs, to go and look at an old ledger in a basement store room. He would normally tell one of his junior clerks which ledger he wanted and the clerk would go down and fetch it, clean it and give to him in his office."

"So what do you suggest we do next?" Roger asked.

"I will continue my analysis and arrange to travel to Sydney next week and you track down what has happened to the manager Mr. Offstrop and the rest of the staff, as I would like to interview as many of them as I can find."

Digger flew to Sydney the following Tuesday, having arranged for Pat to stay with Moira while he was away. Mr. Newgate's secretary had booked him into a very pleasant hotel, overlooking Sydney Harbour and first thing Wednesday morning, he met with the Sydney Security Manager, who had already been instructed to render any help to Digger that he might request.

"I gather this is all to do with the 1938 robbery," the Manager said, after the usual introductions and pleasantries.

"That is correct," Digger replied, "look, the official line is that I am investigating the robbery, since it was the biggest in the bank's history, with a view to seeing what lessons can be learnt, in order to update our security procedures."

"And un-officially, what are you really doing?"

"As you joined the bank after the date of the robbery, I have been given permission to tell you the truth. New information has come to light, which would suggest that the robbery may have been an inside job. We now suspect at least one, maybe two or more bank employees were actually involved and may even have planned and orchestrated the entire theft of the gold coins."

"I see, well I cannot say I am surprised Digger. There have been rumours for years that old Offstrop had something to do with it. As soon as he took early retirement and then went off abroad to live, tongues started wagging, but no-one upstairs would hear a word against him."

"I read in his file that he suffered a mild heart attack and was not at all well after the robbery and went to New Zealand to live, an ageing parent to look after, or something like that."

"I believe he did to start with, but someone I worked with got an unsigned postcard from Mauritius one day and she recognised that the address was in his hand writing. I remember her saying 'he always liked to gloat as to how much cleverer than the rest of us he was', but whether that was a holiday or he had moved there permanently, you will have to find out yourself. Perhaps the Pensions Department will be able to give you his current address."

"That is interesting, has the branch manager been informed that I am visiting him this afternoon?" Digger asked.

"He has and I have told him that I would be coming with you, assuming you don't mind that is."

Before he left for the branch, Digger telephoned Rusty's boss to give him an update and to mention that the Security Manager wanted to accompany him to the branch. He was told to wait for another half hour before he left the office. When he called round to collect the other man, his secretary informed him that he was having an unexpected meeting with his director and that a car had been arranged to take Digger to the branch on his own.

Having purchased a new camera in Perth, before he left for Sidney, along with several rolls of film, Digger took pictures of the front and back of the bank and was in fact in the process of doing this when he was stopped by a policeman, who asked him what he was doing and insisted on going into the bank with him and speaking with the manager, before he was satisfied that nothing untoward was going on.

"The front of the bank was completely rebuilt the year after the robbery, but the back office is pretty much the same as it was then," the Manager informed him.

"Were you or any of the staff working here at the time of the robbery?" Digger asked.

"No afraid not, apart from Mrs. Taylor, that is, but she was just a junior then."

"I would like to speak with her in private if I may, do you have an office I can use please."

"Yes of course, you can use my assistant manager's office, next door to mine. If you would like to make yourself comfortable, I will ask my secretary to bring you some tea and tell Mrs. Taylor to come and see you."

Digger moved in next door and tea and biscuits for two were brought in and a very nervous Mrs. Taylor, knocked on his door.

"Come in Mrs. Taylor," said Digger, rising to meet the lady and shaking her hand before inviting her to sit down and offering her a drink.

"The Manager said I was to talk to you about the robbery that happened here, before the War," she said nervously.

"That's right, I gather from the manager, that you were actually here when it happened. Perhaps you could just tell me what you remember, but take your time, there is no hurry."

Mrs. Taylor slowly told her story and Digger realized that the experience, albeit over twelve years ago, was still very fresh in her mind and she was able to relate what had happened to her that day, with confidence and in detail.

"So let me get this straight, you were not actually in the front office when the robbery commenced, but were in the back office working with Mr. Davis."

"Yes sir, that is correct," she replied.

"Mrs. Taylor you and I are obviously about the same age and I would much prefer it, if you called me Digger."

"Marjorie, my name is Marjorie, Digger. You don't sound Australian!"

"Just a nickname from my youth. So what exactly were you and Mr. Davis doing in the back office."

"Nothing. We weren't doing anything, we were just working on some old ledgers together."

"I was given to understand that the manager was down in the basement, working on old ledgers, so why were you two not down with him?

"Mr. Davis and I had been doing Ledger work together for a week or two, but we never worked down there in the basement, it was just a store and it was filthy and the lighting was poor. I remember that the manager was in a funny mood that day; he only joined us a few minutes before the robbery began and said there was something from the previous year he wanted to check out."

"Did he often work down there on his own?" Digger asked.

"Not that I know of, but he and Mr. Davis were always last to leave the office, so he may have gone down there after I had left, I just do not know."

"So why didn't he come upstairs when the robbery was in progress. Surely he would have wanted to know what was going on in his bank and to check on the safety of his staff?"

"I have never thought about that," she said, "mind you the door to the basement was locked, so he couldn't have come up if he had wanted to."

"Are you sure the door was locked Marjorie?"

"Oh yes, a couple of weeks earlier, one of the clerks almost broke his neck when he leant against the door and fell down the stairs, so from then on, it was locked at all times, whether someone was down there or not."

"What happened when the security men brought the sacks of gold through to where you were?"

"I was frightened out of my life. The door burst open and a man in a mask came in and pointed a gun at us and then a security guard came in, pushing a small trolley, with all the sacks of gold on it and a second robber with a gun came and stood in the doorway behind them."

"You must have been terrified," Digger commented.

"I was, but Mr. Davis told me not to be frightened and to stay calm."

"Can you remember whether the trolley belonged to the bank or the security guards or the robbers brought it with them?" Digger asked.

"Oh it was the bank's trolley. Mr. Offstrop had asked me to fetch him three heavy ledgers a few weeks before and I struggled to carry them through to him and got my clothes dirty, so Mr. Davis ordered the trolley for us, so no-one would have to struggle like that again in the future. He was very considerate like that, Mr. Davis."

"So I hear," Digger said, "if I remember correctly Marjorie, you and the security guard then went back into the front office with the robber by the door, leaving Mr. Davis and the other robber in the back office."

"It wasn't quite like that Digger. The other two did leave, I mean the guard and the second robber but I was told to stay and help Mr. Davis count the gold sovereigns."

"I don't remember reading about that in any of the statements you all made," said Digger, "but please carry on."

"The robber who stayed behind had put one of the sacks on the table and then cut it open with a knife and some of the coins fell onto the floor. He told Mr. Davis and me to pick them up and then count out three piles of two hundred gold coins each, onto the table beside the open sack. While we were picking the coins up, the robber must have been distracted, because Mr. Davis touched my arm to get my attention and then slid three or four coins into his shoe and intimated that I should do the same, which I did. When we had finished counting the coins into the three piles, I was told to go through and join everyone else in the front office."

"And is that what you did?" asked Digger.

"Yes, but as I was just going through the door, I remembered that I had left my handbag on the shelf by the window, so I turned round and asked if I could take it and Mr. Davis said I could and just then, there was a knock on the back door and the robber told Mr. Davis to open it and then that other huge man came bursting in, waving a gun around and I almost fainted in fright."

"So was there some reason that you did not mention counting the coins in your statement to the police?" Digger enquired.

"Well sort of Digger; Mr. Davis made his statement before me and told me that he had said he was on his own when he counted the coins and had forgotten that I was with him and that as it did not matter whether it was one or two of us, could I not mention it in my statement. So I didn't. I was young and still very frightened and Mr. Davis told me afterwards that the robber had threatened both him and me, if they should ever be caught."

"Did you happen to see what happened to the piles of coins you counted out on the table?"

"Not to start with, but as I was getting my handbag, I noticed that two of the piles of coins had gone and the robber was putting the third pile back into a security bag."

"Do you mean back into the bag he had cut, or one of the bags on the trolley?"

"It wasn't the cut bag and I don't think it was one from the trolley, as that was over the other side of the room, away from the window. I am not sure where the sack came from, but I had the sense that it was different somehow, to the others."

"How strange," said Digger, "are you sure about all this?"

"Oh dear, now I am all flustered; I am certain that is what happened, but it was all so terrifying that I might be wrong."

"So when did the big man punch Mr. Davis and knock him out?"

"I don't know, it must have happened after I left, but his eye was bloodshot and his face was swollen, he was lucky that there was no permanent damage."

"What happened to the coins you put in your shoe Marjorie?"

"I brought them in and gave them to Mr. Davis the next day, but he said that the bank would like me to keep them, in recognition of my heroism, wasn't that nice of them?"

"Yes it was, do you still have them by any chance?"

"Oh yes, I could never get rid of them. Would you like to see them?

"I most certainly would, could you bring them in tomorrow for me please."

They chatted for another half hour or so and then Mrs. Taylor returned to work and Digger talked with the manager for a while in his office and then they walked through to inspect the back office together.

"So this room is the same as it was in 1938 then," Digger said.

"To the best of my knowledge it is," the Manager replied, "give or take the odd coat of paint and some new lino on the floor; Oh and we replaced the bars on the windows and back door a couple of years ago."

"Would you mind opening the back door for me please and the door to the basement storage area," Digger asked.

The manager went back to the office to get his keys and returned with the Chief Cashier. First the manager opened the door to the basement and switched the light on, he then used his key to open the top lock and the Chief Cashier used his key to open the bottom lock of the back door. The Chief Cashier then waited while Digger went outside and took some photographs, looking out onto the street from the doorway and then took some from the street, looking into the bank.

He then came back inside and the door was locked once again by the two men.

"Has that door always required two keys to open it?" Digger asked.

"It certainly has," the manager confirmed. "The locks were only upgraded a year ago, but the two key principal has been around as long as I have worked for the bank."

"What is kept in that cupboard on the wall over there?" Digger asked, pointing to a large wooden cupboard on the far wall.

"It's not a cupboard, it's a hoist, to get heavy ledgers up from the basement; those stairs can be lethal, if you are carrying something when climbing them."

"Has the hoist always been there?" Digger enquired.

"I think so, I will check with Mrs. Taylor."

"Would you mind asking her if it was in working order on the day of the robbery, please."

The manager left and spoke with Mrs. Taylor and returned a few minutes later.

"She said it was there in 1938 and it was in excellent working order as it had only been serviced the week before. Why do you ask?"

"Not sure really, just a hunch, that something your Mrs. Taylor told me does not fit with the official record, but hey, look at the time. Is it all right if I come back tomorrow and you and I spend some time rummaging around in the basement."

"Of course it is, but I advise you to bring some work clothes with you and I will organize some extra lighting."

With which they went through to the front office and the manager went back to his own office and Digger went back to his hotel to think about all he had discovered and to ring Moira later in the evening.

"Hi love, how are you and Fred doing today?" he asked.

"We are just fine Digger and I wish you wouldn't call the baby Fred, it might be a girl, remember. How were things in Sydney today?"

"Very interesting, I met a lady who was working in the branch when it all happened and she has thrown a completely new light on the whole incident. In fact, I am going back to the branch tomorrow to check out their basement, so it was a good job you suggested that I brought some work clothes with me."

"By the way, Donny called from New Zealand last night to say they have arrived safely and taken a room with Deborah's friends in Auckland and will probably stay there for a few weeks, while they look for somewhere to rent. He also said that Bertie and Victoria are flying into Sydney this Thursday, not next week as his letter implied and that they will be stopping in a hotel in town, as Vicky was not able to put them up as they had hoped."

"Thursday you say, well perhaps I should arrange to meet up with them. Did Donny say which hotel?"

She gave him the name of the hotel and they chatted for a bit longer and he told her that he was not sure when he would be coming back and she said not to worry, which of course meant, 'come home soon'.

He then called Roger in Perth and they chatted about what he had discovered in the branch and the fact that a sack had been cut open and at least six hundred sovereigns removed.

"Did you take Don Davis's press cuttings with you by any chance?" Roger enquired.

"Yes, but I haven't had time to go through them yet, why do you ask?" Digger replied.

"Well there must be a few cuttings missing from the company's file and I wondered if Don had taken them and put them in his own file."

"Anything in particular you want me to look for?"

"I was reading about the robber who escaped with the money and whom the police hunted, but could not find. They thought he had eventually left Sydney by boat, but I could not discover what happened to him after that, so if you get a moment, would you mind checking Don's file of press cuttings for me please."

Digger arrived at the branch at the same time as the Manager and they went in together and chatted for a while over the customary 'cup of tea' and then went down to the basement together. They set up the extra lighting and began going through all the cupboards and boxes, looking for something which Digger said 'should not be there'.

"It would really help if I knew what I was looking for," the Manager confided.

"I am sorry, but there has to be some reason that Mr. Offstrop was down here and I cannot believe it had anything to do with old ledgers," Digger replied.

"Surely whatever it is, would have gone by now," the manager suggested, after having sorted through another dirty box of old books and files.

"I don't think so. Both Don Davis and the manager left the branch shortly after the robbery and what better place to hide something, than somewhere no-one wants to go. Would you mind giving me a hand moving this large chest away from the wall please," Digger asked.

The two men struggled to move the chest away from the wall and as they stepped on the flagstone that the chest had been resting on, it wobbled under their feet.

"That doesn't feel right," said Digger, "I don't suppose you brought a shovel with you today."

"Afraid not, but I do have a couple of large tyre levers in the boot of my car, which is parked about fifty yards away; it's time we took a break anyway," the manager replied.

They went back upstairs and the Manager got his car keys and the two men strolled down to his car and got the tyre leavers and a rope from the boot and after several cups of tea, they went back down the stairs to the basement.

It took them almost half an hour to loosen the wobbly flagstone enough to lever it up and get the rope under it and lift it out. It only took another five minutes to remove some of the earth and retrieve the first of the Sydney Mint currency sacks that had been buried underneath the flagstone.

"Look at this one," the manger said, holding up one of the sacks with a jagged cut across the top of it, "what do you make of that Digger?"

"That fits with what Mrs. Taylor told me yesterday, how many sacks do we have altogether now?"

"Ten including the one that has been cut open," the Manager replied. "In that case, if there are ten sacks here, what did the robbers use to carry the coins away in?"

"Good question, obviously something else, or the coins never left the bank that day and Mr. Offstrop and Mr. Davis carried them out a few at a time, over the ensuing weeks," Digger suggested.

"So you think they were both in on it then?" the Manager asked.

"They had to be for all sorts of reasons, but when Mrs. Taylor told me yesterday that it was only Don who unlocked the back door to let the big man in, who purportedly carried the gold out to the car, it meant that Mr. Offstrop had already unlocked one lock with his key, before going downstairs."

"So Davis and the robber loaded the gold onto the hoist and sent it downstairs, where Offstrop unloaded it. Very clever, so I wonder where the gold is now?"

"Not only that, but what was in the sacks that were carried out to the car, obviously not the stolen gold coins!" Digger exclaimed.

They finished searching the rest of the basement and eventually emerged back upstairs in the early afternoon and after speaking with Mrs. Taylor again and checking that the gold coins she had picked up from the floor, were genuine sovereigns, they washed and changed their clothes and went out together for a late lunch. After the meal, the Manager returned to the bank and Digger headed back to his hotel and phoned the Melbourne office, to bring Rusty's boss up to date with what he had discovered.

He had just put the telephone down after calling Moira when it rang again and this time it was Roger, to find out how things had gone.

"But if Davis and Offstrop were in it together, how come Davis kept on working, whilst Offstrop disappeared. It sounds to me that not only were the robbers cheated of the gold, but Davis was as well and that Offstrop disappeared with the lot," Roger suggested.

"I agree Roger, I have come to the same conclusion. The robbers were simply a bunch of amateurs put together to create a smokescreen, while the bank's own employees, planned and implemented the perfect robbery. Which of course explains why the wife and children of the getaway car driver, were out with him, having a ride around town, when the bank was robbed."

"So you don't think the security guards who delivered the gold are implicated at all?" Roger asked.

"Absolutely not. The gold coins Mrs. Taylor showed me were the real thing."

"Did you let her keep them?"

"Oh yes, but I did ask her to hang onto them in case we needed them for evidence."

"Have you had a chance to look at Don's press cuttings yet?"

"Sorry, I forgot last night, I will do it later today, I promise."

Digger worked for several hours in the hotel, reading through Don Davis's press clippings, looking for the articles about the escaped robber. Eventually he found an article in the West Australian of March 1938 stating that the police and port authorities had recently searched the S.S. El Burro Volando II, when it docked in Broome, looking for the gold which had been taken from the robbery at the Perth Mining & Commerce Bank Ltd, City Branch earlier in the year.

It went on to say that the skipper, Captain Robert Bannister, had been interviewed by the police regarding the mysterious disappearance of one of the suspected robbers, a Mr. Thomas Raymond whom the police believed had got away with twenty thousand gold sovereigns, being the majority of the proceeds of the robbery. A picture of the suspect taken some years earlier, accompanied the article.

Captain Bannister was reported as saying that the man in question had been taken on as Second Mate in Sydney, under the assumed name of Bob Harwich and had come highly recommended and had carried out his duties aboard ship adequately.

Mr. Harwich had gone ashore in Geraldton and returned to the ship inebriated and had made the mistake of picking a fight with Captain Bannister, who was well known for his boxing ability and promptly knocked the much larger man out cold.

The man was taken to the rear of the ship to recover in the fresh air and it is believed that several hours later, when the ship was steaming somewhere in the region of Shark Bay, he came to and stood up, but became disorientated and fell overboard.

Captain Bannister sounded the alarm and stopped the ship and spent several hours searching for the man, but he was not found. Several crew members are reported as saying that they heard a man cry out, shortly after he had gone overboard and assumed he had been eaten by the sharks.

It is understood that no gold coins were found on the ship and no charges were made against Captain Bannister.

"Hello Victoria, it's Arnold, how was your flight?" he asked, when he telephoned their hotel later that evening.

"Arnold, how nice to hear form you again, the flight was fine thank you; we heard you were in Sydney, some investigation Mac said, to do with the new job."

"That's right Victoria, I was wondering if you and Bertie fancied having dinner with me this evening?"

"Sorry, but we have just eaten Arnold, what a shame, it would have been nice, perhaps tomorrow, if you are still in Sydney. Hold on here comes Bertie, I will put him on the phone to speak to you, goodbye for now."

"Hello Digger, how are you and Moira keeping my friend and congratulations on the baby and the new job, you must be really pleased with yourself."

"Thanks Bertie, we are fine, Moira has had the usual problems, but she was good when I left home on Tuesday. The job is going really well too."

"Some sort of special investigation Mac was saying, anything interesting?"

"As a matter of fact it is, extremely interesting and I was hoping you would actually be able to help me with something," Digger replied.

"What I know about banking, 'you could write on the back of a postage stamp', as my Great Uncle Harry, used to say. What is it you want to know my friend?"

"Were you ever captain of a ship which sailed from Sydney to Broome, called the S.S. El Burro Volando II, by any chance?"

"Goodness, you are going back a bit, but yes I was, why do you ask?"

"By some strange coincidence Bertie, I am investigating the robbery which took place at the Perth Mining & Commerce Bank Ltd, City Branch, in early 1938."

The telephone line went silent.

"Are you still there Bertie?"

"Yes Digger, I am still here."

"I have just read an article in the West Australian Newspaper from March 1938 saying that you were interviewed by the police in Broome, about the disappearance of a certain Mr. Thomas Raymond, who fell overboard in Shark Bay and about the gold he was suspected of stealing."

"Well I am sure you also read Digger, that the gold was not found on my ship and that Mr. Raymond fell overboard and was eaten by sharks."

"You are right Bertie, I did read that, but I would really be interested in talking to you, since you have first hand knowledge of the whole matter, which might help my investigation."

"I really don't think I can be of any help to you Digger, sorry," Bertie said firmly.

"Then you leave me no alternative but to speak with Mr. Raymond myself, or would I be correct in saying, with Mr. Raymond Thomas himself!"

"Damn you Digger, the man saved your life, show some gratitude and leave things alone."

"Believe me, I understand that, only too well, which is why I would rather talk with you about all this Bertie, than with him."

"Look, there's a coffee shop down on the Rocks, I will meet you there in thirty minutes," with which he slammed the telephone down and turned round to face his wife, who was standing there, open-mouthed, aghast at what she had just witnessed.

"Not now Victoria, not now," was all he said to her, before grabbing his hat and leaving the room.

Chapter 17
The Acacia Tree

As Digger walked down to the area known as 'The Rocks' from his hotel, he mulled over in his mind what he was going to say to Bertie and exactly how much of what he had found out, he should share with the man who had become such a good friend over the last two years. It was of course Bertie and Victoria who had been largely responsible for him and Moira leaving England and settling in Australia and for the introduction to Nugget and the job with the bank.

He was first to arrive at the café and found a table on its own towards the rear of the premises and ordered a cup of coffee and a ham roll, as he had suddenly realized he was feeling very hungry.

He waited for ten minutes and was beginning to wonder if Bertie had changed his mind, when the familiar figure of his friend appeared in the doorway and looked around the room. Digger waved and Bertie walked over to join him, ordering a coffee from the waitress as he passed the counter.

Digger stood up and stretched out his hand in the usual greeting and was relieved when Bertie took hold of it and shook it. They both sat down and looked at each other, wondering who should speak first, Digger deferring to the older man.

"It's all right my friend, you can relax, I have calmed down now," Bertie said, taking off his hat and putting it on the table. "I want you to know Digger that I fully realize that the information your investigation has found out about this robbery, has almost certainly placed you in a most difficult situation. So before we begin our discussion, I need to understand the exact nature of the investigation and what will happen with any new evidence which may come to light."

"Sounds fair to me Bertie, what specifically can I tell you?"

"Firstly, whether this is solely a bank review, or whether you have already involved the police in your investigation and secondly, whether any of your findings or discoveries, will be turned over to the police at the end of the investigation?"

"Well firstly, may I say a big thank you, for coming out tonight and for agreeing to speak with me," Digger replied, "and in answer to your questions, it is solely a bank review, which was triggered by something we found out about the man who tried to kill me, out at Southern Cross. The police have not been involved to date and I have no intention of involving them in regard to anything I have learnt so far. As regards my findings and recommendations resulting from the investigation, I will only be presenting those to the Board of Directors at the bank."

"But there is nothing to say that they won't pass on any of your findings to the police, if they so choose," Bertie suggested.

"I guess that is true, but it is twelve years since the robbery and the bank is only interested in recovering the gold, if possible and discovering if its own employees were involved at all. I do not believe that they are on a vendetta against any small time criminals, who may have been dragged into the scheme and it certainly would not be good for the bank's reputation, if it became public knowledge that a senior bank employee, masterminded the whole event."

"I see," said Bertie thoughtfully, "and has your investigation discovered anything so far, that would lead you to conclude that the mastermind behind the robbery was a senior bank employee?"

"Yes, it most definitely has. What I am about to tell you is confidential, but if I am going to ask you to help me, I believe you need to know, all that I have discovered in regard to the robbery. Please believe me when I say, that I am not out to hurt, expose or prosecute anyone, outside of the bank's own employees, who planned and participated in the theft of the gold coins and bank notes."

"O.K. then, I believe you Digger, you tell me what you have found out and I will help you if I am able."

Over the next hour or so, Digger explained in detail about what Hans Schmidt had said to them and how he believed Don Davis and Mr. Offstrop had planned and executed the robbery.

"There are obviously some things which I have not found out yet, so I would be interested to hear of anything you might have picked up during your time aboard ship, with Bob Harwich," Digger concluded.

"Very well, I did have several conversations with Bob Harwich but it is getting late and I am feeling very tired, plus I left a very upset Victoria in our hotel room when I came here to meet you, so can I suggest that we call it a night for now and pick it up again tomorrow morning."

"That is fine with me, where do you want to meet?"

"We had planned to see an old shipmate of mine tomorrow morning, who has a farm outside of town and I don't want to disappoint Victoria or Skip and Edna by canceling the trip, so may I suggest that if you could get hold of a car, we could all drive out there together and you and I could go for a long walk while we are there and I will tell you everything I know."

"Sounds good to me, but I will have to arrange to hire a car first; so suppose I come past and pick you up at the hotel about ten thirty, would that be all right?"

The two men finished their second cup of coffee and Bertie gave Digger a quick update on how Mac and Deborah were faring in New Zealand and then they parted company and returned to their respective hotels.

Victoria was sitting up in bed reading when Bertie returned to the room, anxious to know what had happened at the meeting and what had upset her husband so much.

"I thought you would still be awake and waiting for me," he said, as he got into his pyjamas and climbed into bed beside her.

"What on earth did Arnold say on the telephone that upset you so much and is everything all right between the two of you now?" she asked.

"It was all a terrible misunderstanding and we are good friends again, nothing to worry about Victoria. In fact I have invited him to come for a ride with us tomorrow. Do you remember me talking about Skip and his wife Edna a while back, well I thought it would be good to take you out to see their farm, the Acacia trees should be in flower about now and they are a truly beautiful sight and since Digger was free tomorrow, I invited him to come as well."

"Oh I am so relieved Bertie and I would love to meet your friends and see their farm and it will be good to hear all of Arnold and Moira's news as well."

The next morning Digger was awake early and wrote up all that he had discovered so far, including a separate note about his conversation with Bertie, the previous evening. He then telephoned Roger at home and told him what had been happening.

"So tell me again how you met this man that you are driving off to a remote farm with tomorrow," Roger said skeptically.

"I can't Roger, it's a friend of a friend and he only agreed to speak with me if I promised to keep his name out of it," Digger explained.

"Digger, this is your first trip to Sydney, are you sure it isn't someone already involved in the robbery, who is setting you up?"

"Good point, but I really do not believe so, you will have to trust me on this one Roger."

"This has absolutely nothing to do with my trusting you Digger, it has to do with your own safety, don't forget there has already been one attempt on your life. Look, just as an insurance policy, at least put all of your documents in the hotel safe along with a note as to who this person is. If you return safe and sound you can destroy the note and if you don't, I will know where to look for your killer."

Digger was stunned by this suggestion, but after careful consideration, he did what Roger had requested and deposited all of his paperwork in the hotel safe before he left the hotel.

He then picked up a car from the hire company, bought himself some maps from a local bookstore and arrived outside of Bertie and Victoria's hotel, promptly at ten thirty.

He had been waiting for five minutes when he spotted them walking down the road from the shops, clutching a large paper bag, so he got out of the car to greet them, "Over here Bertie, Victoria," he called out, "been spending all your money this morning?"

"Arnold, it is so good to see you again and looking so tanned and handsome," Victoria said, "sorry we are late, but Bertie only told me about the mosquitoes this morning, so I had to go and get some cream to put on, as I do not want another bought of malaria, thank you very much."

They all got into the car, with Bertie in the passenger seat next to Digger, who handed him the book of maps. It took Bertie a few minutes to locate the area the farm was situated in and to plot a route there, so they were soon on their way and catching up with each other's news.

"So Donny doesn't actually have a job yet?" Digger queried.

"Not yet, but he has been to see several employment agencies and one of them has found him a few days of contract work with the local council, which he starts next week," Victoria explained, "but Deborah was able to start with her Insurance company straight away and the friends of Bertie that they are staying with, Rosie and Brock are a really nice couple. Rosie has known Deborah since she left school hasn't she Bertie?"

"That is correct, she stopped with Rosie and her daughter for a few weeks and had a great time and Brock used to sail with me when I was sailing in these waters and in fact, it was through me that the two of them first met."

"You never told me that before," said Victoria.

Bertie ignored her last comment and said to Digger, "Take the next left up the hill and then turn sharp left again when you get to the top and if my memory serves me correctly, that should be the road to the farmhouse, assuming Skip has not moved it!"

To everyone's relief, the farmhouse was in the same place, but it still took a five minute drive down a dusty dirt road to locate it. When they arrived they could see an elderly couple, sitting on the front porch eating lunch, "Hey Digger go over and ask them if they happen to know where a mean old sea dog named Skip lives," Bertie suggested.

Digger walked up to the couple and called out, "Good morning folks, I was wondering if you could give me some directions please, my passenger in the front of the car, was trying to locate a mean old sea dog named Skip. Do you happen to know where he lives?"

The man jumped up, followed by his dog and walked past Digger, heading for the car, he opened the door where Bertie was sitting, stared in and then ordered his dog to 'seize'. The dog jumped in, sat on Bertie's lap and started to vigorously lick his face.

"Call him off Skip, he is filthy and smells, probably a bit like his owner," Bertie added under his breath.

"Here boy," Skip said, calling the dog to his side and turning round to face his wife shouted, "Edna, it's that old pirate Bertie Bannister and his wife, come and say hello."

Edna came over and hugged and kissed Bertie who had just got out of the car and was dusting himself off and then she gave Victoria the same treatment.

"We heard you were doing well for yourself Bertie, old friend, but having your own chauffeur driven car, I am most impressed!" Skip said.

They all walked up to the house and were taken inside and led into the front parlour, which was only kept for special guests and important occasions and Digger was introduced to Skip and Edna as a Pomey friend from England . As Digger needed to go to the bathroom shortly after arriving, Bertie took the opportunity to say to his friends, "On no account mention that you are in any way related to Ray Thomas, in front of Digger. I will explain why a bit later, but you and I Skip, need to take Digger on a tour of the farm before we leave, all right?"

Skip nodded and said to his wife, "Would you get some food for our guests Edna, while I get everyone a drink."

The atmosphere was a little strained for a while after Digger re-joined the group, but the food and drink and good company and stories from the past, soon lightened things up and everyone enjoyed themselves in each others company.

Victoria and Edna soon became firm friends and when Bertie suggested after lunch that the men take a ride round the farm, the women were happy to announce that they would stay behind to chat.

The three were about to drive off in the car Digger had hired, when Bertie whispered something in Skip's ear and he said, "Hold on guys, I need to get a couple of shovels from the shed," with which, he got out of the car, went back into the house, then went into the shed and came out with a couple of shovels that he put in the boot.

"Where to Bertie?" Skip asked, "anywhere in particular or just a general tour of the farm?"

"How about taking us to that old stock shed you showed me last time I was here," Bertie replied.

"Are you sure about that? I don't think I have even used it since then, not having the stock that I used to. Why don't we go down to the billabong, the acacias are in flower and look wonderful this year."

"Shed first please Skip, then the billabong," said Bertie firmly, "and I can fill you in about why we are really here, not that I hadn't planned to visit you and Edna anyway, you understand."

"I'll believe you Bertie, thousands wouldn't. Take the track heading off at two o'clock Digger and follow it for about three miles, the shed is the only thing on the horizon, you can't miss it."

While they drove, Bertie explained that Digger now worked for the bank that was robbed in January 1938 and was carrying out an investigation to see if any senior members of the bank had been involved in the robbery.

"Digger is particularly interested in your nephew, Tom Raymond and how he and his friends came to be involved in the robbery and how much gold was in the sacks that he carried away from the scene of the crime.," Bertie stated.

"I assume Digger is aware Bertie, that my nephew fell off the back of your boat somewhere between Geraldton and Shark Bay and was drowned or was eaten by sharks."

"Yes he is quite aware of that fact Skip and would be grateful of any other information, no matter how trivial, that you can give him, to help with his bank's internal investigation."

"Sorry to be blunt Bertie, but there is a lot at stake here, are you telling me that I can trust this man?" Skip asked.

"Yes I am," said Bertie, "anything you say is in strictest confidence and will not be written down and used against you, me, or anyone else we might both happen to know."

"Good enough, fire away Digger and I will do my best to answer you," Skip replied.

"Did your nephew have a criminal record before the robbery?"

"He had been in trouble with the police, for fighting and drunkenness, but he hadn't done anything really bad, like that before. He had crewed with me on my ship before I gave up the sea and had done a good job, but when I stopped, so did he."

"So how did someone like him get involved in a bank robbery?"

"This is what he told me," said Skip, "and I don't think he was lying to me, as he was pretty frightened when I got the story out of him. He was in the pub with his circle of mates one night, when a new man came in, well dressed, sharp looking, Tom said. The newcomer bought a round of drinks and got chatting to Tom and the other men. Now one of Tom's friends was a bit of a hard case with a criminal record and he and the new man went off into a corner to talk."

"Did Tom think that the two men knew each other already then?" Digger asked.

"He didn't think they knew each other, rather, that they knew of each other, if you understand what I mean. Anyway, the two men rejoined the group and the local man told a couple of the blokes to disappear, leaving Tom and six others to talk with them."

"Do you remember what the stranger was called?" Digger asked.

"No, Tom said he was about thirty five, average height, nothing that would make him stand out in a crowd, but he thought that he spoke with a slight South African accent. I know in the end, that the local man said they should refer to him as Phoenix, just so everyone knew who they were talking about."

"Strange name, why Phoenix I wonder," said Bertie.

"Tom wasn't sure but thought it had something to do with where he had come from," said Skip.

"So was Tom just brought in for his size and strength and ability to carry the sacks with the gold in," Digger asked.

"Yes I think so. Tom was told that he would have two sacks to carry, each weighing about thirty five pounds, so he said he practiced running with two milk churns, each with three and a half gallons in, to simulate the weight of the cold coins."

"How far was he expecting to run then?" Digger asked.

"They told him about a hundred yards."

"But that doesn't make any sense, because the getaway car was parked right outside the bank," Digger stated.

"No, that wasn't the right car. Phoenix gave all the men twenty pounds the week before to buy new overalls and heavy boots and hats to pull down over their eyes. Well it appears that the man who was supposed to drive the getaway car, which Tom and Phoenix were to use, took the twenty pounds and left town, so Tom roped in a mate of his at the last minute, who didn't properly understand the plan and just parked outside the back door of the bank."

"That explains why he was dressed differently to the rest of the gang and why his wife and children really did not know what was going on then," said Digger.

"Exactly, she had thought she was going into town to do some shopping and was horrified to find out her husband was acting as a getaway driver in a bank robbery. He told the kids it was a game, so they were not at all frightened by what happened."

"Amazing," said Digger, "did Tom say why he punched the man in the bank so hard in the face?"

"No, he never mentioned that, but this is the shed you wanted to see Bertie, shall we all get out and stretch our legs," Skip suggested.

They all got out of the car and walked into the shed and sat down on some upturned crates that they found there.

"Am I right in thinking Skip, that Tom stayed here for a while after the robbery?" Bertie enquired.

"That's right, the driver first took Phoenix to the station, then he dropped his wife and children back home and then brought Tom up to me at the farm. When the driver eventually got home he found the police waiting to interview him and he just kept to his story about breaking down outside the bank and being forced at gunpoint to drive the robbers away, having insisted he be allowed to take his wife and children home first. Since they could not find anything in his house to connect him to the robbery and of course never arrested Phoenix or Tom, they had to let him go."

"You asked earlier, about why Tom punched the man in the face, Digger. I was told that it had always been part of the plan but that in his rush to get away, he forgot to do it, so the man himself, reminded Tom and told him to do it," Bertie informed him.

"How strange, can you elaborate on that please Bertie?"

"It appears that this man Phoenix kept looking at his watch and saying that it was all taking too long and that the police would be coming soon and that Tom should pick up the two sacks and both of them should get out of the bank. Well Phoenix went out first and went to the car and Tom was about to follow, when the man in the bank shouted out, 'hey you big oaf, you are supposed to hit me before you leave, Tom ignored him and kept going, when the man followed him to the door and shouted again, 'hey you, stupid, I said hit me', so he did."

"He had a punch like a sledge hammer, the man must have been mad to have shouted at Tom like that," Skip commented.

"So I presume that this Phoenix took the sacks of gold coins with him to the station then," Digger said.

"No, Tom kept them as part of the deal. The man in the bank gave Phoenix a roll of bank notes and the two sacks of coins were the gangs share of the robbery, except that the sacks only had a few hundred coins in each at the top of the bag and the rest of the bag was filled with stones."

"I was also told the same story as that Digger," said Bertie, "because Tom had practiced carrying the churns of water, he knew how heavy the sacks should have been, so as soon as he picked them up, he knew something was wrong, but just thought that there was less coins in the bag than they had expected."

"No honour among thieves, it would seem," said Digger. "Did he share the coins out with the others or keep hold of them?"

"None of the gang came anywhere near him, the whole time he was hiding here, so he kept hold of the coins himself, besides about twenty that is, which he gave me to give to the driver, when everything had died down."

"And did you give them to him?"

"He wouldn't take them, said he thought the police were still watching him, so I gave him twenty pounds out of my own money and kept the coins," Skip explained. "I still have them hidden away, if you want them."

"I would like to see them, just to check they are genuine, but I don't need to keep them, thank you. Tell me about the money sacks, do you still have them?"

"I do, but they are buried, along with the gun and ammunition they gave Tom."

"What sort of a gun was it, can you remember?"

"A hand gun of some sort. But he couldn't have hurt anyone with it, as the ammunition they gave him was all blanks."

"Are you sure about that?" Digger asked.

"Oh yes, I had the sacks and the gun hidden in this shed, but after Tom drowned, Edna got very nervous every time anyone knocked on the door and told me to bury the sacks and gun somewhere safe, where no-one would ever find them. So I came out to here one evening, must have been about this time of the year and noticed a couple of foxes just down the hill there and thought I would use Tom's pistol to get rid of them, as I had not brought my shotgun with me. Anyway, I caught them unawares and fired a couple of shots at each of them and they simply jumped off and ran away, as the bullets were all blanks."

"Did you or Tom ever hear from this Phoenix again or from anyone at the bank?"

"No Digger, we think Phoenix went off back to South Africa, or wherever he came from, to share the loot with whoever had planned the job and had kept the rest of the gold."

"Do you happen to remember where you buried the sacks and the gun?"

"I think so, in fact the place is at our next port of call, the billabong, so shall we go."

They all got back into the car and Skip directed Digger down the side of another small hill and round a sharp bend, to a stretch of water, with trees lining the bank.

"This is Edna's billabong; it's her favourite place on the whole farm. She just loves to come here and sit and read and swim and fish and sometimes we bring a picnic and sometimes we just sleep out under the starts."

"It's just beautiful Skip and what is the name of the tree with the magnificent yellow flowers over there, just past the rock?" Digger asked.

"That tree is a Cootamundra Wattle," Skip replied, as they were all getting out of the car. "When I buried the sacks it was just a young sapling, but look at it now, it is a magnificent specimen. If you two get the shovels out of the car and meet me by the rock, we can all go treasure hunting."

Digger and Bertie retrieved the shovels from the boot of the car and joined Skip who was now standing on the rock. I had to write a poem to help me remember where the spot was, so here goes, he said and recited out loud,

"Step off the rock and cross the ground
Three whole paces and the treasure's found.
Dig with the spade and sing this song
Neath the yellow blossom, by the billabong."

"Encore, encore," shouted Bertie, "but I think you were a better skipper that you are a poet my friend."

Skip smiled and bowed and then announced, "This is the spot, dig here, its about two feet down and the items are in a small wooden crate."

Digger and Bertie started to dig the hole, but just got in each other's way, so Bertie stepped back to where Skip was standing and watched the younger man work. When Digger stopped for a rest, Skip took over and seemed to be removing twice the amount of earth that Digger had managed with the same shovel. When Skip stopped, Bertie took over and he had only removed a few shovelfuls of earth, when he hit something solid and proceeded a lot more carefully, until he had uncovered the top two inches of a wooden box.

"If you just lever up that corner Bertie, the lid should come off," Skip informed him, which is what he proceeded to do.

"It's only the money sacks I am interested in," said Digger, "I suggest we leave the gun and ammunition here and fill the hole back in."

The sacks were carefully removed from the crate and were passed to Digger for his inspection. Although they were filthy and some bits were now rotten, it was obvious to Digger that they were indeed the sacks which had been used to carry the coins away from the bank and clearly printed across the front of each sack were the words 'Perth Mint'.

The gun and ammunition were left in the box and the lid pushed back in place and the hole filled in. Digger then drove them all back to the farmhouse for their evening meal, which the two ladies had prepared together, while the men were out 'enjoying themselves'.

After dinner Skip took Bertie and Digger to his office and after rummaging around in an old cupboard, produced the twenty gold sovereigns that Tom had asked him to give to the driver.

"They are certainly genuine, just like the others I have seen already. I did say earlier that I did not want to keep them Skip," Digger said, "but to be quite honest, the whole time you are holding on to them, they are a liability to you and put you and Edna at risk of being prosecuted as accessories to a major crime."

"If you want them, you take them," Skip replied. "If Edna knew I still had them she would really go crook at me."

"Well I do have a small budget, to cover exceptional costs, so what would you say about me buying them off you, for fifty pounds?" Digger offered.

"I would say thank you and good riddance, provided you don't tell anyone where you got them from."

"Agreed," said Digger and handed over the money in exchange for the coins, which Skip put into a large brown envelope for him.

The men went through to the parlour and joined the ladies for a last drink and natter before saying their final goodbyes and leaving the farm. Skip and Edna promised to visit Bertie and Victoria either in England or in Spain some time soon, but said that it was unlikely that they would find the time to visit them in Western Australia.

Digger took his friends back to their hotel and then returned to his hotel and telephoned Rusty's boss at home, to tell him that he had finished the Sydney part of the investigation and needed to meet with him to discuss what to do next. It was agreed that Digger should return home to Perth the next day and write up his report during the following week and then fly over to Melbourne the next Wednesday to review his findings with the Board.

Digger arrived in Perth in the early afternoon of Saturday the 26th of August and was surprised, but delighted to find Moira and Nugget and Junie waiting for him at the airport.

Chapter 18
Chairman's Decisions

Digger could tell that Nugget was dying to talk with him about the Investigation, so suggested that he came inside the house to chat, while Moira got his dinner ready.

"I am really sorry Nugget, but I am under strict orders from Melbourne not to discuss anything with anyone at Perth, but if you were to make one or two comments or suggestions, I am happy to pull a face or to smile, if you get my drift," Digger informed him.

"To be honest with you, I never got on with Offstrop and have always privately wondered if he had anything to do with the robbery, in light of his sudden illness shortly after it occurred and his early retirement which followed a few weeks later," Nugget said.

Digger smiled and nodded slightly.

"I assume in light of the new information that Hans Schmidt gave you, that Don Davis was also involved somehow, but since he carried on working for the bank, I presume he was not a major beneficiary from the robbery."

Digger smiled once more and nodded again.

"I have been wondering if you uncovered any other evidence which might link someone else with the robbery; perhaps a bank employee based in Perth!"

Digger blinked and shook his head and without thinking said,

"What on earth would make you say a thing like that Nugget? Surely not because Rusty was not allowed to help me in the Investigation?"

"No, not really, but it did concern me for a while Digger. I knew that I had absolutely nothing to do with the robbery, in

303

any shape or form, so it certainly bothered me as to what might be at the back of that decision to exclude Rusty, because he was the obvious person to assist you, wasn't he?"

"Yes, he most certainly was. Oh, don't tell me you think I had something to do with him being barred?" Digger exclaimed.

"No of course not, my friend, I know you better than that," Nugget replied, patting Digger on the arm, "no, it had to be something I knew, which was relevant, that I did not know was relevant, if you can understand my logic. But for the life of me, I cannot imagine what it could be."

"Me neither, Nugget, the only things I have discovered that in any way might implicate someone from Perth, are the two Perth Mint money sacks, that they used to carry the proceeds from the robbery in, when they escaped from the bank."

Nugget sat there silently considering Digger's last comment and then he gasped and standing up exclaimed, "Well that it is Digger, that is exactly what I know, that someone did not want me to remember."

"What do you know Nugget, what is so special about the two Perth Mint money sacks, there must have been dozens of them around the bank at that time."

"There were quite a few, but perhaps not as many as you might think, as the empty ones were always returned to the Mint at some stage, unless they were kept in the vaults with the coins they contained. But I think I might know how two of the Perth Mint sacks ended up at the City Branch in Sydney."

"Well go on then, tell me!"

"I sent them over by registered post about a month beforehand," Nugget stated.

"Why on earth did you do that?" Digger asked.

"For the best reason in the world," Nugget replied, "my boss told me to and would you like to know who my boss was?"

Digger nodded, half dreading the reply.

"It was Mr. Offstrop's cousin, Albert Offstrop, who is now the Director of Planning in Melbourne and that is the reason that my son was kept away from the investigation Digger, because he knew Rusty would talk to me about it and I would remember sending the sacks across there."

"You could well be right, but I doubt that we could prove any of this Nugget, I would have thought that any Post Book from 1938 would have been disposed of years ago," Digger suggested.

"Not necessarily my friend, I sent it 'Registered Post' remember and that was always a separate Post Book and knowing the manager of that department, it could still be around in one of the post room cupboards somewhere; worth checking when we get to work on Monday, don't you think?"

"I do indeed, but I was not supposed to be discussing the Investigation with you at all, so I suggest you leave it to me and I will get Roger to look for it first thing Monday morning," Digger suggested.

Sunday the twenty seventh of August was Moira and Digger's first wedding anniversary and they celebrated it in style. First he gave her breakfast in bed and a bunch of flowers that Pat had got for him, which she had hidden in the shed.

Next he gave her a card and a beautiful opal brooch he had bought in one of the specialist jewellery shops in Sydney and in return, she gave him a new fishing rod, which Mick had chosen and picked up for her.

After church they went to a restaurant in Perth for a quiet meal together and afterwards met Vi and Mick and the children at the beach and shared a picnic tea which Vi had taken with her.

On leaving the beach, they then went home with Vi and played board games with the children until it was their bed time and then chatted with Vi and Mick for a while, before returning home for a glass of cold ginger beer and an early night.

Somehow Digger had found time to telephone Roger over the weekend and asked him to meet him in the Post Room at seven o'clock sharp, when he knew the Post Room Manager would be arriving for work and to wear some old clothes, as it could be dirty work.

"Let me see now, middle cupboard over there, probably the second shelf from the bottom, if my memory serves me right," the manger said to Digger.

"Well that is amazing," said Roger, who had gone across to the aforementioned cupboard and retrieved the Registered Post Book for the years 1937 to 1942 from the second shelf up and brought it over to where the other two men were standing by the counter.

"You must have a photographic memory, well done, I am most impressed," said Digger to the man.

"My memory is good, but not that good!" said the man smiling, "you happen to be the second person in as many weeks to ask me for that book," he explained.

"Who was the first person to ask you then?" Digger asked, dreading the response.

"Mr. Albert Offstrop, the Director of Planning from Melbourne. He told me that he was over here seeing Mr. Newgate and as he used to work here when we were both a lot younger than we are today, before the War that is, he called in to see me, for a chat. He was telling me that he was having an argument with another director in Melbourne about something he had sent to him in December 1937 and said that he remembered sending it Registered Post; so I said he could check it out in the old Registered Post Book, which was in that cupboard, where you found it, just now."

"Did you leave him alone with the book, or were you with him the whole time he was here," Digger asked.

"I think I was with him the whole time, because we were having a coffee together while he was looking at it."

"Were you two friends when he used to work here then?" Roger enquired.

"Not really, we occasionally played badminton together, but I don't think you would have called us friends."

"Getting back to the book," Digger said, "are you certain that you didn't leave him alone with it, even for a couple of minutes?"

"Yes, well no, that is apart from getting him a couple of sugars for his coffee, I was with him the whole time. He was laughing as he gave me the book back, because he said that he was the one in the wrong and would have to fork out for a bottle of Scotch, for the other director, but before you ask, he didn't tell me who it was."

"Look at this Digger," Roger said, "the page for most of December 1937 is missing."

"Don't look at me like that," the Post Room Manager said, "the page was there when I gave him the book, because I remember there was an ink blot at the top of the page that looked a bit like a whale and we joked about it."

"No one is accusing you of anything, but I will need to keep hold of the book for a while and you may be asked to make a formal statement of what you have just told us," Digger stated.

"Fine by me, I will do it right now if you like," the man offered; so Roger took his full statement, while Digger went up to the office and started to write up his report on the Investigation.

He had been writing for about an hour when Mr. Newgate came into his office and sat down in the visitor's chair for a chat.

"Well Smith, how has it all gone and do you have anything new to report, other than what we discussed on Thursday evening?"

"I certainly do sir, there are some very disturbing developments that we need to discuss as soon as you are free," Digger replied.

"No time like the present," he suggested, "why not come back to my office and tell me the worst."

Digger and Mr. Newgate spent the next three hours together, going over in detail everything that Digger had found out during his time in Sydney, without, of course, revealing the names of his sources. They then went on to discuss Digger's conversation with Nugget on Saturday evening and what he and Roger had learned from the Post Room Manager that morning.

"You have been most thorough Smith, if you will ask my secretary to type up the Post Room Manager's statement and get him to sign it, I will speak with Nugget privately, about what he told you on Saturday. I am obliged to ask you though, why you disobeyed the strict guidelines you were given in Melbourne and told Nugget what you had found out?"

"When Rusty's boss told us that Rusty could not be part of the investigation, I got the distinct impression that he did not feel comfortable with the decision and with what he was implying about Nugget. I guess my time in the army during the war, taught me a lot about people and also taught me to trust my own instincts, it saved my life on at least two occasions and my instincts were shouting out to me, trust Nugget."

"Well done, I heartily concur with your reasoning; I too did not feel comfortable with that decision and did wonder if someone was trying to hide something."

Digger left Mr. Newgate's office and returned to his own and told Roger the outline of their discussion. Roger gave the secretary the Manager's statement for typing and then unpacked the two Perth Mint money sacks from the bag Digger had carried them in and started to carefully clean them with a small hairbrush he had purchased for that reason.

Digger rejoined Mr. Newgate and Nugget after lunch, by which time Nugget had made a full statement about his role in sending the Perth Mint sacks to Sydney without feeling the need to mention his conversation with Digger the previous Saturday. He and Mr. Newgate had both signed the statement and a copy was handed to Digger for the official file.

"Surely you do not seriously believe that the Director of Planning could have had anything to do with planning the robbery?" Digger asked the two senior men.

"We have already discussed that possibility and have come to the conclusion that it is most unlikely that he was actively involved in the planning or execution of the robbery. Having said that, he was instrumental in the decision to appoint his cousin as Branch Manager, in the first place and to sign off his early retirement, in the second place," Mr. Newgate informed him.

"Can you remember the reason he gave you for sending the Perth Mint sacks to Sydney," Digger asked.

The other two men smiled at each other, "Mr. Albert, as we all called him, was very strong on giving orders and very weak on giving explanations," Nugget replied.

"But at least he should know where his cousin is living right now, which could point us to where the gold is hidden, or to where, whatever it was used to purchase, is located," Digger remarked.

"Good point Smith," Mr. Newgate agreed, "I plan to ring the Chairman at home this evening and suggest that we meet privately with him, to discuss the whole situation and see how he wants to proceed, from here. I will see you two gentlemen again first thing tomorrow morning."

As they were leaving the office, Nugget asked Digger to accompany him to his own office, for a private word.

"Mr. Newgate told me the answer you gave to him when he asked you why you disobeyed your instructions and spoke to me about the investigation on Saturday. Since you did not mention the little charade we played at first, I did not mention it either Digger."

"Right you are, mum's the word," he answered.

"I want you to know how much I appreciate the trust you displayed and the friendship you have showed to me, I consider that recruiting you in London, was the one of the smartest things I have ever done, since I started working for this bank. Your Mr. White was completely correct in his analysis of you, he will be very proud when I tell him of your loyalty and achievements."

"I had no idea you kept in touch with him Nugget, how is he keeping?"

"He is well and is talking of retiring next year and having a world cruise with his wife, so maybe we will be able to catch up with him, when he calls in at Freo."

Digger returned to his office and worked late into the night writing up his report and it was gone ten o'clock before he finally got home.

"Moira I'm home," he called out, as he walked into the kitchen and got a bottle of ginger beer from the fridge. Duke came bounding up to him, paws covered in sand where he had been digging for bones in the back garden.

"Hello boy, where is she?" he asked the dog.

The dog turned round and went back out to the garden and Digger followed to find Moira, fast asleep in the rocking chair on the patio. Duke did no more than start to lick her hand and arm which were hanging down one side of the chair and she slowly came to and looked up.

"Can I help you sir?" she said coldly, "I am the lady of the house, but it is probably my husband you want to speak to, but I am afraid that he is away on business, yet again!"

"I am sorry love, but there have been developments today and I had to get my report finished, I did telephone but you weren't in, sorry."

"Well to coin a phrase Digger, 'your slippers are in the oven and your dinner is in the dog', so hard luck if you are feeling hungry, I am feeling tired and fed up and am going to my bed."

"Don't be like that Moira, things are coming to a head, this investigation is really sending shockwaves throughout the bank and I am having to be absolutely certain of what I know and what I think, as careers are going to rise and fall as a result of what I choose to write in this report."

"Goodness and is Nugget one of those involved in all this?" she asked.

"As a matter of fact he is, but how did you know that?"

"Oh, just something that Junie said when she offered to give me a lift to the airport on Saturday and has he been affected, or can't you tell me that either?"

"He has been affected and has been completely exonerated and will probably accompany Mr. Newgate and myself when we meet with the Chairman, later in the week."

"Not another business trip away Digger, Pat might as well move in permanently until this investigation is over," Moira declared.

"Joking apart, I have no objections if you want her to do that, as things are not going to get any better for another month or two yet, in my opinion."

"Well I was joking, but she did say that one of the girls she was sharing with, had a friend who wanted to move in with them and Pat was not keen, so I will speak with her about it. Sit down and I will get your dinner, I didn't give it to Duke, although I was tempted to," she said.

"Thanks love, any mail today?"

"Nothing in the post, but Victoria rang from Sydney and said that they are having a smashing time there and will be arriving back in Perth at lunchtime on Saturday and could we pick them up from the airport. I said we would, so put that in your diary and don't forget it."

"Did she say what time the plane lands?"

"Shortly after two forty five, I think, Oh, and I invited them to stay with us for Saturday night, but she did say that they were hoping you would be able to drive them out to Pinjarra on the Sunday."

"No problem, I can do it after church. Did she mention what they want to do with car?"

"Yes she did, it appears Bertie has ordered one of these new Utes he was telling you about and intends selling the car straight away to help pay for it, so you had better decide how much you are prepared to offer him for his car,."

"Good morning gentlemen," Mr. Newgate said, when Nugget and Digger joined him in his office the following morning, "I had a long conversation with the Chairman last night who was devastated by your findings Smith. He never suspected that bank employees were actually involved in the robbery, let alone, masterminded the whole affair and ran off with the proceeds."

"That could not have been an easy conversation for you," said Nugget, "as I believe that the Chairman and Mr. Albert Offstrop are quite good friends outside of the office."

"Quite so, quite so. Anyway, he slept on what I told him and rang me back at home this morning and suggested that since he already had planned to visit Adelaide on Wednesday, that the three of us fly there as well and we can have a private meeting without anyone in Melbourne knowing what is happening."

"Did you discuss with him the option of going to the police with the new evidence?" Nugget asked.

"I did, but he was completely against it. The bad publicity could ruin the bank's reputation for years, mud sticks you know. Anyway, since Smith here, has clearly stated that he will not reveal his underworld sources and that obviously, they are not going to the police themselves, the Chairman has decided that we should continue to keep the investigation, a purely bank affair," Mr. Newgate confirmed.

"While I think of it, Roger has cleaned the sacks I brought back with me and has found a number on the bottom right hand corner of one of the sacks; does that mean anything to anyone?" Digger enquired.

"That number was put on by me and was the entry number in the Post Room Registered Mail book. I remember that I used an indelible pencil to put it on each of the sacks," said Nugget.

"I will get Roger to check the entry numbers on the pages either side of the one that was removed and see if it fits the range," said Digger.

"I will instruct my secretary to book flights and accommodation for our trip to Adelaide for the three of us, for Wednesday and possibly Thursday and I will see you at the airport tomorrow morning gentlemen."

"Well it's a good job that I have asked Pat to move in this week and keep me company Digger; I really thought I would see more of my new husband than this, in the first year of my marriage."

"Excuse me, but we are now into the second year Mrs. Smith," Digger replied and quickly ducked as a cushion went flying across the room.

"Have you decided how much you are going to offer Bertie for his car?" Moira asked.

"I thought I would offer the three hundred pounds that he paid for it, as we have had the use of it for all of this time," Digger replied, "so when is Pat actually going to move in here?"

"Since I knew you would be here on Saturday to pick up Victoria and Bertie, I suggested that you go and collect her on Sunday after church, that way you can take Victoria and Bertie out to Pinjarra on your own and I will stay here with Pat."

"And how are you coping with your work at the hospital these days, no more heavy lifting I hope?"

"No, they have assigned me lighter duties and sister has even been giving me some of the ward's paperwork to do. Mind you, I am not sure if she is being helpful, or she just hates doing it herself, anyway, my job is working out well at the moment and I am happy to keep going for a few more weeks yet. What time is your flight to Adelaide tomorrow and when will you be back home again, this time?"

"We leave at eight and should be back in Perth about six thirty on Thursday evening all being well and yes I will ring you tomorrow night, even if nothing is changing."

The Chairman met with the three from Perth in the Board Room in the Adelaide Office and spent the whole of Wednesday afternoon and evening, understanding the complexities of the situation and in deciding how to proceed.

"If he had not been the one to bar Rusty from the investigation and had not traveled to Perth the other week and torn that page out of the Post Book, I could have believed that he was as innocent as Nugget here and had just been duped into helping his cousin," the Chairman stated, "but I have no option but to conclude that he was a willing party to his cousin's criminal activities and was trying to hide that fact from Mr. Smith."

"To be quite honest with you Mr. Chairman, I too have come to the same conclusion, which makes his continued membership of the Board of Directors, quite untenable," said Mr. Newgate.

"For the moment gentlemen, I would ask that you leave me to speak with him, but you can expect an announcement about his early retirement from the bank, by the end of the week," said the Chairman.

"What are your instructions regarding the investigation Mr. Chairman?" Digger enquired.

"Well, everyone in the bank is aware by now of what you are doing Mr. Smith, so it is essential that we are seen to be vigorously pursuing those who have defrauded us. You must follow up on all of your leads and track this culprit down, if only to dissuade anyone else from trying something similar in the future. I gather you wish to speak with the Pensions Department to see if they can furnish you with a current address for Mr. Offstrop and I will certainly be asking his cousin for the same information during my conversation with him; have no fear on that account."

"Very good sir," Digger replied, impressed with the man's courage and determination.

They discussed how the investigation should proceed and then Digger looked at his watch and gasped, "Would you excuse me for a few minutes Mr. Chairman, only my wife is five months pregnant and I promised to telephone her this evening, before she went to bed, just to see how she was."

"Of course, why don't you use the office next door; as it happens, there is something of a more private nature that I wish to discuss with your colleagues here."

Digger left the office and went next door to telephone Moira and was surprised to find that Pat answered the telephone.

"There is nothing to worry about honestly Digger, she was just feeling very tired tonight and has gone to bed early; she said you might phone this evening," Pat informed him.

"And there is nothing wrong, she didn't faint again or anything like that?"

"Well yes and no. She told me not to say anything in case you got worried, but she took the dog for a walk earlier, while I was cooking our tea and you know how strong he is, well a cat came out of a gateway and he darted after it, pulling her after him and she tripped and fell over. A passer by helped her up, but I think she was pretty upset, because she left Duke in the street and came home on her own and he turned up ten minutes later."

"Did she hurt herself or the baby when she fell? Do you think she should go and see the doctor tomorrow Pat?"

"She only went down on her knees, but they are badly cut and bruised and I did say to her that if she is not feeling any better tomorrow that I will call the doctor myself, before I go to work."

"Thanks Pat, you are a real friend and please do call the doctor tomorrow, if you even have a slight doubt as to how she is. Please tell her I rang and that I will definitely be home tomorrow night, bye and thanks again."

Meanwhile, the Chairman was discussing the private matter he had mentioned with the other two men.

"This young man Smith has really impressed everyone he has been in touch with Nugget, an excellent choice for a recruit, well done."

"Thank you George," Nugget said to the older man, "I think he will go far in the bank, loyal, intelligent, hardworking and lots of imagination and new ideas."

"Sounds almost like you when you were younger Nugget, but to be serious for a moment, with the anticipated departure of our Director for Planning, it will leave a place on the Board at Melbourne free, so if you and your good lady would still like to move back over there from Perth, Stanley, the job is yours for the asking."

"Thank you George, we would still very much like to move back to Melbourne and Planning has always been something that has interested me, so yes, I am asking."

"Excellent and that leaves the post of Divisional Director for Western Australia free Nugget and I would like to offer that position to you."

"Thank you George, I accept and trust I can fulfill the role as well as Stanley has done during his tenure in the post."

A few minutes later there was a knock on the door and a very worried Digger came in and sat down.

"Everything all right at home with Moira Digger?" Nugget asked.

"I am not really sure, she took a fall while out walking the dog today and has gone to bed. Her friend Pat is staying the night and will call the doctor tomorrow if she is no better."

"Well you make sure you catch the early flight tomorrow and get yourself off home," the Chairman said, "I am sure the bank can manage for a day or two, if you need to spend some time at home with her."

"Thank you sir, I may just do that," Digger replied.

Digger got home in the early afternoon on Thursday and found Moira still in bed, having been told by the doctor that morning, to have a complete rest for at least three days and on no account to go dog walking again, until after the baby was born. He also confirmed that the baby had not been affected by the fall and everything else was in order.

"I told Pat not to say anything about the dog, because I knew what you would say!"

"We have discussed this already Moira and have agreed that when Victoria and Bertie arrive here, they will want Duke to go with them and after what has happened this week, it is probably for the best anyway. Once January has come and gone and the baby is safely with us, we can then think about getting a puppy of our own; all right?" said Digger.

"I know, but he has been such good company during all the time you have been away over the past few months, that I have got really attached to him and can't bear the thought of not having him around anymore," Moira replied.

Digger walked over and cuddled his wife and then asked, "Is Pat coming back here tonight or is she going to her digs?"

"She is going home tonight but will expect us to pick her up after church on Sunday along with all of her things. As you and I discussed, I have told her that she can stay here, even after the baby is born, as she needs accommodation through to the end of February; after which she will probably have to move to another hospital anyway."

Digger went out for some fish and chips that evening and did the weekly shopping on Friday morning and took Duke out Friday afternoon, for what was possibly his last walk with him.

On Saturday morning, he cleaned the house from top to bottom and promised Moira he would look into buying her one of these new Goblin vacuum cleaners she had been talking about for a while now. He made up the spare bed and put out clean towels and only managed to arrive at Perth Airport in time to park the car and rush to the Arrivals lounge, just as Victoria and Bertie were emerging.

There were hugs and kisses and handshakes and great concern shown for Moira's condition, who to everyone's surprise, had got up from her bed and got washed and dressed and was sitting in the lounge to greet them, when they walked into Ruth Street.

Duke, of course, was uncontrollable and had to show them his kennel and run in the garden and his ball and at least half a dozen different bones, before he would relax and just sit at Victoria's feet, looking up at her, with those big sad eyes of his.

While Victoria helped Moira in the kitchen, Digger and Bertie took a walk in the garden, which gave them the opportunity to discuss the current status of the investigation.

"Thank you my friend for being so honest with me," Bertie said, when Digger had finished speaking, "you said you would keep Tom Raymond out of it and you have kept your word.

You can be sure that I will never mention this to any of our mutual friends either."

"Thanks Bertie, for your help and for your trust and for persuading Skip to trust me as well, I won't forget it. All we have to do now is find out where Mr. Offstrop and his friend Phoenix disappeared to and what has happened to the gold."

"Just a thought for you to consider Digger, but I seem to recall that at some stage you mentioned Mauritius to me in one of our discussions."

"Yes I did. It is just possible that Offstrop went there at some time after he had left the bank, but whether it was permanent or just a holiday, I do not know. Why, what have you been thinking?"

"It occurred to me that there is a town in Mauritius named 'Phoenix', maybe just a coincidence, but it might be worth following up at some stage."

"Right, thanks for that, but I think that's the dinner bell sounding, time to eat."

On Sunday they all went to church and then Digger dropped Victoria and Bertie back home at Ruth Street and he and Moira went and picked up Pat and her things; except that Pat had so many things that it took Digger two trips to get everything back to their place for her.

After lunch, Digger drove Bertie, Victoria and Duke out to Pinjarra and deposited them at Vicky's farm, where they found Jenny had been dusting and cleaning and getting everything ready for their stay.

Before he left them to go home, he discussed cars with Bertie and offered him three hundred pounds for the Morris Eight, which Bertie was happy to accept. He told Digger that the Ute was being delivered to Pinjarra the following Tuesday, so since Digger had already withdrawn the cash from the bank, he handed it over there and then, so Bertie could pay the required deposit when the car was delivered to him.

For the next few days, Moira felt that the house in Ruth Street seemed really empty without Duke being there, but with Pat to keep her company, she eventually confided that she was pleased the dog had gone to be with Victoria, his true owner.

Chapter 19
Unexpected Dangers

"Good morning sir, yes I have received a copy of the memorandum from the Chairman saying that Mr. Albert Offstrop had taken early retirement on health grounds and congratulations on your appointment as Planning Director, based in Melbourne," Digger replied when Mr. Newgate telephoned him on Monday morning.

"Thank you Smith, needless to say my wife was delighted when I told her we would be going back to Melbourne and I am pleased to inform you that Nugget will be appointed Divisional Director for Western Australia later in the week; but please keep that to yourself until it is official.

"Did the Chairman happen to mention how Mr. Albert responded when he was confronted with the facts about his cousin and his own involvement at the time of the robbery and more recently, about the disappearing page from the Registered Mail Post Book, over here the other week?" Digger asked.

"As we expected, he denied he had any involvement in the robbery and said that he had simply sent the sacks over to Sydney, to assist with a Security Drill his cousin wished to run, before the gold was delivered. As regards the incident here the other week, he claimed that he simply panicked when he found out that his cousin was suspected of planning the robbery and realized that the Perth Mint sacks might have been used in the robbery and that he might possibly be incriminated because of them, he then agreed with the Chairman that he had acted stupidly and offered his resignation on the spot, which of course, the Chairman accepted."

"I guess that saved the Chairman the indignity of having to sack a fellow director," Digger observed. "Did he say if he knew where his cousin was living now?"

"He says not. The last time he heard from him was ten years ago, when he was living in Napier in New Zealand and thought there was something about an elderly parent, he was looking after. The Chairman did manage to speak with the Pensions Department Manager this morning and obtained an address for you, do you have a pen handy?"

"Hold on a moment please," said Digger, as he took a notepad out of his drawer and a pen from his top pocket, "O.K. I am ready."

"This is where all communications for Mr. Offstrop are currently sent; Box 37, Smiths Place Post Office, Georges Drive, Napier, New Zealand."

"Another Box Number, it would seem that he and Don Davis were playing similar games," Digger commented, "which bank is his pension sent to each month?"

"That would be the Bluff Hill Savings Bank of Napier; it's just a small local bank. We have decided that we would like you to continue searching for the erstwhile Mr. Offstrop, as the Chairman views this latest development, as a serious blot on the bank's integrity and would like to see this miscreant brought to justice, if that is at all possible. He asked me to say how pleased he was that you had managed to retrieve some of the gold coins from the robbery and trust you will be able to locate a few more, before your investigation is over."

"One last question Mr. Newgate, would it be possible for a senior executive at our bank, to speak with someone at his bank and find out what happens to the money each month, as that would give us a real clue as to whether Mr. Offstrop is actually in New Zealand or has moved on to pastures new."

"Good point Smith; I will see what I can discover, although I do not remember ever dealing with this bank before, so it might be difficult to find out this information for you. Meanwhile, I would like you and your assistant, to consider how we should proceed from here, what with your wife being pregnant and all that implies."

"I don't mind going to New Zealand on a trip for the bank Digger," Roger offered, when told of the latest developments.

"To be honest Roger, I feel this investigation is coming to a close and your manager has been pressing for your return and as I happen to know that it could mean a promotion for you, I do not think it is right to stand in your way," Digger replied.

"I see; that's a pity as I have enjoyed working for you. Couldn't I still be seconded to the investigation for a couple of days a week, so I can continue to give you some support when you are away?"

"That is certainly a possibility which I will suggest to him, but I can't afford to be away a lot myself at the moment, as Moira is finding it more difficult to manage each day and she still has three months to go, before the baby is due."

"It's a pity that cousin of yours whom you were telling me about, isn't living in Napier rather than Auckland, he could have asked around for you," Roger commented.

"That is not such a bad idea Roger and to be honest, he is probably much better trained than me, to take on an undercover operation of this nature. I think I will telephone him at home right now and see if he is game for it."

"Arnold, what a nice surprise, are you at home or still at work?" Donny said when he answered the telephone.

"Still at work Donny, how are you both keeping and settling in to life in Auckland?" Digger asked.

"We are both well and Debs has had no trouble settling in, she loves her new job and the people she is working with and we have found a house to rent not far from where her friends Rosie and Brock live and she is just loving it here."

"That is good to hear, but what about you, are you enjoying it and have you found a permanent job yet?"

"It's O.K. here, but in answer to your second question Arnold, not yet. I have been given a few days here and there as a contractor, but it is all basic stuff I did ten years ago and none of the permanent jobs I have looked at have really taken my fancy. As you know, Henry and I were going to branch out on our own and have our own consultancy, but I don't have his breadth of experience and could not do that on my own, not that I really want to anyway!"

"That's a shame, but still, it's an ill wind that doesn't blow somebody some good; maybe I can offer you something that might interest you."

"If it is anything to do with banking; thanks, but no thanks. I would rather be a kept man and go fishing or play golf every day, than go into banking. No insult intended Arnold."

"And none taken Donny, but I do have a problem in New Zealand and I think you are just the man to help me."

"I am all ears, tell me about it," Donny said, trying to sound interested.

Digger spent the next ten minutes giving his cousin the outline of the problem and finished by saying that someone needed to visit the Post Office and the Bank to find out what happens to the mail and the money destined for Mr. Offstrop and in view of Moira's current disposition, he would rather not have to do it himself.

"So what do you think Donny, interested?" Digger asked.

Donny must have considered the matter for a full five seconds before replying, "In principle yes, but let me clarify that for the initial trip, you are prepared to pay all of my expenses and five pounds a day, for as long as it takes, for me to drive down to Napier and see what I can find out about this man for you."

"That's about right, as long as you do not overdo the expenses, as I will have to get anything over ten pounds a day signed off by my manager."

"You have a deal," Donny confirmed. "I do however have work tomorrow, Wednesday and Thursday, but I could travel down on Friday, that would give you time to send me an airmail letter, with all the relevant information in. Hold on a second, Debs is trying to say something."

"Ask him if I can go with you, they owe me some time off work, in lieu of all the extra hours I have put in since I joined," Deborah suggested.

"Did you hear that Arnold? The 'trouble and strife' was wondering if it would be O.K. for her to come with me. A single male always draws attention to himself, whereas in my considerable experience, a married couple go un-noticed."

"It's fine by me Donny, but I guess I should point out that there might be some danger involved here; we are looking for a man who planned and executed the perfect robbery and as I found out to my own cost, even boring old bank employees can become desperate men."

"You make a good point young Arnold, I will not underestimate the opposition and will go prepared for action. Send me the letter as soon as you can and we will make our battle plans. Bye for now, love to Moira."

"Well I agree it makes sense Smith, since he is someone you know and trust and it does save you the task of traveling over there yourself, I just wished you had spoken to me first," said Mr. Newgate, after Digger had informed him of what he had just arranged.

He spent the next hour writing down everything that Donny needed to know and after enclosing a bank draft for fifty pounds to cover initial expenses, took the envelope down to the Post Room.

"I see my old friend Mr. Albert has taken early retirement," the Manager said, when Donny handed over the envelope.

"So he has," said Digger, "and to think we were only talking about him the other day. Just goes to show!"

"Hi love, how are you today?" Digger asked when he got home that evening.

"Not too good, if I am being honest. I know I should have discussed it with you first Digger, but I have told the sister at the hospital that I want to stop work Friday week, the fifteenth. I hope you don't mind."

"Of course I don't mind! My new position as the Senior Internal Audit Manager for the whole of the bank has been confirmed and the pay rise, I am delighted to announce, is substantial. This means that there is no problem whatsoever, with you stopping work at the hospital, for as long as you want to."

"That's wonderful news Digger, well done. But the look on your face says you are not telling me something. What is it?"

"Am I really that transparent?" he asked incredulously.

"Only to me," she replied smiling, "so what is it that you are not telling me."

"They would prefer it, if we moved over east, to Melbourne or Sydney."

"By 'prefer it', what do you mean exactly?"

"After the baby is born, but before the end of May. Most of the branches are over east and they believe that most of my work will be over there; so they are just thinking it would mean less time away from you, if we moved where the work is going to be," he explained.

"Sounds very sensible to me Digger, there is nothing really holding us here in Perth, apart from Vi and Mick and the children and of course our 'weekender' at Pinjarra, which I am sure Ray and Jenny would keep an eye on for us and perhaps Vi and family would use from time to time."

"So you would be quite happy to move over east then?"

"Absolutely, everything I have read and heard about Sydney, really excites me; but you will have to be the one to tell Vi, she is your sister and I cannot imagine for a single moment, that she will be at all pleased with us moving away from her."

"You are right; I hadn't thought about Vi," he said, "so I guess it is only fair that I be the one to tell her. By the way, I spoke with Donny today and have asked him to help me with the Investigation, as we are now looking for Offstrop in New Zealand."

"How far is New Zealand form Sydney?" she asked.

"About three hours by plane, I guess; but why do you ask?"

"I was just thinking that if we did move to Sydney, Donny and Deborah would be our nearest family and not Vi and Mick. So what did you ask him to do for you in New Zealand?"

"A bit of detective work I suppose you would call it. We think Offstrop might be there and with Donny's wartime experience of operating behind enemy lines, he was the obvious person to choose. What has happened to Pat tonight?"

"I am not really sure, she said she was going out with a friend from hospital, but it was all a bit vague and don't you forget that we have promised to give her somewhere to live until the end of February, so the earliest I would want to move to Sydney is the end of March."

"Understood. Any mail?"

"No, but Victoria rang and invited us out there for the weekend, so I said yes, but not until Saturday, as I never know when you are working late these days. I think Bertie has some sort of problem with his new Ute, as he asked if you could take your car mechanics tools with you."

"Are we stopping with them at the farm, or in our own place?"

"Well, when you finally decorate our bedroom and repair all of the broken windows in the house, we can stop in our own place, but until such time as you do, we will be stopping with them."

"All right Moira, I have the new glass and putty in the shed, so I will take it with us and make it this weekend's job, Oh grumpy one!"

"Come on Mac, what on earth are you doing, I have been ready for ages. What did Brock bring that was so important anyway?" Deborah asked, as she walked into the shed, where Mac had been ensconced since Brock had called round an hour beforehand.

"Sorry Debs, just something he asked me to look at for him and I couldn't say no, could I? They have both been so good to us."

"Well are you ready now?" she asked impatiently.

"You go and start the bike and I will get my jacket," he said, pushing her out the door.

Only when he could hear the big Indian ticking over, did he remove the gun he had been cleaning from under the bench and put it into his old army holster, which he then put into his rucksack. He got his jacket from the hook in the hall and within a few minutes they were off on their first New Zealand long distance bike ride.

They stopped in Cambridge for a hot drink and a biscuit and found a small hotel in Rotorua where they had lunch and a leg stretch. Deborah bought a few things from the shops, which she had realized she had forgotten to pack and they were soon on their way on the last leg of the journey, arriving in Napier shortly after three.

He tapped her twice on the leg, indicating that she should stop, so she pulled over to the side of the road.

"What's the matter she asked?"

"We have just gone past Georges Drive, it is back there, about fifty yards. We then travel down for about a hundred yards and Smiths Place should be on the left."

"I thought we were going to book a room in a hotel first Mac, only it is getting late and we need to find somewhere to sleep for the night," she suggested.

"I don't know what time the Post Office closes, so let's go there first and see what we can find out," he said.

She turned the bike round and went back down the road and turned into Georges Drive and then into Smiths Place and found the Post Office, just down a few yards. She pulled the bike over to the side of the road and Mac got off and walked into the Post Office.

The young woman behind the counter tried hard not to stare at his scarred face, but could not help herself.

"I got it in the war," Mac informed her, "it doesn't hurt any more and it is slowly fading away," being the answers he gave to the questions most people normally asked him.

"I am so sorry sir, how rude of me, I really didn't mean to stare at you like that, but my brother has similar scars to you, do forgive me."

"It is quite all right young lady, as I am sure your brother will agree, it is something you have to get used to."

"Thank you," she said, "what can I do for you?"

"I am moving into the area and could do with having a Post Box to have my mail sent to; I believe that you do have provision here for such a service?"

"We do indeed, would you like an application form?"

"Yes please." Mac replied. "It was actually a friend of mine who suggested I came here. Old Offstrop has been having his mail sent here for years, he was telling me."

"That's right he has, long before I started working here, but of course I have never met him, but his daughter is a most pleasant young woman."

"She certainly is," said Mac, un-phased by the unexpected reply, "but it must be at least eight maybe ten years since I have seen her, it would be lovely to catch up with her again."

The young woman looked around the shop to make sure that no-one else was listening and then said, "The third Saturday of every month, she comes in to collect her father's mail, never misses, but I haven't told you that, understand."

Mac winked and smiled, bought a few stamps and left with the form.

He and Deborah then mounted the bike and found a hotel overlooking the harbour and booked a room for two nights. He then telephoned Digger at work and told him what he had found out and organized for the bank to send a parcel to Mr. Offstrop that would be wrapped in bright red paper and would stand out like a sore thumb, when the young woman carried it out of the post office the following weekend. He and Deborah then went down to the restaurant for their evening meal.

After a walk around town in the morning, they went out for a boat ride round the harbour in the afternoon and returned to Auckland on the Sunday, having both had a most enjoyable weekend at the bank's expense.

Back in Perth, early on Saturday morning, Digger and Moira loaded the car with their overnight bag, working clothes and the glass, putty and tools to repair all of the broken windows, plus a few other odds and ends and after saying goodbye to Pat, set off for Pinjarra.

"I knew you were eager to get the windows done, so I told Victoria that we would go to James Street first and then drive up to the farm after lunch. How long do you think it will take you to repair them all?"

"The hardest job is getting the old glass and putty out of the frames, so I really have no idea. Could be a couple of hours, or it could be a couple of days, or somewhere in-between, so lets just agree that I will work till one o'clock and we will then have lunch. After lunch I will replace the lock on the front door and then we will drive up to the farm."

"What is the point of replacing the lock on the door, when we still have broken windows?" she suddenly asked, after there had been silence in the car for at least ten minutes.

"Because I am going to repair the windows at the front of the house first and you told me that you are going to hang those old curtains you were given, on the front room windows today. Did you buy any curtain wire to hang the curtains on, because I didn't get any?"

"Last time we were at the house, you washed all the walls and window frames at the front of the house and you passed me down some items that were in your way and that needed cleaning. Do you remember what they were?"

"Ah, those long rods."

"Correct and would you like to take a guess at what those long rods might be used for?"

"It's a good job for you that my hands are having to grip this steering wheel, or it would be 'curtains' for you, my girl," he said laughing.

The remainder of the journey soon passed and they stopped at the shops in Pinjarra for some bread, cheese, milk and a chisel, as he had forgotten to bring one with him.

They pulled into James Street and parked in front of the house and Digger opened the door and went in, while Moira went round the back to visit the sheep, who had come up to the fence to greet her. She took a piece of twig out of the wool on the back of the big one and made a fuss of both of them, before going round to the big water tank where their water trough was located. It was looking pretty mucky, so she made a note to ask Digger to clean it out for them.

She then went back into the house and took the thermos flask out of the box she had brought and made them both a hot drink and took Digger's through to the big room at the front, where he was working.

"Tea up," she called, "how is it going?"

"Brilliant!" he replied, "that's all the glass out of both of those big windows. That new chisel is just the job for getting the old putty out. The shopkeeper said it would be the right size. The difference it makes having the right tools for the job, you know."

"Would you mind emptying the sheep's water trough for me, it has got all mucky again?"

"I did it last time; they must go paddling in it when we are not here. You will have to distract them while I clean it out, as that big one went for me again. I tell you, if he does it once more, he is going to the butchers!"

"He never bothers me," said Moira, "it's just you he has not taken to. Even Duke gets on with him all right these days Ray said, last time I spoke with him."

"Very comforting to hear that, time to start work again."

Digger spent the rest of the morning putting in the new glass, fixing it with the panel pins and then applying the new putty. Once this was completed, he assisted Moira in hanging the curtains she had been given and they then sat down to enjoy a cold drink and a packed lunch on the veranda.

After lunch, he replaced the old broken lock on the front door, with the new one he had purchased in Perth and had packed his tools away and was about to get into the car, when Moira reminded him of the water trough.

"It can't be that bad, I will do it next time," he told her.

"No Digger, do it now. You wouldn't want to drink out of a filthy mug, so why should the sheep. Unless of course, you really are scared of the big one!" she taunted.

"Right, you call them down to the far end of the fence and I will then jump over and clean out the trough. Do you happen to remember what I did with that old broom I used last time?"

"Where you left it I expect, just inside the shed."

She walked down to the far end of the fence and called the sheep, who meekly went over to her and ate some of the fresh hay she was offering them. Meanwhile, Digger had retrieved the broom from the shed and had jumped over the fence and was almost finished with the trough when he heard her shout out, "Watch out Digger, the sheep have spotted you and are coming your way."

Forewarned is forearmed, so he stood facing the sheep, with the big yard broom at the ready, having completed the cleaning process. He slowly walked towards them and they slowly backed away and as he quickened his pace, they suddenly turned and ran down to the other end of the field, away from the house.

"My hero," she said sweetly, "name your reward."

He turned and half smiled as he said in a sort of Humphrey Bogart tone of voice, "I am going to keep you to that darling," with which he attempted to vault the fence, forgetting that the top strand at that particular point was actually barbed wire and it not only ripped open his trousers, but the side of his leg as well.

He cursed and she went into 'nursey' mode and made him go indoors and remove his trousers so she could bathe the wound.

"I think this needs a couple of stitches Digger, I will put a dressing on it for now, but we need to get you to the hospital and get it looked at. You might need a tetanus jab as well, depending on when you had your last one."

"Right you are, but let me put my trousers on again first. Do we know where the hospital is?"

"I am sure there is a sign in town to it, if not we will have to ask someone. It's a pity I did not have those driving lessons when you suggested it, as it would come in handy right now."

She packed the remainder of their things into the car and closed up the house and then helped Digger into the drivers seat and he drove off down the road. They found the sign for the hospital, almost where she had remembered it to be, went down the road indicated and parked outside the hospital's main entrance.

"Wait here, while I go in and see if they can help you," she ordered.

She returned in a couple of minutes with an orderly pushing a wheel chair and with Moira's help, Digger climbed aboard and was wheeled into the Emergency Ward. He only had to wait about twenty minutes before a doctor came and inspected the cut. He asked a nurse to clean and sterilize it, and then stitched it together with three stitches and gave Digger a tetanus jab as it was over five years since his last one.

A fresh dressing was applied over the wound, by the nurse and when Moira explained that she too was a nurse, they gave her a supply of dressings to last a week and suggested he see his own doctor in a week's time. They then drove up to the farm, where Victoria and Bertie were waiting for them.

"We were beginning to wonder if something had happened," said Victoria.

"Well it actually has," said Moira, who went on to explain in detail, the debacle with the sheep and his entanglement with the barbed wire fence.

"I would have thought that a man with your military training would know all about the dangers of barbed wire," Bertie suggested.

"You would have thought so," said Digger, "but lets get down to the important matters at hand, where is this new vehicle of yours?"

"I thought you would never ask," Bertie replied, "hobble this way," he said, leading the way outside to one of the empty stables.

"Wow what a beauty, do you want to start her up," Digger asked.

"Are you sure you are up to this, what with your bad leg and all?" Bertie replied.

"While I was in France during the war, I had to repair the engine of my lorry, surrounded by the enemy with bullets whizzing around, so believe me, this is a piece of cake my friend; but if you could fetch my tools from the boot of my car, I would be most grateful."

The tools were fetched, the motor started and Digger only had his head under the bonnet for about fifteen minutes, before he declared the problem solved and the Ute was ready for a trial run.

"I'll tell you what Digger, Ray has prepared a pile of logs for us which need picking up, but I am not quite sure where they are. If we go to his place first, we can get him to come with us and show us where they are," Bertie suggested.

"Good idea. Can I drive?"

"Of course, I will go and inform the ladies of our plans," he replied and walked over to the farmhouse where the ladies were sitting on the veranda chatting.

"But I have just made a cup of tea Bertie, have that first and then you can ring Ray and let him know you are coming," said Victoria.

Moira walked over to the stable and told Digger of the change of plans, so he came back to the house with her and washed his hands, while Bertie telephoned Ray and told him of the planned afternoon's activities.

"Ah look mate, I would love to, but I promised I would help Jenny with the Spring Cleaning today and I would hate to let her down," he said sincerely. "Well I will ask her and see what she says. Jenny, Victoria is entertaining Moira at the farm this afternoon and they both wondered if you would like to join them for afternoon tea? You would, right."

"Good man Ray, I heard that, see you in ten minutes," said Bertie.

Ray and Jenny had joined their friends within the allotted timeframe and the men gulped down their tea and the requisite number of home made scones, before bidding the ladies farewell and heading off together in the Ute.

"Next right," said Ray after a couple of minutes on the dirt road. "I am sure the front of my truck is bigger than this, it's a bit squashed in here with the three of us Skipper."

"Let's just be grateful that Duke decided to travel in the back," Bertie replied, "or it would really have been squashed and smelly, to boot."

"Just take the next track on your right Digger and you will come to a clearing where the wood is piled up," Ray informed him.

Digger turned in the clearing so that he had the back of the Ute facing the pile of logs and the front facing the way out.

They all got out and stretched their arms and legs and Bertie said, "Well thanks for fixing the engine Digger that was a whole lot better than the last little trip I went for in her."

"You are most welcome, she drives really well. Is that your axe over there Ray?" he said, pointing to an axe that had been half buried by some fallen logs.

"Thanks mate, I have been looking for that for a week, I wondered where I had left it," Ray replied. "I suggest we just get enough logs to fill the bottom of the Ute, so we can see how she handles with a load on and so we don't do any harm to Duke with logs rolling around the back."

They all went to the pile and between them carried twenty or thirty big logs over to the Ute and laid them in the back so that they would not roll around.

Bertie was just carrying the last of the small logs over, to the jeers of his companions, when Ray remembered the axe and shouted out, "Hey Tarzan, do you think you could manage my axe as well."

Bertie turned round and walked over to where the axe was lying, with the two other men standing side by side watching him, when Digger said to Ray, "What was that movement down by the handle of the axe just now Ray, a bird or something?"

Ray exploded forward shouting as he went, "No Bertie, Tiger snake, leave the axe alone!"

Unfortunately, Duke must have sensed the danger at the same time, because as Ray shouted, he started barking, so the message did not get through to Bertie. He bent over and picked up the handle of the axe and had turned and was about to start walking back to the Ute, when the large striped snake sprang forward and bit him on the ankle.

He shouted and dropped the axe, just as Ray got level with him, so he picked the axe up and severed the head of the Tiger snake from the rest of its body.

"Is it a poisonous snake?" Bertie asked.

"It most certainly is, we need to get you to the hospital fast," said Ray.

Bertie immediately removed the belt from his trousers and strapped it round the thigh of the leg that had been bitten and pulled it tight in order to slow down the spread of the poison.

Ray picked him up and put him in the back of the Ute and climbed in next to him, holding the makeshift tourniquet as tight as he could.

"It's all right, I know where the hospital is Ray," said Digger, "Duke, you come in the front with me. I will go to the farm first, so they can ring ahead to the hospital and let them know we are on our way. I just hope they carry a supply of snake serum. Hold on tight everyone."

As he drove the Ute into the farmyard, he was sounding his horn wildly and Jenny came running up to the back to find out what the matter was. Ray quickly explained about the snake attacking Bertie and sent her into the house to ring the hospital and to tell the others what had happened. Digger was on his way again in less that a minute, having told Duke to get out of the Ute and drove at break neck speed down the hill into Pinjarra. The hospital doctor was ready and waiting for them when they arrived and quickly had Bertie's boot off and had inspected the wound and administered the serum in no time at all.

"What do you think Doc?" Ray enquired, after Bertie had been wheeled into a ward and put to bed.

"I think he has had a very lucky escape Ray. Those old army boots he was wearing gave him a lot of protection, as I think only one of the fangs pierced the leather and actually got through to his ankle. Added to that, his own prompt action in putting the belt round his leg to act as a tourniquet, plus you two getting him here so quickly, have undoubtedly moved the odds of survival in his favour. From what you told me about the size of the snake, it was a fully grown adult and could quite easily have killed him. Could this lady be his wife by any chance?"

Victoria and Jenny came rushing into the hospital ward as the doctor was finishing his statement.

"Where is my husband doctor? Is he dead?" Victoria asked.

"No Mrs. Bannister, he is not dead, he is alive," the doctor replied, "and in my opinion he is a very lucky man. He is over there in the end bed, but please be calm and do not stay for too long, as he needs to rest."

Victoria thanked the doctor and she and Jenny walked over together in the direction he had indicated and as they spotted Bertie in bed Victoria said, a little abruptly, "I really do not think there is anything lucky, in being bitten by a snake!"

West Australian Tiger Snake
Artist – Liz Bartley

Chapter 20
An Undercover Operation

First thing Monday morning, Digger went shopping for some canned fruit, biscuits and tinned meats and took them along to see the Post Room Manager and to arrange for him to box them up and send them to Mr. Offstrop's Post Office Box in Napier.

"It's not going to be cheap sending this lot over to New Zealand," the manager warned him.

"I don't care what it costs," said Digger, "but the parcel must be there by Friday of this week at the latest, understood."

"Anything you say Digger, but I don't have any bright red wrapping paper here, but I do have some green wrapping paper left over from Christmas, if that would do. Do you have a card or letter to go with it?" the manager asked.

"The green paper will be fine, but I don't have a card or letter, just put one of Mr. Newgate's compliment slips in with it, but nothing else. Tell the courier I want to know if there are any problems and if it is held up, I need to know immediately. Mind you, if it is held up, we will probably be changing our courier!"

He then spent the rest of the day reviewing the results of an Internal Audit carried out by his assistant in Geraldton the previous week. Once again the main concern was for the security of the counter staff, plus Digger had one or two new ideas about the bank's internal procedures for handling large shipments of cash as they arrive at, or depart from the bank, by security van.

On Tuesday Mr. Newgate called him into his office to inform him that he had now been in touch with the manager at the Bluff Hill Savings Bank in Napier, regarding Mr. Offstrop's account with them.

"It turned out that he and I had met before, during the time he had worked at our New Zealand head office, based in Auckland. When I explained the reason behind my enquiry, he was quite happy to provide me with the relevant information," Mr. Newgate informed Digger.

"Small world," said Digger, "so what did he say exactly?"

"He said that there was a regular monthly Standing Order, which transferred a small sum to the account of a lady at their Hastings branch, but he knew nothing about her. I gather from what he said that Hastings is just a few miles down the coast from Napier. Once every three months the majority of what is left in the account is transferred to an overseas account with the National Plantation Bank in Capetown."

"Well that is most interesting," said Digger, "I think we can assume that the account in Hastings belongs to the young lady who picks up his mail each month and the account in Capetown is probably his own, but of course we do not know the name he is using there."

"I could try contacting this National Plantation Bank if you wish," Mr. Newgate suggested, "but since I know absolutely nothing about them, or what his connection to them might be, we might just be giving him notice that we are closing the net on him; what do you think Smith?"

"I agree sir, let's wait and see what my cousin finds out this weekend. The parcel was sent off yesterday and should arrive Thursday afternoon or Friday morning, so if I let Donny know that the woman probably lives in Hastings, he can make the necessary arrangements when he arrives there."

When Digger got home on Tuesday evening he was surprised to find that Victoria and Bertie were already ensconced in the spare room, with Bertie getting to know Pat over a cup of tea on the patio, while Victoria was helping Moira in the kitchen.

"This is a nice surprise," said Digger, as he shook hands with Bertie, "I presume you are feeling a lot better now than you were last time we were together. No serious after effects I hope?"

"Not really, my ankle is still swollen and there is some bruising on my leg and foot and it was fairly painful for a day or two, but all in all, I was very lucky, those old army boots of mine, probably saved my life."

"That is exactly what the doctor thought, you must tell me where you bought them so I can get a pair for myself; you certainly gave us all a mighty scare Bertie, that's for sure."

"And thank you Digger, for getting me to hospital so quickly, that too helped in reducing the effects of the venom."

"Did you two drive up in the Ute today, or come by train?" Digger enquired.

"Neither, Ray wanted to pick up some equipment for the farm, from a supplier in Perth, so he drove us up in the Ute and we are getting the train back to Pinjarra tomorrow."

"Very wise, ankles are funny things to mess around with. Sorry Pat, I didn't mean to ignore you, how are you today and how is the new friendship going?"

"I am very well and the new friendship is going well too, thank you for asking Digger," she replied, blushing slightly, "but Moira was struggling again at work today, I think she was very wise in deciding to finish at the hospital next week."

"Next week, I thought it was this week she was finishing."

"I understand that her ward Sister persuaded her to stop one more week as someone was away on holiday, but I am sure that she will be O.K."

"I see, well I hope she knows what she is doing, that's all. Excuse me a minute Bertie, while I get changed into something a bit more casual; I will just say hello to the ladies in the kitchen."

Digger walked through to the kitchen and greeted Victoria and Moira, who then followed him through into the bedroom.

"Where did you put the jewellery box which David in Gibraltar gave us for Bertie? We should have taken it with us at the weekend and given it to them then. What must they be thinking of us Digger?"

"From what David said to us at the time, I doubt that they know we are holding it for them, so stop worrying. I put it up in the loft for safe keeping and will get Bertie to give me a hand getting the case down that I put it in, as soon as I have changed. You haven't said anything to Victoria about it yet, have you?"

"No, I have said nothing, but what difference does it make?"

"None I expect, but it did belong to Bertie and I would rather give it to him privately, so he can show Victoria in his own good time. How long will dinner be?" he asked.

"Twenty minutes," she replied.

Moira went back into the kitchen and Digger got changed and then fetched a step ladder from the shed and asked Bertie to hold it while he went up through the trapdoor in the passageway, to the loft above and passed the case back down to his friend. He then came back down the ladder and the pair of them went into his and Moira's bedroom closing the door behind them. Digger then opened the case and said, "While we were visiting David and his wife in Gibraltar, he asked us to bring this to Australia and give it to you," with which he took the jewellery box out of the case and gave it to Bertie.

"Why thank you Digger, I had no idea that David had asked you to do this, I was not expecting anything else from him just yet," Bertie said, opening the box.

Bertie removed the bracelet and turned it over in his hands, "Oh my, I had forgotten how beautiful this bracelet was. It was part of the things I gave him for safe keeping at the end of the war and had assumed he had sold it, to get his business going in Gibraltar."

"He did tell us that it wasn't quite so valuable now as it used to be, as most of the diamonds are fakes, as the originals got lost or something like that and he had to replace them," Digger explained.

"Is that what he told you? Has Moira said anything to Victoria about it, do you happen to know?" Bertie enquired.

"I told her not to, so I don't think so," Digger answered.

"That's good, because I may decide to give it to Deborah and not to her and would hate for her to be upset over it; so please do remind Moira to say nothing about it, until I have made my mind up as to what to do with it."

"Of course; would you prefer me to keep hold of it for you, until you have decided what you want to do with it then?"

"I don't think so Digger, we are going to the bank tomorrow anyway, so I will just put it in my safety deposit box there, but thanks for the offer," Bertie replied smiling.

On Wednesday Donny phoned Digger in the afternoon and received an update on the mysterious woman who had been picking up the mail for Mr. Offstrop and the probable whereabouts of where he might be living himself, right now.

"Apart from knowing that Mauritius is just off the coast of South Africa, I cannot say that I know a lot more than that about the place," Donny informed him, "but I can tell you that Hastings is a small town about twelve miles away from Napier and that the Post Office in Smiths Place, closes at twelve thirty on a Saturday. It would be my guess that she will take everything back to her own home, sort the mail out there and then post it off on Monday or Tuesday, from a Post office nearer to where she lives. This means that the surveillance operation could take the best part of a week to complete, are you happy to employ me and pay all of my expenses, for that length of time Arnold?"

"Absolutely, we all feel we are getting closer to him now and just need his address in Mauritius, to finish things off. How you manage to achieve that Donny is up to you, but just make sure you let me have all the relevant receipts for your expenses, along with a report of all that happens."

"I will, but don't build your hopes up cousin for a quick result, it may take a few tries before I manage to gain her confidence and find out where she sends the mail to."

"Point Taken; is Deborah going with you again this weekend?" Digger asked.

"Unfortunately not, there is a concert or something she is going to with Rosie and doesn't want to cancel it, so I will be on my own this time. Wish me luck."

"What do you mean, you don't know where you will be stopping," Deborah exclaimed on Friday morning, as Mac was packing his things in the back of the car he had hired the day before. "Surely you will be stopping in that nice hotel we used last week."

"I told you Debs, I will definitely be staying there tonight, but I am not sure after that. It depends on where this mystery woman lives and what she does with the mail she picks up."

"Quite honestly Mac, I do not feel comfortable about you spying on another woman like that, I would hate it if it were me!"

"Like what Debs? I will just be observing her, nothing more. She is probably just an innocent person who is doing a friend a favour and is getting paid for it. Digger assured me that the man he is looking for did not have any children, so she is definitely not his daughter, but has simply been told to pretend she is, I presume to avoid the Post Office asking her any awkward questions."

"Well I still do not feel comfortable about it Mac and make sure you keep me informed of where you will be staying, do you hear?"

"Of course, if I change hotels, I will telephone here and let you know; please stop worrying Debs; this is after all, what I was trained to do."

Mac drove down to Napier stopping at Rotorua for a bite to eat and arrived at the hotel in the early afternoon. He bought a map from the local newsagent and drove round town, checking on the location of all the various Post Offices and hotels and then drove to Hastings and did the same thing there, calling in at a hotel in the town centre and booking a single room overlooking the main street, for the Saturday and Sunday nights. He then returned to the hotel in Napier for his evening meal and telephoned Deborah with the details of the second hotel he had booked himself into. After a couple of drinks in the hotel bar he returned to his room for an early night.

His alarm went off at seven and he was up, shaved, washed and dressed and down stairs having a large breakfast by a quarter to eight. Taking a newspaper from the hotel lobby, he walked to his car and drove to Georges Drive and parked at the bottom of Smiths Place, in a position which gave him a good view of the Post Office entrance.

There were a couple of people waiting in the street for the Post Office to open, an old man with a walking stick and a young mother with a pram, but neither came out carrying a large parcel wrapped in green paper.

By eleven o'clock a stream of customers had come and gone and Mac was beginning to wonder if he was wasting his time, when a taxi drew up and a young woman got out carrying a shopping bag and went inside the Post Office. While she was inside the taxi driver turned the cab round and was waiting outside in Smiths Place for her. She emerged about five minutes after she had gone in, struggling with a heavy green parcel, that the taxi driver put in the boot for her.

Mac waited until the taxi had left Smiths Place and turned right into Georges Drive before he started the car and set off in pursuit, keeping a safe distance behind them, he followed the taxi all the way to Napier's railway station.

He watched the woman get out of the taxi, pay the driver and then walk through the side gate onto the platform and sit down on one of the benches, with the parcel on the seat beside her.

He waited in the car for a few minutes and then walked into the Booking Office and asked when the next train to Hastings would be arriving.

"About ten minutes time sir," the clerk replied.

"How long is the journey time," Mac asked.

"About thirty minutes. Do you want a single or return ticket?"

Mac ignored the question, "And which platform does it leave from?" he asked.

"This side, now do you want a ticket or not sir, as there are other people waiting in the queue behind you."

"Sorry, not sure; please go ahead of me," he said to the old man who was standing behind him.

'So,' he thought to himself, 'she has a Hastings bank account, is waiting for the train which is going to Hastings, the sensible thing is for me to head over there now, so I am already in position when she arrives at the station.'

He slowly walked to the car studying the woman on the bench as he did. She had now taken a magazine from her shopping bag and was engrossed in it. Getting the map out of the glove compartment, he started the car and had a leisurely drive to Hastings and was safely parked in the car park when the train from Napier arrived fifteen minutes after him.

He got out of the car and walked over to the station entrance and watched everyone disembark from the train and pass through the barrier and who should be bringing up the rear, but the woman from the Post Office, with the large green parcel.

"Excuse me madam," he said to her, "you didn't happen to notice a lady in a leather jacket on the train did you, only I was supposed to meet my wife here this morning and she hasn't turned up yet."

"Sorry, afraid not," the woman replied, in a very distinctive New Zealand accent. "There is another train in forty minutes, perhaps she will be on that one, but as you can see, I have problems of my own to deal with."

With which she smiled and walked over to where a taxi was waiting in the station yard.

Mac went into the station but watched the taxi through the window as it started up and as soon as it drove off, he raced over to his car, started the engine and followed it, as it headed north. It had only travelled about a mile, when it turned off the main road and after several rights and lefts, stopped outside a house in the St. Leonards area of Hastings and the woman and her parcel got out and went inside the house.

After about thirty minutes he decided that she was not going anywhere that night and as he did not want to draw attention to himself, drove to the hotel in the centre of town where he had reserved a room and booked in.

During the rest of the afternoon, he checked which Post Office was nearest to where she lived and worked out where he could park the car and observe her, from a safe distance.

He had dinner about seven and went out for a drive around town after dinner, going past the woman's house and noting that the curtains were pulled and the lights were on.

After breakfast on Sunday he decided that he would like to go to church and the receptionist informed him that there was a Baptist church in town and gave him directions to it.

"I am not sure what time the service starts, but I think it is eleven o'clock. I will check for you and let you know if it is different," the Receptionist told him.

He left the hotel at ten forty five and drove to the church and parked down the road from the entrance. While he was searching for the car keys which he had dropped on the floor, who should go cycling past him and pull into the church yard, but the woman he had been following on Saturday.

For the first time in all of this adventure, he started to feel just slightly uncomfortable and waited until the woman had padlocked her bicycle and walked through the church door, before he got out of the car and followed her in.

An usher greeted him at the door and welcomed him to the church and told him that there was still a few single seats down to the left. Mac followed the directions and noticed the woman sitting next to an older lady, with whom she was deep in conversation.

Mac walked past her and sat about three rows in front and about two seats in from the side. He was pretty sure that she had noticed him, but gave no indication that he had noticed her. As soon as the service finished he was out like a flash, into the car and away back to the hotel where he had a light lunch.

He telephoned Digger later in the afternoon and brought him up to date with what he had discovered and they discussed the various options that were open to him.

"Having observed her on several occasions and actually spoken with her now, I just do not believe that she is anything more than a friend or old neighbour, who is doing your man a favour each month. He only pays her enough to cover her expenses and I am certain that she was not involved in the robbery or his current disappearance," Donny stated.

"I agree Donny," said Digger, "but if you come clean and tell her about the investigation, she might not believe you and feel she has to let him know what you have told her."

"Good point," agreed Donny, "but getting his current address in Mauritius out of her is not going to be easy."

"Hey, if it was easy, I would have done it myself or sent Roger, my assistant, over there to speak with her. Perhaps you should get a job at the Post Office she uses, so that you can read the address on the envelopes, or pick her pockets in the queue tomorrow, when she sends the parcel off to him," Digger joked.

"Why thank you Arnold, you have just given me an idea, must go, things to do."

"Hey Donny, don't do anything illegal, I am authorized to pay reasonable expenses, not stand bail for you. Good luck tomorrow."

Having put the telephone down on his cousin, Mac walked downstairs and spoke with the receptionist.

"Excuse me Miss, but I don't suppose you have a large sheet of wrapping paper I could scrounge off you, do you?"

"We don't have any new sheets of paper I'm afraid, but I do have this," she said, holding up some slightly crinkled brown paper, "it's the wrapping paper from a parcel which arrived here last week, you can use that if you don't mind turning it inside out," with which she passed the paper across the counter for inspection.

"Thank you that will do just fine. Just one more thing, you don't by any chance keep your old telephone directories, do you? My wife and I live in Auckland and would find it most useful to have a directory for this area?"

She smiled and pointed to the far wall of the lobby, "You see that door marked 'PRIVATE' over there, well it is actually a large store cupboard and to the right of the door are a pile of old directories and magazines that the Boys Brigade collect every now and then. You may find what you want in there and there may even be one for Wellington, if I remember correctly; please feel free to help yourself."

"Most accommodating of you," said Mac, who then wandered over to the cupboard and found a directory for Napier and one for Wellington as well as some magazines on Carpentry and Model Railways and of course, some back copies of the National Geographical Magazine.

"Do you need some string for the parcel Mr. Smith?" the receptionist called out as he was heading back to his room.

"I do indeed, thank you," he replied and walked back to the counter to collect a small ball of string.

"I do have some sealing wax under the counter, when it is all tied up, if you want to use some," she offered.

"Thank you I will; you have been most helpful. It has just occurred to me that I might need to stay here Monday night as well, can I reserve the room just in case."

"Yes, I can do that for you, just let me know by twelve tomorrow if you do not need it, otherwise we will have to charge you for the extra night."

"Will do and thanks again," he said, climbing the stairs to his room with his pile of directories and magazines.

Mac made up the parcel and tied it securely, keeping the Railway Magazine out to read himself that afternoon. He addressed the parcel to himself in Auckland and then went downstairs and took up the sealing wax offer from the Receptionist.

He took a walk round town in the late afternoon and after a long soak in the bath, ordered the roast lamb in the restaurant, followed by the local ice cream and then a drive past the mystery woman's house in the evening, before going to bed.

His wake up call came at six thirty and he had washed dressed and was eating breakfast by seven thirty, in order to be in his car, waiting down the road from where the woman lived by five to eight. He reasoned that if she was going to a post office before going off to work, then she could be away from home somewhere between eight o'clock and half past.

By nine o'clock he was getting a bit desperate and would like to have driven past her house to see if there was any sign of life, but decided to give it another thirty minutes. By nine thirty he had noticed that several people had looked out of their windows at the mystery car parked in their road, so he decided to drive down the road past the woman's house and park at the other end. As he drove past he noted that the curtains had been pulled and was just about ready to park the car further down the street, when who should come out of the house and be rushing towards him, carrying a big green parcel but the woman herself. He decided to keep going and headed round the corner to the main road and pulled up about ten yards past the Post Office.

He waited until he could see her in his rear-view mirror and then he casually got out of the car, took his parcel out of the boot and placed it on the pavement. He then locked the boot and the car, picked up the parcel, arriving at the door just a few seconds after her.

"Hold on a moment," he said to her, "and I will open the door for you, my parcel is heavy, but yours looks very awkward."

"Thank you, it is," she said and squeezed through the door and joined the queue for the parcel counter, followed by Mac.

As he was standing there wondering what to do next, she turned round and said, "Did your wife turn up safe and sound on Saturday?"

"I am sorry!" said Mac, in mock surprise.

"Your wife, Saturday, the train station, you spoke with me remember and asked me if I had seen her."

"How rude of me, of course I did, I am terrible with faces. No, she didn't; it turned out that the friend she had been visiting had become unwell, so she did not like leaving her. When I got back to the hotel there was a message waiting for me. A bit of a wasted weekend, but never mind! Plenty of time to think and catch up with some reading."

"I think I may have seen you yesterday actually," she said.

"While I was out walking in the afternoon I expect, I got lost and must have walked for miles," he answered.

"Err, no, it was in the morning, I believe we went to the same church."

"I did attend the service at the Baptist church yesterday morning, but I arrived late and had to rush off afterwards, is that the same church you attended?"

"Yes, my mother and I have been going there for years; you were sitting a few rows in front of us, I recognised your face as you walked past our row."

"Not difficult to miss," said Mac.

"I honestly didn't mean it like that," she quickly replied.

"It's all right, my wife says I go around in a dream, sorry if I ignored you, no offence intended. I think you are next."

During the whole conversation with the woman, Mac had been reading and memorizing the address on the label she had used to cover the original address on the parcel. While she spoke with the counter clerk and had her parcel weighed and the correct stamps were applied, Mac took out a notebook and wrote down the details he had memorized.

He was woken from his thoughts by the woman who said, "It is your turn now, I am already late for work and my office is a fifteen minute walk from here, so I will have to dash. Nice meeting you again, goodbye."

"Would it be presumptuous of me to offer you a lift, as I have a car parked outside and am only taking a slow drive back to Auckland today," he offered.

"Oh, thank you, that would be most kind; I will wait for you outside."

He passed the parcel over the counter and it was weighed by the clerk and he paid the postage and went outside, to find the woman standing by his car and in the act of putting her compact back into her handbag.

"My name is Macdonald Smith," he said, offering his hand, "but all my friends call me Mac."

She took the outstretched hand, shook it gently and said, "Lillian Markham, it's very nice to meet you Mac."

They chatted during the drive to her workplace and he discovered that she was a legal secretary in a small solicitor's office and he told her that he was an out of work draughtsman who had recently emigrated from England with his newly wedded wife.

When they arrived at her solicitors office he jumped out of the car and opened her door and she thanked him for the lift and bid him farewell.

Mac drove back to the hotel, cancelled his Monday night room reservation at Reception, packed his bags, paid his bill and left Hastings. He enjoyed a pleasant drive back to Auckland, arriving home in time to have a roast dinner ready for Deborah when she arrived home from work.

"So what was she like this Lillian Markham woman?" she asked over dinner.

"Like any other thirty something single woman," he answered without thinking.

"What do you mean by that?" she demanded, "I am thirty five, in case you had forgotten."

"You are thirty five and gorgeous and I have hated being away from you, for all these days. Perhaps you should come over here and remind me why I love so much," he suggested.

Chapter 21
Outfoxed

Mac was up early on Tuesday morning and had written his report and posted it off to Perth, along with a note of his expenses by mid-day. He then went along to another employment agency that someone at work had told Deborah about and arranged an interview with one of their consultants, for the following morning. He then went home and telephoned Digger who was still at work.

"Well done Donny, to find all that out and get the woman's name and where she works, you have done marvelously well," said Digger, "as soon as I get your report and claim for expenses, I will send a bank draft over in full settlement of what we owe you."

"Thank you Arnold, it has been a pleasure working with you and I had forgotten what fun undercover work could be. I am sure you will be pleased to know that I have an interview scheduled for tomorrow morning which might well lead to a full time job, so wish me luck."

"I do indeed and perhaps once Moira and I move to Sydney next year, we may see a lot more of each other," Digger suggested.

"How did Vi take the news of your impending move over east?"

"I haven't actually told her yet. I did mention it to Mick and suggested that he should say something to her, but he refused point blank and said I should tell her myself, which of course, is what Moira had already said to me."

"Rather you than me, she is not going to be happy about it, having moved from England to be near to you again. By the way, if the new job does not materialize and you want someone to go to Mauritius for you and follow things up there, just let me know."

"If there are any trips planned to far flung places, I am afraid you will be at the back of the queue, but thanks for the offer, bye for now," with which he put the telephone down and walked into Mr. Newgate's office to give him an update.

"That is excellent news Smith, your cousin has done well for us, but I would prefer to read his full report before we decide what we should do next. I am here for another couple of weeks yet, so there is no rush, I don't suppose that our Mr. Offstrop is going anywhere in a hurry."

On Thursday evening Digger asked Moira whether she was doing anything to celebrate her last day at the hospital on Friday, only to find out that she had agreed to stay there for one more week, as one of the other staff nurses had returned to Broome, to nurse a sick parent.

"I am only doing light duties now Digger and I am feeling really well at the moment, but next week will definitely be my last, I promise," she said emphatically.

On Saturday they drove over to spend the afternoon with Vi, Mick and the children and after a visit to the beach, returned to Vi's for tea. She said nothing during the meal and Digger was getting his courage up to give her the bad news, when to his relief, she told him that Mick had broken the news to her about their probable move to Sydney next year.

"Of course I am saddened by the thought of your move across to the other side of the country Digger, but I do understand that you have to do what is right for you, Moira and the baby. Coming out to Australia was the best thing Mick and I have ever done. We love the climate, the beaches, the people, the fresh start it has given us and everything about it here and it is you and Moira we have to thank for that. We would never have made the decision to come, if you had not already been out here yourselves and had not encouraged us to emigrate and were also ready and willing to help and support us, once we had arrived."

"I am relieved to hear you say that Vi, I was honestly dreading the thought of having to tell you," Digger confessed.

"So Mick informed me, I must be a real dragon or something," she said tearfully.

Digger sat there quietly, looking around the room and then he started whistling.

"You are supposed to say, 'No you are not Vi' you cheeky whatsit, you are still not too big to have your ears boxed you know," with which she got up from her chair, walked round the table and sat on his lap and gave him a big hug.

When Digger arrived at work on Monday the 25th of September he went straight to the Post Room to see if the letter from Mac had arrived for him.

"Is this what you are looking for?" asked the Manager, "I thought you might be in for it," with which he passed the letter over the counter. "I assume the green parcel I sent over, did the trick for you then?"

"We think so, but 'lets not count our chickens before they are hatched', thanks for putting it aside for me."

Digger went upstairs and gave the report to the secretary and asked her to type it up and produce at least three carbon copies of it. When it was complete, he gave the top copy to Mr. Newgate, one for Nugget, one for himself and one for Roger, asking them all to study it that afternoon and to meet the next day to discuss it together.

On Tuesday morning at ten o'clock, they all met in Mr. Newgate's office to review their findings.

"Well gentlemen, I think that Digger and his cousin are to be congratulated on an excellent result," said Nugget. "I think we can safely conclude that from the address Digger's cousin obtained from the parcel that the woman in the Post office was sending to Mr. Offstrop, that he is alive and well and living in Mauritius. Would you all agree?"

Digger and Mr. Newgate both nodded and said that they agreed with Nugget, whereas Roger made no movement and said nothing.

"Do we have a dissenter in our midst, Mr. Cousins?" Nugget enquired.

"I think I would prefer to call myself a skeptic, rather than a dissenter sir," Roger replied.

Digger was beginning to feel slightly embarrassed that his assistant had waited until now to voice his concerns about the report from Donny and therefore asked a little gruffly,

"What exactly is it in the report, that you are feeling skeptical about Roger?"

"It is not what is in the report Digger, but what is missing from it, that is worrying me," he replied a little sheepishly.

"There is no need to be shy Roger, please continue," said Nugget, recognizing Diggers apprehension and Rogers embarrassment, "what is it that you think might be missing from the report?"

"The rest of the mail which was sent to Mr. Offstrop sir," Roger replied.

"What mail might that be?" asked Mr. Newgate.

"Last week I spoke with the Pensions Department who handle all the mail being sent to retirees and they told me that over the last month, there had been at least three other communications which had been sent out to all of the bank's pensioners. It struck me that there was no mention in the report of the woman passing any mail across the counter, just the parcel wrapped in green paper and it made me wonder if she wanted Digger's cousin to read the address she had written on the parcel; but perhaps I am being concerned over nothing."

"The old premise of 'if something appears to be too good to be true, it probably is' eh, Mr. Cousins. Why don't you telephone your cousin Mr. Smith and see if he can clarify that point for us," said Mr. Newgate, "and I suggest that we all get together again tomorrow morning at the same time, to continue the discussion."

The three men left the office and Digger told Roger that he wished to speak with him privately in his office, straight away.

"Why on earth didn't you tell me about your concerns before we went in there Roger?" Digger demanded, once the door had been closed, "you made me feel like an uninformed idiot!"

"I am really sorry Digger, I didn't mean to embarrass you just now, honestly I didn't. I laid awake half the night thinking about the report, knowing something was missing and then the penny dropped and I realised what it was. That is why I was slightly late in joining you in Mr. Newgate's office for the meeting. I got in early today and telephoned the Pensions Department in Melbourne and checked my facts once more, as I wanted to be absolutely certain before I said anything."

"Fair enough Roger, well done. I will try and call Donny at home right now and see what he has to say on the matter; you ring Directory Enquiries and see if you can obtain the telephone number of the solicitors office where Lillian Markham works, the name and address are in Donny's report, if I remember correctly."

It took Digger a couple of attempts at telephoning Donny at home, before he finally picked up the receiver.

"Arnold, how nice of you to ring, about the job interview I presume. Well, I have already had one interview for a full time job and I have a second one lined up for Friday, things are looking up for me cousin; did you get my report and have you sent my cheque off yet?"

"Yes I got your report Monday morning and I did your expenses yesterday afternoon Donny, but I am not sure you have actually earned them, to be quite honest with you."

"What on earth do you mean Arnold; I have practically solved the case for you, what more do you want?"

"My assistant Roger has just asked a very interesting question, which I am hoping you can answer."

"Good for Roger, go ahead, I am all ears."

"When Lillian Markham was in the Post Office on Monday, were you able to observe her the whole time she was at the counter?"

"I believe so. Why?"

"You didn't leave the queue or talk to any of the other customers while she was transacting her business?"

"No Arnold, I watched her like a hawk, what's the problem?"

"Your report did not mention her handing over any letters along with the parcel and we know for a fact, that there were at least three other letters which had been sent to the Napier Post Box that month, for Mr. Offstrop."

"As we agreed Arnold, I was waiting in the car outside of the Napier Post office, so I did not see all the other mail that might have been given to her inside. I was just watching for a lady carrying a large green parcel to come out of the Post office."

"I understand that Donny," said Digger, "but at least one of the letters which was sent to him, required a quick response from him, so she would have needed to send it on to him, even if she was in the habit of opening his mail and removing anything of no importance."

"Well I didn't know that of course, but I did watch everything she did and am quite certain that she passed nothing to the clerk on the Monday morning, apart from that parcel."

"Is it possible she could have opened the parcel and put the letter inside?" Digger suggested.

"I really don't believe so; the parcel looked like it had not been touched, apart from having large sticky labels put on, over the top of the labels which your post room had used."

"From what you have just told me Donny, it sounds to me like Roger may be right in his concern over the authenticity of the address in Mauritius and therefore of the whereabouts of Mr. Offstrop," said Digger.

"I hate to admit it, but you could be right. I thought at the time how fortunate I was that she had written the address on the side of the parcel as well as on the top, in big bold clear handwriting and of course it was her who started the conversation not me. Would you like me to get Deborah to ring the solicitor's office she said she worked at, to see if she really did work there?"

"Not to worry at the moment, Roger is checking that out for me, but if we needed you to go to Napier again to check on her next month, would you be game?"

"I would certainly be game, but I might not be available, if I have started a new job by then. But stay in touch and I will do whatever I can to help."

When Digger had finished the conversation with Donny he called Roger into his office.

"I have to inform you Roger that you were quite right to be skeptical, my cousin has just confirmed that there were no letters passed across the counter at the Post Office along with the green parcel," said Digger.

"Oh dear, that suggests that Miss Lillian Markham is not as innocent as we all thought at first, that is a surprise. I have obtained the telephone number for the solicitors office she purported to work at, I guess we need some pretext to ring them and see if she does really exist," he replied.

"If we get a move on, we could just about contact them, before they leave for the night and it gives me the excuse to be brief with what I tell them," Digger suggested, "get me the number please and let me know when someone comes on the line."

Roger dialed the number and waited a while and a lady eventually answered the phone, "Good afternoon, this is Roger Cousins from the Perth Mining & Commerce Bank Ltd, may I speak with one of your senior solicitors please."

"I am sorry Mr. Cousins, but everyone has gone home apart from myself and our senior clerk, can either of us help you?"

"I expect so, but I will just pass you over to my manager, he will explain the problem to you, one moment please," with which Roger passed the telephone across to Digger.

"Good afternoon, this is Arnold Smith, I am the Senior Internal Audit Manager with the Perth Mining & Commerce Bank Ltd."

"Hello Mr. Smith, as I just explained to Mr. Cousins, there is only myself and our senior clerk here at the moment, but can I assume from your title that there is some sort of urgent problem you wish to discuss with one of our solicitors?"

"Yes, that is perfectly correct, but to be exact, it is actually a member of your staff that I have a need to speak with, perhaps you could tell me if she will be in work tomorrow, her name is Markham, Miss Lillian Markham."

"You must have the wrong solicitor's office Mr. Smith, there is no-one called Lillian Markham working here, but hold on a moment please and I will see if our Mr. Jones recognizes the name, perhaps she may have worked here before I joined the firm."

Everything went quiet for a while and then a man's voice was heard down the telephone.

"Mr. Smith, my name is Jones, perhaps I can be of some assistance to you. As our secretary has just informed you there is no-one by the name of Lillian Markham working in this office, but I suspect that someone has been playing some sort of prank on you, I fear."

"Really Mr. Jones, why on earth would you think that?" Digger replied formally.

"I am a member of the Hastings and Distract Drama Society and two weeks ago we performed a play in a local hall, where one of the main characters was a lady by the name of Lillian Markham."

"Oh dear Mr. Jones, I see what you mean. Well thank you very much for the information and I hope I have not detained you both for too long. I trust the play was a big success for the Society."

"Yes, it was actually Mr. Smith, we sold out for three nights in a row and received a good write up in the local press."

"Did you have a leading part yourself," Digger asked politely.

"Oh no, I am the stage manager, but several of my colleagues here, were on stage, in fact our Miss Offstrop, who played the part of Lillian Markham, was quite outstanding, the way she mastered that South African dialect was truly amazing."

This last piece of information had left Digger a little speechless, so he coughed a couple of times, apologized and then said, "What an unusual name, Offstrop, I don't think I have come across that before," he lied.

"It may have been Dutch originally, not really sure," Mr. Jones informed him, "such a shame she will not be around for our next play, as we are trying another one based in Africa, by the same author."

"But I thought you said the young lady was a colleague of yours," Digger probed.

"I did, she was a colleague, but a relative of hers has become very sick, so she felt obliged to hand in her notice last week, so that she was free to go off and look after him. A lovely girl though; so helpful and considerate to others."

"What a shame, good staff are so hard to find these days; you said him, her brother perhaps?" Digger suggested.

"No I don't believe so, I got the impression it was a much older man the way she spoke about him," Mr. Jones replied.

They chatted for a bit longer and then Digger thanked Mr. Jones for his assistance and bid him a very good afternoon. He then turned to Roger and related all that he had just found out from Mr. Jones in New Zealand and suggested that they both think about it overnight and meet again on Wednesday morning in his office, before re-convening the meeting with Nugget and Mr. Newgate.

Digger did not sleep too well on Tuesday night and by Wednesday morning he had run over so many different scenarios in his mind that he didn't know what to think.

When he met with Roger in his office he discovered that he too had gone round in circles in his thinking, so they decided to be honest with Nugget and Mr. Newgate and admit they did not know
what they should do next.

"There is no shame in admitting you are stumped gentlemen," Mr. Newgate declared, "what we have here is a very complex situation and since the bank has waited this long to get it's gold back, a few more days or weeks delay is neither here nor there, in my opinion. Would you agree Nugget?"

"Most certainly I would," Nugget replied, "this is not a life and death situation we are facing, where a decision has to be made today. In my experience, if you do not know what to do, then you should make the decision to do nothing for now and meet again in say, two weeks time from today and see if things are any clearer to us all then."

"So there we have it," said Mr. Newgate, "we will meet again in two weeks time, but I have to warn you that I will be leaving for Melbourne shortly after that, so any follow-up meetings will have to be over in Victoria."

When Digger arrived home on the Friday he found Pat in the kitchen cooking the tea and Moira outside working in the garden.

"Hi Pat what's for tea?" he asked, as he looked in at the kitchen.

"Chicken casserole and just so that you know, Moira did not stop work today Digger. She really has coped well with these lighter duties, much better than everyone expected, so she has the agreement of her ward Sister, to keep going for as long as she feels able."

"Why aren't I surprised. Thanks for letting me know Pat."

He wandered into the garden and sat down on the patio watching Moira on her knees, weeding the roses, she being oblivious to his presence until he coughed loudly.

"Digger, you made me jump, sneaking up on a girl like that! I didn't hear you arrive, have you been there long, help me up will you please?"

"I was watching you work love and have been here for five minutes," with which he walked over, helped her to her feet and turned one of the chairs round to make it easier for her to sit down.

"Did Pat tell you that I didn't leave work today and are you cross with me?" she asked.

"Yes she told me and I am never cross with you, just concerned; but if you feel you can manage working for a bit longer, then you are the best judge of that, not me."

"Oh good. Do we have plenty of petrol in the car as I thought it would be nice to go out to Pinjarra and see all of our friends for the weekend and I told Pat she could come as well, you don't mind do you? I telephoned Victoria today and cleared it with her."

"Of course not, it's a good idea, but one condition, you come as a spectator this time and leave the work to me."

"If you say so, we ladies will just have to drink tea and sit and chat, I am sure we can cope with that. I did remember to repair your work trousers, the ones you tore on the fence and I did order the paint you wanted, so we can pick it up on the way tomorrow. That's Pat calling, time for dinner."

When they arrived at the farm on Saturday, Moira and Pat were greeted by Victoria who took them off into the house and Bertie, kitted out in some old workman's overalls he found in the stables, climbed into the passenger seat besides Digger and they drove away together to James Street.

"Well this is very kind of you Bertie, to come and give me a hand with the painting," Digger said.

"My pleasure my friend, Victoria has been positively starved of female company since we arrived here, so she will have a lovely time with Moira and her friend Pat. Am I allowed to ask how the Investigation is going?"

"Has Donny not told you anything about it then?" Digger asked.

"I have heard all about his new job in Auckland from Deborah, but she has said nothing about the work he undertook for you in Napier."

Digger gave a quick overview of what had happened and how the bank had decided to give it a rest for a couple of weeks, "So you see Bertie, we have hit a bit of a dead end at the moment. Any suggestions or ideas that your wide experience of life and all it's nuances, may bring to mind, would be most appreciated."

"I guess that is my cue for a story, but I will resist the temptation, you will be delighted to hear. It's just the obvious questions which come to mind Digger, for example, does she have a passport, why was she so good at speaking with a South African accent, why a South African bank in Capetown rather than one in Mauritius and did the cousin who only recently left the bank already know any of this?"

Digger sat in silence for a while and then said, "Thank you Bertie, you ask some excellent questions, why didn't I think of any of them?"

"Sometimes you can be so close to a problem that you 'cannot see the wood for the trees', as my great Uncle Harry used to say. But the one question which worries me most is why did the bank have no record of his being married with a daughter? I wonder if that could be something else that your Mr. Davis removed from the company files?"

"I don't know the answer to that, but I will find out next week; but to change the subject, do you prefer to paint walls or ceilings?"

Between them they managed to paint all the ceilings in the house as well as the walls of the main bedroom and the kitchen, before they ran out of paint. By the time they had got back to the farm in the late afternoon, Ray and Jenny had joined the company and an excellent meal and a pleasant evening was had by all, without anyone being bitten or damaged in any way, apart from overeating.

On Sunday they all went to church in the morning and then to the pub for a drink and a light meal, before heading back to Perth.

"Did Bertie tell you about Samuel and Caroline Van Royt's visit next year?" Moira asked as they were driving home.

"No he didn't, when are they coming?"

"They were going to come in May, but Victoria said that they were planning on taking a cruise back to England, leaving at the end of April, so she is not sure what they will be doing now."

"They could come and stop with us, I suppose, but we will probably still be settling into our new house somewhere in Sydney around then," said Digger.

"Why not tell them that and suggest that they come and stay with us in Sydney, in May, the baby should be going through the night by then and they could be our first visitors."

"Good idea, if you don't think it will be too much for you, having visitors with a new baby and all that."

"And all what? There he goes again Pat, fuss, fuss fuss!" she said in an exasperated tone of voice. "When will you learn Digger, that millions of women before me have had babies and have coped with far worse difficulties than having two visitors for a couple of weeks, do you understand that?"

"Whatever you say Moira and don't bring Pat into the conversation. Just don't complain to me if you cannot cope, I will not want to hear about it and do you understand that?" he snapped back.

On Monday morning the 2nd of October 1950 Digger and Roger sat down to discuss the questions that Bertie had raised over the weekend. The first thing they did was to ring Rusty's boss in Melbourne and to ask him to check Mr. Offstrop's personnel file for any mention of a wife or daughter and to find out his full name. He said he would be happy to do that and also offered to make the telephone call to Mr. Albert Offstrop to see what light he could shed on the matter and to find out if there was any family connection with South Africa.

They then spoke with the Security Manager in Perth about finding out some more details about Miss. Offstrop, but were told that he would need her full name and address to be able to do this.

Digger also decided that he would call Mrs. Taylor at the City Branch in Sydney and see if she could shed any light on the matter.

"Hello Marjorie, it's Digger Smith from the Perth office, we met a couple of weeks back you may recall."

"Good afternoon Digger, nice to hear from you again, what can I do to help you today?"

"I was wondering if you ever met Mr. Offstrop's wife and daughter during the time you both worked together in Sydney?" Digger asked.

"Oh what an interesting question," Marjorie replied.

"Really, why is that?"

"Well officially he never admitted to having a wife and daughter, we were all led to believe that he was still single, but you know what a rumour mill a bank can be Digger!"

"Indeed I do," Digger agreed, "so what rumours were circulating?"

"I am not a gossip Digger and do not like to spread rumours about anyone, but since you brought the subject up, one of the older women who had been working in the bank for a lot longer than me, maintained that he had been involved with a young woman while on a safari in South Africa and that he was the father of her child."

"How interesting," said Digger, "there cannot be many bank employees who went on a safari before the War."

"Well no, that's what I thought and then one day in late May in nineteen thirty seven, who should come into the bank just before closing time, but this woman in her mid thirties with a young girl who could only have been about twelve I would say and asked to see Mr. Rutger van Offstrop."

"I don't want to sound a doubting Thomas, but how can you be so specific about the date of all this Marjorie?"

"It was just a few days after my eighteenth birthday and Mr. Offstrop had called me into his office that same morning, to tell me that he was very pleased with my progress and to give me my first raise. You tend to remember things like that."

"I guess you do," Digger replied, "so what happened next?"

"I don't really know, one of the other clerks fetched Mr. Offstrop, who turned as white as a sheet when he saw them standing there and immediately ushered them into his office. They were still in there when we all left to go home and we never saw or heard of them again and the official story which circulated was that they were relatives of his from South Africa, who had just arrived in the country and had called in unexpectedly to see him."

"Ah right then," said Digger, "so that explains it."

"Not really Digger, I was told to take in some tea and biscuits for them all, just before I left for home and I distinctly heard the little girl call Mr. Offstrop, 'Papa'."

"Did you hear any of the conversation between the woman and Mr. Offstrop?"

"No, she spoke with a very heavy South African accent, but she did call him Rutger, which I assumed was his Christian name."

"So if the little girl was about twelve in nineteen thirty seven, I guess that would make her about twenty five now," said Digger.

"I guess so, a young woman in her own right. I wonder what has happened to her now, or perhaps that is the reason you telephoned me today Digger?"

"Partly, we have come across a young woman in her mid twenties who appears to be his daughter, so the information you have just given to me is most helpful. Thank you Marjorie, goodbye."

No sooner had he put the telephone down on his call to Sydney, than Rusty rang with some news about Mr. Offstrop's personnel file.

"Hello Digger, I thought you would like to know that his full name is Rutger van Offstrop and there is absolutely no record of his being married and having a daughter, it looks like we got that one wrong," said Rusty.

"I don't believe so Rusty," said Digger, who gave him an abbreviated version of his recent conversation with Marjorie Taylor.

"I see what you mean," said Rusty, "well I cannot believe that his cousin and the rest of the family did not know about his wife and daughter; I will mention it to my boss who has arranged to telephone Albert Offstrop tomorrow morning. As soon as I hear something, I will call you, bye for now Digger."

It was actually Wednesday afternoon when Rusty's boss telephoned Digger and informed him that he had personally spoken with Albert Offstrop that morning and the picture was now a lot clearer.

"It appears that the Offstrop family did originate from South Africa shortly after the Boer War and they came in two distinct groups, one settling in Australia and the other in New Zealand."

"Was he able to be specific about the locations where they settled in both countries," asked Digger.

"He said they went to Adelaide to start with in Australia and then some moved to Melbourne with Rutger then moving to Sydney on his own and mainly Dunedin in New Zealand. In nineteen twenty four there was some family problem to do with a parcel of land in South Africa and Rutger went across on their behalf to sort it out. While he was there he met a young friend of a second cousin called Simone, fell in love with her and enjoyed a holiday romance."

"So the rumours in the bank were not too far off the mark then!" Digger commented.

"Not far at all. Albert went on to explain that when the family found out about the romance and then discovered that the young woman was pregnant, they were horrified, as were the family of the young woman herself; who forbade her from having any further contact with him. The woman had the baby, a little girl called Carice and Rutger sent her money each month to help support the child."

"Hold on while I write all this down," said Digger, "the mother was called Simone and the daughter Carice."

"That's right, but I did not ask for the mother's surname, I am afraid. Anyway, some time in nineteen thirty six, Albert was not sure of the exact date, Rutger and Simone both arranged a simultaneous holiday to Mauritius, where they resumed the romance and talked about getting married and living together in Australia. They were introduced to some sort of underworld character there, who said he could arrange all the details and transport mother and daughter to Australia for a fee."

"Ah, so that explains the Mauritius link," Digger said, thinking aloud.

"Quite so; well half the fee was paid by Rutger a month or so later and the remainder was due when they arrived in Australia. Albert was a bit vague about the next bit, but he knew that something had gone wrong on the journey and mother and daughter were delayed for about a week and Rutger was naturally getting frantic, as he did not know what had happened to them and when they would now be arriving."

"Very understandable in the circumstances, since they were probably entering Australia illegally," said Digger.

"I hadn't thought about that, but I suppose they were! Anyway, when they did arrive, it appears that they were driven directly to the bank where his wife informed him that the Australian contact had demanded Rutger pay the remainder of the money that afternoon, which indeed, Albert said Rutger paid over to him, after they left the bank."

"So I assume that mother and daughter then lived with Rutger at his house in Sydney," Digger said.

"It appears not. The family were still not happy with Rutger and the arrangement, so Simone and Carice went across to Adelaide and lived with an elderly relative of Rutger's, with him going across to visit them, whenever he could. It became their home and the girl went to school in Adelaide and did well, Albert said she was a bright little thing and all the family were very fond of her."

"So is that where Rutger went after he retired from the bank?" asked Digger.

"For a short period of time, yes it was, but then the elderly relative became unwell and wanted to go to her sister's in

Dunedin, so they all moved across to New Zealand with her, since she had been so good to Simone and Carice."

"Did Albert tell you where in Dunedin, Rutger and family are now living?" Digger asked.

"No he did not. He said he was honestly not sure where his cousin was now living, but knew that his wife had not liked Dunedin and her own parents had become unwell, so she had returned to South Africa some years ago and thought that Rutger had gone with her. He seemed genuinely surprised when I told him that we believed his daughter Carice, was currently living in Hastings, North Island and was collecting her father's mail and sending it on to him."

"Did you ask him if the family could shed any light on the whereabouts of the gold, taken in the robbery?"

"He told me that since he had retired from the bank, that he had given a lot of thought to the subject and the only suggestion he could make was that since Rutger was only fifty six when he retired on 'health grounds', his pension would not have been sufficient to provide an adequate standard of living for them all. He now wonders if Rutger used the money to buy a business of some sort, to provide him with the extra income he needed."

"Did he suggest what sort of business he might have purchased?"

"He did not know for sure but thought that if it was anything, it might be a hotel, as the family had run hotels in South Africa for many years, before emigrating here."

"Well if he did purchase a hotel, or any other business for that matter and we can prove it was from the gold he stole from us, the bank might yet get its money back," Digger suggested.

"That is very true Smith," said Rusty's boss, "and I would like to suggest that it is about time you personally made a trip to New Zealand to speak with the solicitor that the young woman worked for in Hastings and to pay a visit to Dunedin, to track down our Mr. Offstrop, what do you think?"

Chapter 22
The Other Woman

"What do you mean he suggested you fly over to New Zealand and track Offstrop down? He had absolutely no right to give you such an instruction without talking to me first Digger," said Nugget, when Digger informed him on Thursday morning of his discussion with Rusty's boss the previous afternoon.

"It wasn't an instruction, so much as a suggestion Nugget, I am sure he had no desire to go over your head and he is certainly aware that you are the new Divisional director for Western Australia and my immediate boss, now that Mr. Newgate has a new job," Digger hurriedly explained.

"Good, I am delighted to hear it! And if he knows what's good for him, he won't forget it in a hurry either! I want a full report of the whole Investigation from start to finish on my desk by eleven o'clock Tuesday morning of next week, with a copy for Mr. Newgate. This will give us the remainder of Tuesday to study your report and we will all sit down and review it next Wednesday, at the meeting we have already scheduled in our diaries. Is that quite clear?"

"Yes sir," said Digger, slightly taken aback by the obvious anger in Nugget's response and the lightly veiled rebuke to himself.

"I do not want you to speak directly to the man again on any subject, but particularly the Investigation and I will be speaking with my erstwhile colleague in Melbourne myself, once this meeting is concluded; that will be all Digger, you may go."

Digger sheepishly closed the door to Nugget's office behind him and slowly walked back to his own office, not sure what to make of the conversation that had just taken place. He made himself a cup of tea and sat down to think for a while and then called Roger into his office and outlined the work they had to do in the next few days, in order to have the report completed and typed up, by the following Tuesday morning.

As each section was completed, it was passed to Nugget's secretary for typing and the final report was put together and the deadline was met on Tuesday morning, with just an hour to spare.

When Digger arrived at work on Wednesday the eleventh of October, he was informed that the meeting had been cancelled and that both Nugget and Mr. Newgate would be away from the office for several days, as they had both gone over to Melbourne to meet with the Chairman. The secretary said that Nugget had telephoned her to say that the Chairman had called him at home the previous evening and asked him to travel to Melbourne that morning.

"I really have no idea what is going on here Roger," Digger said, as the two men sat down in his office and enjoyed a cup of coffee together, "it must be something to do with the Investigation to call them both across there at such short notice."

"Perhaps they spotted something in the report or Albert Offstrop has come up with some new information," Roger suggested.

"You may well be right, who knows? Still, while they keep paying my wages, who am I to complain, but I must say I was looking forward to going over to New Zealand myself, to put the final pieces of the jigsaw together."

"In view of what happened to you at Southern Cross, being thrown down the mine shaft and all that, I thought you and more especially Moira, would have been relieved that the problem seems to have been taken out of your hands."

"I think Moira might be, but I must be a glutton for punishment or something, but you do make a good point Roger, if I am allowed to go over there and Donny is not available to accompany me, I will insist that they let you come and keep me company, so we can watch each others backs," Digger stated.

"Perhaps you should ring your cousin and find out how the new job is going and whether he would be available to accompany you or not, because you could still get a telephone call from the Chairman, at any time, telling you to go over there and you need to know whether you should mention my going with you or not," said Roger.

"After my conversation with Nugget the other day, I don't think I dare mention anything to anyone, that I have not discussed with him beforehand," said Digger, "but I will ring Donny today. He will still be at work at the moment, so I will call him later this afternoon and see how things stand with him."

"Yes who is it?" was all the reply he got when he telephoned Donny in Auckland, later that day.

"Hello Deborah, its Digger, is Donny there please.

"It's your moronic cousin for you," she said to Donny, but loud enough so that Digger could hear her.

"Arnold, how nice of you to call and how pleasant to hear a warm friendly voice again," were Donny's opening words, said loud enough for Deborah to hear.

"What on earth is going on there Donny," Digger asked.

"My wife has taken it into her head that I have found myself another woman, if you can believe it!"

"Another what? You! I don't believe it. What on earth has made her think that?"

"Goodness knows, I have absolutely no idea what goes on inside that pretty little head of hers. Anyway Arnold, what can I do for you?"

"I was just ringing to see how the new job was going and to say that there is a good chance I will be coming over to New Zealand myself, sometime soon and need to know whether you will be available to accompany me on my journeys to Hastings and most probably, Dunedin."

"The job is about two grades down from what I was doing in Bedford, so it's O.K. but nothing more and I am not sure how long I can do it for, if I am being honest with you. Unfortunately the pay is not too good either, so I am doing a lot of overtime to make up my money, including some Saturday work, so you had better count me out from accompanying you on your trips, in the next few weeks, at least."

"Not really the bright new future you were looking for then," said Digger.

"You can certainly say that again Arnold, particularly with thunder face here, glaring at me."

They chatted for a bit longer, but Digger was aware that his cousin was anxious to sort matters out with Deborah, so he ended the conversation and said goodbye.

"Don't you ever insult my cousin or anyone else in my family again Deborah," he shouted across the room at her, having slammed the receiver down on its holder. "If you and I have a problem, it stays between us, I don't drag your family into it and you will have the good manners not to involve mine. Is that understood?"

She had never seen him so angry before and was taken off guard by the vehemence of his outburst and just nodded and said nothing.

"Now tell me calmly, in words of one syllable Debs, why on earth you should imagine I have been associating with another woman."

They both sat down on the couch together and she started to explain, "I left for work before you today because I had to be in early, just like I was on Monday and waited by the bus stop as usual. When my bus drew up a woman got off and walked away in the direction I had just come from and as she walked past me I thought to myself what a pleasant scent she was wearing, I wonder what it is, as I would like some myself," Deborah paused for breath and watched Mac closely for any reaction.

"Go on I am listening," Mac replied.

"When I came home this evening, I smelt that same scent in our home the moment I walked through the door and I know for sure it is not mine Mac."

"Debs, when my face was damaged in the War, it did something to my nose, I have virtually no sense of smell be it pleasant or unpleasant. I cannot tell if you are wearing perfume or not or what it might smell like if you do; which is why I never use aftershave myself nowadays, as I always ended up using too much and people would not come near me."

"I never knew that Mac, does it affect your sense of taste as well?"

"I suppose it must, which is probably why I prefer sweet to savoury food. But getting back to this mysterious scent wearing woman, have you seen her around here at any other time?"

"Well I have thought about it a lot this afternoon and I am sure she passed me on my way to the bus stop on Tuesday morning when I was a bit later, but I was in a hurry as I did not want to miss the bus and may have been mistaken."

"How strange, but to change the subject for a minute, have you been rummaging around with my papers, in your quest to prove my unfaithfulness, which I keep in the second drawer down in the desk?"

"Of course I haven't Mac, isn't that where you keep your notes on the work you did for Digger?"

"The very same, have you disturbed them for any reason Debs?"

"No, why on earth would I? What makes you ask the question?"

"Well I tend to keep my papers in date order, it makes life easier when you are keeping track of the changes to a drawing; anyway, when I was looking for something tonight, after I came home from work, I realised that some of the papers were out of order and just assumed that you had been in the drawer for some reason."

"Well I can assure you that I haven't Mac, as I said, I could smell that woman's scent the moment I stepped through the door and was far too upset to do anything and certainly not to rummage through your papers."

"Well Debs, I think we have to conclude that someone broke into our house today and has gone through our things. Let us both check the house over and see if anything is missing and you go through every room and have a good sniff, so we can tell which rooms she went into. By the way, did you get a good look at her face this morning?"

"Not really, I would say that she was twenty or thirty, white, average height, slim build and she was wearing a grey coat with a very large headscarf, which covered most of her face."

"You know, that sounds a lot like the young woman I followed in Hastings the other week, Lillian Markham."

They spent the next fifteen minutes searching the house and then sat down with a glass of sherry to discuss their findings.

"There is nothing missing that I can think of," said Deborah, "but your other jacket was almost off the hanger and I would never leave it like that, so maybe she went through the pockets looking for something. I could detect her scent in every room of the house, what about you, did you discover anything."

"Nothing I can think of, except a pencil maybe. I broke one the other night and was too lazy to find the pencil sharpener, so just took a new one from the middle draw of the desk and left it on top with the broken one and it has now disappeared, unless of course, you took it, for some reason."

"Not guilty, I use a propelling pencil, so it definitely wasn't me. We should check the doors and windows to see if any of them have been forced open. By the way, what time did you leave for work today?"

"I was a bit earlier leaving the house today as I had decided to walk to work rather than take the bus. I had realised that I was getting unfit and thought the exercise would be good for me, but it took me a lot longer than I thought it would and I ended up being twenty minutes late, but fortunately the boss was even later, so I got away with it."

"That explains why you weren't at work when I rang you at ten past nine this morning," said Deborah.

"Why did you ring me?" asked Mac.

"We are out of bread and I was going to ask you to pick some up from that nice bakery round the corner from your office, but when I was told you were not in, I was concerned that you had gone back to sleep after I left, so I rang home in case you had."

"Oh I see, how thoughtful of you," Mac replied.

"Yes it was, but it was also the start of my paranoia, as someone picked the phone up and then put it down again after a few seconds. I thought that I had misdialed and was going to ring the number again, but I was called in to speak with the M.D. and forgot all about it, until I came home tonight and smelt the woman's scent."

"So you decided that good old hubby had been entertaining another lady in your home, while you were working your fingers to the bone at the office, eh!"

"Something like that; I am so sorry Mac for doubting you and for being so rude to Digger just now, please forgive me."

"Of course I forgive you Debs and Arnold is very thick skinned where you are concerned, but we have to decide what we need to do next, to discover who this woman really is and why she broke into our home."

"But if there is no sign of a forced entry, how did she get into the house?" Deborah asked.

"We are not the first tenants to live here and we did not have the locks changed, so who knows who might have a key."

"Hold on, that gives me an idea, Rosie always leaves a spare key under a stone in the front garden, I just wonder if one of the previous tenants used to do that and it is still there, I am going to have a look," with which she jumped up and went out into the front garden and returned five minutes later holding a key aloft.

"Have you tried it in the lock yet?" Mac asked.

"I have and it fits and I am going to ask the agent tomorrow if we can change the locks, as I no longer feel secure here, but at least we know how she got into the house, but if it is this Lillian Markham, or whatever her name is, how did she know where you lived?"

"If it is her and it probably is, as a thief would certainly have stolen my camera or your jewellery, or the few pounds I had left in my bedside drawer, she almost certainly did get into the house with the key she would have found under the stone. As to how she knew where I lived, I can only presume that while I was busy reading and remembering the address on her parcel while in the queue at the Post Office, she was equally busy reading and remembering the address on my parcel and I was too dumb to notice!"

"So the ultra smart and highly trained British spy, was out maneuvered by a simple woman eh? I told you that I was not comfortable with you following her, I must have known something like this would happen."

"Rubbish, you knew nothing of the sort, she just got lucky, that's all."

"I presume by your parcel, you meant the out of date telephone directories and magazines you so kindly sent yourself."

"Precisely, I think I need to ring Arnold back and let him know what has been going on here and it wouldn't hurt you to apologize to him either Debs."

Donny rang Digger and explained what had been happening, but Deborah was unable to come to the phone as she had disappeared into the bathroom and was washing her hair while he was talking to Digger.

"So what are you going to do next?" asked Digger.

"I have a similar looking key that I brought out from England with me, so I will leave that under the stone and see if anyone moves it, but of course they will not be able to get into the house," Donny replied, "and we will both keep our eyes open for a mysterious looking woman in a headscarf, but to be honest, there is not a lot we can do, until she pops up again."

"Well thanks for keeping me informed and I am sorry that helping me out has resulted in this unpleasantness for you and your lovely lady wife."

"Thank you Arnold and Debs really thinks you are wonderful too, she is just too shy to say it," Donny joked, "I appreciate your concern, but I don't believe she is dangerous or represents any real threat to us, she is just becoming a nuisance; any way, since I am paying for this call, I will bid you goodbye."

It was Tuesday of the following week, when Mac was early for work and decided to get off the bus a couple of stops before his normal one, that he noticed out of the corner of his eye, a woman in a headscarf, jump of the bus as it was pulling away from the stop. He went into a sweet shop and bought some Polo's and noticed that she had not walked past the shop while he was inside, so he crossed the road, opposite to a shop with large angled windows and watched her in the reflection, as she crossed the road about twenty paces behind him.

He sauntered along for a bit more, looking in the shop windows as he went and noticed she stayed about twenty paces behind him, stopping whenever he did. He turned down a side street and quickly took his camera out of the bag he was carrying and wound on the film, holding the camera in front of him. He crossed that street at a steep angle, so she would not be able to see the camera and then turned first left down another road and stepped into a doorway a few yards down, camera at the ready. As he heard her coming towards him, he stepped out and took her photograph, whilst at the same time saying, "Good morning Miss Markham, this is a pleasant surprise."

She seemed rooted to the spot for several seconds, which gave him time to wind the film on and take a second photo.

"Why Mr. Smith, fancy meeting you here," she said and then started laughing, "I guess we must both enjoy the same sort of films, not to be able to come up with some better lines than that."

"Very true, you and I need to talk, perhaps you will allow me to buy you a coffee and a bun, there is a little café round the corner that I sometimes use."

"The one next to the bakers you mean, I saw you in there last Wednesday."

"Was that before or after, you broke into my house."

"It was after I used the key you foolishly left under a stone in your front garden, to gain entrance to your house as I needed to use the bathroom. I then came into town and noticed you leaving your office and watched as you had lunch with two other men, colleagues of yours, I presume,"

"They were indeed, so after searching through my home and spying on me while I had lunch, what conclusions did you come to, may I ask?"

"I decided that you really were a draughtsman who had recently emigrated from England and that if you carried on eating meals of the size you enjoyed last Wednesday, that you would soon become overweight and not able to spy on and then follow, young innocent women, around their home towns anymore, which might not be a bad thing of course."

He smiled back at her and nodded and they went into the café and sat at his normal table and he ordered two coffees and two buns.

"So, having used my bathroom, why did you then go through the papers in my desk and why did you walk through every other room in the house?" Mac asked.

"I was trying to find out how much of what you told me was true and how much was a lie; so I was checking on your story of being newly married and having only recently arrived in New Zealand and what your real job was and who you were working for."

"Again, what conclusions did you come to, may I ask?"

"That what you told me seemed to be perfectly true, which worried me even more, because if you were not with the Police, or Immigration Authority or the bank, but really were an out of work draughtsman, what were you doing in Napier and Hastings, following me?"

"How did you know I was following you, I thought I had been so careful?"

"I don't mean to be rude Mr. Smith," she started.

"Please call me Mac," he interrupted.

"My real name is Carice Offstrop, but I expect you already know that Mac," she said, "but to continue; I don't want to be rude, but with your scarring, you do tend to stand out in a crowd, if you know what I mean."

"I accept that Carice, but you did not actually see me until I spoke with you at the railway station in Hastings."

"Ah yes, your missing wife, I remember the conversation well. I hope that if a husband of mine should think I had gone missing, that he would show a lot more concern than you did," she remarked. "As it happens, the lady in the Post Office in Napier, asked if my father's friend had been in touch with me yet, to which I replied, which friend would that be and she said, 'the young man with the badly scarred face'."

"A bit of a give-away I guess."

"When I came out of the Post office with that ridiculous green parcel, I guessed that someone would be watching out for me, so when I spotted your car down the street from the Post Office and then at the station and then again at the station in Hastings, I realised it had to be you. I also noticed you drive past the house a couple of times that day, but not having a car myself, I couldn't follow you and then out of the blue, my friend who works as a Receptionist at the hotel you were stopping in, phoned to ask what time the service started at the Baptist Church, which she knew I normally attended."

"Let me guess and she said, 'you can't miss him as he has a badly scarred face'."

"Exactly, but since you were going there of your own accord, not knowing it was where I attended, I decided that you could not be all bad and was no longer fearful of you."

"I am pleased to hear it, as I really did feel most uncomfortable, when I saw you ride past on your bike."

"Good, it serves you right and since I have been honest with you, I trust you will show me the same courtesy and now be honest with me in return."

"Fair enough Carice, what do you want to know."

"Why were you following me and who were you really working for?"

"I was working for the Perth Mining & Commerce Bank Ltd and was commissioned to track down the whereabouts of your father."

"But you are a draughtsman, why would they employ you to follow me?"

"I was at that time an 'out of work' draughtsman, so my cousin Digger, who is the Senior Internal Audit Manager at the bank, asked me if I would like to do him a favour and undertake this little task for him. I should explain that I was involved in all this sort of work during the War, but sadly out of practice."

"You can say that again," she commented.

"I would have thought that you should have realised who I was working for, by the sender's address on the parcel."

"I rang Papa in South Africa about the parcel and he said he had never received one before from the bank and thought it might have been from someone who was out to do him harm, so he gave me the address in Mauritius to put on it and told me to send it off there as soon as possible."

"I see, but what about the rest of his mail? You never posted them to your father when you sent the parcel off."

"I kept the letters for a few days and then asked my Receptionist friend if you were still staying at the hotel and when she said you had left, I sent them off to him. Now tell me Mac, why did the bank employ you to track Papa down, it doesn't make any sense."

"Because of the bank robbery of course Carice, the twenty thousand gold sovereigns your father and his gang stole from the bank in 1938."

The expression on her face and the dropped coffee cup, which smashed the saucer as it landed and spilt coffee all down the front of her dress, gave Mac the distinct impression that this was not something which Carice Offstrop had been aware of, before that moment in time.

The waiter rushed over and cleared away the crockery and gave Carice a tea towel to mop up the spilt coffee with, "Is the lady all right," he asked.

Carice nodded, wiped her dress and handed the tea towel back to the waiter and then stood up and rushed out of the café. Mac quickly settled the bill and rushed after her down the street, calling out, "Carice, Carice, please wait a moment."

She must have run for a good minute before she ran out of breath and slowed down to a fast walk, which gave Mac the chance to catch her up, "Carice, I am so sorry, everyone had assumed that you knew about the robbery and that was why you were helping your father to keep his whereabouts secret from the bank."

"I was still a child in 1938, why should I know anything about a robbery and how can you be sure that my father was involved and to suggest he had his own gang is ridiculous. He is not a criminal, he is a kind and gentle man, why would he do such a terrible thing as to rob his own bank?"

"This is really not the place to continue this conversation Carice, are you stopping in Auckland at the moment?" Mac asked.

"No, I am going back to Dunedin this afternoon, an old uncle is dying and only has a few days to live, I want to be with him; I only came up for a week or so, I have been looking for a new job and of course looking for you."

"My cousin at the Bank, needs to talk with you about your father, can you give me an address in Dunedin where he can reach you."

"Papa owns the Pretoria Hotel in Dunedin, it is just on the outskirts of town, I have an apartment on the top floor, he can contact me there, but please leave me in peace for a couple of weeks so that the family can bury my uncle and mourn him properly, without being disturbed."

"Very well, my cousin is a good man, you will like him, I am sure he will not bother you until you are ready to talk with him."

They shook hands and parted company, she going to the train station and he going to work, where once again he was late and this time his boss had got in before him!

Donny phoned Digger that evening and told him what had transpired between Carice Offstrop and himself.

"So she convinced you that she did not know anything about her father's part in the robbery," Digger stated.

"I would bet my life on it, the information I gave her just shattered her composure and I watched as this articulate, confident young woman became an absolute mess in a split second."

"Well I wasn't expecting that," said Digger, "and you say that the sick relative is an old uncle and that her father is in South Africa, perhaps with her mother."

"Perhaps so, I can't answer that, because I did not ask her the question."

"Fair enough, but what is the name of the hotel that her father owns in Dunedin."

"It is called the Pretoria Hotel but as I said earlier, I am only giving you the name of the hotel on the understanding that you wait for at least a couple of weeks before you make contact, is that understood Arnold?"

"Understood Donny, I just hope she does not skip the country with the rest of the gold that they have hidden away somewhere."

"I think that is most unlikely Arnold, as I say, she was genuinely shocked by the news and could not believe that her father could do such a terrible thing."

"Fair enough, well thanks for keeping me informed and hopefully we can meet up somewhere, if I come to New Zealand in a few weeks time, bye for now."

Digger decided to think about all that he had just heard over night, rather than rush in and tell Nugget, who had hardly spoken to him, since returning from Melbourne at the weekend. That night Pat had gone out dancing with her new friend, so it gave Moira and Digger a chance to chat on their own.

"Poor girl, what a terrible shock it must have been, to find out in that way, that the father you love and respect is a master criminal, it must have been devastating for her," Moira remarked.

"I suppose so," said Digger, "I had not thought of it in that way, I had assumed she was in the know and was helping to cover his tracks."

"You know what assume did Digger," said Moira piously.

"I know, make an 'ass of u and me' and it certainly did this time."

"When will you tell Nugget then, about these developments?"

"I don't know, he was in a foul mood last week, when I told him that Rusty's boss had said I should go to New Zealand, he almost bit my head off. I have never seen him like that before."

"Could it be anything to do with Rusty leaving the bank?" she asked innocently.

"What? How did you know that, when I, who work for the bank, had not heard anything about it?"

"I work with his mother silly and women talk to each other, unlike some men I could mention. It appears that someone he worked with called him an unpleasant name, or something like that and Rusty thumped him for it and he then told Rusty's boss, who suggested he should resign, so he did."

"When did this all happen?" asked an incredulous Digger.

"Some sporting event the weekend before last, I think Junie said."

"Well that certainly explains Nugget's ill humour, I feel a lot more comfortable talking to him now, than I did before, well done love!"

The next day, bright and early, Digger spoke with Nugget's secretary and arranged to se him just after lunch.

"Come in Digger, please shut the door and make yourself comfortable."

"Thank you sir," said Digger and sat down.

"There is no need to use 'sir' with me Digger, I was just in a terrible frame of mind last week when we spoke and I apologize if I treated you unfairly."

"That's all right Nugget, I only heard about Rusty leaving the bank last night, I quite understand."

"Thank you my friend, what makes it all the worse, is his boss and I have never really got on together. We both joined the bank at about the same time and there has always been rivalry between us. He thought he was in line for a Divisional Director's job and was really peeved that I attained the position before him and I felt he took his frustration out on Rusty, something which I would never have done."

"What a rotten thing to do, so what is Rusty doing now, looking for a new job I presume?"

"The banking community is quite a small community and within forty eight hours of resigning, he had been to two interviews and was offered two jobs. He is now working for an English Bank at a greater salary and a more responsible position, so he is well pleased with himself. In fact one of the reasons the Chairman called me over there, was to apologize for what had happened and to make sure that neither I, nor you, nor anyone else for that matter, would follow him across to the new bank. Rusty asked me to give you his new telephone number at work, but I have asked him to give me an undertaking not to poach you, for at least another year; hope you don't mind Digger."

"Not at all Nugget, I am very flattered at your concern, but I am also very happy here and we are both looking forward to our move to Sydney next year."

"I am glad to hear it Digger, but I gather from my secretary that you have some important news from New Zealand, so tell me what you have discovered."

Chapter 23
Flight to South Africa

"What did Nugget say when you told him you knew about Rusty leaving the bank?" were Moira's first words when Digger got home from work that Wednesday evening.

"Hello darling, it's wonderful to see you too, have you had a nice day at work, you haven't been overdoing it, have you?" was Digger's reply.

She walked over, kissed him lightly on the cheek and said, "There, that's all you are getting until I know what happened."

"You sure know how to drive a poor boy wild," he replied.

"Would you two rather I left you alone for a bit," said Pat, not sure what to make of the interaction that was taking place.

"No, you stay and support me Pat; it's just someone's English sense of humour coming to the front, but if you wouldn't mind pouring him a cup of tea, it might loosen his tongue and prevent me from passing out with an acute case of curiosity!"

"Who is being sarcastic now? Thanks Pat," Digger said, as he sat down at the table with the cup she had passed him, "if we are all seated comfortably children, then I will begin; after a few sips of my tea."

"So what was his reaction?" asked Moira.

"He was actually quite pleased that I knew about it and was happy to tell me that Rusty has landed a great job with an English bank, but wouldn't tell me which one, which makes me wonder if it was with Midland Bank, my old employer."

"Why on earth wouldn't he tell you that?" asked Moira.

"It appears that they are recruiting at the moment and he was worried in case I was tempted to follow Rusty and join them too, knowing how well we get on together."

"Oh I see, but you wouldn't want to do that, would you?"

"Certainly not at the moment, I enjoy my job too much and am looking forward to our move to Sydney, which is what I told Nugget."

"Good and what about Mr. Offstrop and his daughter, how did he respond to your news about them?"

"He was just as surprised as the rest of us had been, that she appeared not to know anything about the robbery, but was not at all happy that I had agreed with Donny not to make contact with her for at least a couple of weeks. I explained that Donny had given his word to her and I had given my word to Donny, so he said he would not press the matter and we have left it that I will make contact with her by phone on the thirty first of October."

"Did you give him the name of the hotel she is living in?" asked Moira.

"Yes, I felt I had to or it would seem that I did not trust him. He said that he would get someone in the New Zealand office to check out who actually owned the hotel and to get it valued, so that we had that information handy, once we have tracked down Mr. Offstrop."

It was a week later and only after the New Zealand office had informed Nugget that Rutger van Offstrop owned the hotel and gave him an approximation of what it was worth that he telephoned the Chairman and updated him on what they now knew.

"I cannot believe that you kept this from me for a whole week Nugget and that we have to wait another six days before we make contact. If the daughter is still in New Zealand when Smith makes his telephone call, I will eat my hat. She will be long gone by then, you mark my words."

"He gave his word George and I had to honour that, which is why I have used the time to find out who actually owns the hotel in Dunedin and what it is worth. It means we can get back a large part of the money he stole from us, once we have proved his guilt."

"That might not be as easy as it sounds Nugget. I have had several discussions with the lawyers on that particular matter and they say that proving his guilt in a court of law will not be an easy matter, assuming we can get him extradited, from wherever he may be living and the costs of bringing the case to court could easily outweigh any financial benefits we might be able to get back from him."

"I see and of course the publicity would not do us any good either," suggested Nugget.

"That too, it would appear that our best option would be to get him to admit his guilt and make whatever reparations he is able to make; so tell Smith to go ahead with his telephone call next week and to travel over to Dunedin to visit the daughter, if she has not already flown the coop."

"The Pretoria Hotel, can I help you?"

"My name is Arnold Smith and I would like to speak with Miss Carice Offstrop please," said Digger, a little apprehensively.

"One moment Mr. Smith and I will put you through to the manager."

Digger's heart sank as he waited for the manager to come on the line.

"Good day to you Mr. Smith, my name is Newn and I am the manager of the hotel. Miss Offstrop did leave a message for a Mr. Arnold Smith, should he call, but before I deliver it, I need to know that I am speaking with the correct gentleman, so would you mind telling me who you work for and your position in the company."

"Good day to you Mr. Newn, I am the Senior Internal Audit Manager with the Perth Mining & Commerce Bank Ltd and it was my cousin, Mr. MacDonald Smith, who spoke with Miss Offstrop in Auckland."

"Very good sir, thank you; Miss Carice has asked me to inform you that she has flown to South Africa to visit her father and mother to discuss with them the matter which concerns you and your bank. She expects to be away for about six weeks and will make contact with you on her return, if you would be so kind as to leave me your address and telephone number for her."

"Thank you Mr. Newn, can I ask when she flew out to South Africa?"

"It was Monday afternoon sir, I took her to the airport myself as she was in no fit state to drive there on her own, still being very upset from having attended her uncle's funeral and interment in the morning. She was extremely fond of the old man, as indeed we all were."

"Do you happen to know where in South Africa she flew to?"

"Capetown I believe; now if you would be so kind as to give me the details I mentioned, I have a myriad of things to do, as I am sure you have."

Digger gave the manager his address and telephone number and slumped back into his seat after replacing the receiver back onto its holder. About ten minutes later, Nugget walked in and sat down.

"Tell me the worst, what did she say?" Nugget asked.

"She said nothing but the manager of the Pretoria Hotel Dunedin, where she has an apartment, told me that she had flown to Capetown on Monday afternoon, after attending her uncles funeral in the morning. He went on to inform me that she will make contact with me when she returns from seeing her parents, in about six weeks time."

"Oh dear, the Chairman will be unbearable, he said this would happen, I am afraid that is the last we will hear from Miss Carice van Offstrop, Digger."

"I don't agree Nugget. She said she had an apartment in the family hotel in Dunedin and she did. She said she wanted to spend time with a dying uncle and she did and then she went to his funeral. I believe she has been honest with us so far and that we should expect her to make contact when she returns from South Africa."

"I admire your faith in human nature Digger and really hope you are right, for all of our sakes, but I want you to make contact each week with the hotel manager and see if they have heard from her and let me know the moment you hear anything, whether I am in the office or not."

"Of course Nugget and thanks for your support and trust, I appreciate it."

On the 7th of November, Digger made his first telephone call to the Pretoria Hotel and was curtly told by the manager that Miss Carice was still away and had not been in touch with them.

On the 14th of November, the manager was a little less officious and informed Digger that Miss Carice had been in touch that week. She had asked that Mr. Arnold Smith be informed, should he call, that she had briefly spoken with her father about the matter under discussion, before he had gone off on Safari with some friends. Her father had confirmed that his involvement in the matter, was exactly as Mr. Smith's cousin had stated, during his conversation with her in Auckland.

"Well that at least is some progress Digger, that he has verbally admitted to being involved in the robbery, but a bit worrying that he has chosen this moment in time to go off to who knows where, on Safari," said Nugget. "Keep calling the hotel each week and try asking a few more questions each time, now that the manager knows she is willing to speak with you, although probably he has no idea what the 'matter under discussion' is."

On the 21st of November, the manger was quite chatty and confirmed that Miss Carice was still in South Africa, but had just left for the interior, after hearing that her father had been seriously injured by a very large rampaging buffalo and then bitten by a baboon, which had come into the mission hospital he had been taken to for treatment."

"The Chairman is going to love this Digger; when I told him that Offstrop had gone on a Safari, he said to me, 'You just wait Nugget, I'll wager he gets eaten by a lion and is never seen or heard of again', this will make his day."

On the 28th of November, the manager reported that Mr. Rutger Offstrop's condition had deteriorated, mainly because the baboon bite had triggered a seizure and the doctor at the hospital did not think the injured man had long to live.

The news of his death and burial was given on the 5th of December and Digger duly offered his condolences to the family and enquired when Miss Carice was now expected home.

"The 13th of December sir," said the manager formally, "and she has asked me to inform you that she now holds Power of Attorney for her mother and will contact you immediately she has spoken with the family's solicitor in New Zealand."

"Surely the manger gave some intimation as to whether he believed the report of Offstrop's death was true or just a 'cock and bull, story," said Nugget.

"He played his part very well," said Digger, "and said nothing whatsoever that would make me think he did not believe the information he had given me, to be true."

"We really have no option but to wait for her call, will you be all right to fly to New Zealand in a week or two and meet with Carice and the solicitor, what with Moira being pregnant and due quite soon?"

"Yes, Pat will be staying with her and my sister Vi has said she will come and stop if required and I gather that your own dear wife has offered her services as well. I couldn't possibly miss the final scene of the show as it plays out in New Zealand, could I?"

"I guess not Digger, but if things do change, you make sure you let me know."

Digger telephoned the Pretoria Hotel once more on the 13th of December to be told that Miss Carice had landed in Auckland and was making her way to Hastings to speak with her solicitor and she had said to tell Mr. Smith that he would be hearing from them in a day or two."

It was in fact the following day when the senior solicitor at the very firm she had once worked for, telephoned Digger to say that he had been instructed by Miss Carice van Offstrop, who was acting on behalf of her mother and late father, to meet with Mr. Arnold Smith, Senior Internal Audit Manager with the Perth Mining & Commerce Bank Ltd to discuss certain matters pertaining to the late Mr. Rutger van Offstrop and his former employer and also Mrs. Simone van Offstrop and the widow's pension which was now due to her.

Nugget immediately gave him the all clear to attend the meeting in New Zealand and asked his secretary to book

Digger's flights for the Friday afternoon to Sydney and then the Saturday morning to Auckland.

Moira was a bit disappointed that she would not be able to go with him, but assured him that she and Pat would be able to manage somehow, without him for a few days.

He rang Donny at home to tell him of his travel plans and he immediately invited him to stay with them for the weekend and said he would be pleased to accompany him to Hastings on the Monday and to remain with him for as long as it took.

"What about your job, won't they mind you taking several days off work without proper notice?" Digger asked.

"Probably, but they pay me so poorly and have treated me so badly, that I really don't care what they think, I was going to hand my notice in this week anyway. Do you want me to arrange for a hire car for you, or are you happy to travel down on the back of the bike."

"I would be so fearful of scratching the paintwork and incurring Deborah's wrath yet again, that I think you should book a car for us, but please don't tell her what I just said."

"I won't, your secret is safe with me, see you at the airport Saturday afternoon Arnold, bye."

"What secret is that Mac, which you have promised not to divulge?" asked Deborah.

"Arnold is coming here for the weekend and wants me to go to Hastings with him on Monday and has a fear of motorbikes, so has asked me to hire a car for him."

"Remind me not to trust you with any of my secrets; do you want me to make up a bed in the garage for him?"

"Debs, you are going to be nice to Arnold this time, do you hear me?"

"Just joking Mac, where is your sense of humour, I will be as sweet as pie to your dear cousin, I pwomise."

The flight to Sydney was a bit bumpy and Digger was not feeling to well when he arrived there, so he had a light meal in the hotel's restaurant and an early night to follow.

The plane touched down in Auckland on a nice sunny day and Digger spotted Donny and Deborah in the Arrivals Lounge as he walked through the barrier. The usual pleasantries were exchanged, nothing gushing and they retrieved the car which Donny had hired that morning, from the car park and after a scenic tour of the City arrived at their home around four o'clock.

"Hope you don't mind Arnold," said Donny, "but our friends Rosie and Brock, well really they are old friends of Bertie's, are having a small party tonight at their place and they said we could take you along, so we will just have a light snack now, as Rosie is a tremendous cook and we would not want to spoil your appetite for tonight."

"Sounds great, any chance of a bath before we go out, as the shower in the hotel was not working properly."

Deborah was on the point of saying something extremely sarcastic in reply and got as far as, "What would," when Donny gave her a withering look, which made her completely forget the cutting remark she was about to make.

"Sorry Deborah, what did you say?" asked Digger.

"What would you like to drink Digger, tea coffee or something cold?"

"I would love a cup of tea please," he replied innocently.

"Let me show you to your room and where the bathroom is located, you can have a bath now if you want, I expect you are tired after the flight," said Donny.

Digger thanked him and got some clean clothes out of his case and took the cup of tea into the bathroom and enjoyed a long hot soak. When he had finished Deborah announced that she was going to have a bath, so it gave Donny and Digger the opportunity to go out into the garden together with a cold drink and have a good long chat about work, life and marriage.

"I have to say that the wedding and the first few months of our marriage had gone really well until the other week, when she thought I had been with another woman. For the first time I saw that other side to her, which I guess you know only too well Arnold, when she was spiteful, cold and vindictive towards me. To be honest with you, it quite frightened me to think that the woman I love and who had always been so warm and loving towards me, up to that point, had this nasty vicious streak in her, which she seemed quite unable to control," said Donny with a sigh.

"I have heard enough of Bertie's stories to know that they have been through quite a lot together and I guess you can't go through all the things she has been through, without it having an effect on you," said Digger. "Moira has her difficult moments, but overall there have been no nasty surprises, thank goodness. So tell me, what happened at work when you told them that you would not be in on Monday."

"Just as I suspected really, they told me that if I wanted to keep my job I would be there prompt at nine o'clock on Monday and I told them what a useless outfit I thought they were and that they could keep their rotten job."

"Good for you, life is far too short to spend it working with people you don't like and doing a job you detest," said Digger, "so any ideas what you will do next?"

"Not really, but I did enjoy working for you the other month, even though Miss Offstrop outsmarted me, perhaps I am ready for a complete career change, but don't talk about it in front of Debs please, she was a bit funny yesterday about my losing the job."

The party at Rosie and Brock's house proved to be very enjoyable and ended in the wee small hours, with a slow walk back to the house. On Sunday they all went to church together in the morning and Deborah had arranged for them all to go on a cruise round the harbour with her boss and his wife on their thirty foot yacht, in the afternoon. They went back to her boss's home afterwards, for a roast dinner with their children and several other relatives. Donny, Digger and her boss had a game of cricket in the garden with the children, while the ladies cleared the dinner things away and did the washing up.

"So you played wicket for your local team at home then Mac," said Deborah's boss Neil, "we must get you to play for the office eleven, we need a wicket keeper and Deborah could help the ladies with the scoring and the tea."

"Thank you Neil for the offer, I would love to play for your team, but I would not want to make any commitments on my wife's behalf, if you know what I mean."

"Mum's the word; I will leave it to my good lady to persuade her to come along and help, when the time is right."

"What night do you have team practice and would I be right in assuming that all of your matches are at the weekend?" Mac queried.

"Wednesday night we practice and we normally play on a Saturday afternoon, but with the odd friendly mid week, so what do you think, shall I put your name down for Wednesday night?"

"I would like to say yes, but I am in between jobs at the moment Neil, having quit my last one on Friday. I am actually accompanying Arnold here, to Hastings tomorrow, to assist him in completing an investigation I assisted him with, shortly after we arrived here."

"A bank investigation eh, I would love to know more, but I expect you are sworn to secrecy," said Neil.

"He certainly is," said Digger jokingly, "but Donny did a great job for us in the discoveries he made, which I am hoping will help us close a twelve year old case, to the bank's satisfaction."

"Now that does sounds intriguing, the Managing Director was only saying to me the other day that we should employ an outside agency to check out some of the spurious claims we are getting these days, perhaps we might be interested in hiring your services too Mac. Why not drop me a line with a note of your charges and we will see what we can do."

"Certainly, I would be delighted to do that, as soon as Digger and I return from Hastings."

They got back home about nine thirty, after a very pleasant time with Neil and his family and as they went into the house, Donny pulled Digger back and said quietly, "Please do not mention playing cricket, helping with teas or any other part of our conversation with Neil, I want to give it a bit more thought before I discuss any of that with Debs."

Digger nodded and gave him a knowing smile and after a cup of coffee and a telephone call home to Moira, who said she was 'just fine', went to his room to prepare himself for the next day and then retired for an early night.

They were away just after seven and stopped in Cambridge for a drink and a bun. They called in at the hotel Donny had stopped at before in Hastings and reserved a couple of rooms for the night and then had a light lunch in the hotel restaurant and arrived at the solicitor's office dead on two o'clock.

"Good afternoon, Mr. Smith and Mr. Smith to see Mr. Eaglesham, Digger announced to the secretary-cum-receptionist.

"Good afternoon gentlemen, you would be Mr. MacDonald Smith she said to Donny," who smiled politely back at her, "and you therefore would be Mr. Arnold Smith from the bank, Mr. Eaglesham is expecting you, please follow me."

She led the way through to the back of the building and into a large conference room, where Mr. Eaglesham and Miss Offstrop were seated on one side of a large table, but rose to greet their visitors.

"Basil Eaglesham," said the man as he made his way to Digger and shook his hand.

"Arnold Smith, please to meet you Basil."

Basil then moved to Donny and shook his hand, who introduced himself as Mac Smith.

"May I introduce my client, Miss Carice van Offstrop, whom I believe you have already met Mac."

"Hello Carice, nice to meet you again," said Mac smiling to her.

"Hello Mac and hello Arnold it is nice to meet you at last, I expect you must have wondered if we would ever actually manage to meet each other," she said.

"I can honestly say Carice, that I never doubted it for a minute, from everything Donny told me about you, I knew you were a lady of the highest integrity."

She frowned and said, "Who is this Donny person, I have never met him or her!"

"He means me Carice," said Donny, "the whole world calls me Mac, except my own family who insist on using my childhood name."

"Good for them, my family are the same, but I am not telling you what it is."

"I have ordered refreshments for three o'clock, so shall we get down to business," said Basil.

They all sat down, Donny and Digger took out their note books and Digger took out the file he had brought with him from the bank and the business session commenced.

"The way this is going to work," Basil announced, "is that I will be speaking on behalf of Carice and you will address all of your questions to me. If I cannot answer them, we will adjourn the meeting for a few minutes while Carice and I discuss the question privately, we will then return to the meeting either with an answer, or a suggested date in the future, when an answer will be available, but we sincerely hope that will not be necessary. Is that understood and agreed?"

"That is perfectly clear and agreed," said Digger.

"Good," said Basil, "I first want to deal with the bank robbery which took place in nineteen thirty eight, at the branch of your bank in Sydney, where Rutger was the manager."

He took a document out of a folder and passed a copy across to Digger and Donny and asked them to read it. It was dated the 6th of November 1950 and had been drawn up by Rutger's solicitor in South Africa and had been witnessed by a solicitor's clerk and the solicitor himself. It stated that Rutger alone had been responsible for planning the robbery and that his wife and daughter had no involvement whatsoever. It stated that when he actually told his wife about it, after they had moved to New Zealand, that she was so shocked and disappointed with him, she went home to South Africa to be with her parents who, as it happened, were now elderly and in poor health.

"Is your mother still looking after her parents," asked Digger.

Basil looked at Carice who nodded her approval before he answered, "Mrs. van Offstrop's father died a few years ago, but her mother is still alive, but requires a great deal of care."

"Thank you," said Digger and continued to study the document.

It went on to say that neither Rutger nor her mother had ever told Carice about the robbery and she was truly shocked when the bank's representative informed her of that fact, during their conversation at the café in Auckland.

The document further stated that Don Davis had been a willing participant in the robbery, although he had not been involved until the later stages of the planning, when he had overheard a telephone conversation between Rutger and one of the members of the gang and had demanded a share of the proceeds for his silence.

"Papa told me that Don Davis took several thousand pounds in notes from the robbery, but was never given any of the gold, since now having been a participant in the crime, he could not very easily have incriminated Papa, without incriminating himself," said Carice.

"That was probably your father's main mistake," said Digger, "as it was only through Don Davis talking about his part in the robbery, that this whole investigation got started in the first place."

"Before we go any further Arnold," Basil interrupted, "I need you to sign this document please. It states that as the bank's representative here today, you have the authority to sign on their behalf and that you accept this document to be true and you acknowledge that no blame or recrimination can be laid against Carice or her mother."

"We did discuss this eventuality before I left the office and I can testify that I do have such authority and am happy to sign the document as the bank's representative. Our Chairman is standing by in Melbourne, should you wish to speak directly with him."

"That won't be necessary Arnold, if you and Mac simply sign at the bottom, where indicated."

They both signed the document as bank representative and witness and the solicitor placed the original back in his file and opened another file and took out the next series of documents.

"These documents deal with the marriage of Simone and Rutger van Offstrop, the death of Rutger and Simone's right to a widow's pension from the bank," Basil announced.

He first produced a copy of their marriage certificate, which showed that they had got married in June 1946 in Capetown and again Digger was asked to sign a document to say that he had seen the document and had accepted it as being genuine. Basil informed him that Simone had given her permission for the document to remain at his office for safe keeping and future inspection, should that be necessary.

He then produced two statements made by Rutger's hunting companions regarding the accident and his death. They stated that on the morning of Thursday the 16th of November the party was hunting buffalo when one of the bearers accidentally discharged his rifle, causing the herd to stampede. Rutger, who had positioned himself away from the main party was caught in the path of the stampeding animals and was knocked off his feet by a large male buffalo and then trampled on by several other animals that were coming up behind.

"It must have been frightening for him," Donny commented, "those animals can be quite a size."

The statements went on to say that Rutger had been badly injured from the initial impact with the buffalo and from being trodden on by the other animals, with many fractured ribs and severe damage to his internal organs; but somehow the party had managed to take him to a mission hospital by mid-day on the seventeenth.

The doctor there did his best, but they did not have the equipment to give him a thorough examination and started to make arrangements to have him transported to Capetown. The ward Rutger was in was very basic and as it had been very hot and humid that week the windows had been left open to allow more air to circulate. During the evening of the nineteenth Rutger had dozed off for a while, but was woken by the sound of his bowl of fruit crashing to the floor and as he stretched out to pick up the pieces, a baboon that had come into the ward, bit him deeply on the arm. His cries brought the nursing staff into the ward, who immediately chased the baboon out through the window and cleaned up the wound to his arm and the mess on the floor. Unfortunately the bite had given him such a shock that it caused him to have a seizure, from which he did not recover.

He died in the early hours of the twenty first of November and was buried in the Mission cemetery the following day, with just his hunting companions and the nursing staff attending the funeral. Carice arrived on Thursday the 23rd and paid her respects at her father's graveside and arranged for a simple wooden cross to be erected at the grave until a stone one could be ordered in Capetown and taken out to the village.

Basil then produced the death certificate for Rutger and gave a copy to Digger for the files of the Pensions Department at the bank.

"I believe you will now need to speak with your Pensions Department and confirm that Mrs. Simone van Offstrop is entitled to a widow's pension at the rate of fifty percent of her late husband's pension," said Basil.

"If you will allow me to use an office and a telephone, I can do that right away, but I am sure there will not be a problem in establishing her right to the widow's pension," said Digger.

"I can certainly arrange that for you," Basil replied.

"Thank you," said Digger, "but before I make that call, I would be most interested to know what Mrs. Offstrop, or anyone else for that matter," looking directly at Carice, "can tell us about the gold coins which her husband stole from the bank in nineteen thirty eight."

Basil looked at Carice, who again nodded and he then said, "We are not prepared to answer any more questions for the moment as Carice is still very tired from her long journey, but suggest we meet here again tomorrow morning, at say ten thirty, when you can give us the response of the Pensions Department and we will tell you what we know about the gold coins, albeit very little."

Realizing that nothing was to be gained by pushing the matter at that point in time, Digger replied, "Fair enough, we will meet you here at ten thirty tomorrow morning."

"My secretary will escort you two gentlemen to an office you can use and we will see you again tomorrow, so goodbye for now."

They all shook hands and the secretary escorted them to a small office at the front of the building, with two chairs, a desk and a telephone and Donny asked her if there was any chance of a cup of tea, which was duly brought in to them about five minutes later. Once the secretary had left the two men started to chat.

"If your Rutger van Offstrop was killed by a stampeding buffalo, then my uncle is a Chinaman," said Donny.

"I agree, it is all too convenient," said Digger, "but this death certificate is obviously genuine and we can hardly go to some remote mission hospital in Africa and exhume the body and see for ourselves. Besides, I am sure our Pensions Department, would rather pay out fifty percent of the Pension to his widow, than a hundred percent to him and I suspect that what they are prepared to tell us about the stolen gold, will depend on our answer to that question, so I may as well ring the chairman and see what he thinks."

Digger went over all the details from the meeting with the Chairman, who then went away to speak with the manager of the Pensions Department and rang Digger back in his room at the hotel about two hours later.

"We all agree with you Mr. Smith, that we are bound to accept the evidence of his death that they have given you, in good faith and therefore have no reason to deny his widow her pension. You just need to obtain some more information about her, for example her date of birth, address in Capetown and bank account, so that we can start to pay her what is due each month. Disappointing that they refused to speak about the gold though, you will have to go back tomorrow and see what further information you can find out from them."

"Very well sir, I will do my best, but a thought has just crossed my mind, if you have a moment."

"Of course, what is it?" asked the Chairman.

"A good friend of mine and of Nugget's from England, who also happens to be my cousin's father-in-law, plans to sail back to England shortly with his wife and I know he had thought about breaking his voyage and staying in South Africa for a few weeks. I am sure if we paid for his hotel in Capetown, he would not mind visiting Mrs. Offstrop at home, to personally deliver the gift which the Board of Directors is about to purchase for her."

"What a devious mind you have Mr. Smith, let me think about it and we can discuss it when you return, but do find out if your friend would be willing to undertake such a task on our behalf."

They finished the conversation and Digger brought Donny up to date with matters over their evening meal.

"I am sure that Bertie would be delighted to do that little task for you, but I am not so certain that Victoria would be quite so keen;" said Donny, "but I am glad the bank have agreed to pay the widow's pension to Simone, as she does appear to be the innocent party in all this and it will probably give Carice a bit of peace over the matter too."

"You still believe she knows nothing about any of this then?"

"I expect she knows much more now than she did before and may even suspect that her father was not knocked over and killed by a buffalo, but I do not think she knows for sure that he is still alive and probably has no real inclination to find out the truth," said Donny.

The following day they were at the solicitor's office at ten thirty and after formally shaking hands, sat down and resumed the meeting.

"Well Arnold, perhaps you would like to begin the meeting by telling us what the Pensions Department said about Mrs. Offstrop's request to receive a widow's pension from the bank."

Digger explained that the Chairman had personally met with the Pensions Manager the previous afternoon and that they had agreed that they could see no problem in paying to Simone the widow's pension, now that Rutger was dead.

"If you would be so kind as to give me her personal details, I will arrange for that to commence on my return to Australia," said Digger.

Basil then handed over the details relating to Simone, which Digger checked and placed in his file.

"And now for the other matter you mentioned yesterday, Carice will tell you what she managed to find out from her father about the gold," said Basil.

"When Mac told me about the bank robbery and my father's involvement, I was just overwhelmed, as I am sure you realized," she said, directing her last comment at Mac, who nodded and smiled at her.

"As soon as I got to Capetown I sat down with my parents and asked them to tell me what they had done and why. My father explained that my mother and I entered Australia illegally in 1937, assisted by a criminal gang they had first met in Mauritius. When the gang boss discovered Papa worked for a bank, he said that if Papa did not assist him with a robbery, he would inform on mother and me, to the Australian Immigration authorities."

At this point she stopped for a drink of water and to gauge how the story was going down with her listeners.

"Papa said that the gang boss wanted half the proceeds from the robbery and that he would be responsible for supplying the manpower to rob the bank and agreed to pay them out of his half afterwards. He realized that Papa would be a prime suspect and would need to disappear, once the dust had settled. The delivery of the gold coins gave papa the perfect opportunity to execute the robbery and the rest you already know. A few hundred coins were counted out to pay the gang's immediate expenses and Papa took the rest of the coins out of the bank over the next few weeks. He gave the gang boss the ten thousand gold coins he demanded and kept the remainder for himself."

"Can I ask if your father expressed any remorse for what he had done," asked Digger.

"I am ashamed to say that he didn't," said Carice, "which I gather is the reason why my mother was so saddened when she discovered what he had done and why she returned to South Africa on her own, he refusing to let me go with her. Anyway, a few years later he was contacted by a member of the gang who had tracked us down in New Zealand and told to either give them some more of his share of the gold or help them to plan another robbery, or else the police would get a mysterious tip-off."

"Not nice people at all," said Basil, disdainfully.

"No they weren't, so as a result Papa flew back to South Africa and I moved to Hastings, where of course, I still live, when not in Dunedin."

"If your father went to live with your mother in South Africa, surely the gang would have known where to look for them," said Donny.

"Apparently not," said Carice, "Papa stayed on his own for quite a while and when they judged it to be safe, he married my mother and lived with her in her parents' house, where she still lives today."

"So what did he do with all that gold?" asked Digger, intrigued by the story.

"He bought the hotel in Dunedin with it and of course used some to live on and paid some across to the gang when they came calling in New Zealand. I assume he also used some to send mother back to Capetown. On Papa's death, the hotel passed to mother, but she said she could not possibly want anything to do with it, since it was bought with the proceeds of the robbery. She has therefore, instructed Basil, her solicitor, to make the deeds over to the bank, or to sell it and pay the proceeds of the sale to the bank, whichever you prefer."

Both Digger and Donny were not anticipating this outcome and sat there quietly taking the information in.

"I am sure you will agree with me gentlemen," said Basil, "when I say that this is a splendid offer by Mrs. van Offstrop and will hopefully recompense the bank, in some measure, for the losses it incurred in nineteen thirty eight."

"We would agree with your sentiments entirely Basil and are most grateful for her kind offer. I am sure the bank would want you to sell the property for us, but I will confirm that in writing at a later date."

"Mother did say that she does not need any of the furniture but there are certain personal effects which are family heirlooms, which she has asked me to remove and send over to her."

"Of course," said Digger, "until the bank officially accepts the offer, the hotel and all of its contents belong to your mother, so remove anything which you or your mother wish to keep for yourselves."

The meeting concluded shortly after this and as everyone was saying their good-byes to each other, Carice mentioned to Donny that she planned to be in Auckland at the end of the week, to start looking for a new job and asked him which agencies he had used and where they were located.

"To be honest Carice, they were mostly specializing in the placement of engineers, but I am sure that some of them covered other spheres of work as well. Look, here is my telephone number at the house and you know where I live, so give me a ring when you arrive in Auckland and I will go through all my notes and tell you which ones are worth talking to."

"Thank you Mac and here is a note for your wife, it is the name of the scent I wear, which you said she liked."

Digger and Donny picked up their cases from the hotel and cancelled their provisional booking for that night and telephoned Deborah at work to say that they were on their way back home.

They had a pleasant drive back to Auckland in the afternoon and Digger took them all out for a meal that evening as a thank you for putting him up.

On the Wednesday he caught a flight to Melbourne, where he had arranged to meet with the Chairman and with Nugget who had flown over for a Directors Board Meeting the previous day.

Chapter 24
Surprise! Surprise!

"So what do you honestly think Digger, is he dead or is he alive," asked Nugget, after he and the Chairman had congratulated Digger on a most successful trip.

"To be honest, I am not sure, if he just wanted to disappear, why not simply say that he fell over a waterfall and his body was not found, or he was taken by a crocodile and never seen again; to go to all the trouble of the hospital and statements and a death certificate and a grave and a headstone, seems overkill to me, if you will pardon the pun."

"I am inclined to agree with you Mr. Smith and the Board of Directors met this morning and it has been officially Minuted in the Directors Minute Book, that Mr. Rutger van Offstrop is dead and a letter of condolence will be sent to his widow, but no gift is to be purchased and delivered. We did not feel comfortable with that suggestion."

"Very good sir, I have said nothing to Mr. Bannister as yet, so no harm done there. Did the directors decide what they want done with the hotel?"

"Mr. Newgate has offered to go across to Dunedin and inspect the property with an estate agent and report back to the Board, when a decision will be made, but I expect we will just sell it."

"Miss Carice van Offstrop did say that her mother did not want any of the furniture and fittings apart from a few personal and family items, so we could sell it as a going concern, if we acted promptly," Digger informed him.

The meeting with the Chairman lasted another hour or so and as Digger had been booked into the same hotel as Nugget, they enjoyed a meal together in the evening and Nugget brought him up to date with a few more personal matters.

"Just so that you know Digger, Junie has already spoken with Moira and has arranged for the two of you to spend Boxing Day with us, as I gather you are visiting your sister on Christmas Day this year."

"Thanks Nugget, I will just be glad to have a few days off and relax and do nothing at home. I did speak with your secretary about having the following week off and coming back in on the 1st January, I hope that is O.K.?"

"She did mention it to me and I have signed it off for you, as well as the rest of this week. You have had quite a year one way and another, and with the baby due in the middle of January and your move to Sydney at the end of March, I suspect that nineteen fifty one, will be just as hectic for you, but hopefully a bit less dangerous than this year proved to be."

Digger and Nugget flew back to Perth on the Thursday and hired a taxi at the airport, to take them back to their separate homes. Digger bid Nugget goodbye and went indoors to be met by a very large and cumbersome Moira who was delighted to see him safely home.

After greeting his wife, he looked round the room and asked, "No Pat tonight?"

"She has gone home for Christmas but will be back here again next Wednesday, the twenty seventh and Junie tells me that you are off until Monday week, the first of January, so you have plenty of time to decorate the baby's room for me, as we discussed before you went away."

His brow furrowed and his jaw dropped as he replied, "We are leaving here at the end of March Moira, do we really need to re-decorate the room and won't the agent mind?"

"Digger you promised and no, the agent does not mind, I have chosen the paint, all you have to do is pick it up!"

On Friday morning Digger was woken early by his beloved, who went with him to the hardware shop to get the paint and some new brushes, as he had conveniently left the other ones at James Street. He came back to the house and started to wash the walls and ceilings down and was amazed at the amount of dirt that came off and had to admit that Moira was right in wanting to re-decorate the room that their baby would start its young life in.

Meanwhile, in Auckland, Mac had come back from yet another interview for a job he considered to be beneath him, when the telephone rang and Carice van Offstrop announced that she was in Auckland, staying at a small Guest House, not too far from where they lived.

"Hello Carice nice to hear from you, how is the job hunting going?" he asked.

"Badly Mac, what about yourself?"

"I had another interview this morning, complete waste of time; but I did mention to my wife that you might be calling and she said to invite you round for dinner tonight."

"Are you sure about this, what with me coming into your house un-invited to use the bathroom and all."

"Absolutely, we can go through the agency information I have looked out for you and Deborah and I have a business suggestion we want to discuss with you."

"A business suggestion eh, that sounds intriguing, what time shall I arrive?"

"Somewhere between six thirty and seven would be good, we normally sit down to eat around ten past. Is there anything you cannot eat?" asked Mac.

"I am not too keen on shellfish, but apart from that, I eat anything. See you later," she said and returned to her room to think about what a 'business suggestion' might involve her in.

At six fifty p.m., there was a knock on the door and Deborah went to answer it. She had already decided that if she did not like the look of this woman, who had broken into her home, she was going to tell her what she thought of her and then slam the door in her face.

"Hello Deborah, I am Carice van Offstrop and I come with a peace offering and an apology for entering your home un-invited," she said smiling and handed over a small package, which Deborah accepted and asked her to come in.

The two ladies shook hands and Carice and Mac shook hands afterwards and Mac took her coat through to the bedroom, while Deborah untied her package, which turned out to be a small, but very expensive bottle of perfume that she had not tried before.

"Well thank you Carice, peace offering and apology accepted, can I get you a glass of wine?"

"A glass of dry white, if you have it please," she replied.

"Mac, two glasses of Chardonnay please and there are some beers in the fridge as well. How is the dinner doing?"

"The roast lamb is almost there," he said, "another ten minutes or so, but we could sit down at the table and start with the melon, if you like. Here are your glasses of wine ladies."

Deborah noticed the surprised look on Carice's face and explained, "Mac learnt to cook while he was in France during the War and is much better at it than me, so while I am bringing in the bacon, he is cooking it, so to speak," she joked.

They swapped small talk during the melon course, but got down to the serious conversation of the evening, while eating their main course.

"So what sort of a 'business suggestion' do you want to discuss with me?" asked Carice.

"Well it is mainly Debs' idea, which I wholeheartedly support, so I will let her explain it," said Mac.

"I first met Mac in Spain during the War, when we were both working for the British Secret Service.," said Deborah. "Mac working behind the lines in France and me assisting my father in gathering intelligence about enemy naval movements in the Mediterranean Sea."

"Wow, I was not expecting that," said Carice.

"We were both young and wild and the danger and excitement were intoxicating, but we lost touch with each other until August last year, when we happened to meet up with each other through Mac's cousin Digger, who you met in Hastings this week."

"Oh I see," said Carice, not really seeing at all, where this was leading to.

"We got married in April in Spain and shortly afterwards came out to New Zealand with my Dad and his second wife Victoria, who then went over to Western Australia, where Victoria owns a share in a farm. More wine please Mac, my throat is going dry," said Deborah.

"Do you want me to take over with the story for a bit Debs, or your dinner will grow cold?"

She nodded and Mac continued, "As I told you before, I was a draughtsman in England, but I was looking forward to doing something different with my life when I came out here, so when Arnold, my cousin, asked me to do a bit of detective work for the bank, I jumped at the chance and really enjoyed myself, working with him on the Investigation."

"All right Mac, I will continue," said Deborah, "I noticed that Mac was his old self again while working for the bank, the Mac I had fallen in love with during the War and

425

suggested to him that maybe he should give up being a draughtsman and start being a private investigator. I work for a big Insurance Company and we need someone to investigate spurious claims from time to time and we could definitely put that sort of work, his way. Mac's immediate response to my suggestion, was that in this sort of a job, you should never work on your own, as you need a partner to watch your back, so when he said that you were also looking for work in Auckland and he had already told me how well you had played your role in acting for your parents interests, I suggested that the two of you should team up and form your own firm of Private Investigators, so tell me, what do you think of the idea?"

"Hey, what a wonderful idea Deborah, would you be involved yourself, or stay with your Insurance Company?"

"Certainly to start with I would stay with my current employer, to make sure we still had an income each month, but who knows, if the business picked up and there was an obvious role for me to play, maybe I would join the two of you as well."

"The more I think of it, the more it excites me, I am just not sure what Desmond will say about it though, he tends to be on the cautious side."

"Sorry Carice, but who is Desmond?" asked Mac.

"Desmond Newn, the manager of the Pretoria Hotel, we have been engaged to be married for several years now, but Papa did not approve of my marrying one of the staff, as he called him; but now he is dead, mother has given her blessing, so as soon as the hotel is sold and he can move to a new job in Auckland, we will definitely get married."

"Is he likely to object to the venture then?" asked Deborah.

"I don't really think so, but I owe it to him to discuss the matter with him, before giving you an answer. He is arriving in Auckland tomorrow morning and we planned to have dinner tomorrow night at his brother's restaurant in town, why don't you two come and join us and we can finish the discussion then."

"We wouldn't want to spoil your plans for spending time with your fiancée," said Deborah, but not very convincingly.

"We are spending the whole of Christmas together with his brother and family; do please say you will join us."

"In that case we would love to come and thank you for the invitation," said Deborah.

"Have you thought of any names yet, for our new enterprise?" asked Carice.

"I rather like Smith and Offstrop Investigations Limited," said Mac.

"Oh no!" said Carice, "How about Offstrop and Smith Detective Agency," she suggested.

"I do not think we should use our own names," said Deborah, "my suggestion is The Red Rabbit Inquiry Agency, that is a name people will remember."

"I like it," said Carice.

"I hate it Debbie," said Mac, ducking as she threw her napkin at him.

"Is this some sort of private joke between you two then?" asked Carice.

"It goes back to when we first met and Deborah here, made fun of a poor wounded serviceman, who had slight problems saying his 'R's'. Because she laughed when I said 'Wed Wabbit Wuns Wiot' I got to call her Debs, a privilege no one else in the whole wide world has."

"Oh I see, but it is a good name Mac and I have a sneaky suspicion that the office above my future brother-in-laws restaurant is empty, so we would have somewhere to set up shop, where people regularly come and would easily see any sign we put up in the window."

"Two against one Mac," said Deborah.

"I can see I am not going to win this, so The Red Rabbit Inquiry Agency, it is," said Mac, "assuming Desmond agrees."

The next day they joined Carice and Desmond at the restaurant for dinner and were pleased to discover that Desmond had come round to the idea of his future wife being a partner in an Inquiry Agency, albeit with some reservations.

While Mac and Deborah spent Christmas Day with her boss and his family and Boxing Day with Desmond's brother and his family, Digger and Moira spent Christmas Day with Vi, Mick and the children and Boxing Day with Nugget, Junie and Dora, Rusty being unable to come over and join them that year. Whilst they thoroughly enjoyed the two days, Moira was so tired that she spent the following Wednesday and Thursday in bed recovering, which gave Digger a chance to finish the baby's room in peace and as Pat had come back from her parents on the Wednesday, she was able to cook dinner for them on both those nights.

On Friday they drove to Pinjarra to see Vicky who was back from college, along with Bertie and Victoria, but they made a point of stopping on their own at James Street to check everything out, as Vi and Mick and the children had asked to use the house the following week, to give them all a break from Perth and to give Mick the chance to update some of the plumbing for them.

On Saturday night Vicky arranged for them all to go to dinner at the farm, along with Ray and Jenny.

"Are we allowed to ask if the Investigation is now over Digger," asked Bertie.

"I obviously cannot give you any details, but yes Bertie, it is over. I can say that the bank employee that we suspected of being involved in the robbery is now dead and the bank have closed the investigation."

"Did he die from health problems in the end, although I always thought Mauritius was a healthy place to live?" said Bertie.

"Oh no, it was a hunting accident in South Africa, he never went to live in Mauritius, apart from the odd holiday, that is."

"Please change the subject," said Victoria, "I do not want to hear about any hunting accidents, if you don't mind."

"I am so sorry Victoria, how tactless of me," said Digger.

"What are your plans for going back to Britain?" asked Moira, changing the subject completely.

"I am really excited Moira, Bertie has been speaking with some of the captains he used to know before the War and has arranged a really interesting cruise for us. The only problem is that we leave here on the twenty fifth of January, so I really hope that baby of yours comes on time."

"The last time I spoke with the doctor, he thought it would arrive early rather than late, so I think it is a safe bet you will be able to see him or her, before you leave," said Moira.

"Oh good; anyway we are going back to Auckland to spend some time with Deborah and Mac and then we leave on the second of February on our cruise. We are sailing round the top of Australia to Darwin and then we call at several of the small islands on our way to Singapore, where we are stopping for two nights and then we set sail for Capetown, where we are spending just over a week and Bertie has promised to take me to one of the big game parks to see all the wild animals."

"Lucky you," said Vicky, "I would love to see the big animals in their natural habitat."

"So when do you finally get back to England then?" asked Jenny.

"I honestly don't know, because from Capetown we are sailing up the coast of Africa and then through the Mediterranean and ending up at Barcelona, as Bertie wants to spend his birthday at our house in Spain."

On the fifteenth of January 1951 a baby boy was born to Moira and Arnold Smith, whom they named, William George Smith, after Digger and Moira's respective fathers. He weighed in at seven pounds three ounces and the house in Ruth Street had visitors every day for almost two weeks, who had come to see and hold little Billy, as he soon came to be called. Lots of pictures were taken and posted over to Scotland, so that Moira's parents and Granny could proudly show their first grandchild and great grandchild to all of their relatives and friends.

Victoria managed two trips to Perth in the ten days between his birth and their departure to Auckland and took lots of pictures to take with them, but whether it was to show Mac his new nephew, or to stir up motherly feelings in Deborah, no-one was quite sure.

Ray and Jenny took Bertie and Victoria to the airport in the Ute, which Ray had promised to use from time to time, to keep the engine in good working order, but not use as a utility vehicle on the farm. On their way back from the airport they called in to see Moira and little Billy and Moira could not help but notice the sad look in both their eyes, as they held and cuddled the little one.

"Did you see much of Vi and Mick during their holiday at James Street?" Moira asked.

"Ray picked Brian up on the Monday afternoon and took him back home on the Friday morning, the two were inseparable," said Jenny. "The boy loved working with Ray on the farm and was just a natural, according to Ray, they have already arranged for him to come out and stay with us for the whole of the Easter holiday, Ray can't wait, can you?"

Ray nodded, "He is a great lad and we get on really well together, it's nice to have someone working with me who is willing to listen and learn. Come on Jenny, time for us to go, I am sure Moira won't mind you coming again to see her and little Billy."

"Of course not Jenny, come as often as you like, we love company and all the fuss, don't we Billy?"

"How much longer is Pat with you for?" asked Jenny.

"She has been offered a position at the hospital in Geraldton so plans to leave here on about the twenty fourth of February and spend some time with her family and then travel up there about a week later. You are both very welcome to start staying with us again after that, well at least until we move to Sydney at the end of March."

"Thank you," said Jenny, "we have missed your company of late, on our visits to Perth and perhaps we will be able to come over to Sydney and visit you, once you are settled in, eh Ray?"

"We will have to wait and see, not sure we could both go on a long trip like that together, but you could certainly go over to visit, perhaps take Digger's sister Vi with you," he suggested.

When the plane landed at Auckland airport on Friday afternoon, Mac was there to meet Bertie and Victoria.

"Debs sends her apologies, but something cropped up at work and couldn't get away," Mac explained, "but I have arranged a hire car for you, as you requested Bertie, so let me help you with your bags and we will go and find it."

They located the car and all climbed in and set off for home via the centre of town.

"Did I understand Deborah correctly when she said you had started some sort of agency to do with someone's restaurant," asked Victoria, "only it was a bad line last time we rang you and I did not catch all that she said."

"Sort of correct," said Mac, "we have actually formed an Inquiry Agency and it is situated above a restaurant which is owned by Stephen Newn who is the brother of my partners fiancée, which is very convenient for cups of coffee and cheap meals."

"If I remember correctly, your first day of business was the same day that Moira had her baby," said Bertie.

"Yes it was, but we actually sat and did nothing for the first week as no-one employed us, but we had a little job last week, from one of the customer's at the restaurant, who wanted us to find a missing relative for her."

"Were you successful in the hunt?" asked Bertie.

"Oh yes, it took us three days, but we eventually discovered he had been arrested earlier in the year for his part in a major art robbery and was serving a five year jail term. I think she would rather have not known. But she duly paid our fee and expenses, so hopefully she will tell others about us."

They drove for a bit longer, with the usual small talk taking place, when he pulled up outside a restaurant and pointed to a window on the first floor. Victoria read aloud the sign which was displayed, "The Red Rabbit Inquiry Agency, discretion and full disclosure are guaranteed. No job too small. What a strange name Mac, where did that come from?"

"I can guess," said Bertie, "she was never going to let you forget that Mac, can we go in and see what a real 'detectives office' looks like?"

"Of course, Carice will just be twiddling her thumbs, let's go and surprise her."

They all got out of the car and climbed the stairs to the office and found Carice talking on the phone to someone.

"Hold on please, my partner has just come in and I will see if he is available to come and visit you on the Monday, one moment please."

"Hello Carice this is Deborah's dad Bertie and his wife Victoria, what is going on here?" asked Mac.

"This is the lady we did the work for last week whose male relative we found to be in prison. She says that she has spoken with him on the telephone and with his wife who lives in Wellington and both vehemently claim that he is innocent, the lady says that she has persuaded the man's wife to travel to Auckland and that she hopes to be here over next weekend and would like us to speak with her some time soon after that, in order to prove his innocence and get him released from prison, do you think we should take it on?"

"Absolutely, being in prison is no picnic, but it must be awful if you know you are innocent. Arrange for them to come here on the Monday please Carice."

Carice finished the call and then joined the others who were busy chatting, when she was properly introduced to Bertie and Victoria and then she went on to tell Mac about the other telephone call she had received, while he was out of the office and of the client who had walked in off the street.

"The telephone caller was a man who wants us to track down his lost dog. It appears that they live in Auckland and that they sold their car this week to a man who lives in Gisborne. Their pet spaniel, who both he and his wife adore, was in the habit of sleeping on the floor in the back of the car and they think the dog climbed in while they were showing it to the buyer and was still there when he drove off to Gisborne.

They have his address but he is not on the phone and since they no longer have a car, they would like us to go to Gisborne and find their dog Brutus and bring him home. I thought I could probably handle that on my own."

"It sounds straight forward, we will just need to go round there and get some photographs of them with their dog and a detailed description, as I do not want to have to stand bail for you on a 'dog-napping' charge. We will also ask for the first day of our fee up front, just in case this is a 'wind up' from some competitor we don't know about yet."

"I hadn't thought about that," said Carice, "better safe than sorry. The caller who came in to see me, is one of Stephen downstairs', wealthier customers. He has to go off on business to Sydney tomorrow and is unable to attend a boat auction at the harbour on Tuesday and wondered if we would be willing to bid on his behalf, for a motor boat that he is interested in."

"Surely he must have someone who works for him who could do that for him," said Mac dubiously.

"His business partner is going with him to Sydney and his manger is too well known at the harbour and once people knew that he was the one bidding for the boat, then they would try and force the price up."

"But what if there is something wrong with the boat and he refuses to pay up, we could be stuck with it," said Mac.

"Stephen has since assured me that the man is both genuine and honest, plus I should have mentioned that he is willing to pay five times our daily rate if you will do this for him. Since your father-in-law is staying with you this week and in view of all his years of experience with all sorts of different boats, I thought perhaps you could take him with you and if he was not comfortable with the boat, you just did not put in a bid on it."

"What do you think Bertie, would you be willing to come with me and give me your opinion? I have to say that this is not quite the work I expected to be offered as an Inquiry Agent."

"I would be delighted to accompany you to the auction Mac and may I tactfully suggest that you should consider yourself to be like a 'tramp steamer' which picks up any cargo and takes it to any port, rather than a luxury liner on a fixed route from London to New York, if you will pardon the seafaring analogy. There is probably an opportunity to see the boat and possibly try it out on Monday Mac, might be worth checking that out."

"Point taken, so you and I will need to get together on Monday morning Carice and go through everything before you see our dog lovers and go off to Gisborne and Bertie and I go for a boat ride."

"Very well, I will ring the client and tell him we are prepared to act for him and find out what his limit is on the boat."

"Good, well if you will excuse us Carice, I have two tired in-laws to take home, see you on Monday."

Deborah was late in getting home that night and the dinner was actually on the table and the other three were eating when she finally walked in through the door.

"Dad, Victoria, I am so sorry I was not able to be at the airport to meet you, how was your flight?"

Bertie stood up and gave his daughter a hug and said, "The flight was fine thank you, but you look exhausted Deborah, what on earth is the matter, problems at work?"

"Not really, just an all day review meeting I was involved with, which over-ran as usual, but enough of work, we have a whole weekend to spend together, so tell me all that has been happening in Pinjarra and how Moira and her baby are doing."

They spent the weekend sightseeing together and Mac arranged for them to have Sunday lunch at Stephen's restaurant, where Carice joined them on her own, as Desmond had now returned to Dunedin, to help get the hotel ready for it going up for sale the following week.

"Now you two," Deborah said to Mac and Carice, "no business talk today, this is a weekend and we have guests."

"I haven't noticed it stops you and Neil discussing business whenever we go to visit them," replied Mac, "but Carice and I have nothing to discuss which cannot wait until Monday, have we partner?"

"No partner, but I am interested in hearing about the cruise that Victoria and Bertie are going on back to Europe, it is something I have always wanted to do."

Victoria did not need to be asked twice about her forthcoming trip and described in detail where they would be stopping and what sightseeing they hoped to do, all the way to the point where they arrived at Capetown.

"I gather from Mac, that you know Capetown quite well yourself Carice, so perhaps you could tell us where we should go and what sights we should see," said Victoria.

Carice took up the conversation again and made some suggestions which Victoria noted down, but ended by saying, "I don't know if Mac mentioned that my mother is still living in Capetown with her mother and that the hotel that Desmond has gone back to Dunedin to help to sell, actually belongs to her, well it did, but she has given it to the bank."

"It's all right dear, Mac has explained what has happened, you do not need to say anything more," said Victoria reassuringly, "your mother has acted with great integrity and we all admire her for it."

"Thank you Victoria, I appreciate your saying that. Anyway, some of the items in the hotel actually belonged to her family and in particular there is an old sea chest, which belonged to a forbear of mother's, who sailed the seven seas in the early eighteen hundreds. Whilst she has told me that I can have anything else I like from the hotel, she has particularly asked if I can send her the chest and I was wondering if you could take it with you as part of your luggage, rather than risk it being damaged in the ship's hold?"

"We would be delighted to Carice, wouldn't we Bertie?"

"Of course, anything to help, as an ex sea dog myself, I can understand why the chest is so important to your mother and her family, but I suggest you pack it with books and other items to help it keep its shape and put a strong strap round it, as some of these old chests are not as sturdy as they once were and we would not want to deliver a pile of old matchwood to your mother."

Carice went off to Gisborne on Monday and eventually returned with the lost dog on the Wednesday and delivered him to a very delighted pair of owners, who were only too happy to pay her bill on the spot, along with a large bunch of flowers as a thank you present.

Mac, Victoria and Bertie inspected the boat on the Monday and went out for a pleasant cruise round the harbour, Bertie acting the part of the retired sea captain, who was looking for something to go fishing in and for making short trips up and down the coast.

There were several bidders at the auction but Mac was able to acquire the vessel for a hundred and fifty pounds below his client's maximum figure, who again was delighted with the result Mac had achieved for him.

Carice delivered the chest to Bertie and Victoria on the Thursday evening as they were having their luggage loaded onto the ship on Friday and on Saturday Mac and Deborah drove them to the harbour and waved them off on their cruise..

February in Ruth Street was an interesting month as Digger and Moira got used to playing the part of mother and father and were soon to realize that being a parent was an extremely difficult job. Vi was a regular visitor to see them and often brought the children with her to see their new cousin.

On the twenty fourth of February Pat said her goodbyes to Ruth Street and promised to visit them in Sydney as soon as they were settled and she had saved up the fare and they presented her with a new 'nurse's watch' as a goodbye present.

The Sydney Office were desperate to get Digger over there as soon as possible, as there were several incidents at different branches that they wanted him to look into and as Moira was feeling so well and the agent said he had another tenant waiting for them to move out, they brought their removal date forward and left for their new home on Saturday the third of March.

Digger had gone over to Sydney some weeks before and had found several nice houses in the Balmain area of Sydney, not far from both the hospital and the bridge, which he and Moira had discussed at length. Eventually they came to a decision on which house to choose, so Digger phoned the agent and arranged for a six month lease on the property, with an option to extend it, if they wanted to.

As they were settling into their new home on the fifth of March, the ship that Bertie and Victoria had been travelling on, was tying up at the main dock in Capetown.

"I can't believe you did not have a sly peek inside of that chest Bertie," Victoria said as two of the seamen helped him load it into the back of a taxi.

"You wouldn't want a complete stranger looking into your possessions Victoria, now would you? I just wished I had not suggested putting books inside to help fill it, I think she must have put a complete set of the Encyclopedia Britannica in there. Thanks very much men, for helping me with that, here buy yourselves a drink later," he said to the sailors as he slipped them some money.

The taxi driver took them to the address Carice had given them, where her mother and grandmother were living and helped Bertie carry the chest from the taxi to the front door.

When they got to the front door of the house, it was already half open, so they looked around the garden in case Simone was out front somewhere, but when they could not see, Bertie knocked loudly on the front door and called out, "Hello, anyone at home?"

They heard a lady's voice from the back of the house shout out, "Will you see who is at the front door please Rutger, as my hands are covered in flour at the moment."

Victoria nudged Bertie and said, "That was Carice's father's name, I told you his death was all a sham, this will be interesting!"

The door opened and Bertie said, "We have called to see Mrs. van Offstrop, is she at home please?"

The young boy looked at the two people standing there and called out, "Auntie, it's a man and a lady to see you and another man too, with a large box."

A few seconds later a small petite lady in her mid fifties came through from the back of the house, wiping her hands on her apron and said, "Thank you Rutger dear, you can go and play, I will speak with the lady and gentleman. You must be Mr. and Mrs. Bannister, Carice wrote to tell me that she had asked you to bring the old chest, she really shouldn't have bothered you, but it is most kind of you to deliver it in person, please come in."

"Thank you," said Victoria, "where would you like the box to be put, as it is very heavy?"

"Perhaps your husband and the other gentleman would be so kind as to carry it through to the front room for me," she replied.

Bertie and the taxi driver lifted the chest and managed to carry it over the front step and down the passage and just got it into the front room and lowered it onto the floor, as Bertie was losing his grip on it.

"I have a little car and can take you back to the hotel or ship if you like, to save your driver from waiting," said Simone.

"Thank you," said Victoria, "that would be most kind, Bertie pay the driver please."

Bertie did as he was told and paid the driver, giving him a good tip for his assistance with the chest.

"When Carice told me you would be coming, I was so thrilled as we do not get many visitors these days and a new face always perks mother up for a few days, please make yourselves comfortable while I go and fetch her. There is some cool lemonade on the table, if you don't mind helping yourselves."

The room was a typical Victorian Drawing Room, with large comfortable furniture, faded wallpaper and several ornately framed pictures on the wall. Bertie noticed that they had actually positioned the chest, underneath a very old picture of a bearded mariner, complete with eye patch, cock hat and a telescope.

"I wonder if that was the old captain who originally owned the chest?" he said to Victoria.

"Ask her when she returns," Victoria replied, "do you want some lemonade?"

"Yes please, my throat is parched and I think I may have pulled a muscle in my back, lifting that chest."

"Oh I do hope not," said Simone, entering the room with a very old lady hanging onto her arm. "This is my mother, she is a little hard of hearing and her mind tends to wander a bit, but I will try and introduce you to her, once I have made her comfortable."

The old lady sat down in what was very obviously 'her chair' and Simone got a footstool for her feet and then sat down close to her.

"Mother, these are friends of Carice who have brought the old chest back from Australia for us, isn't that kind of them?"

The mother's eyes searched the room until she spotted the chest and then she half smiled and said something quietly to Simone who repeated it to her visitors, "Mother said thank you, she is relieved that the old captain, that's his picture on the wall and his chest are reunited once more. Mother never wanted me to take it to Australia with me, but it was left to me by my grandmother, so it was mine to do what I liked with."

"Well we are very pleased to have been of service, Mrs. van Offstrop," said Bertie.

"Simone, please call me Simone," she said.

"Simone, I am Bertie and my wife is Victoria, as an old sea captain myself, I can understand the sentimental value attached to the chest."

"Thank you Bertie, but I cannot imagine what Carice filled it with to make it so heavy, she knew it was only the chest which I really wanted, let's open it and see."

"I think I may have been my own worst enemy here Simone, as I suggested she padded it out with some books and things to help protect it," said Bertie, "can I give you a hand with that strap, you seem to be struggling with it."

Bertie went over to the chest and using all his strength managed to undo the belt that Carice had used to fasten it and went and sat down again while Simone went through the contents, which had been wrapped in some old blankets to stop them from rattling around.

"Look mother, the silver candlesticks that Grandpa gave you and which you gave me for my twenty first birthday and there are some vases from India and the rest seems to be made up with these old books and papers, what on earth did Carice send these to me for, I told her I did not want any of them, perhaps the book shop might be interested, but they only offered a pittance last time we sold some of Papa's old books to them."

She piled the books and papers up and then held them out towards Bertie, "Bertie, would you mind carrying these over to the table by the fireplace for me please, I will get rid of them later."

"Do you want me to move the chest to somewhere else in the house for you?" he asked, as he placed the pile onto the table.

"You have done quite enough for me, I don't want you hurting your back any more, even when empty, this old chest has always been very heavy. I see you are looking at that old document, please take it if it interests you, or any more that are there for that matter, I will only end up lighting the fire with them."

Bertie had a quick look through the papers and picked three which he said he would like to have, along with a book which was on the subject of the Spice Trade and was obviously very old.

"Can I give you something for these he asked?"

"Certainly not, after the service you have done for mother and me in bringing the chest back, I won't hear of it," she replied.

They all chatted for a bit longer and then as promised she drove them back to the ship, where they had decided to stay, until the start of the safari, which Bertie had organized for them.

When Simone returned from the ship she asked her nephew to go to the workshop and bring the tools she had looked out the previous day, into the front room and set them down next to the chest.

"Wish me luck mother," she said, as she picked up the large screwdriver and started to undo the screws holding the false bottom in place. After removing the first six screws, she took a break, as her arms were sore and although little Rutger had a go himself, he was not strong enough to turn any of the screws which were left.

"Give the screwdriver to Auntie dear I feel strong again now," with which she took hold of the tool and slowly removed the remaining six screws from the bottom.

"Pass me that wet cloth please Rutger, so I can wipe all the dirt off the bottom. Good, now I can see the marks uncle made, when he fitted it all those years ago. Now pass me the chisel and the mallet please." The tools were duly passed across and placing the chisel on the lines drawn on the false bottom, she hit it as hard as she could with the mallet and as she hit it the last time, the wood splintered into three smaller pieces, which she was able to remove using the chisel and the pinchers in turn.

"Look at all those gold coins Auntie, what are they?"

"They are called sovereigns dear and uncle put them in the chest many years ago, before you were born, so that one day, when things got a bit difficult for Auntie, just like they are now, I would have a little nest-egg to help me. Wasn't that thoughtful of uncle?"

Once Bertie and Victoria got back to the ship and were in the confines of their own cabin, Victoria blurted out, "Well go on, tell me, what was in those papers you were so excited about?"

"I don't know what you mean Victoria, just some old papers and a book, I thought they might be of some interest to me on the long voyage back to Spain."

"Don't you come the innocent with me Bertie Bannister, I know you too well, you could hardly contain your excitement back there, what are they?"

He spread the papers out on the bed and studied them carefully, "This one is a chart of the Seram Sea in Indonesia and this one is a chart of the Sulu Sea in the Philippines and this one is a map of one of the islands, which I believe to be located in one of these two seas."

"But these charts are ancient, surely there will be much better up-to-date charts around these days and the map is not in English so what use is that to you?" asked Victoria.

"Whoever owned these charts has written one or two notes on them himself, but my Dutch is not good enough to work out what it says, but I do know enough Dutch to realize that the other map of the island has got a reference on the back of it, to this book on the Spice Trade, which is why I picked it up as well."

"Very interesting Bertie, but why the great excitement when you saw them?"

"Because I believe this," holding up the map of the island, "is a treasure map and Simone's forbear is none other than the Dutch Sea Captain, Pim de Zwolle, a notorious cut-throat and pirate of the late seventeen hundreds. This could be the map of his hoard of treasure, which has never been discovered."

"Or it could be a map of where he buried his pet parrot and how do you know it is this Pim character anyway?"

"I have seen his portrait before somewhere and read a little of his history, I am certain that is who it is," said Bertie.

"Even if it is, what do we need this buried treasure for Bertie and let's face it, you really are too old for those sorts of adventures any more."

"Well we will see Victoria, we will see. Where would you like to eat tonight?" he asked.

"How about that hotel Simone drove past on the way back from her house, it looked very posh and I feel like being posh tonight."

"Your wish is my command; I will go and see the Purser and see if he can arrange a table for us, I won't be long."

The Purser rang the hotel and told them that two of their passengers, a Captain and Mrs. Bannister would like to book a table for that evening, but unfortunately the restaurant was full according to the manger, so Bertie and the Purser started to discuss other 'posh' options.

"I had better go back and check with her," said Bertie, "or I am bound to make the wrong choice, see you soon."

Victoria could not understand the dilemma, it was obvious which hotel to choose, so Bertie went back to see the Purser, only to be told that the Manager of the hotel had rung back to say that he had made a mistake and that they did have a table free and hoped that the Bannister's would be able to come.

"Well that sorts that one out then," Bertie said to the
Purser, "could you book a table for seven tonight and a taxi for
six thirty please."

When they arrived at the hotel they were asked to wait at
reception as the manager wished to speak with them
personally.

"Captain and Mrs. Bannister, I am so sorry for all the
confusion, but the party for eight that had booked in for six
forty five, turned out to be a party for twelve and as they are
such good patrons of this hotel, we obviously could not turn
them away."

"So what are you saying to us exactly?" Bertie demanded,
"I hope you are not attempting to turn us away instead."

"Goodness me, I would lose my job if I did such a thing,
no, I have spoken with the owner of the hotel about the matter
and he has insisted that you dine with him and his wife
tonight, compliments of the hotel of course, in his private
dining room, if that is acceptable to you both."

They looked at each other and Victoria smiled so Bertie
said it would be acceptable and they were escorted to the
owner's private room, where his wife was already present and
waiting for them.

"Hello Captain Bannister, Mrs. Banister, we are so sorry
for this mix up, I am Aileen Strong, it is very nice to meet you
and please call me Aileen."

"It is nice to meet you too Aileen, my name is Victoria and
my husband's name is-"

"Let me guess, she interrupted, "my husband believes he
might already know you, if so, your name is Robert
Wilberforce Bannister, or Bertie to your friends. Am I right?"

"You are completely correct," said an amazed Bertie, as he
shook her hand and sat down next to Victoria, "there cannot
be more than half a dozen people in the whole wide world

who could possibly have known that. So the big question Aileen, is who is your husband?"

"Here he comes now Bertie, see if you recognize him," she said.

The man was about Bertie's age and height, but wore a full beard which hid a lot of his features, but there was something about the way he walked into the room and stood there looking at Bertie that seemed to ring a bell from the distant past.

"Give me a clue," said Bertie, "something about you is familiar, but I am just not sure."

"The Training Ship Mercury," said the man.

Bertie could not speak and his eyes filled with tears as he struggled to find the words, but eventually stood to his feet and looked the man straight in the eye as he said, "Derek Strong, but it can't be you, you were washed overboard and drowned in March eighteen ninety five as we were coming round the Cape of Good Hope on our way back from Melbourne, I have mourned your death for the past fifty six years."

"It is me Bertie and I am sorry I never let you know I was still alive, but originally I was too angry and then I was too embarrassed, but our paths have crossed on several occasions, you just never recognised me."

"How on earth did you survive in those terrible seas we experienced round the Cape?"

"For a start, I was not washed overboard, but I actually dived off the boat on purpose. While I was out fixing the bowsprit I saw this young woman drifting past in a small boat and she waved to me in desperation and before I knew what I was doing, I had dived off and caught hold of a rope that was trailing in the water behind her boat."

"Did the young woman survive as well as yourself?" asked Victoria.

"I certainly did," said Aileen, "but why not pour everyone a drink Derek and then you can start to tell them our story."

"A good idea," he said and filled their glasses with the champagne the waiter had brought in while they had all been talking.

"A toast," he said, "to the wonder of life and all of its mysteries."

"To Life," they all repeated and drank their champagne.

THE END

Epilogue

The refining pot for silver
And the furnace for the gold;
But the heart of man is tested,
By the maker of his soul.
The foolish man his house will build,
Upon the shifting sand
And be surprised and outraged
When the storms of life and the daily strife
Roll in and knock it down.
Come close my friend and listen
For my story's told and done,
But yours has yet to find it's end,
With adventures still to come.
So be bold and brave and forthright,
In adversity be strong,
Be like the tree which stands straight and tall,
In Blossom by the Billabong.

6th April 2012 LS

Lightning Source UK Ltd.
Milton Keynes UK
UKOW041556110812

197410UK00004B/4/P